WHAT IS FORGIVEN

A World War II Mystery

by C. F. Yetmen

YPSILON & CO PRESS

Ypsilon & Co. Press
Austin, Texas

ISBN 978-0-9988890-0-9
Library of Congress Control Number: 2017905274

Text set in Electra
Book design by Adam Fortner
Cover by David Provolo
Author photo by Samantha Eisenmenger

For my mother

"The German people should know by now that the people of the United States hold them in no fear, and in no hate. It is true that the Germans have taught us the horrors of modern warfare, but the ruin that lies from the Rhine to the Danube shows that we, like our Allies, have not been dull pupils."

Justice Robert H. Jackson
Excerpt from the opening statement
before the International Military Tribunal
Nuremberg, November 20, 1945

chapter one

Wiesbaden, Germany, October 1945

The man's pale face was cracked, the scars of his ordeal revealed under the ribbon of sunlight streaming through the dirty window. Just under his chin, a ridge of pink paint hinted at the jowls that told his age, but the same paint gave a youthful rosiness to his cheek. He looked at Anna with near-black eyes, his expression defiant and expectant, as if they were engaged in conversation and it was her turn to reply. A light warping torqued the canvas in its frame, and a small tear was visible at one corner, but it was nothing that wasn't fixable. Anna lowered her face toward the painting as it rested on the swatch of cloth the conservators used to protect the precious inventory, and when she was sure no one was looking, she ran her hand across the rough paint, feeling its texture on her fingertips. She knew she shouldn't touch it, even with gloves, but the temptation was too great. The familiar sounds of army boots squeaking on the waxed floors and the low rumble of American voices continued in the near background, and the sun illuminated the dust in the air. She inhaled the distant oily scent and exhaled it for a long time, sending a cloud of tiny particles swirling toward the ceiling. She considered what the *Man in a Green Jacket* had endured in order to arrive here, into her care. Months in a damp cellar wrapped in bed sheets alongside a few dozen of his fellow travelers had not diminished the gleam in his eyes nor weakened the set of his shoulders. It was a painting that told of another time. What would the man say, if he could speak?

"Let's get you back home," she said. "You've been very patient." She turned the painting over on the work table, which was really just one of the old oversized doors from the back of the building balanced on a pair of smaller folding tables.

She was so engrossed in reading the gallery and exhibition labels on the back of the painting that she didn't notice Cooper step into the workroom.

"Frau Klein? Can you speed this along, please?" He stood in the half-open door, rolling the sleeve of his uniform down his arm. "The new hire will be here soon. Let's meet up in my office." Captain Henry Cooper was her immediate superior—she his translator and assistant, he an architect assigned to safeguard Germany's damaged monuments and restitute its stolen art for the Monuments Men unit Anna had fallen into a job with. It was no small task, for sure, and one made all the more interesting by Cooper's penchant for ignoring the military's protocols.

"I'm almost done here." She turned back to her work, adjusting the table lamp to get a better look at the hodgepodge of stamps, labels, and numbers that told the painting's story. Anna knew by now the familiar stencils of the ERR, the Einsatzstab Reichsleiter Rosenberg, Hitler's ruthless art thieving unit. She made a note of the markings on the condition report part of the long and repetitive intake form, following the established protocol. This canvas, an oil painting of a seated man looking over his left shoulder, likely belonged to the same collector as the dozens of others she had catalogued over the last few days. The Nazi cataloging stamps on the back told that it had been taken from a Jewish family in Frankfurt. Thanks to meticulous Nazi record keeping, the Americans had already made good progress on connecting the paintings with their rightful owners. The only problem, and it was a big one, was finding those owners, if they were even still alive. Of all the Jewish collectors whose paintings they had identified, the Americans had not found a single one yet.

"Is that another one of the Morgenstern collection?" Cooper appeared next to her and leaned forward on his elbows, his face close to the canvas. "How many does that make?"

"Twenty-nine so far. But this is the most valuable I've seen. It's by Emil Nolde."

Cooper leaned over the painting, studying the topography of the canvas. "I have to say, I think I like these crazy Expressionists. They are growing on me."

Anna straightened to put some space between them. His casual proximity still made her uncomfortable, even though he meant nothing by it. Americans were always standing too close and talking too loud. After working with them for almost three months, she still wasn't used to it.

"Who is this new hire?" she asked. Whoever he was, he was getting his own office and a personal welcome from Cooper. "He must be pretty high up. Is he from America?" Maybe it was a famous curator or art historian. Anna pictured a fusty man with heavy glasses and English tweed jackets. She watched as one worker wheeled a desk chair past the door and another followed, carrying a desk lamp. Anna had been asking for a lamp for her tiny desk for two weeks and had been told there were none.

"Nope. From Frankfurt. And it's a she. Frau Eva Lange, of the Staedel Museum." Cooper's marble-mouthed German made Anna smile. "Lots of knowledge about the goings-on during the war, so she should be a real help in terms of finding owners and catching the bad guys. Haven't met her, but Captain Farmer says she's top-notch. Even the bigwigs vouched for her."

He grinned. "That'll make the guys in Munich take notice of our little operation."

Munich was the bigger, more prestigious Monuments Men Collecting Point, dealing with major collections stolen from Jewish collectors in Vienna and beyond. The ramshackle Wiesbaden Collecting Point run by the bespectacled and starched Captain Walter Farmer was, by contrast, not as glamorous, although it was at this moment in possession of thousands of works of art from German state-owned collections, which the Nazis had hidden in a salt mine, as well as a few pieces stolen and looted from private citizens. Hundreds of crates from the Merkers Mine had been delivered weeks ago, and since then, the smell of salt hung in the air and soaked into everything. The workers joked that it was like being at the beach but without the sun or the sand or the fun.

"Do we have the list of people who have arrived at the new displaced persons camp yet? The one near Frankfurt?" Anna opened the window, fanning herself uselessly with her sweating hand. She had read about the new camp in the town of Zeilsheim that had been established specifically for the survivors of the concentration camps. The Americans' original plan to house the nearly-dead victims alongside homeless German civilians and war prisoners had been a disaster, and a visiting American senator had made a stink to the American military government. Now the survivors had their own camp, run by themselves, with extra rations and medical care.

"It's still a mess. I've got a man headed over there this afternoon. He can try to get a list. Did you get a previous address for Mr. Morgenstern?"

Anna sorted through the papers on the table. "Just for his gallery, as listed on the labels." She found the note she was looking for and deciphered her own handwriting. "Braubachstrasse. In the old part of the city, near St. Paul's church. It was destroyed in 1944. No information on where he lived."

"It's a long shot to locate him. You know that, right? I doubt we'll find a single owner or even a family member of any of these collectors." Cooper waved an irritated hand over the paintings stacked along the walls. "The best we can hope for is that they show up here with their ownership and provenance documents intact. Anyway, I need you to move a little faster with getting all this sorted. You really don't need to memorize each painting. We have other work to focus on."

Two workers carried a large metal desk into the adjacent room. A crash echoed as a drawer slid out and hit the terrazzo floor. One man cursed at the other, who laughed as they maneuvered the desk through the doorway.

"What about her Fragebogen?" Anna asked. "Did you check Frau Lange's Fragebogen?" She should have known better to bring up procedural correctness and bureaucracy with Cooper, but she couldn't help it. Rules were rules, and all Germans had to complete the Americans' questionnaire that whittled Germans' loyalties down to a series of checked and unchecked boxes. *Yes, I was a Nazi, but I didn't mean to be.*

Cooper nodded. "Frankfurt even signed off on it—she's squeaky clean. That's good enough for me." He checked his watch. "Hurry up, will you? Be upstairs in five minutes."

"I look forward to meeting Frau Lange." Anna hoped she sounded enthusiastic. She finished logging in the painting on the intake form, filling in the identifying numbers from the stamps on the back, and checking one last time for any other damage. Before she set it back in its crate, she took another look, as if to say good bye. Once the paintings were crated, they were put into storage and their paperwork filed away. It might be months or years before anyone saw them again. Until a valid claim was filed by an heir or other party, these valuable and treasured pieces were officially the responsibility of the US government. Unofficially, Anna had made it her responsibility. It was the least she could do.

Eva Lange was no fusty matron in a tweed suit. The woman sitting across from Cooper's desk when Anna arrived was tall and elegant, her stockinged legs tucked at an angle, crossed at the ankle, and completed by a pair of delicate dark red pumps. Her straight back and folded hands spoke of a certain upbringing, but the worn, gray wool suit that hung on her frame, much too warm for the heat of day, echoed the tough times. Her blond hair was pulled into a roll at the nape of her long neck, and her skin, although smooth, was the color of dishwater. She had spruced up with some hyacinth-smelling perfume, and the anemic stain of red on her lips gave her the appearance of a colorized photograph. The woman's gaze slid somewhere over Anna's head as she scanned the meager office.

Anna reached for her own hair. She felt shabby in the men's pants and boots she wore along with her dingy, faded blouse. The woman stood when she saw Anna and extended a hand.

"Hello, I am Eva Lange," she said in English, which Anna assumed was for Cooper's benefit.

Anna returned the greeting and pulled the chair from her desk alongside Cooper. Anna and Cooper shared an office, with her desk under the window next to his, but she had the feeling that she was interrupting. Anna looked at her boss. He was returning to his old self now that his job at the Collecting Point was once again secured. They had been working together for a little over a month and had gotten off to a rocky start. Cooper was unaccustomed to Army protocol and driven by an earnest desire to do good in a bad world. Now, chastened after having taken the matter of a stolen painting into his own hands, he was trying to toe the line. Anna amused herself with the knowledge that she had saved his job and that, technically, he was in her debt. It was like a little coin she kept sewn into the hem of her pants, hidden from view but ready to be cashed in if needed. But no one had yelled at them at all this week. Cooper hadn't broken any rules, she hadn't told any lies, and everything had been *by the book*, as the Americans liked to say. It was only a matter of time before he was back to his old self.

Cooper was beaming. Anna had never seen him so happy to meet any German. For him, Germans were objects of suspicion. He tried to hide it but didn't succeed.

"Frau Lange comes to us from Frankfurt," he said, scanning a paper in front of him. "The Staedel Museum." He gestured as if the museum was right next door. "Very impressive, Frau Lange. An actual qualified person. Welcome."

Eva Lange smiled, and Anna felt a cool breeze waft across the room.

"Thank you, Captain. I am honored to be here. And it's Fraulein, not Frau." She cocked her head to the side, steadying her eyes on Cooper. "I have never been married."

Anna saw color rise in Cooper's cheeks.

"You have very impressive qualifications, Fraulein, as I said, so we'll put you to good use." Cooper smiled and then looked down at the papers in his hand, pretending to scrutinize something in detail.

Anna caught herself rolling her eyes and making a sucking sound with her lips, which she covered by pretending to clear her throat. She felt stupid and out of place, as if someone had erased her part in a play.

Cooper remembered she was in the room. "Frau Klein, would you run over to the front office and make sure all the needed papers are in place? I want Fraulein Lange to start right away."

"I checked with them on my way in," Eva said, "to be sure they have everything, which they do. So, I guess I am all yours." She smiled. "Is that how you say it?"

"Excellent. Anna will see that you get your papers, and then I'll go over the rules of the building with you. Who can come and go. What stays. Who has the keys, et cetera. We tightened up security, so you'll need to watch yourself." He nodded and pushed his chair back.

Eva Lange fidgeted with the bag she held on her lap. "Yes, of course. I understand."

Anna considered the new woman's credentials. She was young for someone with such an impressive resume, especially considering that after 1933, the business of museums was a particular interest of the Nazis, and by 1937, they had raided most of them, taking what they wanted for themselves and declaring the rest "degenerate." In 1933, Anna had been eighteen years old. If Eva was ten years older, that put her very close to Cooper's age now, and would have made her twenty-eight the year the Nazis declared their war on art. Anna tried to do the math.

"Were you at the Staedel long?" Anna heard herself ask.

Eva Lange jerked her head as if she had forgotten Anna was there. "I was there until 1939, when everything was moved out to the country for safekeeping. After that, there was no work for people such as myself. Unless, of course, you joined the Party. They took a special interest in museum curators, as you know."

"So you must have known Jacob Morgenstern?" Maybe Fraulein Lange would prove useful, even if she was annoying.

Eva made a show of searching her mind. "No, I don't think so. Should I?"

"He was a dealer in Frankfurt. He had a gallery in the Altstadt. I thought you might have crossed paths."

"No, I can't say that I recall. But, you know, there were so many galleries in Frankfurt before the war. My memory might be failing me." She regarded Anna, waiting for the next question.

"What did you do after you left the museum? How did you live?"

Eva Lange turned in her chair to face Anna. "I moved in with my father and did menial work to earn a few marks. Cleaned houses for a while, then I was a cook. I worked in the barracks, cooking for the troops."

"Oh. I thought that was a Frauenschaft job," Anna said, referring to the Nazi women's guild. "For the fatherland and all that."

"Not necessarily," Eva said. "There were ways around that. If you were clever. I am sure you were in the same boat?" She turned her attention back to Cooper and addressed him, tossing Anna aside. "I am so very grateful to you, Captain. As you can see from my qualifications, I will be able to help your work very much."

"Yes, you will be a fine addition to our little team. We need all the help we can get. I'm up to my armpits in art, and I'm starting not to enjoy it anymore. I'll be happy to have you on board." He turned to Anna, getting back to business. "Frau Klein? The credentials?"

Anna pushed her chair back under her desk. She swept a cold gaze over Cooper and Eva Lange as she stood, hoping to reassert some upper hand, but Eva caught her eye and added a satisfied smile for good measure.

"I'm sorry, I have to finish my work downstairs," she said. "The paintings are waiting to be shelved. I can get the papers for you when I finish."

Cooper's eyebrows twitched as he straightened in his chair. He paused before he spoke through a long exhale. "Very well, Frau Klein. I shall get them myself. You are dismissed."

As Anna lingered in the hallway, she was surprised to find that she was seething. The way Cooper had sent her on a clerk's errand and swooned over this woman's qualifications. How he had dismissed her, literally. The way Eva Lange had flirted with Cooper, her academic prowess wrapped in an elegant package with long legs. An entitled, smug package.

She took the stairs two at a time, as if to outrun the anger that was quickly turning into jealousy.

"Frau Klein, is everything all right?" The question from Karla Albrecht, the young woman behind the reception desk, slowed Anna's pace. She had only been there a week and was trying to make herself useful. Earnest and pretty, Karla, too, had taken to wearing men's pants, a bold move for someone in such a visible post. Her job was to support the field officers and staff in whatever way was needed, which meant that mostly she relayed messages between people who passed by her desk throughout the day. She was like a human message board.

"Fine. Thanks, Karla. And how are things with you?" Anna approached the desk, happy to have an excuse to take a break.

"Who is that woman in Captain Cooper's office? Is she new?" Karla pushed the big round glasses she wore up the bridge of her nose. Anna suspected the glasses were purely aesthetic, hand-me-downs from a grandmother perhaps, intended to make the wearer seem smarter. Karla was serious about her job; her young, porcelain face was set in an expression of earnest analysis that made every conversation take on the air of a mystery that needed solving. She was much prettier than she knew, with her thick brown hair pulled back from a heart-shaped face, a long slender neck, and the upright carriage of a dancer. Everything about her was delicate, except her personality, which was fearless.

"Yes, she is. Eva Lange. From the Staedel in Frankfurt."

"Fancy. Is she going to work with you?"

"I think I'm going to work *for* her, the way it sounded to me."

Karla chuckled, but then her face turned serious. "Want me to keep an eye on her for you?" She nodded and provided her own response. "I'll let you know if I see anything."

"You do that." Anna made a show of a furtive glance around the lobby, as if they were hatching a plot together. "And keep me posted," she whispered.

"Yes, ma'am." The fake dramatics were lost on Karla, who straightened the papers on her desk and turned toward her typewriter. "Now, I better get back to work."

"Enough chitchat," Anna agreed. She put Eva and her lipstick and her hyacinth perfume out of her mind and headed downstairs.

Amalia played with her braid, twisting it around her finger and pulling the end into her mouth. She sat on the bed that she now shared with Anna and Madeleine since Oskar had moved in and begun sleeping on the sofa. The four of them sharing what was left of Madeleine's apartment–a living room, kitchen, and bath–made for very close quarters, but so far, aside from a few grumblings about elbow room, they had managed well enough. Madeleine, the oldest and dearest friend of Anna's late mother, had taken them in when they showed up on her doorstep in the summer. They had become an improvised family of sorts, and Anna dared hope that things would settle down into a routine, even if a difficult one. She lay back on the bed and stared at the crumbling plaster on the ceiling.

"What did you do all day?" Anna directed her question at Oskar who was in charge of Amalia, her six-year-old daughter. At age ten, he was the best babysitter she could find, even if he was one to run loose in the black market and return home with untold treasures, like an egg or a small bag of real coffee. Anna never asked how he got them.

"Oh, we went here and there." The boy shrugged. "Don't worry. We were good," he added as he collapsed himself onto the ground next to her. His eyes twinkled. "We have some fresh bread for supper."

Anna shook her head. "Don't tell me. I don't want to know." She had gotten very good at not knowing. It was a skill that had served her well for the last decade. Until she got a stronger foothold into the new world, she was resigned to relying on the old habit, even if she knew it was wrong.

"This came today." He pulled an envelope from the pocket of his pants and handed it to her. "It was under the door."

Anna pushed herself up onto her elbows and regarded the envelope before taking it. It was official and American. A little shockwave pushed through her body. The officials were not in the business of mailing good news to Germans. She had not even told Oskar about the letter she had received from the UNRRA, the United Nations Relief and Rehabilitation Agency, in charge of refugees, with which he was registered. That letter threatened to upend his young life all over again, just when he had gotten a small toehold. And, since she was now his unofficial guardian, the letter threatened her with the same.

She shoved that thought out of her mind and took the envelope, tearing into the flap with her index finger. She skimmed the one-page letter inside, looking for the verbs that would indicate whatever action was being imposed upon her by the great American military. Her breath caught in her throat.

"What's wrong?" Oskar asked.

Anna's eyes floated over the words: *requisitioned, housing, billeting, officers*... She folded the letter back into the envelope.

"Nothing." She smiled. "Some official nonsense about new rules. Nothing to worry about."

"I don't believe you." Oskar snatched the letter from her hand and ran into the kitchen.

"Oskar, give it back." She made only a feeble attempt, sinking back onto the bed. He was right. The *Amis* were requisitioning Madeleine's house to billet officers. They had two days to get out, or they would be forcibly removed. No assistance was offered or provided, no appeal allowed. Their little home was being taken away. She had known it was a possibility, but she had thought they might be spared. Now she felt stupid for expecting anything different. She closed her eyes and tried to think.

"This says we have to leave, doesn't it?" Oskar tossed the letter onto her chest. "It says the *Amis* are moving in here."

"Is that true, Mama?" Amalia whispered. "Where will we go?"

"It will be all right," Anna said, fuming at Oskar. "Don't worry."

Amalia tugged on a ragged fingernail. She was so small, so vulnerable. *Dammit. Just when things were looking up.*

"Tell your stinking *Amis* they should put that letter where the sun doesn't shine," Oskar said. "Damn *Amis* think they can take everything. Like they haven't already."

"That's enough from you, Oskar. Go and put on some water so you can take a bath. You are filthy." She turned to Amalia. "*Maus*, don't you worry. I will fix it. And as long as we're all together, everything will be all right." She considered if this was a flat-out lie or a kind of prayer. They had two days. She would talk to Cooper first thing in the morning.

"But where will we go? And who will live here in Auntie's house? It's her house. Will the *Amis* live here?" Amalia's whines grated on Anna's nerves.

"I don't know, *Maus*. I will find out tomorrow."

The front door scraped on the wooden floor as it opened. "Auntie!" Amalia called and tumbled off the bed to run and greet Madeleine.

The old woman appeared in the doorway from the small foyer and held out her arms to sweep Amalia into an embrace. Madeleine was the only one among them who appeared unchanged by the war and its tragedies. She had suffered, too. First her son, Bernhardt, was killed in the Great War and then her husband Otto had succumbed to the strain of life in the Third Reich. The final blow came when her best friend—Anna's mother—died in the bombing of Vienna that past March. Even as the war staggered to its inevitable gruesome end, it had taken more. They had come so far, but it had not been far enough. Still, Madeleine could pull herself up by her bootstraps and see the possibility of things getting better. Most days, Anna was happy to even find her bootstraps. Pulling herself up was another story.

"How are you, Auntie?" Anna stood to take Madeleine's bag from her. "*Maus*, let Auntie sit down. She's very tired."

"Not at all, my dear." Madeleine put a hand on Anna's shoulder. "Stop fussing. You have enough to deal with." She smiled. "How are things with our Americans?"

"Well enough. Nothing much to report today."

"No masterpieces today? Or is it becoming old hat already?"

Anna laughed. "A few. I did work with the odd Old Master. It was a typical day."

Oskar returned from the kitchen and greeted Madeleine with a respectful formality that Anna found endearing. He half-bowed and almost clicked his heels together as he took her hand. "Frau Wolf, good evening."

"*Hallo*, you little rascal," Madeleine replied. "What have you been up to?"

"I am heating water for the bath, if you would like to have one," Oskar said. "I don't really need it."

Amalia giggled and held her nose. "Yes, you do, too. You smell."

The two children began laughing and Anna shooed them out of the room. "Go clean up, both of you. I need some fresh air in here."

Madeleine sat on the sofa and looked at Anna. "So, really, nothing happened today?" Her eyebrows rose under a direct gaze.

Anna busied herself with imaginary wrinkles on her blouse. "No."

"You, my dear girl, are a terrible liar." Madeleine crossed her legs and leaned back against the deflated sofa cushions.

Anna deflected. "There was a new hire at the Collecting Point. A curator with big credentials. I find her irritating, but it's nothing."

"Irritating? In what way?"

Anna searched for a plausible reply that would not give away the churning feelings. She cleared her throat. "She is a know-it-all. Sort of arrogant. Kind of inserted herself into things. And now I have to work with her."

"I see. Inserted herself between you and Captain Cooper, you mean?"

Anna shook her head. "No, of course not. She's just…well, she's rude. To me."

Madeleine smiled. "And not to Cooper, is that it?"

Anna crossed the room and began pulling clothes from the drawers in the big walnut wardrobe in the corner. "I think it's time I did some wash. Would you like me to wash your dress?" She gestured toward the blue cotton dress Madeleine wore.

"No, it's still fine, I think. Why don't you sit with me for a minute?" She patted the cushion next to her.

Anna was stuck. She felt like a school girl as she sat down, dutiful.

"Auntie, I know what you think. I know what everyone thinks, but it's not like that."

Madeleine chuckled. "I don't think anything, my dear. And that's not even what I want to talk about. I want to talk about the other thing."

"What other thing?"

"The letter."

A surge of heat behind her ears made the skin on Anna's cheeks begin to prickle. Her eyes moved to the envelope from the housing authority that lay on the bed. The letter about Oskar from the refugee agency was in her bag. Two life-upending letters. "What letter?"

"Don't ask, 'what letter?' You know what I mean."

Anna heard herself start speaking. "I'll go talk to the refugee people about Oskar. He has a home; they don't need to concern themselves with him. I'll get it straightened out. " She closed her mouth.

Madeleine shook her head. "You haven't answered him, have you?"

Anna said nothing, waiting for Madeleine to explain.

"He is still your husband." Madeleine patted Anna's hand as if to wake her from a daze. She smiled, but her eyes did the opposite.

Madeleine was talking about a different letter than the one about Oskar or even the one from the housing agency. She meant the one Anna had received from her husband, Thomas, at the end of August. The one telling her he wanted them to come home to their little village in Thuringia in the gentle, tree-covered hills near Weimar. The home she had left when it became part of the Russian sector. She had stashed the letter in the desk after reading it only once. She could not bring herself to read it again, even though she sensed Thomas's hand in the smooth strokes of the ink. She could see him sitting at his desk in the bedroom of their house, the light from the window highlighting the worry on his face. In the weeks since the letter had arrived, his words hung over her every moment. The only thing that distracted her was the work at the Collecting Point.

"Yes." What else could she offer?

Madeleine shook her head. "It's not right of you to leave Thomas hanging on the line like that. Don't you care about him even a little?"

"Of course I care about him. He's my husband. I love him. I just don't know how to tell him, that's all." She sank into the cushion. "How can I tell him we aren't coming home?"

"He deserves to know, my dear. And there will be legalities to deal with."

"Legalities?"

"Yes, of course. You'll need to file for divorce. You can't stay married under these circumstances. You must let him go, Anna. You can't have it both ways."

Anna shook her head. "I can't do that. Not to Thomas. Never. I could persuade him to come to Wiesbaden and be with us here, in the American sector." She knew this was impossible. Thomas hated the Americans almost as much as he hated the Nazis. He was happy in the Russian sector. He had said so in his letter.

Madeleine patted her arm. "Then do it. But tell him the truth so he can make his own choice. You are being unkind. How long have you had the letter?"

"Three weeks only." Anna tried to act as if it had not, in fact, felt like an eternity. "I haven't had much time to think about it."

"You held your breath for months to hear from him, and now you don't have time to send him a reply? Shame on you, child."

Anna hated when Madeleine scolded her. She heard her own mother's voice and she knew she deserved it. She thought of her husband and the life—the entire world—she had left behind that were now so removed, as if she had read the story in a book. She tried to muster an emotion that would be appropriate, but all she felt was fear.

"Thomas is a good man, and he deserves a future. I understand that you don't want to go back into the Russian sector. But if he is rebuilding his life there, then you must let him go. And the Americans won't let him back here so easily either. He is a communist; he will have to say so on his Fragebogen. The *Amis* won't like that at all. You hear the news, don't you?"

Anna exhaled and looked at her hands, as if they held some answer. Thomas had a house and, as a doctor, an official position in the Russian occupational government. Were the Russians also kicking Germans out of their houses? Maybe if they all went back, they would at least have a place to live. No, it wasn't worth it.

"Divorce?" The word came from a small voice in the doorway. "Mama?"

"*Maus*, you aren't supposed to be listening." Anna stifled a groan. She held out her hand for her daughter who stood clutching her doll, her eyes wide between a tangle of undone braids. "Come here." She wanted to comfort her, but Amalia turned and disappeared into the bathroom, slamming the door behind her.

"She'll be all right." Madeleine stood up. "I'll get the rations put away."

"There's something else, Auntie." Anna reached for Madeleine's hand. It was getting dark inside as the light of the late summer evening faded, but Anna waited to light the candle on the side table. The dim light felt like a protective barrier. She held the letter up.

"What's that?"

"The house has been requisitioned. We have to be out in two days." Anna passed the letter to her, but Madeleine didn't open it.

Madeleine sat down on the bed. A few strands of her silver hair had come loose from their bun and trailed down her back. Today she looked like an old woman, which she was, but she never appeared that way to Anna. She was defeated. Anna surmised that her thoughts were with those she had lost. Madeleine had remained steadfast and abiding while everything went to hell around her. But now, the war had finally unmoored even her.

Madeleine tapped the folded letter on her knee in a steady rhythm, her silhouette outlined in gray on gray. Anna blamed herself for this turn of events, as if she had brought the Americans' attention to the house, even though she knew the eviction had nothing to do with her. The home was relatively intact, the plumbing functioned, it had a roof and a door, and thus was desirable property for the Americans. As the occupation settled in, more and more *Amis* needed places to stay. And she had noticed a lot of visitors at the Collecting Point, other Monuments Men from Munich, and officers with loud voices and big strides taking up space in the halls. Cooper had been preoccupied with meetings that took him away from doing the in-the-field work that he enjoyed more. Everything was changing again already. She had found a good job with the Monuments Men, and Cooper had been her advocate for a better job with more pay. She had gained a toehold that turned into solid footing and could see a path emerging into her future. When the letter from Thomas had come, asking her to return to an entirely different future, her choice had been almost immediately clear. She loved Thomas, even his idealistic commitments to a communist system in a world now devoid of any scrap of idealism, and he was father to a daughter who thought he hung the moon and stars.

She knew his beliefs when she married him, before bright, blinding lines were drawn and people had to make life and death choices about what they believed. During the war, the Nazis had hunted communists with unrelenting cruelty, stringing suspects up from the light poles in the same town square in Weimar where she and Thomas had once spent warm Sunday afternoons together, walking and talking as if nothing else mattered. But when those beliefs became a threat to their safety, he became darker and furtive in his ways. It was a matter of survival, and she went along, keeping ears and eyes closed for the sake of Amalia. But at night she woke, gasping and sweating, from nightmares of his face on the lolling heads of the bodies hanging next to the now-silent fountain in Weimar's central square. Even when it was clear that the Russians were no benevolent conquerors, he never faltered in his devotion to their ideology.

But she saw no future in communism, no matter how much Thomas saw one, no matter how much he wished for it. A more scrupulous or pragmatic woman would have taken this chance to return to her husband who was sure to be rewarded for his communist loyalties with a choice position and special perks, like milk and eggs and bottles of vodka. In the Russian sector, they would have a roof over their heads, and not be evicted into the street on a moment's notice. Her husband, the eminent doctor, had stature, and by extension, so would she. She might even have electricity and reliably running water, and Amalia would go to school every day instead of running around the black market with Oskar. But it would come at a steep price. There was a reason the *Amis* despised the Russians. All the Americans' talk about freedom and justice and opportunity—they believed it. It was not an abstract concept, it was their way of being. And it was starting to rub off on her.

And already so much had changed. Anna was now responsible for a boy who had no one and nothing. He didn't even know the truth about how much had been taken from him. That was another secret Anna kept. The secrets were beginning to pile up inside her like garbage, and she had to think to keep them straight. As they sat in the dark, she worried once again what would become of them. For a moment, her new life had looked so promising. But, of course, that was in her own mind where unpleasant tasks were ignored and she created her own reality. She hadn't even told Thomas that she wasn't coming back. He hadn't any idea what had happened to them, and she didn't even have the decency to tell her husband that their paths had separated.

She took Madeleine's hand. "I'll talk to Captain Cooper first thing tomorrow. I'm sure he can stop us from being evicted. Please don't worry."

Madeleine sighed. "This is a fine ending to the story. They sit over there in their Collecting Point trying to return every scrap of paper and oily canvas to their rightful owners, but they have no issue with snatching my home out from under me. Isn't that wonderful? And now we are out on the street."

chapter two

"Come on, Frau Klein, look alive, would you?" Cooper swatted her on the arm with a file folder on his way to his desk. "Lots to do."

Cooper's arrival made Anna jump. She had been lost in the list of the Zeilsheim camp residents, which Karla had plopped on her desk with great satisfaction first thing that morning, whispering, "I thought you could use this." She had leaned in, her sense of drama in full swing. "I need it back before lunch. Farmer wants it recorded and filed."

Now Anna closed the folder on the list she was working on and fed a sheet into the typewriter, trying to look busy. Cooper had taken Eva Lange with him to the countryside, documenting damage to some old cloister. Anna tried to ignore the fact that she and Cooper used to go together. Why was she typing up reports rather than translating in the field, as she had been doing? "Your field reports from yesterday are on the desk," she muttered.

"What's gotten into you, Frau Klein?" Cooper slammed the stack of file folders on the desk. Anna spun around in her chair. Even before Eva Lange's arrival, he had become distracted and short-tempered once or twice, but now he was in a full rage.

"Excuse me?"

Cooper wiped his brow with his handkerchief. Their shared office was hot, and the humid breeze from the open window didn't help. He had spent most of the morning downstairs in Eva Lange's office next to the conserver's studio, where bespectacled men with serious faces pored over damaged paintings. When Anna had seen him, he had been irritable, already once criticizing the way she had logged the painting details from the Morgenstern collection into the catalog, even though she had done it in the same meticulous way as always. Now he was shuffling papers between folders and ignoring her.

"Excuse me?" Anna repeated. "What have I done now?"

"These files are a mess. You know I like them to be alphabetical. These are in some other order. Chronological? What the hell?" Cooper threw up his hands.

Anna turned back to her work. "I haven't done those files. Those are the ones from downstairs. You took them off my desk this morning before I had a chance to finish them, remember?" She began typing again, pecking hard at the keys.

Cooper exhaled and sat down. "Anyway, I need them sorted right away. And here." He handed her Eva's questionnaire and the letter of introduction that had gotten her hired. "Make sure these get downstairs in the personnel file."

Anna snatched the files from his hand. "Yes, sir. Right away. What's gotten into *you*? You've been nothing but rude all day."

Slumping in his chair, Cooper pulled open the center drawer of the desk and rummaged around before slamming it shut again. "Goddammit. Never mind. I'm sorry. We've hit a rough patch with the higher-ups. Politics. Total nonsense. It's taking up all my time. I can't..." He stopped. "I shouldn't be taking this out on you. Please, carry on. Don't mind me."

Anna nodded and turned to sort through the files. "All right." She typed one report and then another, feeling his presence behind her, gauging when he had calmed down enough for her to broach the issue of her impending homelessness. As she listened for his movements and formulated her approach, she stopped typing.

"Anna? You all right?" Cooper asked. "You seem out of sorts, too. You feeling okay?"

Anna bit her lip, keeping her back turned. She faked a laugh without turning around. "Yes, of course. It's the heat. In a few weeks, I'll be complaining about the cold. It's always something." She felt stupid and shifted the papers around to buy herself a moment. How to ask Cooper for his help with the housing problem? He was already on edge. She decided to wait until after lunch. He was usually in a good mood then.

"If you say so. Listen, can you show Fraulein Lange around a bit today? Maybe take her to the canteen for lunch? Help her fit in? I think she'll be a great help to us."

"Of course," Anna said. "I am glad she is helpful. She can help me with this Morgenstern collection."

"I've already put her on it. She says she now remembers hearing of a dealer in Frankfurt who sold the art the Nazis stole but then didn't want to keep. If she can get her hands on some of his files, we can see if any Morgensterns went through him. An address might turn up. It's a long shot, but that's the kind of knowledge we need."

Anna regretted making the offer. Morgenstern was her project. She had been carefully documenting all the pieces, making note of all the labels, and she wanted to be the one to find their home. Now he was setting up the Lange woman to take credit for it. "Very well," was all she said.

"You know we're all in this together," Cooper said with deliberate condescension, "We're *all* the good guys."

Anna nodded. "Right. Thank you for the reminder." The words she wanted to say would not form on her tongue, so she continued typing to see if they might force their way out.

"Look, Frau Klein, are we having a problem? Because if we are, I'd sure like to know about it. I don't have time for this emotional nonsense, I've got work to do and so do you." He appeared at her side and leaned against the edge of her desk.

Anna pushed her chair back to create some distance between them. "I'm fine, Captain. It's just that…" She fidgeted with the papers on the desk. *Were they really all the good guys? Did good guys throw old women and children out of their houses?* She blew air through her pursed lips, as if to propel the words. "We've been told we have to move out."

"Move out? Who has to move out?"

"We—Madeleine and the children and I—have to move out by day after tomorrow. They requisitioned Madeleine's house." She felt better having let the words go, but hearing them spoken out loud gave them more weight. It made everything more real.

Cooper rolled his eyes. "That's not going to happen. I'll talk to them. They'll have to find somewhere else. Do you have the paperwork?" He held out his hand.

Anna pulled the letter from her bag. "We'll have to go to the DP camp." Her voice cracked and Cooper caught her eye.

"Don't worry, all right?" He held her gaze. "Trust me, won't you?"

"I do trust you. But can you fix it by tomorrow?" She hated this, asking for help, feeling vulnerable.

"Sure, I can." He put the letter on the table. "Consider it done. You're not going anywhere." His eyes moved past her and into the hallway, as the footsteps of a cohort passed their open door. Cooper shot a look at one of the men, whom Anna didn't recognize, and then shook his head as their eyes met. The other man kept walking.

"What was that about?" she asked.

Cooper shook his head with more energy. "You trust me? Now, can I trust you?"

"Of course."

He gestured for her to lean forward and tilted his head toward her ear.

"You've noticed the State Department types hanging around the place?"

Anna nodded, but she hadn't seen any more visitors than usual.

"All right. Here's the short version." He leaned closer. Anna could smell the coffee on his breath and felt its warmth on her cheek as he spoke. She stared at the floor where his boots were almost touching hers. "The suits stateside are stirring all kinds of bullshit about the art we have here—the German National Gallery stuff? We're worried they're going to pull our funding and rescind our orders. And then they'll ship all this art stateside and put it in their museums. They put out a press release about it a couple of days ago. I thought Farmer's head was going to shoot straight out of his collar."

Anna had only encountered Captain Farmer briefly, but found him to be matter-of-fact. But of the rest of the *Amis*, she was never quite sure. They were so big in their ways and so entitled, which was understandable. And the art stored at the Collecting Point now was worth millions, not to mention how prestigious having ownership of it was. Taking it to America would mark the utter downfall of German culture. It was poetic when she thought about it. *Of course, that's how it will go.*

"So, it's true. That's what the plan was all along, wasn't it?" She gave Cooper a side glance, not daring to turn her head. "I suppose you've earned them. The spoils of war."

"No, that's just it, you see? There's a group of us who are flat out against this." His voice was steady and unemotional, as if he were giving a routine order for the hundredth time, but his eyes darted into the hallway.

"What do you mean?"

"I mean, I need you to keep eyes and ears open. Not everyone is on the same team around here. Get it?"

Anna's heart sank. With the events of the past days, her attachment to the Collecting Point and the work of the Monuments Men had been her one touchstone. The one thing she knew was right. Now the *Amis* really did want to take the German's art, and their whole operation was in jeopardy. She felt more tired than ever.

"Come on, Anna. You know me. I can't speak for the idiots in Washington, but this was never the plan."

"It sounds like you're going to make trouble," Anna said. *I can't afford to lose this job. Not now.*

Cooper sat up and grinned. "I like to incite trouble. It's one of my best talents. If I can't do it in the Army, where am I going to do it? The U.S. Army is the perfect place. Besides, things are starting to get boring." He winked. "Don't worry. Let me know if you hear any loose talk. And we have to make sure everything is battened down tight. Everything is by the book. I mean it. We can't afford any mistakes."

He checked his watch. "I need to meet Fraulein Lange downstairs. We have a meeting with the curators. Let's talk about this later. Steady on, Frau Klein." He patted her on the shoulder and turned on his heel. "There's lots to do."

"And my housing?" she called after him.

"Leave it to me," he said as he disappeared down the hall.

Anna stared at her typewriter. She decided she would trust him. Anyway, she had no choice.

The small storeroom was set up like a warehouse, with large shelves to store the paintings lined up against the wall, leaving only a narrow space to walk through. Anna squeezed past the frames protruding from the shelves, catching glimpses of painted faces and lively strokes of landscapes. She wanted to stop and look at the bounty that the Collecting Point had acquired, but she was not supposed to be alone in the storeroom, which was secured under Cooper's lock and key. Anna had fished the keys from Cooper's desk drawer knowing he was in a meeting with Eva. She checked the custody card in her hand again. One of the digits on the registration number for the *Man in a Green Jacket* painting was missing. She had noted it when she went to file the card with the rest of the conditions reports. With an incorrect number, the painting could be misfiled, or worse, misplaced. She wanted to be sure everything was by the book, as Cooper said. No room for mistakes now. She estimated she had about ten minutes before she would be missed.

Anna sorted through the canvases, many of them stripped of their frames. She recognized the Velasquez she had logged in last week and the small Goya. Her daily interactions with masterpieces of art had not yet become routine, and she remembered every detail. When her hand reached the spot where the painting should be, there was a noticeable gap. The slot was empty. She checked the paintings around it, slowly at first, then with a little more urgency. Her cheeks warmed as her heart accelerated.

"It's not lost," Anna said to herself. "It's not lost. There's a reason for this." Had a conservator pulled it for another round of work? She decided to be irritated rather than concerned. That one custody card was the last one in the inventory and she wanted to finish the file and get on with her work.

Anna sorted through the paintings for another five minutes before giving up. The painting wasn't there. She had looked again and again in the place where it should be, where many of the other Morgenstern pieces were, all sorted and numbered and organized as they should be. She recognized many of the paintings she had recorded, which had come from a cellar in Bensheim, a picturesque country town fifty kilometers to the south. The paintings had belonged to a Jacob Morgenstern, a gallery owner in Frankfurt, but the stamps on the back provided no address or further information. The collection would have been taken over by an Aryan business partner who had been forced on the Jewish collector, thanks to the Nazi laws. Anna was learning how the Nazi art theft program had worked so well. First they passed the laws that stripped Jews of their businesses and their property. Jewish-owned art galleries were "Aryanized," forced to sell their inventory to more suitable owners—meaning Aryan—for far less than it was worth. Those forced sales moved most art out of Jewish hands, but that wasn't enough, of course. In the end, the Nazis stole what they wanted either from individual collectors or from art museums. That this collection existed at all anymore was a miracle, as most Aryan dealers unloaded their new inventories quickly, selling them to anyone who would take them for well below their market value, just to be rid of them. There was no record of who the Aryan proxy owner of this collection had been, but Anna was surprised these paintings had eluded the many dealers buying up the art cheap on Hitler's orders. The enormous Fuehrer Museum in Linz that Hitler planned to house his hostage art had thankfully never come into being. Anna's work with the Monuments Men would serve as her small act of penance for what her people had done. She vowed to learn all she could about the work they were doing, not just to be useful to the Americans—although keeping her job was enough motivation—but also to help set things right, to keep her eyes open after she had kept them shut for so long.

But now something other than her ever-present hunger made her stomach shift. Something was wrong. She considered the chain of command the painting had traveled along before reaching its spot in the storage room. She had logged it in, or at least she was fairly sure she had. Cooper had sent all the logged paintings downstairs to be photographed and assessed for damage, so one of the conservators, or even Eva, had been involved in that. Then it would have been loaded onto its palette by one of the German workers, or a GI, and brought in here. Access to the Collecting Point was heavily controlled ever since the large shipment of masterpieces from the National Gallery in Berlin had arrived at the end of August. Nothing went missing from storerooms. Her stomach did another twirl. There was no logical reason for the painting to not be in its spot, safe and sound, and she knew it, no matter how many explanations she gave herself as to where it might be. She squeezed Cooper's keys in her hand. If she had not come down here in the first place, would anyone have known it was missing? Not for a while, at least not until there was a reason to crate the painting or move it. She scanned the rows and rows of canvases and frames as her heart began to pound. This was not *by the book* at all.

She turned off the light and cracked open the door. Peering into the hallway, she was relieved to see it was empty. She quickly stepped out and pulled the door closed, locking it in a quick motion and then heading toward the stairs.

"Frau Klein?"

The voice behind her made Anna jump. She turned to see Eva Lange a few steps behind her. *Where had she come from?*

"Is everything all right?" The woman smiled, but there was neither friendliness nor concern in her eyes. She knew the rules and she knew Anna had no business being in the storeroom alone.

"Yes, thank you." Anna shoved her hands in her pockets. "And you? How was your first day?"

Eva Lange regarded Anna for several beats before answering. "All good. There's so much work to be done. I am happy to be of service."

Anna nodded and turned to extract herself from the conversation.

"Were you looking for something?"

"Excuse me?" Anna turned to face Eva but took a step back to indicate she was leaving. She wanted to end the conversation.

"In the storeroom. Were you looking for something?"

"I was double-checking on an inventory number. Everything's fine." *Go ahead and tell Cooper. I know you want to.* She turned to go. "I need to get upstairs."

Eva nodded. "I came to tell you that Captain Cooper is looking for you. He was wondering why you weren't in the office."

"Fine. I'll find him. Thank you for your help," she lied.

The woman's voice droned. What was she saying? At the back of the group of Collecting Point workers who had been summoned to the main hall, Anna stood on her tiptoes to catch a glimpse of the new Monuments Man—a woman, in fact—who was imparting some crucial information. Karla was standing nearby and shot Anna a quizzical look. She was relieved to know that she wasn't the only one to not understand the woman's speech. Anna returned the look with a shrug and gave up trying to see. Instead, she stared at the backs of the men in front of her, subconsciously searching for Cooper.

"...And so, we must be vigilant about who comes and goes on the premises, and we must be meticulous in our work," the woman said in a raised voice that finally carried to the back of the group. "It is imperative that we cross our t's and dot our i's; the scrutiny of the United States government is upon us, and we must ensure that our work is above reproach. We, and what's left of the civilized world, cannot afford for this work to end." The woman officer ended with a flourish, clearly designed to motivate the troops, as it were. The group responded with an affirmative grunt before dispersing in a low hum.

"What was that about?" Karla asked. She sidled up to Anna and crossed her arms.

"I guess she's some new Monuments Man." Anna shook her head.

"Woman."

"Right. Not sure what she was saying, though. Sounded serious."

Karla nodded. "I'll find out and let you know." She had found herself another spy mission. Anna tried to stifle a smile but did a poor job. Karla was a breath of fresh air—young and enthusiastic—ready to get on with the adventure of her life.

A face in the crowd of *Amis* turned toward them. It was Corporal Long, the guard who was usually posted outside the front gate. Anna had had several encounters with him, often asking him for a favor of some kind. Usually he obliged, his good nature getting the better of him. But he wasn't looking at Anna. He was staring at Karla, and no one else. Anna followed his gaze to let him know she saw him, but he was too distracted by the fact that Karla was looking back at him, a flush rising in her cheeks. Anna grinned at the sweet display and found herself face to face with Eva.

"Oh, hello," Anna stammered, her mood now soured.

"Frau Klein." Eva's imperious tone reverberated and turned heads. Anna's eyes searched for Karla to pretend to ask her an important question, but the girl had seen Eva coming and vanished. Anna was stuck exchanging pleasantries, wishing she had been as quick as Karla. Eva was determined to have the upper hand in every conversation, which Anna would have thought funny if it had not been so annoying. Why Cooper didn't notice it was beyond her.

"Ah, ladies. Frau Klein, Fraulein Lange." Cooper approached them with outstretched arms as if he planned to gather them both into an embrace. He stopped just short, patting each on the shoulder and looking around before he spoke. "Glad I found you both together. We have work to do."

"Who was that woman?" Anna asked.

"Major Edith Standen," Cooper said. "She's come up from Munich to help us get our act together. And also to take some of the private collection art back with her. We'll be focusing only on state collections from now on. Private restitutions will be handled by Munich."

"Does that mean she'll take the Morgenstern works?" Anna felt a wave of panic.

Cooper cocked his head. "I know it's not as exciting, Frau Klein, but trust me, we'll have our hands full." He grinned. Anna had not seen him smile in days.

"What was the Major saying about the eyes of the government being on us?" Eva asked. "What does that mean?"

"I'll tell you more later. For right now, let's just say we have to keep our noses clean and not screw up."

Visions of the missing painting floated into Anna's mind. Her ears burned as they always did when she tried to hide something. She knew Major Standen's speech had something to do with Cooper's recent bad moods. Why wasn't he telling her anything anymore?

Cooper continued. "Here's what needs to get done. Number one, we confirm the inventory for the shipments that came in last week. Make sure everything is stored where it's supposed to be and that all is in order." He thrust a carbon copy of a list at Anna. "Not the most exciting work, but essential to our survival, if I may put it that way. Once we get this bureaucratic bullshit behind us, we can get back to doing the real work." He smiled at Eva. "You're in good hands, Fraulein Lange." Their eyes met for a beat before he turned back to Anna. He pointed a finger at her. "Anna, I mean, Frau Klein, you're in charge. Report back to me by noon tomorrow. It might be a slog, but let's get it done, okay?"

Anna nodded and skimmed the list. It comprised maybe fifty paintings, which shouldn't take long, provided things were where they were supposed to be. "We had better get going," she said.

"And, number two," Cooper interrupted.

The women waited to hear his next assignment.

"Anna, I called the housing people and went as high as I could go. They need Frau Wolf's house for two visiting colonels who are here for some military trials. All the hotels are full and so are the barracks. I had it explained to me that it was either you move out of your house, or I'll have to move out of mine to make room."

Anna's heart sank. "Okay."

Cooper held up a hand. "I'm not done. I even got on the horn to the regional government people to see if they would override the requisition, but no-go there either. I just want you to know that I did try."

"Okay," she repeated.

"But here's what we're going to do. Fraulein Lange, I believe you live with your father in a house—where is it?"

"Kopernikusstrasse." Eva was hesitant.

"And you told me earlier it's a big house? We all know big houses are high on the list for requisitioning."

Eva nodded slowly, her face skeptical.

"Right. So, Frau Klein, you'll move in with Fraulein Lange. And since you are both employed by us, I will have the housing people mark the property as home to multiple families, which will keep it out of the firing line. At least for now."

Anna was horrified. Live with Eva? This imperious woman who acted like she knew everything? "But, Captain, there are four of us," Anna said. "I'm sure Fraulein Lange doesn't have room for us all."

Eva said nothing. Anna stared at Cooper. What was he thinking? Move in with a total stranger? That was his solution?

"When would this be?" Eva finally asked, her voice low.

"Tomorrow," Cooper replied. "After work sound okay to you, Frau Klein?" He looked at Anna, his hands on his hips, as if waiting for a petulant child to cooperate. "It's either this or the DP camp, with its lice checks and typhoid powder and overflowing bathrooms."

"I guess." Cooper was right. She had no choice.

Eva was similarly resigned to their fate. "Yes," she said. "I will tell Father tonight." She had not looked at Anna once.

"Great." Cooper rubbed his hands together and rocked back on his heels. "Fraulein Lange, you go ahead and get started on that list. Frau Klein will be along shortly."

Eva took the list from Anna's hand and was gone without a word. Anna considered that Eva was just as irritated and shocked as she was. Now, Anna would have no respite, not even at home. She would be living with the irritant.

Cooper smiled and cocked his head. "Okay, so it's not ideal, but you have to believe me. It's the best I could do. There's not a room to be had in this town, especially not on such short notice."

"How long do you think it will be? I'm sure it's not ideal for Fraulein Lange either. Or her father."

"That I can't say. But I'll stay on it. You'll get your house back,

I promise." He took a step toward her. "I have a meeting. I'll come check on you two later. And, Anna? We're still friends, right?" He tilted his head slightly to one side and smiled. The chest pocket on his jacket under his name tag had come unbuttoned and Anna reached up to fix it before she could stop herself. She pulled her hand to her chest, and took a step back, embarrassed at her instinct.

"Of course we're friends." She cleared her throat.

Cooper bit his lip and paused before he spoke. "Good. We need you, don't you forget that."

chapter three

"Do you know where this goes?" Eva held up a small painting of a man in a green jacket.

Anna blanched. The frowning man, rendered in dramatic strokes, a plume of gray hair floating around his head, gazed at her from the canvas. It was the painting that had been missing from the Morgenstern collection earlier. It had no business being mixed in with the collection she and Eva were logging in.

"Where did you find that?" Anna asked, the question sounding more urgent than she intended. The two of them had been working in the storeroom on the inventory that Cooper had assigned for well over an hour, but they had kept their distance from each other. Anna kept her back turned and hadn't watched Eva, preferring to ignore her altogether. They hadn't spoken ten words to each other in the cramped little room.

Eva shrugged, "It was right here." She gestured to a slot between two paintings along the back wall. "But it's not on my list. Is it on yours?" She tilted the canvas toward the overhead light. "Emil Nolde. One of those crazy Expressionists."

"Yes, that's right. It shouldn't be here at all." Anna grabbed the painting, which caused Eva to raise her hands as if to apologize for having touched it. "It belongs next door in the other room with the Morgenstern collection. How on earth did it get in here?"

"I have no idea," Eva said, a defensive tone creeping into her voice. "I've never seen it before in my life. You were in charge of the Morgenstern collection, weren't you?"

Anna ignored the question. She leaned the painting against the wall by the door. "I'll put it back later." *I have to get Cooper's key first. Without him knowing.* She returned to the task at hand to change the subject, flipping through the remaining pages of the list to see how many more she had to go. "How are you coming with your list?"

"I still have a lot to do." Eva shuffled through the papers. "You?"

"Me, too." Anna stole a glance at Eva, who she assumed was making a mental note to report the misplaced painting to Cooper and blame it on Anna.

Eva bent to pick up a painting off the floor and lay it on the bench she was using as a desk. For a while, the only sound in the stifling room was the scratch of pencils on paper. The salt hung in the air; even months after emerging from the salt mines, the paintings still bore a distinct scent that got into your skin. Anna inhaled, happy for the familiar smell. They worked side by side in silence for another fifteen minutes.

"I think Captain Cooper's plan will work out," Eva said finally. "We only have one bath, but we do have a spare bedroom with a heater in it. It might be a little small, but I think you will all fit."

"And your father? What will he say?"

"Oh, he'll be happy for the company. I leave him alone all day stewing in his books and his thoughts. I think he'll like having someone other than me to talk to."

Anna nodded. "It wasn't my idea, you know. I had nothing to do with it."

"I know. It's a round-about solution and we have no choice but to abide by it. I know how Captain Cooper is."

No, you don't. What is that supposed to mean? Eva had turned her attention back to the list on the table. She was beautiful and elegant. And available. Aside from the anemic and enthusiastically ignored anti-fraternization laws, there was nothing stopping her and Cooper from being more than colleagues. She would be a nice diversion for him, maybe even more than that. And, for Eva, he was a golden ticket to a better future.

"It's only ten minutes from here." Eva said, her voice softer now, like a sister giving advice. "You'll want to bring your winter clothes. It will be cold soon enough."

They continued working, Anna focusing on the brushstrokes that morphed into faces and bodies and trees and buildings, her eyes focusing and unfocusing as her mind wandered. After her recent experiences with lies and more lies, she was hesitant to trust anyone, much less a total stranger. But Eva wasn't a total stranger. The *Amis* had vetted her, and she was clean as a whistle. And, anyway, they had no choice.

"You're worried, aren't you?" Eva didn't look up when she spoke. "I can tell."

"I don't want to be a nuisance. I have two children and an elderly woman in tow." It was part of the truth anyway.

"I understand." Eva straightened. "It's hard to remember how to help each other. At some point, we must learn to be normal humans again. Neighbors. Friends."

"Yes. Normal humans."

Eva smiled and shrugged, turning her palms upward in a questioning gesture. "And anyway, we have no choice."

Anna smiled at Eva's apparent mind reading. She imagined they were only two of a million women just like them, adrift and lonely, trying on their new lives, trying to bring something good out of the darkness. *Damn you, Cooper.*

The room at Eva's house on the Kopernikusstrasse was small, but the four of them were used to close quarters. A tall window looked on to the street, the direct view blocked by a sheer curtain that covered the bottom half of the window. Heavy cinnamon-colored drapes reached to the ceiling, and the wood floor was warmed by a patchwork of overlapping rugs. An iron stove in the corner promised warm nights once the cold set in, assuming there would be any firewood. On the wall above the large bed hung an ornate mirror with a flowery gilded frame that reflected the overhead light fixture of candle-shaped bulbs hovering just above their heads. Two cots were set up against the perpendicular walls, making a square of beds around the middle of the room. It was comfortable and more than adequate, even a little fancy. Anna ran her hand along the top of the night stand where a clock and a lamp shared the limited space, as if to check if their new home was real.

"I know it's a bit cramped, but it's only for sleeping." Eva handed Anna a stack of towels. "Make yourself at home anywhere in the house. I thought at least this way you'd have a private space."

"It's perfectly fine, thank you." Anna waved a hand to indicate she had taken it in. The children tiptoed around, as if to not fully commit their presence to the room in case it was taken away from them. Amalia wore an expression that looked like she had just eaten something terrible and was waiting to spit it out politely. They were grateful and uncomfortable at the same time.

"We'll have dinner at seven o'clock." Eva rested her hand on the door knob as she looked at them.

"I'll help you with that as soon as we are settled." Anna lifted her bag onto one of the cots. It would only take her five minutes to put away their meager belongings.

When Eva had closed the door and left them alone, Madeleine sat down heavily on the bed and put her bag on her knees.

"Will this be all right, Auntie?" Anna took the old woman's hand.

"Yes, child, it will be fine."

"Just until you get your house back."

"At least it keeps us out of that camp."

It had been hard to leave the apartment. Madeleine had herded them out the door with her usual cheerful stoicism. "Let's hope the *Amis* take good care of the place," she had said as Anna choked back tears. Amalia and Oskar had said nothing, but Oskar made a point to take the picture his adoptive mother had painted. It was a simple landscape that was his sole meaningful possession and he carried it under his arm in a white-knuckled grip. Amalia dragged her doll Lulu by the hair and clutched her little cigar box of treasures. That left

Anna to drag the one suitcase with all their clothes down the stairs while Madeleine took a last look around before locking up. They left the key with Frau Hermann, the building's supervisor, who grumbled about having to deal with loud Americans and their dirty boots in the hallways. Frau Herman was impossible to please, and her constant complaints made Madeleine laugh. "I'll miss you, Ingeborg," she had said to the woman, and Anna knew she meant it.

Anna watched Oskar make room for his painting on the windowsill, leaning it against the glass and taking a step back to admire it. Amalia found a spot for Lulu on her cot and Anna left them to get settled. She found Eva busy in the tiny kitchen, sawing at a stale loaf of dark bread with a dull knife.

"Hard as a rock," she muttered, whacking the crust with the knife.

"Let me." Anna took the knife but only managed to push the loaf around on the cutting board. "We should sprinkle some water on it and put it in the oven." She felt awkward and self-conscious. Eva always acted as though she were Anna's superior, both professionally and personally. Now, sharing a living space, Anna had no idea how to act. She wanted to be useful, but she didn't want to be the maid, either.

Anna indicated the pan of potatoes frying on the stove. "That smells good."

"Lard. And there's a little bit of ham left over. I get more rations tomorrow." Eva wiped her hands on the rag that draped over the edge of the sink. "And, anyway, I'm going to sell some things at the black market to get a little extra money. We are lucky to still have a few belongings here that we don't need."

"I wish I had something to contribute," Anna said. "But I'll get my rations later in the week. Amalia gets cereal and milk in hers because she's still young enough. And Oskar is a black market master. He can get just about anything."

"Ah, there's the silver lining." Eva smirked.

Anna pretended to be occupied with the bread to avoid any further talk while Eva pulled plates from the cabinet.

"Oh, good, we have enough," she said. "I wasn't sure we would. So many dishes were smashed in the bombs."

If Eva was trying to make her feel like a burden, she was succeeding. Anna stared at the bread and considered her options. She had to make this work, or she was out on the street. What's more, she had to get Eva to want to make it work, since Eva had all the leverage. It was her house, after all.

"Did you get a chance to put that Nolde painting back?" Eva pulled forks from a small basket on the kitchen table.

"Yes," Anna said. She had snuck it in when Cooper had been off on a field visit. It had taken all of five minutes, and this time she was certain no one had seen her.

"I wonder how it got misplaced. We simply can't have mistakes like that," Eva lectured.

An indignant irritation simmered in Anna's chest, but she held her tongue. It hadn't been her mistake, but there was no use arguing.

"I look forward to meeting your father," she said instead. The old man had been sequestered in his room taking a nap. "I hope we won't be a bother to him."

"I told you, I think he'll like having you here," Eva replied, her tone neutral.

Anna could not get a foothold in the conversation. She tried one more time. "And your mother? Where is she?"

"She died right after we moved to Wiesbaden. The war, the deprivations, it was too much for her."

Anna nodded. *So much death.*

"And my brother, he was sent to France. He died there." Eva's eyes darted back and forth, gathering up the memories in her mind. Her face shrank, losing a bit of its life. For one breath, Anna almost felt sorry for her.

"I'm sorry. My parents are dead, too. In the bombs in Vienna. I've never even seen their graves. They were buried together with all the other bomb victims."

"And your husband?"

The question took Anna by surprise. "What about him?"

"Tell me about him." Eva put the forks down. "Don't you miss him?"

It felt as if the air around Anna had gone very still. The question pierced the part of her that lay dormant under all the rubble of her current life. She swallowed. Could she get the words to come out?

"Yes, I do miss him," she said focusing out the window where a tiny yellow bird flitted to and fro on the windowsill, pecking at invisible delicacies. "Very much."

"But?" Eva asked.

"But? But we aren't together now. Things are not the same."

Eva leaned back against the table and folded her arms. Her head tilted to one side as she looked at Anna straight on for the first time that evening. "What's he like, your husband?"

Anna exhaled. "He's a doctor. A kind man. Generous. Always thinks of the greater good. That's a blessing and a curse."

Eva nodded. "He didn't serve? You are lucky."

"He ran our local clinic and hospital. He was deemed unfit to serve due to his terrible back. And anyway, he is older."

"And now?"

"He is still running the clinic. He has a job...with the Russians. That's where he is, where we came from, Amalia and I."

"You don't love him anymore?"

Anna's face burned. The yellow bird tilted its head, first one way then the other, before hopping to the edge of the sill and flying away. Anna's eyes followed its flight into a tree across the street. "It's not that. Thomas is staying in our village, and I am...well, I'm staying here. It's just not that simple anymore."

"I understand. A blessing and a curse." Her face relaxed. "I think if we are going to be living together, we should call each other by our first names, don't you? I'm Eva." She smiled.

"Anna." They shook hands to seal the deal.

"And I'm glad you are here. All of you." Eva picked up the forks. "Let's have dinner. I'll get Father."

They served the sizzling potatoes at the Lange family dining table, now surrounded by mismatched chairs and one short stepladder, which Amalia sat on. The house was simple and traditional, with little adornment except for the piles of books that grew out of the floorboards. A tall wooden bookshelf teetered against one wall, overstuffed with more books and papers, most of them art reference and some literature. Anna could imagine the family in another time, enjoying animated discussions at the table where the six of them now sat. Eva's father, Manfred Lange, was a slight man with an airy cloud of white hair that hovered over his pink head. With his big watery eyes and raspy breath, he was like a shrunken ghost in corduroy pants. His dentures were too big for his mouth and clacked when he wasn't speaking. They muffled his speech so that Anna had to ask him to repeat himself an uncomfortable number of times until she recognized the sounds. He had been kind to the children and attentive to Madeleine, and the evening had proceeded with small talk and polite laughter. Anna was anxious that at any moment the conversation would turn to wartime activities or beliefs or affiliation, but none of that was on the menu this evening. Instead, Dr. Lange talked about his work as a curator of German art at the Museum for Kunst und Gewerbe in Hamburg before the Great War and in the years between the wars as well. His knowledge of art ran deep, and he spoke with a wide-eyed love about the subject without resorting to snobby condescension or fake lamenting about the plight of art under the Third Reich. Art was the family business, and the father liked sharing his passion with his daughter. His childlike enthusiasm about his work, the artists he knew, and his adventures, made Anna forget about her self-consciousness at being a freeloader and enjoy the company. Even Amalia and Oskar listened intently to the man's stories and laughed at his mischievous jokes. Madeleine relaxed, too, and shared a smile with Anna that said she was happy to be there. A small wave of relief washed over her and Anna dared to relax a little.

Now it was late, and Madeleine and the children had already gone down to bed. Eva and her father sat side by side on the worn sofa while Anna perched on a chair from the dining table. The room was small and well worn, flickering in the light of two candles as the northern wind crisped the air outside. Anna felt chilly, but she ignored it.

"It was different back then," Dr. Lange was saying. "People cared about knowing things, they asked questions, they read books, they debated ideas. The museum was a fantastic place to work. Every day was an adventure. Then everything went black. At first you can't quite fathom it, that such a thing would really happen. That your colleagues are suddenly banned from work. Banned from work? Can you imagine? But you go on. You show up every day. You keep the work going. It's temporary, you think. Someone somewhere will come to their senses and things will go back to normal. Then people start disappearing. They move away, sell everything, and get on a train to France or on a boat to England or America. And still you think, 'I will see you soon. We will have dinner at the Atlantic like we used to, and the work will continue.' But that doesn't happen either. And then there's a war, and suddenly you know things will never be the same. The thugs are in charge, with their ignorant niceties, their false patriots. Now it's all flags waving and hateful speech. You wish you could leave too, but it's too late. You feel like a fool for not having seen it coming. The borders are closed. And the people salute, and the books burn, and any thinking man can see it's a travesty, that the lunatics are in charge. But thinking is not allowed any more. And then, you are an old man, and the land you love has been utterly destroyed." He took off his glasses and wiped his eyes. "I'm sorry. It's no use raging this way, but I can't seem to stop once it starts."

Eva took his hand and squeezed it. She gave Anna an apologetic look.

"Did you lose many friends, Herr Doktor?" Anna asked. "Your colleagues? Do you know what happened to them?"

He shook his head. "I don't know and I don't dare imagine. I don't think I will ever get over it. I'll never be able to face up to what's happened here. To what we allowed to happen. Right under our noses. We are supposed to be a civilized people."

"Father, don't upset yourself," Eva whispered. "It's late. You won't be able to sleep."

"What about the art in the museum? What happened to it?" Anna pressed. She felt invigorated by the old man's honesty. Outside of Madeleine, she had heard no one speak with any clarity about what they had been through. Mostly people wanted to sweep everything under the rug and forget about what had happened, or worse, pretend it never happened at all. Any conversation was a minefield. Everyone wanted absolution, and to get it, they would lie, turn a blind eye, or rationalize even the most obvious crimes.

"When the bombing started in Hamburg, we packed up the paintings in crates and put them in the cellar. We took turns guarding them, living down there, sometimes for days at a time. Eating boiled eggs and bread. Eventually, there were not enough of us left and we had to abandon them. That was in '43, sometime in the winter. When I went back to check on them months later, they were gone."

"We think they were put in the salt mines along with the other collections. For safekeeping. At least, that's what we hope," Eva added. "But let's talk about something more cheerful."

"And then you came to Wiesbaden." Anna changed the subject.

"We came after that, mostly for my mother's health," Eva replied. "There were better doctors and treatments here. We were lucky to inherit this house from a great uncle on my mother's side of the family who had no children of his own. But it was too little, too late." She regarded her father, who stared at his lap.

"Is she buried here at the cemetery?" Anna pointed to the window and the cemetery beyond.

"No, she's at the Sudfriedhof, the one down past the train station. Do you know it?"

Anna shook her head.

"Oh, it's beautiful there." Eva leaned forward. "On nice days, I go visit her and talk to her. Just sit on the grass under the trees. It's the only place I feel truly safe and at ease." She cleared her throat. "As if she's really there. I know it's silly, but it makes me feel better." She turned to her father and spoke softly. "Let's get you into bed now, Papa. It is very late and I think it's getting a bit chilly, too."

Anna stood and helped Eva get the man to his feet. "I will make sure the children don't bother you, Herr Doktor. You can send them on an errand if you need anything. Oskar is very resourceful. They won't be any trouble."

He took Anna's hands in his and looked at her, his eyes swimming behind the thick lenses. "I am glad you are here, Frau Klein. It's nice to have little ones in the house and I enjoy your company. And I know Eva likes having you here, too. She may not let on, but she'll warm to you. It takes her a while."

Anna squeezed his hands and wished him a good night. Then she made her way to their little room and closed the door behind her.

Anna sorted through the palettes of paintings, now neatly arranged according to their inventory lists. She had been through them so many times that she almost knew them by heart but decided to check everything once more, before they turned in the inventory. She was so engrossed in the work that she had not heard the door open behind her.

"What are you doing in here?" Cooper asked, startled. "Jesus, you scared the hell out of me." Anna jumped and let out a shriek, dropping the papers, which scattered across the floor. They both laughed as she fanned herself with mock drama.

"I was finishing the list and double checking Eva's work. We agreed to check on each other to be safe," she said, stooping to pick up the papers.

"Great. I came down here to check on things myself. We can do it together." He bent to help her. "You want to read or sort?"

"I'll sort," Anna said. "I like to see the paintings."

"Right," Cooper said as he straightened and helped Anna to her feet. "Here we go."

They proceeded through the list. Cooper read out the name of each painting along with the artist and the inventory number on the back as Anna pulled each painting from its slot on the shelf and verified the dimensions listed and any other distinguishing features noted. It was vital that each painting be fully documented in order to avoid any future spurious claims or openings for deception. "Shenanigans," Cooper called them. Everything was as it should be: the swirly Max Ernst, the Ernst-Ludwig Kirchner with the big white clouds, the scowling Max Beckmann, all were in their designated spots. She hadn't cared much for the German expressionists until she had come to this place where she could be close to them. It was something to be alone in a room with a painting, to touch it, to turn it over and see its secret underbelly. In a museum, they are lit just so, like a woman made up for a big party. But here the smell of the oil paint that stuck to her clothes, the texture of the carved frames under her fingers, made the pictures take on a human dimension. She sensed the labor that went into their creation, the movement of the brush in the layers of paint. She had come to know the pictures intimately, having studied them and logged in their every feature. She wondered where

Jacob Morgenstern had hung these paintings. In his gallery or at his home? In the living room for all to see? Or back in a bedroom, to be lived with more privately? She pulled out a Kirchner painting of a Berlin streetscape, just as Cooper said its name. It was small, no bigger than a hand towel, and colorful, awash with blues and bursts of red. She liked the way Kirchner painted the women with feathered hats like plumage sprouting from heavily colored faces; their bodies shaped like stretched-out hourglasses, so they resembled peacocks strutting along the street.

"*Berlin 1913*," Cooper said.

"Here," Anna replied, turning the painting over to follow along as he read out the numbers stamped on the back. "All good."

She held the painting up to better catch the light. "Even when I didn't like most of the crazy Expressionists, I always liked Kirchner."

Cooper slid off the table and they stood side by side, regarding the painting. Anna was keenly aware of his presence. She felt the need to keep her body in check, to avoid any accidental moves so as not to brush up against him. She sensed, too, that he was doing the same, standing very still.

"Amazing how he does that—it's beautiful and ugly at the same time," Cooper said. He shuffled the papers in his hand.

"You know he was trained as an architect?" Anna said. "But that was only to please his parents."

"I think he's better off being a painter," Cooper said. "If I could paint like that, I would have done the same." He took the painting from Anna's hands and held it so she could see. "What do you think?"

"I like it, too. I was sad when I heard he had committed suicide. I wish he had held on a little longer."

"Mmm," Cooper said. "What might have been. A lot of that going around." He put the painting back and picked up the list. "You heard from your husband?"

The question came out of nowhere and was a slap in the face. She had expected him to start reading out names again, picking up where they had left off. Instead he ambushed her. "Stop asking me," she said, staring down at the painting. It was a weak defense, but it was the honest one.

"You wrote him?" Cooper stepped toward the racks of paintings, as if creating a physical distance would diffuse the energy that had charged the air in the room. He made a show of casually sorting through the paintings on the shelf in front of him.

"Not yet. But I will. It's not so easy." She cleared her throat and turned her back, pretending to shuffle the papers.

She resisted filling the silence with an idiotic comment. She didn't want to write the letter telling Thomas that she was not returning to the life he was building for them. Even if she could rationalize leaving him, she couldn't rationalize taking his daughter from him in the process. She was so tired of mighty political forces exerting such intimate influence on her life. First the damn Nazis with their total intrusion into everything she did and thought and felt, and their total war and their total downfall. Now the supposed Allies, who had only acquiesced to get along in a marriage of convenience, were already redrawing the lines. It was pulling her in two directions. But she had the freedom to choose this time. *Yes.*

"Anna?" Cooper said. "I was only making small talk. Is everything okay?"

She turned her attention back to the list. She didn't like having secrets. At least not as many as were starting to stack up on her. "There's something I need to tell you."

"Oh?"

"I didn't tell you at the time, but now I think I should have."

Cooper turned to face her. "Tell me what?"

"The other day, I took your keys and came in here to check on a painting I had logged in. The number on the condition report didn't match. There was one digit missing, so I wanted to check on it and finish up the inventory."

Cooper pursed his lips and waited.

"And when I went to find the painting, it wasn't here." She paused for Cooper's response, but he continued to wait.

"It was the Nolde painting. *Man in a Green Jacket*. It should have been filed right here." She walked over to the shelves at the far end of the small room and put her hand on the frames that leaned against each other like books in a library.

"But." It wasn't a question as much as an expectation.

"But it wasn't here. We looked for it everywhere, in here and in the Collecting Point, but it was unaccounted for."

"We?" Cooper folded his arms across his chest. "Who is 'we'?"

"Eva and I. But— "

"You took my keys and came down here when you know that's against the rules? After everything I told you yesterday? I notice you keep saying it *was* missing, so I'm going to assume that you're about to tell me it's not missing anymore. At least, that better be what you're about to tell me."

"Right. It's not missing anymore."

"Show me."

She pulled the small canvas in its golden frame out from between its neighbors, saying a silent prayer of thanks. She scanned the now-familiar face that stared out at her and held the painting up for Cooper to see.

"Looks good to me." He was irritated more than relieved. "Now, let's talk about my keys. Do we need to go over the rules again?"

"I won't do it again. I promise." She set the painting down on the table. She wanted to say that three weeks ago he wouldn't have been bothered at all. But that was then. Things had changed.

"I'll spare you everything I'm thinking right now, Frau Klein. But remember what I said. Everything by the book. All the time. And that includes you. Are you *trying* to make things worse? I'm sure the painting was being cleaned or photographed or something. Had you not gone poking around, there would be no need for these dramatics." He took a breath as if he would continue but then stopped.

Anna stared at the painting to avoid his eyes and not let him see the crimson rising in her cheeks. The man in the green jacket regarded her, imperious and oblivious to the problems he was causing. Cooper's rant caught her off guard, but she was glad she told him. Something still wasn't right; she sensed it. Her eyes moved across the canvas as she considered how to respond. In the corner of the painting, they froze. Swallowing hard, she picked up the picture and held it under the light, tilting it so she could see where the canvas met the frame. She scanned the surface and examined the other corner, leaning in as close as her eyes could focus.

Cooper groaned. "Oh, for Christ's sake, what is it?"

Anna cleared her throat. "This painting had a tiny tear on the canvas. I made a note of it on the custody card. It was just under the frame, here." She pointed to a spot on the bottom right-hand corner and waited for his response. Her heart lurched in her chest.

Cooper put his face close to the canvas and their heads touched as they both strained to see.

"I don't see a tear," Cooper said.

"I don't either." Anna held her breath. She checked the other corners. Had she misremembered its location on the canvas? There were no tears on any of them. Cooper never would have known if she had kept her mouth shut, but now she had pointed out her own mistake. If it *was* her mistake. Something didn't sit right with her.

"Check the custody card. I bet it'll clear this up. "

Anna went white. "It's at home. At the Lange house, I mean."

Cooper pressed his lips together. "And what's it doing there, if I may ask?"

"It's in the pocket of my other pants. I can get it, right now. It won't take long, you'll see."

"No, no. Don't bother, Frau Klein. Bring it tomorrow. We'll address this then. It can wait. What's another breach of protocol between friends?" He gathered up the papers and slammed them on the table to straighten them and then stopped, staring at the wall and saying nothing for several moments. He blinked several times in rapid succession before closing his eyes and letting out a long sigh, as if he were in pain. The smiling face she had so relied on had transformed into one of deep frustration. It unsettled her. In this new life of hers, Cooper had become her rock. And now she was making mistakes.

He opened his eyes but kept his focus on the wall. "Better put that back before it gets lost again." He pushed the painting toward her.

"But, Captain…" Anna started to re-argue her case.

"But, nothing. Just check the custody card. And anyway, it's possible that you entered the information wrong in the first place. It happens."

Anna was incredulous. "I know I didn't. I'm sure of it."

Cooper shook his head. "Not good enough, Frau Klein."

She pushed past him to return the painting to its slot. She knew she was right, even as she pushed it onto the shelf and turned to look at Cooper.

"I don't want to see you down here unaccompanied anymore," he said, stepping aside to show her the door. "From now on, you stay upstairs. If you need to come down here, you tell me," he paused, "or one of the other officers." He locked the door and made a show of shoving the keys deep into his pants pocket. "Understood?"

chapter four

The light was fading when Anna opened the door to the Lange house. The warm air was welcoming, even if it felt stuffy and smelled of mothballs. She heard voices from the living room and was happy to see Madeleine and Eva's father sitting together, talking. At a glance, the room was untouched by war, the holes in the wall that revealed the wooden structure and the boarded-up window panes along the east wall now cast into the shadows. Madeleine laughed at something the old man said and he nodded, as if to convince her of an outrageous story he was telling. It was a charming picture, the two of them sitting comfortably together and sharing a tender moment. But with the evening light waning, and no electricity in store again, the scene marked the beginning of another uncomfortable night.

"Anna, *hallo*." Madeleine opened her arms as Anna came to kiss her cheek. "We were just talking about how things were when we were growing up. It turns out Herr Doktor Lange and I are almost of the same vintage."

"1871 was a good year," Herr Lange said, "and, please, I insist you call me Manfred. After all, we are living together. We are practically a family." He smiled. "And you, Anna? It was a good day? Why don't you have a seat and join us?"

Anna perched on the edge of the couch next to Madeleine to be polite and encourage the two elders to continue their conversation. She really wanted to retreat and take a few minutes to collect herself. The fight with Cooper had shaken her, but it was more than that. Something about the Nolde painting wasn't right. She couldn't put her finger on it, but she knew it to be true. What was it that was putting her so ill at ease? She couldn't approach Cooper with the vague accusation that *something* wasn't right. But at the same time, she couldn't shake the idea that the *Man in a Green Jacket* was trying to get her attention.

"Where are the children?" she asked, as a way to shift her mind.

"I sent them to the market earlier with a few books and things Eva wanted them to sell," Herr Lange said. "I told them to see what they could get for them. I said to be home by dark, so I expect them any minute. And Eva should be along shortly, too. She said she would find us something to eat."

Anna's face dimmed but he waved his hand to assuage her. "Don't worry, child. They are fine. Oskar is a good boy, and smart. He wants to be useful. So I gave him a job. Those books mean nothing to me anymore, so why not see if we can get something for them? People can use them for kindling now that winter is coming." He chuckled at the irony of selling books for burning.

Anna was too tired to protest, even though she did not like to think of the children at the black market and resented this strange man for sending them there. People traded for all kinds of sinister things, and pimps and pedophiles had found a comfortable spot to operate, as long as the *Amis* made only infrequent searches. She had to trust that the kids would be smart.

"I need to have a short rest before we tackle dinner. Will you send Amalia to get me when she gets home?" she asked.

Madeleine patted her hand. "You look tired." She nodded her reassurance.

Anna retreated to the bedroom and closed the door behind her. The room was even more musty than the rest of the house and felt cold and damp. It was a small space for the four of them to share. She put a hand to the small tiled heater out of instinct, even though she knew it wouldn't be lit until the temperatures dropped near freezing. It would be good for Oskar to find some firewood for the house soon, before it all disappeared. The winter would be long and cold for all of them. She pulled the heavy velvet drapes closed, shutting out the world and stirring up a puff of dust from the floor. The fine plaster dust particles coated virtually all surfaces in German houses, so fine as to be virtually unnoticeable. But when disturbed, they rose as little clouds of memory of the bombs and the fires. Anna paid them no mind anymore.

She fished through the pockets of her other pair of pants and found the Nolde custody card. She flattened the crumpled paper and read the painting's description as she had entered it. *Nolde, Emil,*

Man in a Green Jacket. Collection Jacob Morgenstern. Under notes, she had typed *canvas slightly damaged at bottom right.*

She sat on the bed and stared at the wall. *Slightly damaged.* No mention of a tear. But she knew she had seen it with her own eyes. There had been so many custody cards and so many notes on so many paintings. Had she made a mistake about seeing the tear? Or had she thought *damage* was a clear enough descriptor? Her thoughts swam circles in a murky pool of questions threatening to pull her under. She willed the thoughts from her mind. *I'll check the painting again tomorrow. There's a perfectly reasonable explanation.* In the meantime, she had other things to attend to.

She reached into the bag of belongings they had brought from home and dug around until she found the letter from the Americans informing her of the eviction from Madeleine's house. From Amalia's cigar box perched on the nightstand, she pulled the stubby pencil the girl kept amongst her little treasures. She pulled the edge of the curtain away from the window and positioned herself to let the light fall onto her lap. She turned the letter over to its blank side and began writing.

My Dear Thomas…

The pencil hovered over the paper, unsure where to go next. *Have you written him yet?* Cooper's voice floated into her head. No, that was not why she was doing this. Cooper was not the reason. She took a deep breath and tried to clear her mind of everything that was pushing or pulling her in some direction. She wanted to start from somewhere that was pure and free from rationalizing. No justifications. No excuses. *No lies.* She wanted to say what she felt, not what she thought she should feel, or what her husband wanted to hear, or even what was the right thing to say. But she was unsure of what it was that she really felt.

First, I want you to know that Amalia and I are safe and that the journey that brought us to Wiesbaden was as uneventful as could have been hoped for. The truck we were riding on broke down outside the town and we were very lucky to find Madeleine still in her house and willing to accept us with open arms. If it had not been for her, I don't know what we would have done. I know you must have been very worried about us, and I am sorry our leaving caused you pain. The memory of our parting fight haunts me to this day, and I prefer to remember us as we were during the happy times, when Amalia was a baby. Remember how we sat in the garden in the summer and watched her chase the butterflies, feeling so content in our pretty little spot on earth, even as it was catching fire all around us? I suppose it was naive to think we would come out of that hell unscathed, although for a while I thought we had. But I see now that no one has made it through untouched. Even those of us who may look the same, or act as we always have, know that we are all forever changed.

But I have not changed so much that you would not recognize me. I still love you and I love our family. I think often of you and imagine how you are spending your days and how your life is. Do you think about what life is like for me and Amalia now? You might be surprised. I am working for the Americans. I was lucky to get a job because of my English. I am a translator for a captain who is working with the group that saves the art and monuments. Maybe you read about them back in April when they found all the art stashed in the salt mine? And at Neuschwanstein? The unit I work with is dealing mostly with safeguarding the art from German national galleries in order to return it when things are rebuilt, whenever that is. I have seen Rembrandt and Goya paintings up close, held them in my hands even. It is like working in a great museum. I have also been inventorying a beautiful private collection owned by a Jew who likely perished in one of the camps. It will be up to the Americans to decide what do with the art, but I hope some heirs will turn up eventually. It's all such a big mess.

Amalia is well. She misses you, as you can imagine. Even with the meager food, she has grown and her hair is now past her shoulders. She wears it in braids mostly, which Madeleine fights with her about every morning, as I am usually rushing too much to stop and do it. Amalia asks for you all the time, and I tell her that you miss her, too. I know that you do. Madeleine has been a great source of comfort to us and has even forgiven me for allowing the Amis to take away her home in order to billet some officers. I feel as though that was my fault, even though probably there was little I could have done. We are now living with a new friend who works with me, and her father, a lovely man. They both worked in museums before the war. It seems these days I am surrounded by art types, which reminds me of my own childhood when my uncle would invite us to his gallery openings. That life, and ours together, are so long removed that it feels like they belong to someone else, and I feel very far away from everything I ever knew.

She stopped writing. The gap between her life with Thomas and her life now was so wide that it threatened to swallow her if she dared step into it. She had been circling its perimeter for weeks now, avoiding writing this letter and avoiding looking into that precipice. Now she was peeking over the edge, her fingernails dug into the solid ground for fear of sliding into the void. She inhaled, folded the paper into fours, and slid the letter into her bag, which she kicked under her cot for good measure. At least she had started.

As if on cue, she heard the thunderous footsteps of Oskar and Amalia in the foyer before the bedroom door sprang open to reveal their dirty little faces.

"Mama." Amalia lunged at her. The smell of her was sweet and a little earthy, like the soil in a flower pot. Her cheek was cold against Anna's. "I missed you."

"I missed you, too, *Maus*. All day long." She held onto her daughter a little longer before Amalia squirmed away. The little girl perched on the edge of the cot and tugged at her shoe with both hands. Anna laughed and grabbed the little foot to untie the laces. "It's easier if you do it this way," she teased.

Oskar stood in the doorway, hands shoved into pockets, eyes blazing. He had something to say but was waiting to get the lay of the land, in case they were in trouble. That was his usual way. Anna smiled and motioned for him to sit down alongside her. "Come on, boy. Tell me all about your adventures."

Amalia jumped in and started in the middle, with Oskar filling in details to paint a fuller picture. He was very patient with Amalia, and kind, as she rambled and provided opinions on things she could not possibly understand. Herr Lange had given them a stack of five books on art history, and Eva loaded a little cart with some bedsheets and an old rug before sending them off to see what they could fetch. Cloth could be used to make clothes and rugs could double as winter blankets. People wanted the strangest things, and maybe, if you were lucky, someone with the money to spend—usually an *Ami* looking for souvenirs or gifts for people back home—would turn up and buy your pitiful wares.

"Why would anyone buy books when there's so little food and other necessities?" Anna asked. "That makes no sense."

Oskar shook his head. "You can put them in the fire," he said, and then quickly added, "to help the fire. Not to burn the books on purpose. I know that's bad. I mean like for kindling."

"I see. Good point," Anna hadn't thought of that.

"And, also, farmers cut up the paper and use it in their soil. To help things grow."

Anna's eyes widened and she conceded she had never thought of that, either. Was there anything Oskar didn't know?

Oskar puffed up a little and continued the story. "Anyway, when we first got there, we walked through the crowd. I do that to see if there are policemen or *Amis* lurking around. Sometimes the *Amis* are there to buy, but sometimes they are there to police. You can tell the difference."

"There were no *Amis* at all today," Amalia contributed.

"So we picked a spot right on the edge, by the street, because that way you can see the police coming and can run out of there."

"And then what happened?"

Amalia glanced at Oskar before she continued. "We waited a long time."

"Not that long," Oskar interjected. "Maybe an hour."

"It was a man. In a car. He drove up and bought everything."

"Really?" Anna asked.

Oskar chimed in. "No one paid much attention to us. I started taking the books out one by one and walking around and offering them to people, but no one was interested. One lady took a closer look, she even flipped through the pages, but then she said, 'no, thank you.' She was looking for cigarettes. Then the car pulled over and the man acted like he was going to get out, but then he saw us and rolled down the window. He was older, and he had on kind of fancy clothes. He asked what we wanted for the books. I was standing holding up the big one with the painting of the horse on the cover. He must have liked what he saw because he asked us how much right away."

"He wasn't even American," Amalia added. "He was German, like us."

"I told him we wanted a hundred Reichsmark and he laughed at me, but I told him it was a rare book, that all the others like it had been burned, and that it was worth a lot more than a hundred Reichsmark, which only buys you one lousy stick of butter anyway. And I said, 'don't you think this beautiful book is worth a stick of butter?' And then I told him books with art in them make men seem more interesting than they actually are."

Anna laughed at Oskar's sales tactics. "And? What did he say?" She ignored the thing that was needling her about the children peddling wares to God knows who at the black market. Buying was one thing, but selling felt like something else altogether.

"He laughed like you did, and then he said he'd give me three hundred for all the books and everything on the cart because I was such a good salesman. He was dressed fancy, so I thought I could get more from him. We could have waited to sell everything separately, but I then thought we better take the offer, so I said that's fine. That's enough for a dozen eggs, you know. So he got out and put everything in his car. After he drove off, we found an old farmer woman who still had eggs to sell." His eyes darted to Amalia and Anna followed them. A hint of a blush rose in Amalia's cheeks.

"She gave us six eggs," Amalia chimed in. "So we still have money to go back for more tomorrow. And everybody gets a whole egg for dinner." She offered a flat smile.

Anna scanned between them, her eyes searching their little faces. "Is there something you're not telling me?"

Two small heads shook, eyes wide and lips sealed. Anna squinted her eyes as if to scrutinize them. "Are you very sure?"

Two small heads nodded.

"Because you know you must tell me if anything strange or frightening happened. Did someone approach you?" Visions of greasy, moist-lipped men in raincoats assaulted her brain, unsettling her. "You must tell me right away."

Two small heads nodded again.

"Can you get us some American cigarettes to sell?" Oskar asked. "We can make a lot of money with those."

Anna scrutinized him. What was he up to? "I'll see what I can do." She held up a finger. "You had better not be keeping secrets from me. Understand?"

Two small heads bobbed up and down, mouths sealed and eyes unblinking. Anna did not feel reassured.

◆ ◆ ◆

When they emerged to face dinner, Eva had just walked in the door.

"There's mail for you, Anna," she said.

"What's this?" Anna said as Eva handed her the envelope. Another official letter made her heart jump. She looked at the return address. United Nations Refugee Relocation Agency.

"Is it about Madeleine's house?" Eva offered.

"I think that's a different agency," Anna said, turning the letter over in her hands.

"I can't keep them all straight," Eva said. "It's like alphabet soup, between the UNRRA and the MFA&A and the OMGUS and whatever else they have. That must be a job all to itself, the naming of official military agencies."

Anna smiled. "I'll open it later." This letter was about Oskar.

"You should open it now," Eva said. "Sometimes it's good news."

"Usually not," Anna said. On impulse she handed the envelope to Eva. "You open it and tell me what it says." It was something she might have done with her best school friend years ago, when drama was attached to every missive from a boy or potential suitor. She was surprised at her own forwardness, but Eva happily took the letter and smiled at her as she tore open the flaps.

"You'll see," Eva said, "I have a good feeling about this one." Anna was grateful for the effort to soothe her nerves, even if she didn't believe a word.

Eva scanned the paper and chewed on her lip. Her expression was neutral, then confused, then dismissive. "I think they have the wrong person," she said. "This is about Oskar." She handed the letter to Anna. "It says he is to be returned to the camp, that he has to go home…to Poland of all places. It must be a mistake."

Anna skimmed the words as her ears began to ring. She tried to appear calm because she knew it was no mistake. The refugee agency had found the right Oskar. Her Oskar was indeed from Poland, but he didn't know it. When she and Cooper had found him in an abandoned villa months before, the UNRRA had found that he had been adopted through the Nazis' hideous Lebensborn program. Oskar had been born in Poland and taken from there by Himmler's SS nurses, who thought stealing blond Aryan babies from their mothers was good for the Reich. The thought of it made her want to retch, as did the letter in her hand. Oskar knew he had been adopted by a Gestapo officer and his wife, but he thought that was because he was a war orphan. He had enjoyed the good life as a child of the elite and loved his mother dearly. The father was mostly gone, doing God knows what, and the family had indoctrinated the boy into Nazi life—he wanted for nothing, after all—and he had bought into the story completely. When Anna had found him, he hated the Americans, and he hated her for working for them. He mourned the death of his mother most of all after she and his father had died in the bombing of Darmstadt in late 1944. After that, he had roamed, as many children did, before being sent to live with his mother's brother, who wanted little more to do with him than to use him as a sentry for the art he was hiding in the basement of an abandoned villa. But Oskar had come around, and Anna had even been able to reunite him with one of his mother's amateur paintings. That was what had gotten Anna into the mess with the art dealer known as Konrad Schenk, and nearly cost Cooper his job.

"What do you think? It's a mistake, right?" Eva repeated.

Anna shook her head as the words on the page blurred in front of her eyes. "Oskar knows he was adopted as an orphan from the war in

Poland. But this says he's not an orphan at all. That his birth parents might still be alive and looking for him. And that they are rounding up all the Polish orphans—or non-orphans, I guess—and re-educating them to return to Poland."

"Re-educating? That sounds horrid."

"Sounds familiar, is how it sounds." Anna pictured Oskar in the camp being taught Polish and being told that everything he knew to be true about himself was a total lie. That he was a pawn in a game, and that the adults he trusted had betrayed him repeatedly and without any regard for his well-being. His little psyche had already been battered and dented beyond measure, but he had finally found a home that made him happy.

"What will you do? What will you tell him?" Eva leaned in. "Whatever you decide, I will help."

Anna shook her head. "Nothing for now. I don't know what to do. It's not up to me. It's his birth family, and he's only a child. But he's already lost two mothers. As far as he knows, his real mother and his adoptive mother are both dead. How much more can one child take?" As if to reply, her mind flashed away from Oskar and onto the plight of Jacob Morgenstern, who had probably endured unspeakable suffering before succumbing to a terrible death. The posters that were appearing on the walls along the Wilhelmstrasse answered the questions for her. They showed the mountains of corpses from the camps, the hollowed eyes of survivors gazing down on the streets of Germany. *These Shameful Acts: Your Guilt.* The posters admonished. *You watched quietly and tolerated silently.* She had seen one a week ago, then they seemed to multiply, confronting Germans around every street corner. She felt plenty guilty, she just didn't know what she could do about it. So, the answer was that the child and all Germans would take as much as was doled out, and if we couldn't handle it, then it was too bad. *This is your great guilt. You are responsible.*

"Oskar loves you; I can see it. You can fight for him," Eva said.

"But what if his birth mother is looking for him? How can I take her child? Can you imagine her anguish, all these years? And now maybe she has a glimmer of hope?"

It was not about Anna; she knew this. Nothing was about her. What was best for the boy was what mattered. She folded the letter and returned it to its envelope.

"I am not important. It's what he wants that matters."

"But he is only a boy. He can't possibly understand the consequences of such big choices. And anyway," Eva paused before going on, "is the UN really asking him for his opinion? That's not how I read the letter."

"No, they're not. But I am," Anna replied. "He deserves that much."

Eva squeezed Anna's arm. "If I can help, I will."

Anna nodded a thank you and watched Eva retreat into the kitchen. "He brought us eggs," she called after her. "For our dinner."

chapter five

"Where are we going?" Anna climbed into the jeep, pulling her bag onto her lap.

"On an errand. Don't worry, it's sanctioned," Corporal Bender said, sliding into the seat next to her with a big grin. "Ever been to Darmstadt?" Bender, the supply clerk from the Air Force base at Erbenheim, was an ally, a kind of fixer whom Anna had relied on to get her out of a jam a few weeks back. He and Cooper were good friends and cut from the same cloth; not suited for military discipline but happy to play along, as long as it got them what they wanted. Luckily, they were both motivated toward doing good, a trait not all of their fellow GIs shared.

"No. Is there anything left of it?"

"Eighty percent destroyed. That means twenty percent is left. That's the part we're going to see."

"And why do you need me?"

"I need a translator to help sort through some files. They told me they'd provide one, but last time they said that, I showed up and no one was around to help me. This time, I'm coming prepared."

"What kind of files?"

"Just looking up some stuff, checking personnel records mostly."

"Aren't those records in English?" Anna asked.

"Ours are. But I'm checking yours. That is to say, the Nazis'. We gotta make sure the house is squeaky clean, if you know what I mean." Bender tried to cover his slip of the tongue and Anna let it go. He gunned the engine and they lurched forward out of the Collecting Point courtyard. Given the chill of the overcast day, Bender had outfitted her with an American combat jacket that had seen better days. The name insignia had been torn off and the jacket smelled of smoke and sweat and things that Anna didn't care to consider. Although the filth of it repulsed her, she was happy to have it as Bender tore through the streets of Wiesbaden and the wind whipped cold around her. She pulled the jacket closed around her neck. What kind of personnel records were they going to investigate? She decided to wait and be surprised.

They rode unencumbered out of town and along the Wiesbadener Landstrasse. Anna inhaled the fresh air and tried to enjoy the gentle rolling of the hills even under the jeep's rough ride. She tried to study Bender in her peripheral vision. He was a good-looking guy, quite young and robust. Where he was from? She knew only that he and Cooper had served together in Italy at some point in the war, which had bonded them forever. His loyalty to Cooper was unwavering in ways that Anna found admirable. Everything seemed simple around

Bender. Things were either right, or they were wrong. Either he could fix them, or he couldn't. Usually he could.

"Yes?" Bender grinned. He had caught her staring. Anna looked away, embarrassed. As they bumped along, he settled in, gripping the steering wheel with his left hand, resting his right on the seat back behind him. "So tell me how things are going with you? Everything okay? Heard from your husband?"

"Why does everyone keep asking me that?" Anna heard herself snap. "Suddenly everyone cares so much about my marriage. Aren't there other things to worry about?" She shifted in her seat. "No, all right? I have not heard anything more from him. Nor has he from me, for that matter."

"Okay, okay. Sorry," Bender said. "I was just making conversation. We can talk about something else." He exhaled with a whistle and shook his head. "How about…how are things with the inventory going?"

Anna's ears burned. She tried to smile and move the mood back to neutral ground. "Going well. I like the work; it's interesting. I hope Captain Cooper is happy."

"You like working with Fraulein Lange? The beanpole?"

"I guess. We are living with her, you know." She paused before adding, "It was Cooper's idea."

"I heard," Bender said. "He told me all about it."

Anna hesitated. "Did he tell you anything else?"

"About?"

Anna shrugged. She didn't know what. About any feelings he had for Eva? But she didn't dare ask. She thought about the shift she had felt between herself and Cooper, that even in their formal professional relationship, something had changed despite his repeated assurances that they were "still friends." She was ashamed to shine a light on what her concerns meant, even in the recesses of her own mind. "About anything. About the rumors from the State Department? How is that going?"

"Oh, that's a complete mess," Bender said. "No doubt about it. The fellow who visited last month gave a glowing report to State. All about what great work is happening at the Collecting Point, how important it was, how Americans should be so proud."

"That doesn't sound so bad."

Bender shook his head. "Now some joker from DC is creating rumblings that say the exact opposite. He came for one visit last week, and next thing we know, memos start flying about how the place isn't secure, how it's leaking, how we can't guarantee the safety of the art." He exhaled. "It's all bullshit, of course. Something's changed and they're covering their asses. Just not yet sure why. So, there's lots of private meetings and conversations, trying to get to the bottom of what they're really after. We have to come up with some counter-offensive. Of course, the building is secure, it's under twenty-four-hour guard and surrounded by razor wire. The water they see on the floor is to keep the humidity up. They know that, we explained it when they were here."

"And what does Cooper say?"

"He sees the writing on the wall. He's been worried about some kind of shenanigans. It's a lot of valuable art. He expected it even before the rest of us saw anything coming down the pike. He's pretty savvy that way."

"It's because he doesn't trust the Army," Anna said. "This explains his mood at least."

"Yeah, he's been no fun to be around. He knows there's going to be a fight."

"He is a good man."

Bender nodded. "One of the best." He turned to face her. "We are lucky to have him on our side. Don't you think?"

Anna wasn't sure what else to say. The wind whipped her hair out of its clip and she held it down with one hand while cinching the coat around her neck with the other. The ride to Darmstadt was maybe forty-five kilometers, and it seemed like at the speed they were going it would take forever. She stared out over the countryside, which was largely untouched by the bombs that had hit the cities. Here and there, lonely farmhouses marked the landscape. Sometimes the jeep would pass people walking along the road, city folk heading out to the farms to trade for food—a few eggs, maybe some butter. The joke was that farmers were now the richest people in Germany; their barns lined with the silver settings and silk rugs from the city elites who had traded them, desperate for food. Mostly, Anna saw bedraggled people wandering along and wondered what journey they were on. Old men pulling handcarts, women carrying tiny children, lanky boys with dirty knees marching along as if hobbled. Thoughts of Oskar seeped into her brain, and the familiar sense of panic rose, like floodwaters in a riverbed. The letter said an UNRRA person wanted to talk to Oskar and that he should deliver himself to the displaced persons camp the following week. She had not yet decided what to do about it. What if he didn't show up? Would they come arrest him? Would they arrest her, as his guardian? Would they give up and go away?

"Corporal, do you know anything about the plans to repatriate the war orphans from Poland?" Bender might know more than she, and anyway, he was resourceful.

He nodded, eager to display his knowledge. "I heard something about it, yeah. They found a bunch of files—SS files, I guess they were—that had information about the kids the Nazis took from Poland. Of course, the SS didn't bother to include pesky details like who they stole the kids from, but they have stuff like dates and cities and the ages and genders of the kids. Well, babies, really. I guess it's like a big puzzle they are trying to piece together." The jeep slowed as they entered a small town that looked to be nothing more than a main street and some empty buildings. "Does this have something to do with the boy?"

"I got a letter." Anna exhaled to gather her nerves. "He's to report to the camp." She turned to Bender. Saying it out loud made it real. She tried again to rein in her panic, but she couldn't stop the tears welling up. "I don't know what to do."

The emotions overtook her, like a tsunami, crashing over the barrier she had so carefully erected. Her resistance swept away, broken and scattered in the deluge. She let it go and wept, knowing she was making him uncomfortable and not caring much. She cried for Oskar and for herself and for her marriage and for her daughter, who would grow up without her father. She cried for her shame about her feelings for Cooper and for her husband whom she loved with an ache that lived deep in her chest. The tears came easily, hot and comforting, the release completely palpable in her being, like a rusty valve opening and purging its rancid water. She heard her own sobs, as if from a distance, and felt the convulsions of her chest. She must look pathetic, ridiculous, helpless. She didn't care.

The jeep took a hard turn and then came to a stop in a side street. Bender placed a tentative hand on her back and pulled her closer, just enough to wrap a comforting arm around her shoulder. He said nothing, only his hand pulsed like a steady heartbeat as he gently patted her arm. For a long time she reined in her sobs, taking deep breaths between each convulsion, feeling more and more embarrassed at her outburst. After what seemed like a painfully long time, she opened her eyes, ready to re-enter the world. Bender was holding out a handkerchief on a flat palm, and she was glad to take it without meeting his eyes.

"It's even clean," he said. "My mom sent it. She knew I'd need it."

The handkerchief smelled of starch: clean and citrusy. It was the cleanest smell Anna had smelled in months. It smelled like a sunny day, just like the ads promised. She inhaled deeply with the cloth over her nose.

"Nice, huh?" Bender leaned his face close to hers. "You know what?"

She shook her head.

"Turns out you're still a human after all. Here you thought you were tough as nails, you taking on every piece of bullshit that came your way in the lousy, stinking war and this lousy, stinking peace. Lots of people lost their humanity, forgot how to care about others. But yours is still there. Right here. So, guess what?"

Anna wiped her nose, unable to look him in the eye.

"You win. They didn't get to you, Anna Klein. And you're going to be fine." He squeezed her arm as if to reassure a child.

Anna felt self-conscious, stupid, and totally free at the same time. Bender's reaction put her strangely at ease. What was with these Americans?

"I am so sorry, Corporal. This is completely unprofessional. I apologize." She dabbed at her eyes. "I don't know what happened."

"Nothing to apologize for. Things piled up on you, and you had to clean house. Listen, we'll figure out how to do right by the boy. I know you want what's best for him. We just don't know what that is yet." He patted her shoulder. "But we'll figure it out. And you're the best man Cooper's got on his team, so we need you."

"I'm not sure I'm the best man," she said, "not anymore."

Bender revved the engine and turned the jeep back onto the main road. "You are. I'd bet on it," he said.

The drive into Darmstadt became more and more oppressive, like a descent into hell. To say the city was eighty percent destroyed was a kindness. It was all ruins. Maybe they meant that eighty percent of every building was destroyed, Anna thought, because there was nothing more than the hollow façades and a few roofs and cupolas; there were no actual buildings. The place was strangely organized, with the rubble cleared to keep streets open. But it was not a place at all. It was the shadow of one that had been here, and the people walking through the streets were ghosts.

"Where did the people go?" Anna asked.

"You mean the supposedly lucky ones? I guess they left. Not much for them here." He slowed the jeep to allow a group of bedraggled women to cross the narrow street. When he sped up again, Anna had the distinct sensation of the air turning colder, the sky dimmer. It was like driving through a skeleton, with some of its skin and flesh still attached. Here and there, the black, empty eye sockets of window frames stared, hollows in the remaining brick walls that had survived while their wooden interiors had not. Her eyes landed on odd details like a wrought-iron bracket that had once held up a shop's sign and now still clung to its wall. Or the gate to a fence that had melted into oblivion. Rats scurried along to mauled rooftops and an acrid smell hovered. They drove on, the ruins rising around them, closing in and suffocating her. If the aftermath of the bombs was the stuff of nightmares, what had the night of the bombing been like?

"Oskar's mother was killed in one of these raids," she said. "His father, too. He was Gestapo." She craned her neck to see into the destruction. "I wonder where he lived. Not that it matters."

"We're headed to Gestapo headquarters...right up this street," Bender said. "Take a look. It's incredible. Like it wasn't even touched."

The building was indeed intact, with only minor injuries. A few other buildings around it were the same, standing like defiant little outliers among the rubble. That the Gestapo headquarters, of all places, survived, seemed like an especially cruel cosmic joke. Bender nodded as if reading her thoughts. "The jail was in the basement. Not one of the prisoners was even injured. Not by the fire anyway. Poor bastards." He got out of the jeep and motioned for Anna to follow.

"What, me go in there?" she asked, pointing at the building.

"Yeah. It's US Forces Darmstadt Region offices now. Come on."

Anna climbed down from the jeep, stopping to try to fix her hair. The oversized jacket made her feel like a child wearing hand-me-down clothes that didn't quite fit, but she was happy to have the added protection; it provided a layer between her and the world. She followed Bender into the building.

The moment her feet crossed the threshold, she wanted to escape. The air inside was stuffy, and there was a heaviness to it that made her skin crawl, as if she were being touched by a manifestation of the Gestapo itself. The place had clearly been a police station, taken over by the Gestapo and now by the Americans. It had the cold, resilient fixtures and the wear-and-tear of a place accustomed to hard treatment, where you leave niceties at the door. Anna tried not to consider what horrible acts were perpetrated within its walls, and when Bender installed her at a desk in the far corner of a large room, she was reluctant to even sit in the chair, for fear she would somehow be trapped. A flickering light overhead buzzed erratically, setting her nerves on edge.

Bender kept her busy for the next hour, bringing her stacks of files to review. She translated the entries on the various forms and reports. The files were either police records, surveillance notes, or other Gestapo paperwork. It was unnerving to see the kinds of details the secret police knew about people's lives, their comings and goings, their friends and associates. How they could twist innocuous behavior into suspicious activity or even criminal offense. She checked her watch every five minutes in the hopes that it would be time to go home.

"Is this really helping?" she asked Bender when he dropped another stack on the table. So far, nothing she had translated seemed to interest him; he compared names on various lists and sighed periodically. "What are you looking for?"

"Just making sure that the people in our employ are who they say they are. Those questionnaires everyone fills out are not completely reliable, if you get my drift."

Anna squirmed. "Did you check on me, too?"

Bender winked. "You checked out a long time ago. Besides, you aren't from these parts, so there's not much to find. Unless you came for a visit and were up to no good."

Anna chuckled. "Hardly." She scanned the sheet in front of her; it was a list of teachers and administrators employed by the local school during the years from 1939 to 1941. Working at a school usually meant you were a dutiful Nazi Party member, since you were on the front line of educating the Reich's future.

"So you've checked on Eva, too?" She was being nosy, but she could convince herself that maybe it would be good for Eva to know if the Nazis had kept records on her. "She was in Frankfurt for a time before she came to Wiesbaden."

"Well, Frau Klein, do you have misgivings about your new friend? The one who has taken you in and given you shelter?" Bender's eyebrows raised as his smile widened.

Anna blushed. "I was joking," she said. But she wasn't, not really.

"Fraulein Lange is clean as a whistle, as far as we know. Or she kept her head down. What do you know about her?"

"She worked at the Staedel for a while and then she said she did menial jobs, cleaning and cooking for the troops. That's all I know."

Bender was distracted by a stack of papers in his hand. He squinted at the one on top. "What did you say the boy's last name is? Your boy, Oskar?"

"Grünewald," Anna said. "Why?"

"His father was Gestapo, you say? Take a look at this."

Anna took the paper Bender handed her and scanned it. It was a letter addressed to some functionary whose name meant nothing to her. She focused on the signature at the bottom, where Bender was pointing. Peter Grünewlad.

"Oskar's father?" she asked.

"Probably. Seems he was pretty high up."

"For sure. I know his name was Peter. And Oskar said he was gone a lot. To Czechoslovakia, I think."

"Those weren't pleasure trips." Bender frowned. "What's the letter about?"

Anna scanned the text. "Oh, of course. It's a tip about a presumed art collection in a house here in Darmstadt. Gruenewald says he suspects the art dealer who lives there is hoarding art illegally and with this letter he is dutifully passing on the information. He mentions a house in the Elisabethenstrasse…says the art dealer's name is Steinmann. This is from 1942, so pretty late in the game. I don't dare think of what happened to the poor man."

"Steinmann, huh? Make a note and see if anything at the Collecting Point is attached to that name. Just for grins," Bender said. He handed her the rest of the stack. "There might be more stuff in here, if you're interested. Seems pretty prolific. You can tell the boy his dad was good at his job. I'll be back in a few minutes and then we can call it a day."

Anna jotted the name onto a scrap of paper and pulled the stack of papers toward her to straighten it. The pages reflected a bureaucracy of an evil machine with departments and sub-departments that kept everyone busy sending memos to their superiors about what they ate for breakfast that day to prove they were the very best Nazi. There were letters congratulating staff on jobs well done, from the factory inspections to the cleanings of the jail. Budget reports, signed off by Gruenewald. Requisition orders for office supplies. Anna marveled at how mundane the business of killing was. Memos to the main office in Frankfurt, copied to the general office in Berlin, and reverse. Endless streams of paper, just like she had seen at the Collecting Point. She shook her head at the banality of it all. Behind a sheet summarizing personnel timesheets, there was a letter on the stationery of the Reichssicherheitshauptamt, the RHSA, the sight of which made her blood run cold. The RHSA was the department in charge of Jewish deportations. This letter was addressed to the head of the Gestapo office in Darmstadt, a Robert Mohr, informing him that a train, originally scheduled to depart Darmstadt on 11 June 1942, was to be delayed due to damage to the tracks in Lublin and Chelm. Anna looked up. Lublin was in Poland. *Why would one train from Darmstadt be directly affected by tracks in Poland?* Something uneasy stirred inside her and she turned the page. This time the letter from the Gestapo head to his underlings, which included Peter Gruenewald, outlined plans for thc rescheduled train, which had now become two trains, leaving Darmstadt on 30 September. The letter referred to a list of instructions sent by RHSA regarding who was to be placed on which train. The people were slated for what the Nazis called "emigration" or "resettlement to parts unknown," a euphemism to end all euphemisms. Anna took a deep breath. The "deportees" were to be placed under curfew immediately upon receiving their deportation notices, which were to arrive on 15 September, two weeks before the trains were scheduled to leave. The Gestapo was instructed to collect all taxes on property supposedly owed by the deportees and to search and clear their apartments no later than two days before departure. Old people, prominent citizens, and veterans of the Great War were to be sent to Theresienstadt in Czechoslovakia, and all others, including women, children, and infants, were to be sent to Lublin. Anna exhaled and swallowed hard.

She took her eyes from the paper to scan the room. It was on the first floor, a large room that had likely once been filled with desks for police offers and later the Gestapo thugs she was just reading about. Big windows let in plenty of light that showed off the dust hanging in the air and floating from the documents stacked to eye level on rows of tables. People, mostly Americans, came and went, and some sat and wrote furiously in ledgers. She had no idea what they were doing or what the function of this place was now. It was official and industrious without producing any actual discernible results. But when Anna considered what all these documents showed, what they proved, and what the people sitting in silence were learning—it suddenly became a hallowed place. She made herself return to the papers and turn the page. There were memos of details concerning the logistics of housing the Jews who were to be held in a school for two days before departure. Then there was something about the train's scheduled stops to pick up Jews from outlying towns before it arrived in Darmstadt. Another memo was about expenses and personnel, including overtime for staffing at the school.

Then, without warning, she found herself staring at the names themselves. Pages and pages of names, dates of birth, and places of residence. People born in 1876, 1864, 1869, 1917, 1930, 1940 and every year imaginable. An infant only six months old and her family of six, all sent off together. Grandchildren and grandparents. Young men, old women, school girls, scrappy-headed boys. Mothers and daughters. Anna's stomach lurched and she felt her insides seize. She clenched her teeth to suppress the bile rising from her stomach. Slowly she turned the pages and scanned the names. The scene on the train platform played in her mind like a grainy film. The guards and their dogs. Scared children who could not possibly grasp the horror of what awaited them, clinging to terrified parents. Anna had known what was happening to the Jews. Everyone knew. But they could not *imagine* it. And so everyone looked away, out of fear, and out of shame, too. And, out of incomprehension.

She tried to remember what she was doing in June of 1942. Amalia would have just turned four years old and Thomas had been working at the clinic for a year. She could only recall happy times, afternoons spent lying on the grass in the warm summer sun, complaining about food rations and nosy neighbors who couldn't be trusted. Anna recalled seeing a contingent of slave laborers in the village, digging a ditch along the road. They had come from the camp at Buchenwald, she was told. Mostly Russians, the newspaper said. She remembered hurrying past them so her own discomfort would be assuaged and short lived. Out of sight, out of mind, after all. And there was plenty you could keep out of sight in those days. You could pretend that Germany was winning the war, that the war was honorable somehow. You could tell yourself that it would all be over soon, that things could not go on this way, that Hitler was crazy, and that any day now, he would get his. Because someone—someone *else*—would take care of him.

Bender appeared from behind one of the tall shelves that obscured the entrance to the room.

"Lange, right? Eva Lange? That's her?"

"What?"

"The woman at the Collecting Point. What's her old man's name?"

Anna shook her head back into the present. "Manfred. He's a doctor. A Ph.D., I mean."

"Yep. Found him. Take a look. Director of the Museum for Kunst und Gewerbe, right?"

Anna took the folder. "Yes, that's right. Why were you looking for him?"

"I wasn't. I was looking for her, since you asked. Still didn't find anything on her, but found this fat file on him. Apparently, it got moved here when he came from Hamburg. The Gestapo leaves no man behind."

Anna made a face. "Is it bad?"

"You tell me. The sins of the father and all that. You done with these?" He rested his index finger on the stack she had been reading.

Anna was only too happy to replace the pages and straighten the pile of papers. "This has important information in it. About the transports. Shouldn't the authorities have these?"

"They do have them," Bender said. "I imagine they'll be shipped off to Nuremberg for the trials any day. Most everything in here will. That's why I wanted to make one last check." He patted the pages. "What'd you find?"

"Things I wish I hadn't," Anna said.

"I have no doubt." Bender picked up the folders she had finished. "Back in five minutes."

Anna turned her attention to the Manfred Lange files. Here was his work history, a copy of his Reich passport, and his registration papers. The photo attached showed a much younger man, although the photo could not have been more than ten years old. There was no doubt it was the Herr Lange she knew, but the man looking up at her was full of life and energy. He held his head in a confident way, his gaze focused on the camera. Identity photos from the Third Reich tended to show people's faces tinged with something like worry, or trepidation, like they wanted to run away as fast as they could once the photo was taken. But Manfred Lange appeared happy to be photographed. His occupation was listed as art historian, and his date of birth as 29 June 1871. All consistent with what Anna knew about him. She flipped the little cardboard folder of his work permit over. Underneath was a membership card to the NSDAP, the Nazi Party. Again, his unapologetic face stared out at her. Member number 149578. So he had been a party member. Anna twinged a little. Had he told her he had been a party member? People with important jobs usually had to be, and it didn't necessarily mean they were true believers, or even sympathizers. Still, it bothered her.

She scanned the room trying not to appear furtive but failing. She quickly flipped pages to see if she could find his Fragebogen, the questionnaire the Americans would have made him complete. But it wasn't there, of course, because these were the Germans' files, not the Americans'. Deeply uncomfortable, she flipped back to the party membership card. The date of issue was 20 April 1933. Hitler's birthday. Manfred Lange had been what the Germans called a March Violet—a late bloomer. March Violets were those who joined the party right after Hitler had seized full authority in March of 1933. Many with elite jobs and who considered themselves to have standing in society, rushed to join the party in order to be on the right side of the power grab. Probably that's what Manfred Lange had done, too, like millions of others. She closed the folder indicating she was ready to go. She wanted to be out of the building and far away.

"Find anything we should know about?" Bender asked, as he held the door for her.

"No," she lied.

"Okay. I'll take your word for it," he said, climbing into the driver's seat. The air had turned colder and the sky was socked in with dense clouds. "Looks like we're in the clear for now. At least with the folks working for us." He shot her a look.

"Should you have let me see Herr Lange's information?" Anna retaliated to deflect any further line of questioning.

He smiled as he started the engine. "Probably not," he said, "but I can't help it. I'm so nosy."

chapter six

"Where were you? I couldn't find you at all yesterday." Cooper was flustered and irritated but a smile appeared when Anna looked up at him from her desk. Things had piled up while she was out with Bender, so she had come in early to catch up. Anna honestly couldn't remember if Manfred Lange had mentioned being a party member; she could only recall that he was very against the Nazis' attitude toward art and free speech to the point where the memories had upset him. She hated that these misgivings lived on and probably would forever. One day, Amalia would ask her what she had done in the war.

"I went with Bender to Darmstadt. I thought you knew about that," she said. "He told me he had checked with you."

"That's right. Of course. Was it a successful trip?" He sat down in the chair next to her table, intent on something.

"I think so. He asked me to help him translate some paperwork. He was checking on some personnel? I didn't find anything."

"Sounds like good news. For us, anyway. We already had to fire some people when their past caught up with them."

"Because they were party members?"

"Or worse. Makes sense, but we had to let some very qualified people go. And with all these government types breathing down our necks, we can't afford a single screw up. Washington is just waiting for something to go wrong so they can scrap this whole operation." His face sank back into the shadows it had carried for the past weeks. He leaned forward and dropped his face into his hands. Anna felt sorry for him.

"That won't happen," she said. "You will make sure of it." She placed a hand on his shoulder. Without looking at her, Cooper took her hand in his and held it in place, his face still buried in his other palm. His grip on her hand sent a surge of energy through Anna's core.

They stayed this way for several beats, Anna's hand wrapped in his. She noticed for the first time that Cooper's hair, a dirty blond, was hinting at gray at the temple. His tall body was folded into the chair uncomfortably, knees and elbows touching at an awkward angle. The distinctive, starchy smell of his pressed, clean uniform combined with another scent, maybe the pomade he used. He smelled slightly of tobacco and salt—not smoke, but a sweet, pungent smell. She would know that smell without seeing him. Anna was terrified someone would walk in, but she didn't want to break the moment either. She turned her hand under his so their palms met, and she allowed herself to enjoy the sensation for a brief moment before sliding her hand out from under his, slowly, as if not to wake him. He still did not move when she reached over and stroked the hair on his temple with one fingertip. Then she put her hand back in her lap and felt her breath catch in her throat. She stood and walked out of the office.

Inside the women's bathroom, Anna stared at herself in the mirror. She tried to look into her own eyes, but could not. After a few seconds, she could not even recognize herself. The features of her face were disjointed, random parts assembled without any coherence. She bared her teeth, now yellow and held together by gums that were receding from malnutrition and neglect. Her skin was sallow and uneven, her eyebrows overgrown. Everything about her was worn and tired. She felt ugly and disconnected from her body, even though she could feel its aches and pains, the constant backache and the searing stabs in her hip that were remnants of her pregnancy. She tried to see herself through the eyes of others. How did she appear, next to the Americans? Many German women were much better maintained than she was. She had taken to wearing pants and men's boots every day, out of sheer convenience. She liked the way she could sit in them, on the floor or on a stool with legs splayed and knees acting as armrests. This was one less thing to worry about, and they made her feel like she had some control. She thought about Cooper and how he must see her, especially compared to Eva's long, elegant lines and feminine dress. She gave herself a stern look. "Stop it," she told her reflection. "Don't be such an idiot." She wanted to slap herself and was about to do it when the door opened.

"*Hallo*, Anna," said Eva, closing the door behind her. Anna smiled at Eva but made a show of washing her hands to avoid her eyes.

"Everything all right with you?" Eva sidled up and smiled at her in the mirror. "Where were you yesterday?"

"Darmstadt. They wanted me to help translate some files at the Gestapo office. Where were you last night? You missed dinner?" She decided to turn it into a question rather than an accusation.

Eva touched her hair and examined herself in the mirror. "Helping on a report for Captain Farmer. About the painting restoration work." She turned on the tap, which produced a sputter of ice cold water. "Gestapo? What kinds of files?"

Anna detected a shift in the energy between them. "The *Amis* are checking on the people who work here. Apparently, they already had to fire several people who turned out to have been party members, so now they want to be extra careful." She tried to sound detached, to not let on that she knew anything. What good would it do to mention what she had found out about Manfred Lange? He hadn't lied to them exactly; a man in his position would have been expected to join the party to safeguard his livelihood. He wasn't the one employed by the *Amis*. There was nothing in the file that said he had committed any crimes. And anyway, are the sins of the father really to be laid upon the children? If that were the case, all Germans would be unemployable for decades to come. She added that rationalization to the gratitude for the roof over her head and pushed Manfred Lange's party history from her mind.

Eva rubbed her hands together under the trickle of water. "Well, I've been upstairs all morning, in the file room. I need some fresh air, I think. Want to go for a smoke?"

Anna noticed a cut on Eva's hand. "Are you bleeding?"

Eva waved her off. "I cut myself opening a box the other day. I was rushing and the scissors slipped. It keeps opening up again when I move my hand. Not enough nutrition, I guess."

Anna pulled the towel off the rack and passed it to her. "Here, use this." She peered at the scab, which had dark red patches around it. "You should clean that out so it doesn't get infected. Can you get some medicine from the *Amis*?"

Eva took the towel and held it against her palm. "I will. So, do you want to get some fresh air?"

Anna shook her head. "I've got things to do, sorry. This afternoon?" She patted her hair because she thought she should make the effort.

"Can't," Eva said. "I'm going with the Captain to a meeting."

Anna looked at Eva's reflection in the mirror. "With Cooper? What meeting?"

Eva shrugged. "I don't know, some meeting with Captain Farmer. He said to be ready at two. And to bring a note pad. I guess he needs a secretary."

Anna faked a smile that she knew was unconvincing, but Eva was too busy checking her complexion in the mirror to notice. Anna took the chance to get away.

"I must run," she said with exaggerated urgency as she headed to the door. "I'm supposed to be upstairs." It was not a total lie, but outside in the hall she took a left instead of a right turn toward the stairs and then took a walk through the back corridor, careful to not draw attention to herself. Her skin was burning and her heart pounding. A dark feeling spread into the pit of her stomach, which she recognized as something like jealousy. Why was Cooper taking Eva to the meeting and not her? She thought he had wanted to confide in her earlier. Had she cut him off? Why did she care? And what was the meeting with the director about?

She took a deep breath and stopped walking. To her left, the door to the store room stood slightly open when it should have been locked.

She scanned the empty hallway in both directions, paying particular attention to the closed door of the ladies' room. She put her hand on the door knob and poked her head into the dark room.

"*Hallo*?" she said. Then louder, "Hello? Anyone in here?"

She pushed the door open further and went inside.

"It's possible that I finally do have a screw loose, but didn't I tell you that you weren't to be in the storeroom unaccompanied anymore?" Cooper was almost barking.

Anna shifted uncomfortably in her chair. She had come straight upstairs to look for him and found him standing in the hallway chatting with another *Ami*. When she had pulled him aside, trying to disguise her urgency, she saw the other man raise his eyebrows at Cooper and give him a knowing smile, which irritated her.

"Yes, you did, but…"

"And you went in anyway. And now you're sitting here in my office telling me that a painting is missing. Again."

Anna winced at his snarling tone.

"Only I, Farmer, and Standen have a key to that room," Cooper said. "And none of us were in there yesterday, I know that. Both of them were gone to Frankfurt for a meeting."

"Well, someone forgot to lock it at some point," Anna argued. "The door was open and no one was inside."

"So you went in? You realize if anything really is missing or awry, you're going to be the first one they look at."

Anna glanced over her shoulder toward the door. "Something *is* missing," she hissed.

"So you said. But explain to me again why you were there in the first place? If the door was unlocked, you should have told me." Now he glanced toward the hallway.

Anna leaned forward so their faces were close enough for her to see the fine laugh lines around his eyes. "I thought someone was inside—I thought it was you—and I wanted to make sure that's why the door was open. But no one was there. I was going to leave when I noticed that one of the frames was pulled out from the shelf. I went to push it back in so it wouldn't fall and I saw that the painting that should have been there was gone." She paused and then cut him off, anticipating his next question. "I know that collection like the back of my hand, Captain. All the paintings are in alphabetical order by artist. So, George Grosz, Ernst Ludwig Kirchner, Franz Marc, Emil Nolde…"

"Yes, yes." Cooper made a get-on-with-it gesture with both hands.

"It's the Kirchner," Anna said. "*Berlin 1913*. It's not there anymore."

"Could be someone took it to work on the frame. Or to photograph it."

"You said yourself that no one with a key had been down there. And anyway, no one cares about that collection. You told me everyone is more worried about the National Gallery paintings. The Morgenstern collection is sitting there, fully inventoried and documented. It's a completed job. Why would anyone take one of the paintings?"

As he mulled over her question, a tiny spark of panic appeared in Cooper's eye. She leaned forward. "Captain, do you know where your keys are?"

Cooper rolled his eyes and leaned back, pushing his chair away from the desk. "Oh, come on, Frau Klein, of course I know where they are. They're here, in my desk." He pulled open the middle drawer and fished out a key chain, which he dangled in front of her with a smirk. "And if I'm not here, they're in my pocket. I do keep track of them."

"All of them, all the time?" Anna eyed the chain with more than ten keys on it. "How would you know if one was missing?"

Cooper smirked, dropped the keys onto the desk, and began sorting through them with his finger. Finding the key in question, he lifted it up and held it in front of her face. "There it is. Look at that," he scoffed. "Why do you think it's my keys that are being hijacked? You can't blame me for everything."

"Because I have taken your keys and you didn't know." She braced herself for Cooper's anger, but he shook his head.

"I know you take my keys. I trust you," he lectured. "I told you not to go down there alone as a way to protect you, not because I think you're up to something. I don't want you to get caught in the line of fire."

"What do we do now?" Now Anna glanced toward the doorway, and she tuned her ears to any approaching footsteps. Cooper's office really needed a door.

Cooper cradled his head in his hands. "This is about all I need right now. What do you want me to do? File a report?"

"Aren't you meeting with Farmer this afternoon? You could talk to him about it then? Maybe he's got the painting. To show it to some VIP. Don't they do that all the time?"

Cooper stopped. "How did you know about that meeting?"

"Eva told me she's going to the meeting with you. Am I not supposed to know?" Now Anna heard a rising conversation in her own head.

Cooper exhaled sharply. "Just forget you heard about it. I'll explain later." He paused to look her in the eye. "Trust me?"

Anna shrugged. “Whatever you say. What will you do about the painting?” She wasn’t sure she trusted him at all.

“I don’t know yet. I need to think for a minute.” Cooper stood and walked to the side of the desk where Anna was sitting. He paced back and forth for a few moments then half-sat on the edge of the desk in front of her. He leaned close and beckoned for her to move in, too. Anna straightened and looked up at his face. “I’m trying to keep you out of some stuff that’s happening. It’s to protect you, understand? To protect your job here. So for now, don’t tell anyone about what happened, got it? I mean it, not a single soul.”

Anna started to speak, but his raised palm stopped her. “That’s all. Let’s plan to meet again tomorrow after lunch. Out in the courtyard on the loading dock, okay?”

Anna nodded again. It all sounded a bit overly dramatic to her, but then Cooper was fond of the big gesture. She returned to the real subject at hand. “Are you going to lock the storage room?”

“You bet your ass,” Cooper said, taking the keys from his desk, then catching himself. “Pardon my French,” he added. “I’m headed there right now. Do you need anything else from me?”

Anna had a flash. “Yes,” she said. “I know it’s probably not possible, but could I get a travel pass to go to Frankfurt for the day? It would be for CCP business, if you authorize it. I could take the train.” She made a pained face. “Nothing untoward, I promise.”

Cooper looked confused. “Where in Frankfurt?”

“Gestapo Headquarters.”

Cooper laughed. “Oh, a nice day trip that is. What CCP business is it, or am I not allowed to ask?”

“I am looking for Jacob Morgenstern,” she said. “I think I can find him there."

"I hate to break it to you, Frau Klein, but I don't think many Jews are hanging around the Gestapo office in Frankfurt."

Anna cocked her head, acknowledging the joke. "No, the lists. They kept immaculate lists of who was transported where and when. I saw them when I went to the office in Darmstadt with Bender. Jacob Morgenstern was from Frankfurt. If he was transported from there, they will have a record. Maybe that will shed some light on what happened to him."

"I thought all that stuff was going to Nuremberg for the trials?" Cooper changed the subject.

"Yes, I suppose it is. That's why I need to go soon, if it's not already too late."

"You're not going to let this Morgenstern fellow go, are you? You know he's probably dead. And we have more pressing stuff to deal with. Even Fraulein Lange told me she couldn't find anything on him."

"I think we are wrong to write him off, Captain. Not every Jew died in the camps." She rethought her choice of words. "We didn't manage to murder all of them. That camp the refugee people set up in Zeilsheim is full of survivors. Why not Jacob Morgenstern? Don't we at least owe it to him to try a little harder?"

Cooper stood and walked back to his chair, sinking into it with something like bemused resignation, like a husband whose wife has asked for something he knows he won't refuse.

"All right, you go to Frankfurt, Frau Klein. But I can't spare you for a whole day and it wouldn't look right anyway. I don't want anyone noticing that you're gone. There's a train that leaves for Frankfurt at around seven hundred. You go first thing in the morning and be back here on the lunchtime train so we can meet in the afternoon. I'll need you back here by thirteen hundred. Fill out the form for me and I'll sign it. If anyone asks, you're headed to pick up some urgent paperwork from HQ." He checked his watch. "Leave it on my desk and I'll get to it after my meeting." He patted her shoulder with a firm hand as he walked past. It was the kind of pat a coach gives a player when he sends him onto the field. It meant Cooper had moved on and was back on his own agenda. At the door, he stopped and turned, index finger pointed sternly in her direction. "Not a word to anyone about that damn Kirchner, do we have a deal?"

"Yes, sir, we have a deal. Thank you, Captain."

He winked and turned on his heel, his shoes squeaking on the terrazzo floors. Anna watched him go and then pulled the travel form out of the drawer and fed it into her typewriter.

Amalia sat on the front stoop of the house on the Kopernikusstrasse playing with her doll. When she saw Anna, she made a good show of being displeased.

"*Maus*! How are you?' Anna dropped her bag and sat down next to her. "Did you miss me all day? What are you doing out here?"

"Auntie is taking a nap, as usual. Herr Lange told me to play outside. I was walking around the cemetery, but there was a funeral so I came here and waited."

"Where's Oskar?"

Amalia shrugged. "I don't know. He went off to get food. Left first thing this morning without me. But he said he's bringing me a present."

"I see." Anna hugged her knees to her chest and leaned close to her daughter. "Tell me what else is going on. I feel like I don't really see you so much anymore. I'm sorry I'm so busy at work."

"It's all right, Mama. I understand." She worked at a knot in Lulu's hair.

Anna rested her chin on her knees and gazed at the trees that lined the northern edge of the cemetery. Would she ever again feel settled in a place? At home? Safe? Wiesbaden was nice enough, but she had no roots here. Not even a place of their own. Would she one day be able to claim the city as hers?

"Can I ask you something, *Maus*?"

"Okay," Amalia said, using the Americans' word that she had adopted as her response to most things.

"Do you like it here in Wiesbaden?"

"I guess so. But I miss our house, Mama. I miss having my own room. And I miss Papa."

"I know you do. I do, too. I try not to think about it too much. It makes me too sad."

"Me, too. When can we go home again?" She stopped as a thought came to her. "We can take Oskar with us, right? He'll come, too?"

Anna bit her lip. "You know, you are very brave," she dodged. "You came all this way and you've learned to be such a big girl. I am so proud of you." She wanted to say how it was so unfair that the war had taken her childhood away, but of course it was even more unfair for all the others whose lives had been taken. And if you were Jewish, or disabled, or undesirable in any number of ways, the war had tortured you first. To lose only your childhood meant you had come out well ahead.

Amalia turned to face her mother, staring at her with an intensity that Anna hadn't seen before. Amalia's eyes fired and her mouth was set. She was suddenly much older than her six years. It took a moment before she said, "We aren't going back home are we?"

Anna closed her eyes. Amalia knew more than she let on. She had overheard conversations and put the puzzle pieces together, all without the benefit of an explanation or even words of comfort. Anna had let her inaction go far too long.

"*Maus*, we can't go home." Anna took Amalia's hands in hers. "It's not our home anymore. It's not like it used to be, not how you remember it." She gave the tiny hand a little squeeze. "It'll never be that way again, not for us."

Amalia nodded. "I know that. The Russian soldiers. They scare me. I don't want to be with the Russians." Her face started to crumble, but she put it back together quickly, almost imperceptibly.

"I am sorry, *Maus*. I wish it were different." The fear of Russian soldiers had been drummed into them, not just by the Nazi propagandists, but by stories from women in the line of the Soviets' advance from the east. Even if you didn't know the specifics about the rape and torture and killing, the cloud hung low and dark over everything, and the word alone conjured a cold chill in your gut. Germans had been made to understand that the Russians were barbarians and animals, and therefore worse than the Nazis, who kept their killing clean, organized, and industrious.

"But it's not up to you," Amalia recited the words that Anna had always came back to. "I know, Mama." She focused on her mother's eyes. "It's okay."

"I hope so," Anna said. "I'm trying to make it okay."

Amalia nodded and looked at her shoes. "We are divorcing Papa?" Her voice choked and this time she couldn't catch it. She began to cry softly because she already knew the answer. The street had fallen quiet and Amalia's tiny sobs echoed in the rustling of the trees.

Anna found her own voice cracking. Why had she chosen this moment to have this conversation? They could have had a nice afternoon. But, of course, the conversation had been sitting there, like a package on the kitchen table that needed opening. There would never be a good time. She squeezed Amalia's hand again and nodded. "Yes, I may have to divorce Papa. But you are not divorcing him. He's still your Papa and you will see him. When everything calms down, he can come and visit you. And he will love you just as he always has. That doesn't change at all."

Amalia's tears spilled onto Anna's hands. Amalia had seen this coming. Maybe she had talked it over with the more worldly Oskar. Perhaps he had already helped her understand. "I don't even remember that much about Papa anymore," she said. "Do you think he remembers me?"

"Oh, *Maus*, of course he does. You are the most important thing to him. But the adults have made such a huge mess of this world, that now he has to be with the Russians and we have to be here. It's not fair, but we have to live with it."

"But who will take care of us, Mama?"

Anna took a deep breath and straightened. "I will. I'm going to take care of all of us, you'll see." She almost believed it. They sat for a few more minutes, watching people walk by, dragging jugs of milk or pushing carts piled with crates and bundles and baskets of belongings. Now and again a car would pass, usually an American one, leaving behind a puff of exhaust that swirled in the gusts of wind. Anna was so lost in thought that she didn't see Oskar come running through the trees until Amalia called his name.

He crossed the street without looking, hiding something behind his back, his smile reaching from ear to ear.

"What did you bring me?" Amalia stopped crying and wiped her nose with the back of hand. "Show me."

Oskar kept his hands hidden, playing a game of *Guess which hand?* with Amalia, until he coaxed a giggle from her. When he finally produced a Hershey's chocolate bar, the kind the *Amis* handed out to children, she squealed with delight and jumped up to tackle him.

Anna smiled and picked up her bag, thankful for the distraction. She left the two of them, lost in their own world on the stoop, examining the words on the packaging and taking turns putting it to their noses and inhaling. She resisted the urge to lecture them about saving it for later. When something so good falls out of the sky, it is okay to enjoy it all at once. *That's what Cooper would say.*

She pushed the door open and went into the dim calm of the Lange house. She could hear dishes clanking in the kitchen and found Madeleine there, washing the plates in the hot water from the stove.

"*Hallo*, Auntie," she said, kissing her on the cheek. She dropped her bag and picked up a dish towel. "Let me help you."

Madeleine smiled and handed her a plate.

"Thank you, child."

"How are things here?" Anna whispered. Living in someone else's home she was always unsteady, waiting for a change of heart, the decision that the situation was not working out after all, that maybe they would be better off elsewhere.

"It's been very quiet. I napped this afternoon; Manfred read. He's sleeping a bit now. The children were out."

Anna caught a hint of a smile. She nudged Madeleine with her shoulder. "And?"

Color rose in Madeleine's cheeks. "And it was a pleasant afternoon." She pulled a plate from the gray water. "Manfred is a very interesting man."

Anna smiled. "I'm glad." She had noticed that Madeleine and Herr Lange often sat on the sofa next to each other and that he doted on her, giving her books to read, bringing her a blanket, or turning on the light so she could see better. It was nothing more than that, but Anna was happy she had found a companion. The two women stood side by side, Madeleine passing dishes, Anna drying and stacking. Anna tried to put the business with the missing Kirchner out of her mind, but that only left room for remembering that Cooper and Eva were having meetings without her. Meetings she was not supposed to know about. She decided to focus on more important things.

"Auntie, can you fetch the rations tomorrow? Or send the children? I'm going to be tied up at the Collecting Point all day."

"Of course," Madeleine replied. "I'll send Oskar and Amalia. Manfred and I planned to take a walk down into the park. If he's feeling up to it."

"I hope the weather will cooperate," Anna said, scanning the sky through the kitchen window. The weather was always on the verge of shifting, uncommitted and transient. Or maybe it just felt that way to her.

"He has a coat I can borrow. From his wife." Madeleine stacked the plates and moved them to the table. She shook out the small towel and hung it on a hook to dry. Anna sensed there was something she wanted to say and was trying to find the right way in. She smiled and took Madeleine's hand. "I'm happy you're comfortable here."

She chuckled. “You mean you’re glad I’m not alone all day, cooped up, and losing my mind?”

“No, that’s not it at all. I’m glad that this arrangement is working out well. I hope it won’t be much longer, though.”

“I’m not counting on anything changing anytime soon.” She wiped her hands on her skirt and scanned the small kitchen as if something else needed her attention.

“Is something on your mind?” Anna prodded.

Madeleine folded her hands in front of her the way she did when she was about to make a pronouncement. She searched for the right words and made a few false starts before she finally spoke.

“Well, all right. Since you ask, I’ll say it.”

Anna craned her neck in exaggerated interest although she wasn’t sure she wanted to hear any big news. “Say what?”

Madeleine took a few steps back. She peered out the door toward the empty living room and lowered her voice. “I don’t quite know. It’s Eva. I hate to start rumors, you know, but I think she has a secret. There’s no reason for her to tell us anything, I know that, but I think she’s keeping it from us quite deliberately. Which I can understand, of course, because people will talk. And she seems like a nice girl.”

Anna was confused. “What do you think she’s doing?”

“Oh, I hate to even say it. What if I’m wrong? These things are so personal. It’s none of my business.”

“Auntie, come on. What is it?”

“All right.” She forced herself to continue. “I think she and Captain Cooper are seeing each other? What I mean is, I think they are having an affair. Of some kind,” she added, as if there were more than one kind.

Anna bit her lip and stepped in closer. "What makes you say that?" she asked, her tone more concerned than she liked. She decided not to say anything else, in case her voice cracked. She made a face to show she was waiting for an answer in a disinterested way.

Madeleine fretted. "I don't know exactly. She comes and goes so much."

"Oh, that." Anna waved her hand. "She told me she was helping finish a report for the director last night. She wasn't with Cooper." She scoffed at the idea.

"No, she went out again last night after curfew. You know I don't sleep much. I heard her go."

"But how do you know it's Captain Cooper she's seeing?" Anna's tone turned argumentative. "Maybe it's some other *Ami*."

"Has she said anything to you?"

"No, but maybe she wants to keep it private. People talk, like you say."

Anna sat down on the kitchen stool and dropped her hands into her lap. She had no right to feel any of the feelings that flooded her. Jealousy, fear, anger, sadness. Loneliness. Betrayal. She wanted to escape her own being at that moment, to leave herself sitting there on the stool in that apartment on the Kopernikusstrasse in Wiesbaden and to be somewhere else. And to be someone else entirely.

Madeleine took her hand. "Listen, child. I don't presume to know what's going on with you, but I knew enough that this would upset you. I didn't want to say anything. But finally had to. I saw them today. Together."

"You did?" Anna's heart sank.

"This afternoon. They were walking along the Bahnhofstrasse."

"So? That hardly means anything."

"But it's not the first time I've seen them."

Anna shook her head. "Auntie, they work together. They are probably on some Collecting Point business." But she couldn't actually think what business they would have in the Bahnhofstrasse in the middle of the day.

"Why were you in the Bahnhofstrasse?"

"Me? I was out on a visit to the post office. You know I go a few times a week to see if anything has arrived for me. Or for you."

"They've been going on a lot of field visits and Cooper takes her to meetings. That's probably what you've seen," Anna argued.

"Anna, she's snuck out after curfew every night we've been here. I can hear all the footsteps on these creaky floors. I even watched her go through the window." She gestured at the kitchen window, which opened onto the sidewalk. Anyone with any flexibility could climb out easily and hop onto the pavement.

Anna peered out the open window. An overturned crate was set just below, providing just enough of a step to ease the exit and entry. She turned back to Madeleine. "In the middle of the night?"

"Yes. Heads out on foot toward the cemetery. That's as far as I can see. But I thought with the curfew, she must be meeting an *Ami*. Why risk getting picked up otherwise? Would she tell you if she was seeing Cooper?" She paused a beat and put her hand under Anna's chin to catch her eye. "Maybe she knows you wouldn't like it?"

Anna made an exasperated gesture. "Why wouldn't I like it?" Her voice was loud and she caught herself. "Why wouldn't I like it?" she whispered. "It's got nothing to do with me. What they do is not my business. I am there to work and that is all." She paused, and then added, "I hope they don't get caught." Faking concern for their well-being was a plausible cover for the raw feelings she was having trouble concealing. And Madeleine knew her too well, anyway. But Anna continued the ruse rather than confess her roiling emotions. She wiped her hands on the towel. "Right. I will check on the children and then I'll go to the room. Are you coming?"

Madeleine smiled. "You go ahead. I'll go check on Manfred and see if he needs anything."

Anna kissed the old woman on the cheek. "Thank you for looking out for me, Auntie." She stopped at the door and turned. "Do you remember what time it was when you saw them today?"

Madeleine thought for moment. "It was somewhere around two-thirty? I'm not sure, but I would say between two and three. Does that matter?"

Anna shook her head. "Not really."

The front door opened and Oskar and Amalia piled into the house, slamming the door behind them. Anna went into the foyer to chide them for making a commotion, but their wide-eyed faces stopped her.

"What's happened?" She reached for Amalia who buried her face in Anna's pant leg. "What's going on?"

Oskar took on the air of a protective and wise big brother. "A strange man came up to us. We were sitting on the stoop and he started asking us questions."

Anna opened the door and looked up and down the street, but the sidewalk was empty. "What, just now? What kind of questions?" She hadn't seen any man when she had looked out the window.

"If we lived here, if she is my sister, how old is she, what's her name..." Oskar thrust a thumb in Amalia's direction. "That kind of thing." He shook his head. "He wasn't scary, just kind of creepy with all the questions. I mean, what does he care?"

Amalia squeezed Anna's leg. "He said he liked my doll."

"And then he asked if he could see the doll. That's when I said, we have to go, and we came inside. Weird, huh? Creepy old man."

"Did you tell him anything?" Anna asked.

"Nope, not a thing. I'm smarter than that, Frau Klein."

"I know," Anna conceded. She locked the door and then went to the kitchen window, which overlooked the street. No one was outside. "What did he look like?"

Oskar's eyes scanned the ceiling as he painted a picture. "Old, maybe fifty, older than you. Kind of fat, skimpy hair, and a long black mustache. Dressed pretty nice, pants and jacket with a tie. Kind of a blue tie. His face was wrinkled and his teeth were really bad. Right?" He looked to Amalia for confirmation.

"Yes, yellow and wobbly looking. He had dirty shoes and hands," Amalia said. Her low-to-the-ground vantage point provided unusual details.

"And you told him nothing?"

"Nothing. Not even when he asked about you."

Anna's chest tightened. "Me?"

"Well, not you exactly. He asked if the lady that lives here works for the *Amis* at the Collecting Point."

"And you said?"

"Nothing, I told you."

It occurred to Anna that the man might have been asking about Eva and not her at all. It didn't make her feel any better.

Madeleine squeezed Anna's arm. "It's nothing, Anna." She was trying to reassure her, but they both knew it could be any number of things. Children vanished off the streets all the time; pimps and pedophiles were always on the prowl. People sought favors from Germans who worked with Americans; thieves and thugs searched for easy targets.

"You two go to our room and let me talk to Auntie." She shooed then along. "And, Oskar?"

He stopped and let Amalia go ahead.

"Be very careful." She mouthed the words for emphasis. "If it happens again, tell me right away, yes?"

"Yes." He acknowledged her concern, trying to play the streetwise urchin, but she could see he was worried, too. She waved him into the bedroom.

"It's nothing, child," Madeleine repeated. "Oskar is nothing if not smart."

Anna agreed something had shifted again. She walked to the kitchen window and closed it. What the conversation with Madeleine had introduced—Eva and Cooper's secret trysts—had made her uneasy. Now the questioning stranger with the yellow teeth had turned unease into worry tinged with actual fear. And she had been so distracted by the prospect of Eva and Cooper that she hadn't noticed the man outside on the stoop.

"Let's not tell anyone about this, agreed?" she whispered to Madeleine. "Not even Manfred. No need to alarm him." His peace of mind was not her primary concern, but it made for good cover for now.

"Of course." Madeleine squeezed her hand. "There's nothing to tell."

She left Madeleine to putter around the living room, straightening cushions and wiping the dust from the furniture, a pointless Sisyphean task that she nevertheless enjoyed. In the bedroom, Anna found Amalia on her cot, playing quietly with Lulu, who had acquired a new dress made from an old handkerchief. Oskar sat on the floor flipping through a book of old photos of Berlin that Manfred Lange had given him. He stared at each one for a long time before turning the page. Anna lay on the bed for a long time, listening to Amalia's sweet playful whispers and thinking about the events of the day. The episode with the stranger made her feel vulnerable, and she ached to have someone to talk to, someone to make her feel safe. She reached into the bedside table and pulled out the papers and pencil.

I thought today of the times I visited you in the clinic, when Amalia was just a baby. Before things got so bad. We would bring you a lunch and eat at your desk, or if the weather was nice, at the little table out by the hospital kitchen. I remember some days you looked so tired and worn, but you never stopped. When the young girl from down the street gave birth, you were up all night with her. She was so frightened, without her family. I brought soup for you both and some hand-me-down clothes from Amalia. I think of her often, too. Did they take her baby from her? With no husband, she didn't stand much of a chance. I am sure you know what happened, but you didn't tell me and I was happy to not ask. I liked the idea of creating a world that I could control by not letting unpleasant things in. But that's not how the world works. We have no control over anything do we? The things that happen to us, the things we create for ourselves, they are all a series of circumstances aligning in a certain way. All we can do is decide how we view them.

My love, what do you think about when you put your head on your pillow at night? Are you still living in our house? The address on your letter was from the hospital, so I can only assume that our house, too, has been requisitioned by the Army for billeting officers. How is your Russian Army treating you? Our Army is not too bad; I daresay they are fairly kind and reasonable. Of course, there are opportunists and bad apples, the GIs who harass women on the streets or try to coerce favors. And there are as many German women willing to play that game, too. Although I suppose it's not unreasonable to think that something like a true love could bloom in this landscape.

The pencil stopped and she drew circles in the air above the paper, waiting for the next thought. But she was too tired. She folded the paper and stared at her outstretched legs. Outside the small window, the wind rustled the trees and she could hear footsteps on the street as the day wound to a close. Would Eva be back for dinner tonight, or would she be out again? She put the pencil down. Eva was an adult and allowed to live her life. Anna was a guest in her house. It had nothing to do with her.

chapter seven

The train station building had been damaged in the bombings, so the inside was a lot like the outside: open to the sky and elements. Anna made her way through the partial ruins to the platform for the train to Frankfurt. Most Germans had no money or means to purchase a ticket or even permission to travel, so the trains were mostly used by American VIPs or soldiers. Civilians were not so rare as to cause undue attention, but Anna still preferred to go unnoticed. The less interaction with any authorities the better.

She gave her travel document to the MP at the entry to the platform, and he waved her through with barely a glance. At 6:45 in the morning, the passengers were mostly men with attaché cases and officers in their pressed service uniforms heading to meetings at headquarters in

Frankfurt. She tried to look confident and official but instead kept checking the address of her destination: Lindenstrasse 27. On the map she had borrowed from Cooper, she could see it was due north of the train station, and she hoped it was along a street car route. Otherwise it would be a long walk she didn't have time for, given that she had to be back by lunchtime.

She noticed an older officer, a major, who took up position a few feet from her, waiting for the train that had just been announced. He smiled at her and she returned the greeting, which he took as an invitation to approach her.

"*Wohin fahren Sie?*" he said in heavily accented German.

"Frankfurt," Anna replied. "I speak English." She held up her credentials. "Interpreter."

He squinted at her papers. "Ah, on official business, I see, Anna Klein. Where in Frankfurt are you headed, Fraulein Klein?"

Anna hedged. The *Ami* might not be making idle conversation or even chatting her up. She was obliged to answer any American's questions, after all. "Lindenstrasse. I am on business for the MFA&A." She didn't bother to correct his assumption that she was unmarried.

"Ah, right. The Monuments Men. They're digging up more history are they?"

She smiled. He took a few steps closer. The name tag under an impressive stack of ribbons above the breast pocket of his jacket read Stuart. She wished Stuart would go away.

"How's that working out, with the Monuments Men?" he asked.

"It's a very good job," Anna said. "They do important work."

Major Stuart gave a little snort. "I guess so." He pulled out a pack of Lucky Strikes, shook a couple of cigarettes loose, and offered one to her. She declined with a wave of her hand.

Stuart lit up, snapping his Zippo with the flick of a wrist, and then deposited the lighter into the pocket under his ribbons. He acted like a man supremely in charge, unquestioning and unwavering, like a school principal familiar with every trick a student could attempt to pull. It made the corners of his mouth turn downward in a constant look of superiority. He inhaled and stared into the middle distance as if to absorb the admiration he felt Anna must be bestowing on him.

"Have you been to the Collecting Point and seen the art?" she asked, trying to sound naively enthusiastic. "I haven't seen much of it myself, of course, but it's quite spectacular."

"Yes, it is." He took another long pull off the cigarette and exhaled. "In fact, I was there the other day, meeting with Captain Farmer. That's a pretty cozy arrangement they have."

Anna smiled agreeably, hiding the realization that she now knew exactly who she was talking to. Stuart was one of the men giving Cooper his nightly ulcers. She could see why Cooper was so miserable. "Yes," she offered. "Everyone seems very hardworking. And so smart." She wished she had accepted the cigarette.

"Sure, they are. They're a bunch of museum wonks and architects. They're like pigs in slop right now."

She decided to play along and made a quizzical face to show perhaps her English was not up to his idiom. Getting him to talk might prove helpful to Cooper's cause.

"They care more about the art than anything," he added helpfully. "More than reparations or budgets or justice, let's say." He rocked back on his heels as he blew a plume of smoke into the air.

Anna waited for him to offer more on his own, but she sensed that he had said all he was going to say to a strange German civilian on a train platform. She changed the subject. "Do you know Frankfurt well?"

"Not really. Just the restricted zone." He looked sheepish. "I try not to venture out too much. Not a lot of sightseeing to be done."

"You are stationed there?"

He shook his head. "No, I'm visiting." Sensing the opportunity to impress, he turned his face toward hers. "I work for the State Department. In Washington."

That explained his attitude, Anna thought. "Oh, my," she said, feeling utterly stupid. "That's so exciting. What do you do there?"

His already wide face expanded into a condescending smile. He pointed his Lucky Strike at her. "Can't tell you that. That's classified."

"Of course. I shouldn't have asked."

"Suffice it to say, I deal with war reparations and financial matters."

"Like the art at the Collecting Point? Are those war reparations, too?"

He was on a roll now. "Well, of course they are. That's how it works. That's how it's always worked."

"Yes. Spoils of war, is that how you say it? So the art belongs to America now?"

The rumblings of the approaching train were beginning and snapped him out of his posturing. "Look, Fraulein, no offense, but these are military matters that don't concern you or any German." He closed the subject by leering at her though a slow blink. "Where did you say were going?"

Anna hadn't said where she was going and couldn't think of a reasonable evasion. "Lindenstrasse," she answered. "Gestapo headquarters."

"What the hell do you want there?"

"Checking against personnel files," she said. "To make sure that all the employees are who they say they are." She knew this would only lead to more questions. She took a small step back.

"Hmm. Strange job to send a civilian interpreter on," he said. "Why not send whoever's in charge of personnel?"

Anna made a show of agreeing with him. "Normally they would, but they couldn't get away today. And since I can read the German forms, they told me to go. So here I am." She rolled her eyes for added effect.

"They must trust you a lot to send you on this errand," he said. "Since it's totally against protocol. And anyway, you're better off going to the HQ building. The Lindenstrasse building has been mostly cleared and the files sent to headquarters. All of that stuff is going to Nuremberg, so I don't know how much luck you'll have." He looked down at her feet and then slid his eyes up her body. "When we get to Frankfurt, I can give you a lift to HQ, if you like. Since you are on official business."

The train approached, screeching to a long, loud stop that prevented Anna from responding. She wanted to tell him to jump in front of the engine, but instead she stepped aside to make room for the opening door and the trickle of exiting people, all focused on their next destination, keeping eyes down or staring straight ahead. No one was meeting a waiting loved one or making a rendezvous. No one looked at anyone at all.

Anna hesitated but decided a ride would be her best bet, especially if headquarters was, in fact, the place she needed to go. And maybe a car ride with Major Stuart would yield more information. "Yes, thank you, Major. That would be very helpful." She held up her papers. "I believe my carriage is back there." She pointed to the car marked for Germans only, a kind of third-class commuter car. Stuart responded by smirking and gesturing in the direction of the somewhat sleeker car reserved for American officers.

"My car will be at the entrance to the train station." He said over his shoulder as he pushed to the head of the line. "If you find me, I'll give you a lift. But I have no time to wait."

The IG Farben building, where the allied command had set up shop, loomed in the ruined landscape like a beached whale carcass. The long, narrow building curved away from them as the car approached, as if to try and make it appear smaller. Its six wings intersected the massive spine, giving the impression of a giant bone fragment. The staff car Anna and Major Stuart were riding in took a full minute to pass just half of the building to reach the entry that was located in the center where a little rotunda gaped like an open mouth. Upon arriving in Frankfurt after a loud and bumpy hour-long train ride, she had exited her car quickly in order to not miss the *Ami's* offer for a ride. An imposing row of black and khaki cars with attendant soldiers met her outside the station, waiting to be found by their riders, and she had found Major Stuart easily among the push of uniforms. He had waited for her, pretending to fuss with his lighter as he stood prominently displayed next to the enormous Plymouth with the white star on the door. It was the first time she had been in a proper car in months, and she enjoyed the luxury of riding in a closed vehicle for a change. It meant that she arrived at the imposing building feeling partially intact and ready to face the mighty United States Army on its home field.

She pressed her cheek against the car window to get a glimpse of the large American flag fluttering on a very tall flagpole, which was required given the enormity of the building. No ordinary small flag would do here. If General Eisenhower was inside the building, then where would his office be? There must be a thousand to choose from.

"Magnificent, no?" Stuart said as he offered his hand to help her out of the car when it came to a stop at what seemed like a kilometer from the door. To his credit, he had not made any advances toward her in the car. Anna would not have been surprised but she chose to focus instead on Jacob Morgenstern and the reason she was there.

"Gives me a thrill every time, I admit it," Stuart declared to an invisible audience. Anna eyed him as they walked to the entrance, which, although comparatively tiny, was still formidable. German industry had built the massive building, the war and its dark business of manufacturing the Zyklon B pesticide gas that the Americans said had been used in the gas chambers sustained it, and now, ironically, it would hatch Germany's future. No wonder it was so damn big. It was like the brains of a giant machine. She quickened her steps to keep up with the major's authoritative stride as he led her to a small reception desk in one corner of the rotunda. What would happen if she announced to the soldier behind the desk that she would like a word with General Eisenhower himself?

Stuart spoke in a tone and volume that ensured anyone within the vicinity would hear. Flashing Anna a smile, he enjoyed being the man in charge. She played along as best she could, although the exchange felt like a farce and she was embarrassed by his narcissism. Stuart explained to the man at the desk that Anna was there on official business and needed access to the Frankfurt Gestapo records. The officer waited for more information, and when none was forthcoming, he cleared his throat.

"Which Frankfurt Gestapo records, Major Stuart, sir? There's about three roomfuls of them as far as I can tell. And not all organized yet, either."

Stuart consulted Anna. "I don't know. Which records, Fraulein Klein?"

Anna bit her lip and thought before she spoke. She had told him she was checking on personnel at the Collecting Point, so that would mean the police records. Or maybe administrative files? But those were useless to her. She decided to take the chance.

"The transport records, actually." She smiled amiably at the desk officer. "From 1942 onward," she added, thinking it would make her seem focused on the task. The purchase records that had come with some of Jacob Morgenstern's paintings showed that he had still been living in Frankfurt in 1942, so it was a reasonable starting point. She eyed Stuart to see if he'd notice that she was not asking for party files as she had claimed, but he was busy polishing his sunglasses on the sleeve of his uniform.

The clerk, too, was unfazed. "All right, please wait." He pushed a button on an intercom system and asked the voice that answered for an archivist. He pushed a clipboard at her, asked her to sign in, and checked the credentials she provided against the name and unit she had entered on the form. "Someone will be down in a moment."

Anna and Stuart took a few steps back from the desk. "Looks like you're all set," Stuart said, awaiting her gratitude.

"Yes, thank you, Major. You are very helpful."

"Glad to do it." He made a show of checking his watch. "I have to get to my meeting. Don't like to keep those generals waiting." He offered his hand and she took it, giving it a professional, no-nonsense shake.

"Have a good meeting. And I hope the rest of your visit is productive, as well."

"I hope you find whatever you are looking for," he said, taking a few steps backward while holding her in his gaze. "If I'm back around the Wiesbaden area, maybe I'll stop by and check on you. Next week I'm in Nuremberg, of course, but maybe after that." It was not a question and Anna didn't treat it as such. As Stuart walked in the direction of the large metal door that led to important places, Anna caught the clerk at the desk looking at her with bemusement. He shook his head as he turned back to his ledger.

The clock on the wall read ten forty-five. Anna had less than thirty minutes before she had to get back to the station for the noon train to Wiesbaden. She had been sorting through the piles that a nice American woman kept placing in front of her, as if it were a challenge to see how many of them she could get through.

"You wanted Gestapo, you got it," she said, dropping another round on the table. "They kept excellent records, and they were very busy. I don't know how much time you have, but I'm sure it won't be enough." She shook her head and pushed the sleeves of her sweater up above her elbows. "I would help you, but I don't have time for all the stuff I'm supposed to be doing. Be sure you don't get the pages out of order, all right? And tell me when you're done so I can get them back in the boxes."

"When does the trial start?" Anna asked.

"Not until 20 November, but it takes time to get this stuff over there and put away, you know? I'll be glad when it's gone."

Anna signaled her sympathy and turned her attention back to the stack in front of her. The woman disappeared between the skyscrapers of shelves that looked both completely disorganized and somehow sorted at the same time. If you knew where to look, you would find what you needed. The trick was knowing the system. Anna ran her finger down the list of names that were alphabetized, but she didn't dare take a chance by only checking the names starting with M; once in a while, there was a name in the wrong place. She tried to put out of her mind that the lists she was studying proved without a doubt what Germans like her had suspected: that the Nazis had tried to wipe an entire race off the face of the planet. Here was the proof, the machinery of an evil, twisted, horrific idea writ into mundane reality through orders, requisitions, plans, and logistics. It was more than she could bear, but she pushed on, knowing that her desperation would serve no one at this point. She had to find Jacob Morgenstern. She owed him that much. It might be too late to save him, but she would make sure he was not forgotten.

As the time ticked on, she began to flip through the pages faster than she wanted. There were so many names and she felt guilty for glossing over them, each one someone's mother or brother, daughter, or grandfather. Each one a human being with dreams and fears, loves and stories. Each one of them terrified at the moment this roster was created. Again, the images of children clinging to their mother's hands, the dogs lunging, the guards shouting, the looming train cars, and the crowds on the platform swarmed her mind. She had stood on the very same platform only two hours ago. While the *Ami* was busy impressing her with his car and his Washington connections, neither of them had paused to give any thought to what had happened in the same place just months earlier. Stuart was so proud to go to Nuremberg, but he had taken not one breath out of his day to consider that he was walking in the same footsteps as the poor souls he was supposedly vindicating. It was no abstract notion; it was recent history, only a few hundred days removed. How much things had already changed. How the world was moving on, leaving the unpleasant, the ugly, and the painful behind in search of the new. The Americans had turned their attention to the communists, without even a respectful mourning period, even if just for appearances' sake. The new enemy was declared, the gun sights were turning, and the wretched of this war were already being forgotten.

She decided she had time for one more folder. This one was the transport dated 11 June 1942, departure from Frankfurt's main train station. A smaller group of people this time. Was it because they were the last to be identified? Once the Nazis had cast the first net, they kept tightening and tightening the opening until no one could avoid being caught up in it. The groups of people originally exempt from arrest and deportation—Jews married to Aryans, Jews with one Aryan parent—in the end, none of them were safe.

She re-focused her attention and found the register. Although there were perhaps fifty people on this list, she saw him right away. It was as if the names had been typed in bold. Not just Jacob Morgenstern, but all the Morgensterns. Elizabeth Morgenstern, age forty-seven, Meira Morgenstern, age twenty-four, Samuel Morgenstern, age one year. Three generations of the family. Anna inhaled and turned the page to find the notes on the train's journey from Frankfurt to Lublin, followed by a two-day stop in a place called Izbica. From there, the train went to its final destination: Sobibor. She had never heard of Sobibor, but that didn't matter. She knew exactly what it was. Anna pushed her horror aside for the moment and looked at the clock again. She pulled out a scrap of paper and copied down the names and the address: Feldbergstrasse 12. That must have been the Morgenstern's house. She scanned the pages for any other information that might be of use. The name of the Nazi officer authorizing the transport. The date.

Then she stood, lightheaded and eyes swimming with tears. Before she closed the folder, she glanced around the room. No one payed her any attention, so she took the paper with the Morgensterns' names and slipped it into her bag. She closed the folder, added it to the top of the teetering pile, and went to look for the librarian. Finding the woman at the end of a long alley of shelves, she thanked her and wished her luck with the rest of her work.

"Thanks," the librarian said. "I hope you found what you needed. And I hope whatever you found will help make something right."

"I think it will," Anna said. She had ten minutes to make her train.

chapter eight

Late for her meeting with Cooper, Anna ran the distance from the Wiesbaden train station back to the Collecting Point. The train from Frankfurt had been delayed due to an Army transport, and although it was not her fault that she was late, she hated to keep the already tense Cooper waiting. Holding up her papers to the guard at the gate who idly waved her through, barely acknowledging her, she slowed to catch her breath and compose herself as she approached the stairs. She pulled open the large wooden doors and stepped inside, making her way to Cooper's office to check her desk for any notes. This had become their most reliable way of communicating.

Eva stood at the file cabinet, sorting through the folders, lost in her work.

"*Hallo.*" Anna dropped her bag on her chair. No note from

Cooper. She checked her watch. She was almost thirty minutes late. "What's going on?"

Eva jumped and wheeled around when Anna spoke. "Good Lord, you scared me. I was caught up in these files." She pushed the drawer closed and smiled at Anna. "Where have you been?"

"Has he been asking for me?" Anna said. "I know I am very late, and…"

"Who?"

"Captain Cooper," Anna said. "Who else would I mean?"

Eva rolled her eyes as if to chide her own stupidity. "I thought he was with you. Where were you?"

Anna deflected the question. She didn't have time to explain. "I am late for a meeting. I will see you later." She started to leave and then stopped to pick up her bag with the Gestapo list inside, sliding it on her shoulder.

Eva said nothing as she watched her go, and Anna had the distinct feeling that something odd had happened, but she could not tell what. She went downstairs. Karla was under her desk, tugging at the electrical cord connected to her desk lamp.

"Is it broken?"

Karla pushed her glasses up the bridge of her nose. "Nah, just a wobbly connection. It acts up sometimes."

"I'm still waiting for my lamp," Anna said.

"You can have this one if you want one that only works half the time." Karla emerged from under the desk and sat on the floor, cross legged, as she wiped dust from her face.

Anna smiled. "I like your pants." She gestured at Karla's gray tweed men's trousers that she'd cinched with a big brown belt around her waist. The effect made her look like a walking hourglass, pant legs swishing around as she moved. It had made Anna feel an instant kinship to the young girl.

"Thanks." She pulled herself to her feet. "I started wearing them when I started playing the cello. My mother made me play an instrument and I chose the cello because you get to sit down in an unladylike way, which drove her crazy." She chuckled as she wiped her hands on her thighs. "But then I ended up loving it, so I wear pants so I can practice as soon as I get home. Now it's all I do. Give me a Beethoven cello sonata and I'm a happy girl."

"You are an old soul, I think."

Karla shrugged. "That's what my mother used to say, too. I like old, beautiful things. That's why I like this job. Now, what can I do for you?"

"Do you know where Cooper is?"

"I think he's out back. He wasn't happy, Frau Klein. You're very late." She waggled the screwdriver at Anna.

"I'm not that late," Anna defended. "And anyway, I need a favor."

Karla perked up and gave Anna her full attention. "Yes?"

"Can you get a list of employees from the Staedel Museum? During the war years or before? The *Amis* must have one somewhere by now."

Karla nodded slowly, her eyes wide. "Yes, I can. I know just where to find that, too. It might take a bit of doing."

Karla wouldn't divulge her secret source, so Anna let the mystery lie. "I knew you could, Karla. Thank you."

"Jesus, Frau Klein, where the hell have you been?" Cooper barged up the stairs from the basement. "I told you thirteen hundred. You're nearly an hour late."

Karla dropped her head back into the workings of her typewriter. Anna resisted the urge to point out it was a little over thirty minutes, indignant now that he was exaggerating. "I'm here now," she said. "The train was stopped due to a transport. There was not much *I* could do about that." She made a face as if to blame him directly for the Army's transportation issues.

Cooper snorted and shook his head. "Damn Army," he muttered. "Always getting in the way."

"Shall we meet now?"

"Can't now," he replied, checking his watch. "And not here, anyway. There's something I want to tell you and this isn't the right place."

"Oh?" Anna's skin prickled. He was going to tell her about him and Eva. Or that she was no longer needed. Or perhaps both.

"Well, when?" she asked, taking a step back to indicate that she, too, had somewhere else to be.

Cooper looked around. "Dunno. Maybe tomorrow? I'll let you know. Did you find what you were looking for? In Frankfurt? Did you find Jacob Morgenstern?"

Anna nodded. "Yes. A place called Sobibor. Him and his whole family."

"Sobibor? That's one of the camps in Poland. Damn."

"Yes." She didn't know what else to say, so she changed the subject. "Look, Captain, why don't you tell me now? I am terrible at waiting, and you are putting me on edge with all this secrecy." Her anger about Morgenstern had found an exit and was pouring onto Cooper. She couldn't stop herself.

"Would you keep your voice down, please, Frau Klein?" Cooper hissed, eyes focused somewhere past her shoulder. "There's no secrecy; don't be ridiculous."

She hissed back through clenched teeth. "Ridiculous? You have a lot of nerve. I am not the one sweeping things under the rug. I am also not the one carrying on with the staff, and I am not the one negligent in my duty." Her face flushed and her ears burned. She felt both foolish and exhilarated. Her anger about Jacob Morgenstern's fate had found an outlet but hit the wrong target. But now she had said it, and she braced herself for the worst. At least it would be over soon.

Cooper grabbed her by the elbow and pulled her down the hall, pushing her into an alcove. His eyes blazed and his breath was heavy.

"What in God's name has gotten into you, Anna? You have been nothing but surly and secretive yourself, I might add. No word from your husband. No plans to contact him." His mocking tone imitated her. "You waited to tell me about your housing situation. And you didn't even tell me about Oskar. I had to hear that from Bender."

Anna had not expected his turning on her. He was supposed to be confessing his relationship with Eva. How the work had brought them closer. What a wonderful woman she is. She scanned his face, but he was waiting for her to say something. Her anger caught up with her and she resented his accusations.

"What am I supposed to be telling you, Captain? My innermost secrets? How about you tell me yours, then?" The words caught at the back of her throat, making her gag slightly. "I am none of your business. Do you get mixed up with every woman that works for you? I know you won the war and all, but even so. And meanwhile, things are going missing and paintings are disappearing, and you don't care."

His eyes searched her face as if trying to discern where her anger was coming from. He started to speak and then stopped himself.

Anna jumped into the breach. "And anyway, why do you worry so much about my husband? Why don't *you* write him a letter? That is my business, my family, and it's got nothing to do with you. You carry on with your affairs and leave me alone." She couldn't bring herself to make the accusation directly, lest it become real once and for all. If she didn't say it, there was a chance she was wrong.

Cooper took another step closer. Now she was pushed against the wall of the alcove with his body only inches from hers. Anyone passing in the hallway would probably assume they were stealing an intimate moment together in the middle of the work day. But he was zeroed in on her face, his jaw working. Anna retracted backward to create some space between them, hoping no one would see.

"Okay, you got me there, Anna. Yes, things have gone a little off the rails around here. And, yes, I know there's a painting missing. And, yes, if it makes you feel any better, it's keeping me up at night. Don't think for one second that it's not."

Anna nodded in agreement. "Well, good then. What do you intend to do about it? What if there is a thief inside the Collecting Point? I know no one much cares about the Morgenstern collection, but surely a missing painting is a problem?"

He paused, tilted his head and regarded her differently now. As if something new had occurred to him. Softening slightly, he smiled. "Actually, I think if you were to go check on the Kirchner, you'd see it's back in its place all safe and sound."

"What?" Anna said.

"It's back in its spot now. Right where it belongs."

Anna shook her head and heard herself stutter. "But how?"

"There is no thief, Anna. So you can relax. At least about that part. Now, what else were you accusing me of?"

Anna raised her eyebrows. "I think it was you accusing me."

"Oh, right. Your attitude. Frankly, it's unpleasant and unhelpful."

"My attitude, Captain, has been quite good, given the fact that you are never available, you are distracted and irritable and your mind is elsewhere most of the time. I thought we had important work to do."

Cooper conceded. "Yes. I think you have me there. But you're overestimating me, Anna. Does it make you feel better to know that I'm not sleeping?"

Anna sensed the shift in his attitude, feeling something inside her catch, like a gear that had been out of synch. It was both pleasing and then almost instantly disconcerting.

"No, of course not, Captain," she said. "It does not make me feel better." She caught his gaze and held it for a handful of heartbeats. They stood, their eyes locked. She dared not move.

"Good. Because it's not how I want to spend my nights," he said, unsmiling.

She cocked her head to one side. "Are you playing with me, Captain?" she asked, shifting her weight on her feet. "I never know when you are serious."

Cooper tilted his head back so he was studying Anna from under his brow. He said nothing for a few long moments, and Anna became self-conscious.

"Have you ever seen photographs of the Chicago fire?" he asked.

The question took Anna off guard. "What? No," she said. "What Chicago fire?"

"The Great Chicago Fire of 1871," Cooper said, expanding his arms as if putting on a show. "Destroyed the whole city. Started by a cow, they say."

Anna stared at him.

"Nearly the whole damn city was obliterated. In the photos, it looks just like Berlin and Dresden look now. Nothing but skeletons of buildings left standing."

Anna waited. Where was he going?

"And, see, some twenty years later, the whole city had been rebuilt. And not just rebuilt, it was resurrected as something new. Something beautiful and glorious. They called it The White City. Did you hear about it?"

Anna shook her head no. "I was not alive then," was all she could offer.

"No, of course not. I wasn't either. The point is, the city was reborn. The Great Columbian exposition. You've heard of that, right? It was an architectural masterpiece," he said. "Like nothing the world had ever seen. It was an ideal. Not just an architectural ideal, either, but a place that allowed people to flourish, to live and be happy. To enjoy what little lousy time we are given on this earth."

Anna didn't know what to make of this turn in the conversation. What on earth did some burned-down American city have to do with anything?

He held up an admonishing index finger. "I want you to know, Frau Klein, that life is short. Shorter than you think. You know that, of course. I know that sounds silly coming from someone like me saying it to someone like you at this point in the grand sweep of history. But it really is. Life is incredibly short. But it can go from ruins to unimaginable glory in no time, if you set your mind to it." He took a step back. "That's what I intend to do."

Anna nodded, as if to appease a ranting inmate. Before she could speak, Cooper added, "After the fire, a lot of folks said that Chicago should go back to the way things had been before. That the fire was caused by the people's immorality, as some kind of Godly payback. But smart people didn't listen to that. They knew the way forward was to be bold." He stopped. "To do the thing that was difficult. The thing that no one imagined."

He took a deep breath, stemming the emotions that had come over him. The talk about Chicago, the city he loved, transported him away from the dank hallway in the old museum in Wiesbaden, away from a war-ravaged country with no food, no comforts, and an uncertain future. He saw the potential for a new, exceptional world that she could not yet imagine. His American mind saw the things the Nazis had taken from her—not the least of which were freedom and possibility. *Hope*. It was as if he had a key to a door that he had already opened when she was still stumbling in the dark trying to find her way.

"But was it the right thing to do?" she asked. "Just because it was beautiful doesn't mean it was right. Was it the best solution for everyone affected? Or were there casualties along the way? And weren't there people who got left behind, who got nothing from the gleaming new city? I am sure there were people who would have been better off if it had gone back to the way it was."

A smile expanded over his face. They were both comfortable talking in abstracts, in conceptual, noble ideas. It's what Anna liked best about him—his unwavering love for ideals, for humanity, coupled with a decided difficulty in dealing with actual people in the real world.

"Change is the only way forward," he said. "That's how we progress. As a species." He chuckled. "Otherwise we become fundamentalists, wanting everything to go back to how it was in the good old days that never existed anyway. You know we can't go back." He pointed at the pants she was wearing. "Did you wear men's pants every day before now?"

"What does that have to do with anything?"

"I'm pointing out that you have already changed. When I first met you, you were flustered and worried and afraid of everything and everyone."

"Excuse me?" Anna tried to say more, but he put a hand up to stop her.

"Then you realized it was all on your shoulders, that you had to push ahead. When we found Oskar, you didn't let him go, you didn't abandon him."

"I don't abandon people. It's not my nature," she said, defensive.

"Point is, you chose to help him. You chose to fight for him and you made his life better."

"Sometimes fighting for something is the right answer," she argued. "If it is important enough."

"Important is not the issue. Right is the issue."

"Exactly my point."

Cooper laughed and shook his head. "You got me. I thought I could pull it through, but I couldn't. Yeah, I do think rebuilding a great city to be better than it was before was the right thing to do. And, yes, people were left behind. You're right. But we can't have it both ways, can we?"

Anna smiled. Now he had her. Out of nowhere, a wave of desire sent her reeling. She wanted to take his face into her hands, to feel his skin under her touch, to inhale his scent, to taste him. It was as if a long sleeping part of her had woken up, prodded by the aching loneliness she felt daily, the heavy burden on her shoulders to put their life back together. They both stared at each other, not moving. In the dim hallway, the light played on the contours of his face, outlining his jaw and casting his cheeks into shadow. She resisted the urge to touch him with all she had and allowed herself the idea that he felt the same.

He took a step back as if to escape her imaginary grasp. "And anyway, as I said, Herr Kirchner is back in his spot. You can check for yourself. All safe and sound."

He began to walk away, taking a few steps before turning around. "I told you it would be okay." His expression was neutral, but his eyes darted back and forth, searching his mind. Anna thought he was going to say something else, but instead he shoved his hands into his pockets, turned, and marched down the hall.

As soon as Anna opened the door, she knew something was wrong, even before Amalia came running at her, shouting and hysterical. The air in Eva's house seemed flat and thin, as if there was less of it filling the space. She caught her daughter as she bulldozed into her, dropping her bag and trying to keep her balance. "*Maus*, what is it? What's happened?"

She picked up her sobbing child and made her way into the living room where Madeleine and Manfred Lange sat side by side on the sofa looking shell-shocked and pale.

"What on earth?" Anna asked.

Madeleine started to speak and then stopped, making a second run after clearing her throat. "It's Oskar."

"What's happened?"

"They took him away, Mama. They came and they took him, without asking. They made him go. He was kicking and crying."

"What? Who made him go?"

Madeleine put a hand on Anna's arm. "Two women from the refugee agency. They knocked on the door asking to see you. I told them you weren't here and they asked to see Oskar. I tried to hide him, but he came out to see who the visitor was. They told me we had no right to him, that he was a Polish orphan and he had to come with them. I put up a fight, and so did Manfred. We tried to stop them. But they just took him. No belongings or anything."

Anna felt like she had been set on fire. "Where did they take him?"

"That's just it, they didn't say. When I asked them, they kept insisting he was part of Lebensborn, and that he needed to be returned to Poland, to his parents. Anna, I thought his parents were dead? He kept saying the same thing. Did you know about this?"

Anna slumped into the chair next to the sofa. "I got a letter. It said that Oskar was supposed to return to the DP camp to be interviewed by the refugee agency, that there was evidence that the children in the Nazi's Lebensborn program, who were adopted in Germany, were not actually orphans, that there are hundreds of Polish families looking for their stolen children, and that Oskar is likely to be one of them."

Madeleine and Herr Lange sat in silence, staring ahead, processing the information. Amalia crawled into her mother's lap and buried her head into Anna's shoulder. After a few moments, Madeleine said, "But that can't be, can it? Stolen? From their families? And now they have to go back, after all this time? The boy doesn't even speak Polish. And what if his family is dead?"

Anna was at a loss. She had allowed the clock to run out. She never thought they would come looking for him—and how did they find him anyway? The irony was absurd. Now the supposed good guys were stealing people's children?

She fished through her bag with one hand to find the UNRRA letter. When she found it, she handed it to Amalia.

"*Maus*, will you open that for me, please?"

Amalia unfolded the letter and held it so Anna could read it.

"The letter I got came from the UNRRA agency at Camp Lindsey. I'll go there and straighten this out."

Amalia began crying again. "Mama, don't let them keep Oskar," she said. "They can't just take him away from us."

"No, they can't," Anna lied.

"Promise you will get him back?"

Anna knew she was in no position to promise. Amalia's faith in her was less than steadfast. After all, she had so far failed to produce Amalia's father, even after months of promising to do so. She could almost feel her daughter's mistrust, which the girl was willfully over-riding in her desperation.

"I can help," said Madeleine. "Surely someone will have some compassion and see the light?"

Herr Lange cleared his throat. "Those people that came did not look like they had much compassion," he said. "They were no better than the Nazis we just got rid of, if you ask me. Coming in here and taking a screaming child from his home. It's not right. Not right at all."

Madeleine sat next to him and patted his hand to calm him.

"Did they say anything?" Anna asked.

"They asked him a lot of questions he couldn't answer: What was his real name, where was he born, when was he adopted. He was so upset, he didn't say anything at all. Then they picked him up and dragged him out. Does he know about any of this?"

"He thinks his birth mother is dead," Anna replied.

"The neighbors came out to watch, of course," Manfred said. "It was like old times."

Amalia cried quietly and Madeleine picked up Lulu, the doll, who had fallen to the floor, and handed her to Anna. Then she stood and thoughtfully straightened her skirt, as if to buy herself some time. She pulled the switch on the lamp on the end table and exhaled when a dull glow filled the now dusky room.

"At least the electricity is on," she said. "I'll find us something to eat while the lights are still on." She left the room, squeezing Anna's shoulder as she passed. The three who remained—Manfred Lange in his spot on the sofa, his hands resting on his knees like a statue, Anna sunk into the old armchair, and Amalia folded onto her lap—looked a sorry sight. Anna sat, listening to the clanking of Madeleine arranging plates in the kitchen and wondering how the world had become so thoroughly upside down.

When Eva stepped into the living room, tentative and curious, she said nothing at first. She dropped her bag and sat next to her father, taking his hands in hers.

"What's happened?" she whispered to Anna.

Anna recounted the story with Manfred Lange filling in details. Amalia stopped crying but sniffed loudly and returned to the verge of tears by the end.

"That's the craziest thing I've ever heard," Eva declared. "The Americans are taking our children? Why can't they leave well enough alone? The boy is happy here. Why take him from his family?" She shook her head. The room fell silent again.

Madeleine came from the kitchen and Anna signaled to her to take Amalia, who had made herself dead weight on Anna's lap. Madeleine sat down on the other chair, and after Anna had moved the girl to Madeleine's arms, she tapped Eva on the elbow and beckoned her to follow her to the kitchen.

The warmth of the kitchen was comforting, and the steam rising from the pot of lard soup that Madeleine had put on created a feeling of home. Anna stood at the stove to warm herself and idly stirred the liquid, turning the flame down underneath to keep it from scorching.

"What is it?" Eva asked. "Did I say something? What will you do?"

Anna exhaled and looked out the window. "I'll ask Cooper to help me. I don't know what else to do."

Eva shrugged. "Why would you hesitate?"

Anna considered the question. "I hate to ask for favors."

"This is hardly a favor. The boy's future is at stake."

Eva was right. Anna could no longer go it alone. The Nazis had drilled mistrust and suspicion into daily life. People had to have it to survive, and that suited the Nazis fine. But that wasn't normal and it was no way to live. She was beginning to see it now, although asking for help still made her feel beholden.

"I don't like owing people," she offered.

Eva chuckled. "What do you think you will owe him if you ask for his help?" She folded her arms and waited for an answer. Anna skirted the question.

"I know there are benefits, quid-pro-quos, with the *Amis*. I like the scales to be even. At least I like it to seem that they are."

Now Eva laughed outright. "I don't think that will happen anytime soon. The scales will be tipped in the *Amis'* favor for a long time yet."

"I know. But of course I'll do whatever I have to for Oskar. He needs me." Anna wrapped the dishtowel around her hand. "And I need him, too. He's good to Amalia, and he helps me so much. He makes her feel safe. And anyway, he deserves a good life. He's done nothing wrong."

"Ask Cooper. He'll help you if he can."

Anna wanted to ask Eva if Cooper was helping her, too. What were they doing on the secret outings from the office when they said they were in a meeting? Why was she sneaking out at night to see him? The words swirled around in her mouth, but she could not let them escape for fear of sounding childish or petty, or worse, jealous. It wasn't her business anyway.

Eva regarded her with curiosity. "You have no idea, do you?"

"About what?"

"About how highly Cooper thinks of you. He told me about how you returned Oskar's mother's paintings to him, at some considerable risk to yourself. How you took a chance and went up against the *Ami* bosses and got Cooper his job back. I think it's Cooper who owes you. Do you really not see it?"

Anna felt discomfort in every bone of her body. If she could have stepped out of her own skin at that moment and gone away, out of the reach of Eva's voice, she would have sprinted for the door. "I don't know what you mean," she stammered. "I was only doing the job he asked me to do."

"Nonsense. You did more than that. Anna, he relies on you. He's told me the story of your going to the Nassauer Hof all alone to meet with those art dealers at least ten times. How you got mixed up with those two art dealers who tried to cheat the *Amis*."

"He told you that?"

"He mentioned one of them is ratting out the other, so there may not even be a trial. He turned on him and admitted everything to get a better deal from the *Amis*."

"Really?" *Why didn't Cooper tell me?*

"So, you should ask him, Anna," Eva said. "Ask Cooper. He can help you."

Why was Cooper confiding so much in Eva and barely speaking to Anna at all? The gnawing jealousy seeped back into the empty spaces inside her, filling them with an unpleasant churning.

"And you? Is he helping you, too?" Anna asked. This time she couldn't stop herself. Whatever Eva's intimacy with Cooper was, it was better to know. Enough was enough.

A slight shadow crossed Eva's face. "Is that what people are saying?" She made a short jerky motion to straighten, as if someone had prodded her from dozing off. "Do people talk about us?"

Anna shrugged. "People talk. Even if there's nothing to talk about." She waited, but Eva didn't offer a reply. "Is there?" She wanted to ask about the overnight excursions, the secret meetings, the plum assignments. Of course people talked, especially when there were things to talk about.

A deep blush rose so quickly into Eva's cheeks. She fumbled with her hands and then picked up the spoon to stir the pot, turning her back to Anna.

"You don't have to answer that," Anna said, suddenly feeling sorry for her. "It's none of my business. Forget I asked." She took the bowls that Madeleine had set on the table and held one out for Eva to pour soup into. "Let's eat now."

Eva looked to want to say something but then didn't. She ladled soup into the bowl and then held the spoon suspended over the pot, waiting for the next bowl. When Anna held it out, she poured another serving. "We have a bit more tonight, since Oskar's not here," she said quietly, nearly in tears. Mentioning Oskar's name shifted the energy of the conversation back into reality, away from scandalous outings and furtive meetings. Oskar needed her help. What Cooper and Eva did, whatever they were keeping from her, was their own business. She would worry about Oskar.

chapter nine

Anna ran her finger along the names in the phone directory that Cooper kept under the telephone on his desk. He had made his own additions in the margins of the official printed version, which included the name she needed. She lifted the receiver, hoping to make the call before Cooper returned from downstairs. She had last seen him guiding a group of visiting important types around the library that had been set up on the first floor. Reference books and photographs provided research material for guiding the workers in determining questionable provenance or ownerships or even artist signatures. It was an imperfect science to be sure, but the arrangement was quite impressive given the circumstances. Cooper was very proud of all they had accomplished, having personally seen to getting books shipped from museums and universities in America based on the lists that scholars from places like Yale and Harvard had provided him. Eva had brought books from her father's library, too. Cooper was trying to convince the important types of the value of the work required to secure the Collecting Point's future, but it would put him in a bad mood. That was the bad news. The good news was that it would take him a while, giving Anna time to complete her call.

She waited for the exchange and read out the number to the operator. While the line rang at the other end, she sat down in Cooper's chair, perching on the edge to ensure a quick escape, should anyone come in.

"Bender," the voice on the other end mumbled, distracted.

"Hello, Corporal, it's Anna Klein. From the Collecting Point?" Her voice rose into a question unintentionally.

"Hello there," Bender said, his voice smiling. "What can I do for you?"

"Captain Cooper is asking you for a meeting. Are you free this afternoon at fourteen hundred hours?" The calls could easily be listened to by nosy operators and others. The ruse of setting up a meeting with a superior officer seemed a legitimate reason for a German to be making a phone call. She didn't dare say anything more on the phone.

"Sure, I can do that. Your place or mine?" Bender asked.

"Here in Wiesbaden," she said. "I will meet you at the door and show you in."

"I can find my way."

"I think it's better if I meet you at the door," Anna insisted, "if you don't mind."

Bender caught on quickly. "Yes, of course. I'll see you at fourteen hundred. Thanks for the call."

Anna hung up and returned to her desk. She checked her watch. It was only ten in the morning. Her thoughts floated back to Oskar. What was he doing? How scared he must be. How much he must hate her. With all the visitors at the Collecting Point, it had been impossible for her to get permission to break away and see him, and Cooper was distracted anyway. Bender was her best hope.

The pile of untyped reports on her desk had grown, and she saw the paperwork through the eyes of a critical visiting dignitary who might interpret it as more evidence of ineptitude. She scooped up all the papers on her desk, dropped them into the bottom drawer, and kicked it closed with her foot. She straightened up Cooper's desk, throwing away the silver chewing gum wrappers he had rolled up into balls and lined up like little soldiers on his desk.

Satisfied that the place was presentable, she pulled a report from the top of her now-secret pile and started typing, her eyes deciphering Cooper's scribbles like second nature now. She had read so many of his reports that she knew his handwriting from memory, its loopy o's and oversize t's, all vertical and dominant, like towers in a skyline. But her mind wouldn't leave Oskar and the camp.

As she typed, her mind journeyed on, this time to the mystery of the Kirchner painting. It was indeed back in its spot. She had snuck into the storeroom to see it for herself but had only taken a quick glance. The building was crawling with officials, and she didn't dare get herself caught anywhere near a painting. But it was there, *Berlin 1913*, in its golden corniced frame, just as she remembered it. She glanced into the hallway as she typed, awaiting Cooper's return so she could ask him about the painting again. Maybe they could go take another look at it together, just to be sure. She chewed on her lip, her hands hovering over the typewriter's keys. Something wasn't right. When the familiar cadence of footsteps approached in the hall, she began to type, conditioned. Cooper appeared in the doorway.

"Frau Klein, you have a visitor." Cooper stepped aside, his palm turned up to present the unseen guest.

Major Stuart's head appeared and gave Anna a starry smile, pleased that he had surprised her. He extended a hand as she struggled to get to her feet.

"So nice to see you again, Fraulein Klein."

Anna shook his hand and said, "Yes, likewise." She grimaced at Cooper for an explanation.

"Major Stuart was here for a tour of our security…again. He's working on a report for the State Department," Cooper announced. "Then he mentioned he'd met you on your way to Frankfurt yesterday. He thought it would be nice to say hello."

"I thought you were going to Nuremberg," Anna said.

Stuart's chest puffed slightly. "You mean for the trial." He cut a glance in Cooper's direction to make sure he had heard. "That's not for a few days yet. And I need to get this art business settled before I go. Washington is very interested in the work you're doing, and I aim to let them know about it all in detail." He held Cooper in his gaze.

"Major Stuart has been asking lots of questions to make sure he gets everything in his report just how he wants it," Cooper recited. "No stone left unturned." He rocked back on his heels as he shoved his hands in his pockets. "And, now, he's here to see you, *Fraulein*."

Anna cringed. "It certainly is nice to see you again, Major. I am very grateful that you helped me yesterday."

"Did you find what you were looking for?" Stuart asked. "I hope it was a fruitful expedition."

Anna knew what was coming next. She nodded. "Yes, very. Actually, I found some information that will help us return a collection to its rightful owners."

"How nice," Stuart said, meaning the opposite. He turned to Cooper. "Captain, I wonder if you could arrange a car for me to the train station. I'm on the eleven hundred train and I should get going. But first I'd like a quick word with Fraulein Klein."

Cooper coughed out a *yes, sir* and turned on his heel, catching Anna's eye in the process. He was seething. Anna flashed a tiny smile that tried to reassure him. Of what, she wasn't sure.

With Cooper gone, Stuart perched himself on the edge of the desk in a half-sitting position, fingers interlaced as he gestured. "Look, Fraulein Klein...Anna...May I call you Anna?"

Anna nodded and sat back in her own chair, pushing it away from the desk to create a more comfortable distance between them. Stuart reeked of some kind of cologne. Did he always perfume himself so heavily to inspect security systems at military facilities?

"As I said, Anna, I will be going to Nuremberg in about a week or so, and I'm looking for a competent assistant. A translator. But more than that. An adjutant, if you will."

Anna raised her eyebrows.

"And...I'd like to transfer you out of here and take you with me to Nuremberg."

"Excuse me?" Anna said. "Me, go to Nuremberg with you? But doesn't the Army appoint you an adjutant? Why me?" She wasn't altogether sure what he thought an adjutant did.

Stuart smiled and she noticed how big and straight his teeth were, like perfectly aligned roof tiles under fresh snow. She had never seen teeth like that, not even on Cooper.

"Yes, you come to Nuremberg…as my right hand." He paused for effect. "It's a promotion, of course. And you'll be right in the thick of history, just imagine it." His eyes glazed.

"But, I have…I live here," Anna sputtered. "My family lives here. And I…I can't…" she paused to get her bearings. "I have children and an elderly aunt…" She wasn't sure if Stuart's offer was an invitation or an order. Was she obliged to follow his orders? She took a breath and gathered her thoughts.

Stuart was unfazed by her revelation. "I know you have children. I know it's actually Frau Klein, and I know you have a husband, too. But he's not here, is he? You didn't bother to correct my assumption about your marital status, so I assume you consider that situation irrelevant." He leaned in. "Look, I can get housing for all of you. And the schools are starting in Nuremberg soon. How old are your little ones?"

Anna dodged the question. She had no interest in letting Stuart into her life, and his interest made her uneasy. She leaned further back in her chair. "Major, you are very kind, but I believe my work is here. And my aunt won't want to move; she is frail and old and has lived here most of her life. And anyway, to be honest, I like it here." She redirected the conversation back to his favorite subject: Stuart. "What exactly will you do in Nuremberg?"

Stuart was happy to bite. "Well, as you know, I'm a liaison to State, that is, the Department of State in Washington. That's where I'm based and where I'll return when this is all over. In Nuremberg, I'm an attaché, which is to say I'm an advisor on military matters. To the Secretary of State. And others in the administration." He waited for a beat, then continued. "At the trials, I'll be dealing with protocol and other formalities to make sure everything flows as it should. An invisible job, some might say, but also a crucial one."

Stuart leaned forward even more, his face so close that Anna could see the trace of shaving cream stuck to the hairline by his ear. "Anna, what I'm offering is a big promotion. More money, more status for you. Captain Cooper mentioned what an asset you've been to him, but I'll be honest, you don't want to stay here. This operation is shutting down soon. The Army doesn't want to invest any more resources in this art nonsense. The Monuments Men and all this art will ship back to the States and you'll be left without a job. You have to think of your future. You're the breadwinner now, aren't you? People are depending on you." He dropped his voice to a whisper as he turned his mouth toward her ear. "So you see, I believe I can offer you more than Captain Cooper can."

Anna wanted to open the window to let air into the suffocating room, but she didn't want to stand up and invite any movement on Stuart's part. He had become predatory in his narcissism, a man used to getting his way. It would not do to make him mad at her. She smiled and crossed her legs, leaning forward slightly to respond to him with feigned interest.

"Of course, I'm very honored that you would think me worthy of such an important job. You can understand that it's a lot to think about. You took me off guard, and I don't want to seem ungrateful. Perhaps I should give it some more thought and discuss it with my family."

Stuart appeared pleased. "So, you'll think about it." It was a statement and not a question. "Then let's meet for a drink, say, day after tomorrow? You can give me your answer then. You can understand that it's a rather urgent matter, with the trial starting soon. There is so much left to settle before the proceedings can begin. We'll need to hit the ground running." He smiled. "You won't want to miss a minute."

"Major, the car is here." Cooper appeared in the doorway, flushed and flustered, as if he had been running to break up Stuart and Anna's tete-a-tete. "Were you able to finish your business?" Anna had never been so happy to see him.

"Indeed, we have." Stuart stood and extended his hand. "It has been delightful. I look forward to our drink on Thursday. Shall I send a car to pick you up at, say, nineteen hundred?"

Anna nodded uneasily but tried to muster enthusiasm in her voice. "Where shall we go?" She shook his hand, which he held longer than she liked.

"We'll have to go to the Eagle Club. Not much else to choose from in Wiesbaden." He let go of her hand. "Nuremberg will be better." He turned on his heel and marched to the door. Cooper stepped aside to let him pass. "Thanks for the tour, Captain. I'll send a copy of my report to Captain Farmer. I'm sure he'll pass on the details to you." He tucked his cap under his arm and started down the hall. "No need to see me out. I know the way."

Cooper waited until Stuart was safely down the stairs and out of sight. "Nuremberg will be better?" he asked in a mock tone that was half caveman and half clown. "So, what's that all about? Is he stealing you away from me?"

"He's trying," Anna sat down. "Wants me to go to Nuremberg. As his *Adjutant*." She laughed.

"Oh, that's rich," Cooper said. "But first he's taking you to the Eagle Club to sweeten the pot."

"In a car," Anna said. "Not a jeep, even. He has a staff car, with a driver and a roof." She could tell Cooper was irritated, but she enjoyed teasing him. It covered up the fact that she wished she didn't have to go to the Eagle Club with Major Stuart, that she hadn't had the courage to turn him down, that now she had to play the game a little longer before she would upend it, breaking all the rules of quid-pro-quo that were understood and expected. Perhaps even demanded. The whole thing made her desperately uneasy.

Cooper's face betrayed his agitation. He was going through the same thought process as she was. German women did not get drinks at the Eagle Club without paying for them.

"So you'll go?" He sat down at his desk.

"To the Eagle Club?" Anna asked.

"To Nuremberg. I can't stop you."

"I am going to the Eagle Club," Anna said. "That's all I know." She considered the whole exchange with Stuart. "Can he force me to go to Nuremberg?"

Cooper picked up a stray paperclip and began to unbend it. "If he really wants you to go, he can find a way to force you. It's not exactly a free country."

"What if I refuse?"

"You know that would be unwise, Anna."

"He told me that the State Department is set on shutting the Collecting Point down and that it will happen soon." She pulled her chair closer to his desk to get his attention. "If that happens, I'll be out of a job."

"Did he now? I figured as much, but it's good to know I'm not losing my mind just yet." The muscles in his jaw worked and he exhaled. He still had not looked at her.

"They'll send you somewhere else. Back to the States."

"Probably."

Anna stood and opened the window, letting the fresh air in to dissipate Stuart's cloud of cologne. She looked out at the Bahnhofstrasse, at the traffic of American cars and Germans on bicycles going about another day of undoing and rebuilding. Large, bulging clouds hovered in the western sky that had faded into an anemic blue. She had no idea what to do. Stuart expected more of her than the official job requirements, she knew that. The thought disgusted her. But what scared her more was the idea of having to start over one more time, just when she had gotten a toehold. She turned to look at Cooper and caught him staring at her. He swallowed, his jaw clenched.

"I don't know what to do," she said.

Cooper came back to life, leaning back in his chair and folding his hands behind his head. "I'm sure Nuremberg, the trials, the whole thing...It'll be very exciting," he said to the wall opposite him. "Right there, in the thick of things. Justice being doled out. How satisfying. Could turn everything around for you. And think how proud your husband will be." He made a face of mock surprise as if he had just remembered something. "Oh, that's right. Your husband. Sorry to say, but I don't think he's invited to Nuremberg, Anna." Now his eyes focused on her.

His words stung. She had not expected him to lash out. Now she was mad, too.

Anna cocked her head. "No, I suppose not. It would be too many *Amis* for his taste, probably."

"Definitely one too many *Amis*. And too much democracy and freedom, too, probably," Cooper echoed. His mouth turned down in an expression of revulsion. He opened a file on his desk with such force that he ripped the cover.

"Captain…" Anna started and then stopped.

Cooper flipped through the file, his eyes locked on the pages. She stared at him for several moments, the silence between them like a wall. She willed him to look at her, but he didn't.

When the tears started to well and her face burned, she turned her chair toward her desk and fed blank paper into the typewriter. "I have work to do," she said, but now she, too, was staring at the paper in front of her.

"I'll say you do." Cooper scraped his chair back and headed to the door. "Best get to it."

Anna shook a Lucky Strike from the pack. She rarely smoked, usually saving the cigarettes to use as barter for a favor or a few extra grams of bread in her rations. But more and more, she felt the need. She borrowed a light from a young *Ami* waiting by a jeep near the Collecting Point entrance and then returned to her spot at the far end of the steps, out of the flow of foot traffic and, she hoped, inconspicuous, at least to a passing glance. Cooper had disappeared, and she had not seen Eva all day. They were together, she thought, unable to help herself. The smoke rose from the cigarette in a fine mist, and she watched it for a while, twirling the filter between her fingers. Taking a long inhale, the heat filled her lungs, and she took pleasure in exhaling, purging the smoke and the nagging jealousy along with it. After one or two minutes of this, she felt slightly better and bent over, putting the glowing tip of the half-smoked cigarette under the edge of her shoe to extinguish it. She saved the remaining portion and put it back in the packet.

"Mama?" The little voice came from somewhere far in front of her, and she craned to find its source. Amalia was on the outside of the fence, jumping up and down and waving. Anna raised an arm to wave back and then made her way down the stairs and toward the entry gate. Now what?

"*Maus*, what are you doing here?" She hugged Amalia. "Has something happened? I told you to stay with the grown-ups."

Amalia held up an envelope. "This came today. Someone pushed it into the door frame. Auntie said it was important. Is it from the refugee people? About Oskar?"

Anna took the envelope. "Did Auntie send you to give it to me?"

Amalia shook her head and turned sheepish. "No, she's taking a nap. I decided to come see you. It's so boring at the house without Oskar."

"I know, *Maus*. But you are not to go out by yourself, I told you." Anna stroked her daughter's cheek. She had been so distracted that she had not really seen the changes that had taken hold in the little girl. She appeared older, not bigger, but somehow wiser, with a clarity in her eyes that Anna had not noticed before. She was almost seven, at least in years, but Anna knew there was no such thing as a normal seven-year-old anymore.

She changed the subject. "Your hair looks so pretty today, *Maus*. Did Auntie do those braids for you?" If she kept talking, she could delay learning how this letter would disrupt her life anew and tamp down the worry about Amalia being alone on the street.

"No, Fraulein Lange did them. Before she left the house." Amalia paused, anticipating her mother's next question. "I didn't ask her to; she said she wanted to."

"She did a nice job," Anna said. She meant it, too, but she felt guilty for not having the time to do Amalia's hair herself. She had always liked doing it, even when Amalia protested, which was almost all the time. "I hope you didn't give her any trouble. Like you do to me, you little monkey," she teased.

"I was good. I promise," Amalia said. "And Fraulein Lange said she would do them for me every day, if I wanted." She eyed the letter, expecting Anna to open it.

The return address was the familiar UNRRA stamp. What the hell did they want now? Anna took a breath, tore the envelope open, and unfolded the paper inside. It was only a half sheet, some kind of certificate. She scanned the title and the various boxes that had been filled with Oskar's information: his name, birthdate, place of adoption, and so on. All things she already knew. "I think this is his paperwork from the refugee people, to show that he's been registered?" She turned it over, but there was nothing on the back. "I will check with them when I go over there. Hopefully, a bit later."

"Hi there, Anna." Bender had come up from behind them and startled Anna. Amalia took a step closer to her mother.

"Hello, Corporal," Anna said. "I hope you haven't been looking for me."

"Haven't even made it into the perimeter. I was just coming up the street." He checked his watch. "Fourteen hundred on the dot." He tapped his wrist and grinned. "Hello there. You must be Amalia." He extended his hand. Amalia shrunk back into the folds of Anna's pants.

"It's okay. I'm a friend of Captain Cooper's."

"Her English is not so good yet." Anna cocked her head to indicate to Amalia to shake Bender's hand. The girl obliged and then immediately retracted her hand.

"I think you took her by surprise. She will warm up to you." Anna bent down and took her daughter's face in her hand. "Thank you for bringing me the letter. Now, you run along straight back to the house. I'll be home for dinner."

Amalia deflated. "But I want to stay with you. You weren't doing anything when I got here. You were just standing here."

"I was waiting for Corporal Bender; we have a meeting. So you run along home. No stops on the way and no talking to anyone." She stood up and admonished Amalia with a pointed index finger. "Do you promise me?"

Amalia nodded, sullen now that she had lost her mother's attention again. She began walking north, in the general direction of the Lange house, hands shoved into the pockets of her dress, feet kicking at invisible pebbles.

"Go on, child," Anna called. "Run."

Amalia obliged and began trotting. Anna watched her until she disappeared around the corner.

"Where is she going?" Bender asked.

"Home. She came to give me this." Anna waved the paper. "Actually, this is what I wanted to talk to you about."

"Sure, shall we talk here, or would you rather go somewhere else? I'm guessing since you arranged to meet out here, you don't want to go back inside. Won't they miss you?"

"Not for a few minutes. This won't take long, I hope. Besides,

Captain Cooper and Fraulein Lange are nowhere around. They're the only ones who might notice."

Bender agreed, oblivious to her insinuation. Anna even paused to give him the chance to comment, but he said nothing, instead taking the paper from her hands. "Then let's go around the corner. Less traffic there."

They walked the few steps to the north side of the building where a smaller side street was lined with a few trees. Mostly intact, once-charming houses lined the side opposite the massive Collecting Point building. A small pile of concrete rubble looked like it had been a garden wall. Bender gestured for her to have a seat on a large chunk. She sat and waited as he read the form.

"Okay, so this is about Oskar? He went to the camp?"

"They took him. From the house. Just came and took him. And now I don't know what to do. I should have hidden him, or lied, or done something, but they were too fast. They came while I was at work."

Bender shook his head, keeping his eyes on the paper. "Yeah, they can move fast when they feel like it." His face darkened. "This is a transport notice. Looks like they are moving him to a special camp set up just for these kids. It's in Bavaria. See, down here." He pointed to the name in the bottom left corner.

"What?" Anna took the paper. "When?"

Bender sat down next to her and pointed to the date. "Looks like in about a week."

"What? No. That can't happen. We have to stop them. They can't just take him away from me." Her knees threatened to buckle under her. "Can they?"

Bender exhaled. "Technically, they can do whatever the hell

they want. You have no rights to speak of, and neither does he—no adoptive parents, no birth parents, nobody. Except you, I mean. He's a ward of the state, in effect." He rested his elbows on his knees. "But, let's think for a minute. We can figure something out, I'm sure. Did you tell Cooper yet?"

"Not yet. I haven't seen him. And...well, he's been busy."

"No kidding. He's for sure got his hands full with all the State Department bullshit going on. Pardon me."

"You mean that Major Stuart?" Anna asked.

"Oh, you've had the pleasure?" Bender rolled his eyes.

"I will tell you all about it. But first we have to figure out what to do about Oskar. Do you think you can help me? I can't let him go without a fight."

"Have you talked to Oskar or seen him since they took him?"

Anna shook her head no. "I haven't been able to get away today. I feel so terrible, I'm not sure I can look him in the eye."

Bender stood and pulled her up by the elbow. "Well, the way I see it, we've got no time to lose. Let's go."

"Now?"

"Yep. Now." He checked the address on the form. "It's not far. I'll get us a jeep; you go get your things. I'll meet you at the gate in ten minutes."

Anna stopped. "Where do I say I'm going?"

Bender pulled her along as he started walking. "You'll think of something. Come on now, you're getting good at this."

The din in the main hall at the camp was overwhelming. Hundreds—could it be thousands?—of children of all ages were chattering, some running and playing, some sitting in groups, some leaning against the walls. The sound echoed off the tile walls and doubled, quadrupled even. Were all these children stolen from their families? Anna's mind reeled. Bender took Anna's elbow and they walked along the edge of the burbling crowd to a man in a khaki uniform.

"You in charge of these monkeys?" Bender asked. The man replied by cupping his hand to his ear and shaking his head. Bender repeated himself, shouting this time. The man made a so-so gesture with his hand, and Bender crooked a finger indicating he should follow them outside. Anna trailed behind the two men, scanning the teeming gaggle of kids for any sign of Oskar. None of them paid her any mind and no hopeful faces looked up at her. These kids had turned to each other for the comfort and hope that adults had repeatedly denied them.

When she stepped outside, her ears were ringing, and she joined Bender and the UNRRA man, who were consulting a clipboard the man had brought with him.

"Oskar," Bender was saying. "What's his last name, Anna?"

"His adoptive family name is Gruenewald. But I know his Polish name was Novak. Is he here?"

The ride from the Collecting Point had taken only ten minutes, so they were not far from the center of town, but it felt like another planet. The whole city was divided up into different little planets: the American planet, with its comfortable beds and hot dinners; the lucky German planet, where roofs were mostly intact and water ran sometimes; the destroyed planet, which was reduced to rubble that little armies of men shoveled from one place to another; and this, the camp planet, with barbed wire around its edges and a forced atmosphere of normalcy imposed on a truly abnormal circumstance.

The man in khaki was irritated at their presence, and Bender was ready for a fight. "Is there someone else we can talk to?" he asked, terse and impatient. "We know the boy is here; I've got the paperwork."

"Gimme a second, please," the man said. The mustache that perched awkwardly on his upper lip twitched as he ran through the names, reading under his breath.

"He's blond with blue eyes, about this tall," Anna said, offering a measurement with her hand at shoulder height.

The man chuckled without looking up from the list. "Lady, they're all blond and blue eyed. That was the point." He turned to Bender, ignoring Anna. "When did he come in?"

"Yesterday," Anna replied. "He was taken from my house yesterday." The man's lazy attitude infuriated her, but Bender's aggressiveness helped. With an American at your side, it was easy to feel entitled.

"Oh, well, if it was yesterday, then he's still being processed. He's over there in the processing center." He pointed his pencil in the direction of a building behind them that looked just like the one that was in front of them.

"Right. Thanks." Bender took Anna by the elbow again. "Let's go." They marched across the open yard, Anna noting that the buildings were so huge you felt like you were walking in place, making no progress at getting any closer. Bender pulled her along, his strides long and fast. He wasn't much taller than she; he was more fit and probably quite a bit younger. He had the robust quality of a sturdy farm boy that was made even more endearing by his easy way of outsmarting everyone.

"Sorry to rush, but you know these bureaucrats, they will suck the life right out of you if you let them. Best to light a fire and get them a little steamed. We don't have all day. When do you need to be back?"

"I said I was going on a supply errand with you, so I can't be gone very long."

"Especially if you don't have any supplies to show for it." Bender laughed. He gave her a little push, like a brother would tease his sister. Anna smiled and pushed back. "I should have brought you some more typewriter ribbons. I will remember to keep some in my pocket, just in case."

He pushed open the metal door and ushered her into the cold, dark lobby. Stairs climbed along one side, and offices were set up behind a glass partition on the other. Without slowing to read the directory that had been written on a chalkboard on the wall, Bender barged in. Two women looked up from their desks.

"Looking for a kid who was brought in yesterday. Where would he be? I was told I can find him here."

The women stared at him.

"You speak English, yes?"

A sour-faced woman pointed at the ceiling, indicating he should go upstairs, which Bender did, taking the steps two at a time. Voices, some high-pitched children's voices, some droning adults' floated in the stairwell, their places of origin unclear. The offices were spare, with piles of paper everywhere, just like at the IG Farben building. The peace was proving very friendly to paperwork. She followed Bender around as he asked for the right person, expecting answers and making incremental progress. He was like an anti-bureaucracy weapon. Anyone else would have been turned around and dispatched back to where they came from at every turn, but thanks to Bender's persistence, the two of them quickly found themselves knocking on the door of someone with a corner office.

A tired man with a kind face and soft skin that was sallow with overwork and worry opened the door. Anna knew the look instantly. Thomas had it, too. It was the lifeless pallor of a good soul trapped in a bad situation, a soul unable to ease the suffering that it confronted and unable to stop trying.

Bender replayed the situation and the man listened, nodding, his eyes darting toward Anna at intervals to ensure she was agreeing with Bender's account. When the American had finished, the man offered them the chairs opposite his desk, which they took and waited.

"Tell me the boy's name again?"

Anna cleared her throat. "Oskar Gruenewald is his German name." The man thought for a moment. "Yep, he's here. Talked to him this morning."

"You did? How is he?" Anna shifted forward in her seat. "Can I—" Bender held up a hand to stop her.

"He shouldn't be here," Bender interrupted, stern and officious. "The boy has a proper home. He's not an orphan. He's well taken care of."

"I don't doubt that," the man said. "That's not the issue. If it were, my job would be a hell of a lot easier."

"Then what is the issue?" Anna asked.

"The issue, my dear lady, is that it has come to light that many thousands of children were taken from their parents in occupied Poland beginning in 1942. These are not orphans, these are stolen kids. Thousands of them."

Anna deflected her shock at the number. If there were thousands, then Oskar was no special case. She tried anyway. "But that's been known for a while. And Oskar was adopted here. He had a family here. He is a German citizen."

"So said the Nazis. That hardly makes it fact," the man replied. "And so were all the others. But now we've got parents in Poland coming forward to find their kids. They've got names and photos. They've got the dates and places where they were taken. They've got rights, too, you know."

Anna slumped in her chair. She had not let herself think of the flesh-and-blood parents with photos and names who were coming for their children, but of course they were. If Amalia had been taken from her, she would be walking from Poland right now in bare feet to find her. Just the thought of it made her insides ache.

The man watched her for a moment and then said, "Now you know how I feel. It's an impossible situation. When you break all the rules of simple human decency, when you turn all of civilization on its head and violate the most basic structures—children and parents, families, for Christ's sake—how can we be expected to put that back together? Children aren't objects. People are not *things*. We can't return them like…"

"A piece of art," Anna mumbled, staring at the floor.

"Right," the man said. "I'm a doctor, and although sometimes we doctors like to think we are God, it turns out we're only human after all." He leaned back in his chair.

"All right, well, at least tell us where Oskar is, can you? And can you tell us if there are parents who are making a claim on him specifically?" Bender asked.

The man leaned forward and shuffled through the papers on his desk. "Yes, I can tell you where he is, and no, I cannot say if any specific claims have been made. That's another department." He pulled a piece of paper from a file as thick as a novel and held it up. "Parental claims will be dealt with at the Special Centers, not here."

"Where are those?" Bender asked.

"Nearest one right now is in Munich. That's where all these kids will go. They're not set up for this here—this is a refugee camp, not a kindergarten. My job is to prepare them for the transport to Munich, for the language education, and for their eventual return to Poland as best I can."

"What kind of a doctor are you?" Anna wanted to know what made him qualified for such a horrible task.

"Psychiatrist. I provide therapy for them. Help them process this new turn of events. At the center, they will have more intensive intervention, like daily language lessons."

Anna couldn't take any more. She pushed the chair back as she stood up, putting her hands on the desk. "I want to see Oskar. I won't let him go to some special center. If his mother comes for him, if she can prove she is his loving mother, I will deliver him into her arms myself, with a heavy heart but a clear conscience. But this? No. I cannot allow it."

The man shook his head. "Listen. I understand your anguish, really I do. But the UNRRA officers are authorized to deliver any child they believe to be unaccompanied to us for processing. Haven't you seen the signs?"

Anna had seen the signs but had chosen to ignore them, thinking they could not possibly apply to her and Oskar. They said exactly what the man in front of her was telling her. UNRRA child welfare investigating officers, as they were called, had the right to take any child or demand their appearance at hearings with the officials. Obstructing, hiding a child, or in any way hindering this work would get you hauled to a military court for trial and sentencing.

Bender had tired of the conversation about bureaucracy and injected some urgency back into the meeting by also rising to his feet and clapping his hands together. "Right, then we'd like to see Oskar. Can you help us with that?"

The man was relieved to be rid of them and the reality of the painful situation. "That I can do," he said, pushing back his chair. "I will take you to him." He glanced at the paper. "He'll be going out soon. I suggest you say your goodbyes today. It will only traumatize him more if you visit him repeatedly. Best to make a clean break."

"I'll wait by the jeep," Bender said, as they rounded the corner in the hallway and spotted Oskar, sitting dutifully on one chair in a row aligned next to a door. Anna stopped short, knowing that rushing toward him was not what he would want. She waited for him to look up, but he didn't. No one else was in the hall; it was a sterile affair that was a cross between a hospital and a school. The walls were painted a dingy white, and the frosted windows let in only a cold light that shifted when the wind blew through the trees outside. Fluorescent lights flickered overhead, removing any life from the scene. Oskar sat, staring at his hands folded in his lap, one leg kicking against an imaginary annoyance. Maybe he was kicking her, Anna thought. She waited, but still he did not look up. She walked slowly and sat down on the chair beside him, folding her hands in her lap and studying the top of his head. This was the Oskar she had first encountered in the basement of the villa two months ago. Angry, defiant, scared. She could sense his seething at the injustice being meted out to him.

Again the adults in his life had let him down, had played him for their own purposes. And now she was one of them.

She cleared her throat, trying to think of what to say.

"So you came to say goodbye then?" Oskar said, not turning his head.

"No, I came to get you out of here. But they won't let me." She knew better than to sugarcoat anything with him. "But I am not giving up."

"They say I am Polish. That I have to go back to Poland. That I may have parents there searching for me." He shrugged.

"Yes, that's what they told me, too."

"But I thought all my parents were dead. My real ones. And my German ones," he added.

"I thought so, too."

They sat side by side, not looking at each other, instead addressing the crack in the opposite wall that ran from floor to ceiling. Anna didn't know what else to say, so she waited.

"So they lied. About me. About who I am. The people who took me lied to everyone."

"Yes, they did."

Oskar's legs kicked and his feet scraped the floor. He sat on his hands and leaned forward. In the distance, a thunder clap announced a rainstorm.

"Did my mama know? My German mama? That I was stolen? Why would she let them do that?"

Anna shook her head. "I don't think she knew that they lied. I think she wanted someone to love, and a baby to take care of, that's all." What unbelievable bastards the Nazis were. There was no limit to their depravity. It was as if their sadism knew no bounds or reason. She took Oskar's hand in hers and gave it a squeeze.

"I'm running away," he whispered and turned to face her. His face was streaked with tears, his eyes red rimmed and thick. "But don't worry, I won't get you in trouble. I'll just go back to being on my own. I can do it." His hand balled up under hers.

Anna swallowed hard to keep from blurting out that this was a terrible idea, that they would catch him and bring him back, and then probably not treat him so nicely. Instead she nodded. "Where will you go?"

"Dunno. Wherever. Nobody wants me anyway. I'll figure it out. I'll be eleven soon."

"But what if your mother in Poland wants you? What if she's been missing you this whole time? What if you have a family, maybe brothers and sisters waiting for you? If you run away, they'll never, ever find you."

"I don't want any more mothers," Oskar said. "They leave you. I'd rather be on my own." He turned away. "And anyway, you're not my mother. You can't help me. They told me. You didn't have any right to keep me. If I had never gone with you, they wouldn't have found me." He sniffed loudly. "Doesn't matter. You can't help me, nobody can help me. I'm running away."

They sat side by side, his legs kicking again.

"Will you tell Amalia something for me?" he asked.

"Sure."

"Tell her to be careful. Not to talk to anyone."

"What do you mean?"

"That man who came to the house, the one who knocked on the door and asked all the questions? I've seen him before. He hangs around the black market a lot. A few times he's been there not doing anything, just kind of standing around."

Anna bent down so she could see Oskar's face. "Is he there looking for little girls?" she said it flat out and hoped he would understand her meaning.

Oskar shook his head. "I don't know. I've never seen him do anything. I didn't figure out it was the same man when he came to the house. I remembered later where I had seen him. He always wears the same suit with the blue tie." He wiped his nose with the back of his hand. "Anyway, tell Amalia to steer clear, now that I can't look out for her."

"I'm not giving up on you," Anna said. "I've asked the *Amis* for help. I'll do whatever it takes to keep you." She took his hands in hers and put her face next to his ear. "You can still believe in me. I am not abandoning you. If you have a mother who wants to love and take care of you, then she can have you. But until that happens, you are mine to watch over, and I won't let you down. This I promise you." She pushed the thought of Oskar's birth mother to the back of her mind, where all the things she couldn't face resided.

As if a switch had been flipped, Oskar burst into tears, quietly at first, then in gaping, craving sobs interspersed by an agonized silence. She pulled him close and wrapped her arms around him. His fingers grasped at her jacket, tugging at her as if to bond himself to her. Now her tears flowed, too, and a pain washed over her, immersing her in a fog that obscured everything around them. Nothing about what was happening was right. It was all so wrong that it was almost unrecognizable.

"I won't let you go so easily, my sweet boy," she whispered. "We need you. Amalia needs you to look out for her."

From the corner, Bender cleared his throat, and when Anna's eyes found him, he was motioning to her that it was time to leave. "It's starting to rain," he whispered, "we need to get back."

Anna gave Oskar a hard squeeze. "I will be back for you. You are safe here for two more days. The Americans are going to help me get you out of here. Just be brave for a few more days."

Oskar pulled away not meeting her eyes.

She pulled him back, wrapping her arms around him. "And you promise me you won't run away."

He nodded, his resolve gone.

He slid off her lap and waited for her to go. Anna kissed him on the head and walked toward Bender who looked like he was ready to catch her in case she collapsed.

"Will you tell Amalia that I miss her?" Oskar said. "And tell her not to go to the black market without me."

"I will," Anna said. Bender put a hand on her back, gently, and they began walking as she looked over her shoulder one more time. Standing in the hallway with his hands shoved into his pockets, Oskar looked so alone that she thought her heart would shatter.

"It's going to be okay," Bender whispered.

"You don't know that."

"True," Bender said. "But I believe it. And by the way, a Frau Niemeyer? She said to tell you hello."

Anna smiled. Maria Niemeyer had been Oskar's de-facto guardian during his previous days at the camp when he had been a temporary inmate. He had been brought here as a displaced person. Maria had watched over him, had kept him out of trouble until he could come home with Anna. A kind woman with the hard edge of someone who had survived with only her child, Maria was homeless and without family and living in the camp with few prospects. She was at the mercy of the enormous forces that were shifting from the old state of being to a new one, with no clear spot for her to land—in a permanent limbo. The camp had already claimed Oskar once, and now it had him again. At least Maria could watch him, even if she was powerless to help him.

"Maria? You saw her?"

"She's downstairs at the desk. She wants you to know she's looking out for the boy. Got all teary, too, when she mentioned it. I didn't catch everything she said, but she wanted you to know."

Anna tried to hold some gratitude for Maria's kindness and spare a thought for her friend's plight. It provided a little solace. When they made their way out of the building, Anna looked for Maria at the desks behind the reception, hoping to thank her, but she wasn't there.

chapter ten

When Anna opened the door to the Lange house, the light was dim. The living room curtains were drawn even though it was only the afternoon. She heard scuffling from the sofa.

"Amalia?"

"She's out with Madeleine," Eva cleared her throat as she spoke, her voice cracking.

"Everything alright?" Anna stood in the foyer, ears primed on the adjacent room.

The room brightened as Eva opened the curtains one after the other. The meager light from the rainy day fell into the room as she strode around to each window, methodical. Anna was about to ask what was going on when she saw a man sitting on the sofa.

"Oh, I'm so sorry," she stammered. "I didn't..."

"Good afternoon, you must be Frau Klein." The man stood to greet her as if nothing out of the ordinary had happened. "My name is Spitzer." He was maybe in his early fifties, with the smooth face of someone who had spent his days on easy, indoor pursuits. A smile sat comfortably on his open face. He was as calm as Eva was flustered.

Anna shook his hand. "I don't mean to interrupt," she said, preparing to exit.

"Nonsense," Eva said, now moving around the sofa, fussing with the cushions as a way to cover her straightening her blouse and checking her hair. "You're not interrupting. We were going to have a coffee. Join us? We have the real thing." She didn't look at Anna.

"Oh? Well, all right." Anna scanned the room. Something was off, but she couldn't tell what. Everything appeared to be in its place. Had the furniture moved? No. The books were all in place on the shelves, the desk under the window the same as always. Spitzer and Eva exchanged glances, but Anna pretended not to notice as she took a seat in the straight-backed chair across from the sofa.

"So, you're the co-worker I've been hearing about," Spitzer said, retreating to the corner of the sofa.

Anna nodded. She wished she had some equal insight into who Spitzer was. Had Eva ever mentioned a boyfriend or any romantic interests? She hadn't. "Yes, that's me," she quipped. "And housemate, now."

"It's a fine house, isn't it?" Spitzer leaned back, comfortable in his surroundings. "I've always liked it."

"Are you from Wiesbaden, Herr Spitzer?" Anna asked, taking the cup of coffee that Eva offered. She inhaled deeply without thinking, the aroma too delicious and too rare to ignore.

"Once upon a time, yes," Spitzer said. "But the war made nomads of us all, didn't it? I was returning to the area to see my sister when I heard that Eva was here. We go back a long time."

Eva set a cup down in front of him and then sat on the sofa at a conspicuous distance, leaning into the armrest as if to stay out of his reach. She kept her eyes on the steaming cup she balanced on her lap.

"What is your work with the *Amis*?" Spitzer looked at her intensely, a deep scar on his left cheek noticeable when the light hit it just so. It was a dueling scar, the kind boys in university fraternities inflicted on each other in sword fights. To have a scar, a *Schmiss*, was to wear a badge of bravery. His was quite deep and ran almost straight along his high cheekbone. Another smaller scar crossed it, making a kind of inverted crucifix shape, with the shorter scar nearly in line with the folds of his cheeks around his nose. Anna knew this was supposed to impress her, but it didn't.

"I'm a translator, although these days there's not much of that happening. Too much to do in the way of inventorying and typing reports. I do whatever is required."

"Yes, must make yourself useful, I imagine. With a plum job like that, you want to be sure you keep it." He laughed, but there was a meanness in his tone, just under the surface, that cooled any conviviality. She nodded and took a sip of the coffee, feeling a familiar armor steeling her against revealing too much about herself.

"What do you do?" Anna changed the subject. Eva still hadn't said a word or looked up. Was she embarrassed that Anna had walked in on their assignation? Was she afraid?

"I'm an accountant." Spitzer was sheepish. "Not as glamorous as the arts, but important nonetheless." He turned toward Eva. "Hopefully, there will be more work soon. When people have jobs and businesses re-open. Until then, not a lot for someone like me to do, since I don't speak much English. I do speak French, so perhaps I might try my luck down in the Saarland, if I can get there." He tried to catch Eva's eye, but she avoided his gaze.

"Yes, that might be a good idea. Or Paris, even?" Anna tried to move the conversation along, but it was hard with Eva's silence absorbing all the energy from the room.

"Where did you say Amalia is?" She tried addressing Eva directly.

"They went into town to pick up the rations. I'm afraid they got caught in the rain." Eva's voice cracked again when she spoke, but she smiled at Anna. Her eyes were rimmed in red.

Anna glanced at the clock above the fireplace. Dinner with Stuart was only two hours away and she felt a wreck. She drained her coffee and put down her cup. As if reading her cue, Spitzer stood and straightened his jacket. "Speaking of rations, it's my day today, too. I best be on my way. I was hoping it would stop raining, but I don't think it will." He extended a hand. "It was delightful to meet you. I hope our paths will cross again."

Eva rose, too, but kept her eyes down on the sofa, as if she were waiting for something to appear. Spitzer made his way to her and kissed her on both cheeks as Anna headed for her bedroom to offer them privacy. She needn't have bothered; Spitzer was out the door within moments and Eva appeared in Anna's doorway. She looked relieved.

"I'm sorry I interrupted." Anna kicked off her boot and rubbed her foot. "I'm so embarrassed." She made a face to try to lighten the mood.

"Not at all," Eva folded her arms across her chest. "I should apologize." But she didn't offer any more detail.

"He seems like a nice man."

"He's married." Eva sighed.

"Oh." Anna pulled off the other boot, not sure what else to say. She sat, waiting.

Eva brightened a little. "Do you want to borrow anything for your dinner tonight? A dress maybe?"

"Sure," Anna said, if only to make her happy. "But first I need to warm up. I'll help you clean up the dishes later."

Eva waved her off. "I'll do it. Let me know when you're ready."

She left Anna alone to switch her damp blouse for the old blue sweater that had belonged to Otto, Madeleine's husband. It was a bulky cable-knit thing that made her itch and feel claustrophobic, but it was warm. She pushed her icy feet under the blanket. For a few breaths, she stared at the wall and thought of Oskar. Her powerlessness over his fate chewed at her. Fixing a world that had gone so wrong wasn't going to be easy. The blows just kept coming. Some you could dodge, but some landed squarely on their target. Her hand found the box under the bed and pulled out the paper and pencil she had stashed. Leaning against the lumpy pillow and angling the page toward the remaining afternoon light streaming through the window, she re-read what she had already written, before starting a new paragraph.

The weather here has turned toward winter now, and I worry about how we will cope. Maybe we will be lucky and have a mild season, but of course that's silly. I worry about everything from the moment I get off this miserable bed and put my feet on the icy floor until I am back here at night, cold, hungry, and tired. In between, I worry for Amalia, not just for her safety today, but for her future. Her life. The Americans seem decent enough, generally, but many of them still despise us. What would be their motivation to see a Germany that flourishes, with happy and healthy children who grow up to create a world that is better than the godawful mess we've made for them? Do the Amis care about the big vision, or is it expediency and profit they are interested in? Some days I can't tell. Perhaps it is easier where you are? Are the Russian soldiers kind to the people? Your letter said it was safe for us to come home, and maybe it is exactly that: safe. I do want to be safe, but I also want to know what the cost is for my safety. Is the cost my future? Yours? Amalia's future as a free-thinking, happy person?

I worry about living under a new tyranny. The Americans are so free it seems, but they have a tyranny all their own to suffer. I see it in the men I work with. They are burdened with being the standard-bearers for right, for justice, for liberty. But they are human, too, and they fail more than they would like. Now, especially, they bear an enormous cross of righteousness that weighs down on them. When the world is utterly destroyed, the temptation for greed and profit, for taking advantage, or for taking the easy road, is so great. But the Amis set themselves up as the defenders of all that is good in the world. And now they have to live with that, too. When I have time to think about these things, I want to talk to you. I miss our conversations. We would have a good laugh about the Americans and their ways, or maybe even about the Russians and theirs. But it's not so funny now that there is so little of "us" left and so much more of "them." I often feel lost and unmoored, as if the gravity under my feet will fail and leave me to float, without any direction or purpose at all.

She lifted the pencil and thought for a moment. Did she have the heart to tell Thomas the truth? Up until now she had been honest; everything she had written was the truth as she felt it. But there was something that could gather her back into the pull of gravity, that placed her feet firmly back on the ground. Something that allowed her to see a way forward, even if that way was only the next few days. Since getting the job with the *Amis*, she had felt as if she and Amalia were on a train that was beginning to pull out of a station, ever so slowly, but she was on it. What lay ahead she wasn't sure, but the train felt safe. Not in the way she had felt safe before, but in a way that held the promise of something better. Her thoughts drifted and she began to doze off, the pencil slipping from her hand onto the floor. The sounds of Amalia and Madeleine tumbling into the foyer, their bag and footsteps thumping on the floor, woke her nearly an hour later. She checked the clock. Stuart's car would be here in an hour. Anna swung her feet onto the floor and willed them to move.

"No, that one is better," Eva said as Anna held the silk burgundy-colored dress to her front. "It's got a more flattering neckline." She had been watching Anna sort through the oversized wardrobe in her room. Eva sat on the bed surrounded by dresses and skirts and blouses, all from before the war and somehow spared being sold or bartered for necessities. What would have been the most normal ritual between two friends was now strange and out of time for Anna. She couldn't remember when she had last made any effort about what she wore, having acquired all of Madeleine's husband's pants and turned them into her daily uniform. On the one hand, she didn't give a damn about dressing up for Stuart, but on the other hand, she had no other clothing options than the chunky trousers and boots. Eva had happily volunteered her wardrobe, and the two of them had spent the last thirty minutes in Eva's room sorting through clothes like two teenagers.

"What do you think the Eagle Club is like?" Eva leaned back against the wall, pulling her legs up to her chest. "I bet they have some decent food there."

Anna shrugged. She was secretly curious, a little excited even, but she didn't dare let on.

"Do you think you'll go to Nuremberg with him?" Eva asked.

"I don't know. I have to worry about Oskar first, and…" Anna caught herself before she said anything about the mysterious paintings. She had promised Cooper they would keep it between themselves, at least for now. The only reason she agreed to go with Stuart was to keep him happy and to see if she could get him to reveal any more information about his plans for the Collecting Point. It was a sort of spy mission. She felt a little like Mata Hari, or at least that's how she was explaining it to herself.

"And what? Your husband? You have to talk with him first?"

"Yes," Anna lied. Thomas had not entered into the equation in her mind at all. She had no intention of accepting the offer from Stuart, but Thomas was not the reason. She held the dress out at arm's length. "Shall I try this on?"

"Of course." Eva pointed to a screen in the corner of the room and Anna slipped behind the panels to change. Stepping out of the pants and into the slippery dress felt alien and otherworldly. The armor of the heavy pants and boots was gone, her legs and shoulders exposed. She felt naked and vulnerable and was sure she smelled terrible.

Eva tossed a pair of stockings over the screen and then dangled a pair of delicate red shoes with tiny gold buckles on the straps. "Try these. I always wear them with that dress."

"I feel silly." Anna stepped out to show Eva the outfit. "And cold."

"A scarf and coat will fix that. Is that how you want to do your hair?"

Anna put a hand to her dry hair, but before she could reply, Eva jumped up and took a brush to her scalp. "Just a nice twist at the neck here will do the trick." She tugged Anna gently by the hair and together they walked to the dressing table where Eva pinned and tucked everything into a neat little hairstyle. "There." She took a step back. "All set."

Anna regarded her reflection. She had lost so much weight that in the dress with its V-neck and her hair pulled back, her neck appeared longer than she remembered. She straightened and turned her head to get a side view. She didn't quite look like herself, but she was recognizable at least. Older, more tired? Wiser? *Perhaps*. Braver? *Yes*. She smiled just enough to not reveal the gap of the missing tooth she had lost earlier in the summer. It was a passable look.

"What is Major Stuart like?" Eva sat back on the bed and began pulling together the dresses she had laid out.

Anna paused. "Very sure of himself," she finally offered. "Very American. And married."

"I think he's handsome." Eva spoke into the wardrobe as she hung up the unused dresses. Was she jealous? "But then they all are, aren't they, the *Amis*?"

"Not all. That General Patton doesn't do much for me."

Eva feigned a swoon. "Oh, he's the best."

Anna pretended to punch Eva and they both laughed.

"You know, you should go with Stuart, instead of me. You're single. He's on the prowl. You could take the job in Nuremberg."

Eva's face fell and she shook her head. "No. I can't do that."

"Why not? You go tonight. You can say I fell ill." Anna liked the idea more and more. Why hadn't she thought of it before? Eva would be much more open to his advances, which would no doubt make him happy, and perhaps distract him from the Collecting Point.

"No." Eva hung the dresses back in the wardrobe. "He asked you, not me." She turned and forced a smile in Anna's direction.

"But I don't want to go, and you said yourself you think he's handsome."

Eva pressed her lips together and shook her head harder. "Out of the question." She pushed past Anna to the dressing table and rummaged in the drawer before pulling out a black lipstick case. "Here. This one goes with that dress." She held it up for Anna to take.

"Thanks." Anna squinted at the color, a dark red, the deep shade of a heavy port. It was far too dark for her complexion, but she accepted it anyway.

"I'll feed Amalia and put her to bed. Don't worry about anything."

Anna wanted to ask if Eva planned to sneak out that night. Were her secret rendezvous the reason she turned down the offer to accompany an American major to the Eagle Club? Or was it because of this man, Spitzer? There was hardly a better offer in town. Anna regarded her friend out of the corner of her eye as she applied the lipstick. She was busying herself putting the clothes away, studiously avoiding looking at Anna.

"You don't have plans?" Anna tried a different approach.

Eva looked confused. "Plans? What plans would I have?"

"I thought maybe there's someone in your life?" Anna hated prying, but she forced herself. "I thought maybe you and Herr Spitzer...?"

"No." Eva's tone changed. "Not tonight." She closed the wardrobe door, pushing it the final measure with her hip.

Anna tried to pull Eva back onto her side. "I understand. Thanks for taking care of Amalia."

Eva pointed at the clock on the small nightstand. "You better finish getting ready. He'll be here soon. I'll start the dinner." She put her hand on the door knob, but Anna caught her arm and gave it a squeeze.

"Thank you, Eva. I promise I'll tell you all about the Eagle Club. Maybe I can sneak something out in a napkin for you."

Eva softened. "I hear they have fresh fruit. Can you imagine?"

Anna smiled. "Damn *Amis*."

"Damn *Amis*." Eva laughed.

chapter eleven

The rain turned all the dust from the rubble to a fine silt that stuck to everything. Potholes in the street became invisible pools, sinking people ankle-deep into dirty water, soaking their only shoes and generally making everything worse. Major Stuart waited to open the car door until his driver had brought the umbrella around to his side.

"Okay, let's make a run for it," he barked, as if it were an order. "Stay close and we can make it up the stairs." When Anna stepped out of the car, a stiff wind blew droplets of water at her sideways, hitting her square in the back. The dress was indeed far too thin for the weather, which had turned much colder, and Eva's beautiful shoes were stained with water. She held her skirt down with one hand and bounded up the stairs to the Eagle Club alongside Stuart, who at least took care not to go too fast. A wood-faced guard opened the enormous door and suddenly they were inside where it was dry and calm, with soft strains of jazz music floating from another room under the sounds of laughing and chatter. The air smelled of cooking and cigars, and the place oozed with the spoils of victory. In here, under the large mosaic-worked dome, life was good, the war was only a memory, and the makers of the future enjoyed dinner and dancing, thanks to the Red Cross. As Stuart took her coat, Anna wanted to retreat and hide. She felt shabby and less-than, even the dress and fancy hairstyle couldn't cover the tell-tale signs of her status. The fact that the only other women she could see were wearing American WAC uniforms or carrying trays of glasses into the dining room, didn't help.

"Should I be here?" she whispered to Stuart as he returned from the coat check, pocketing their tickets. "I don't think I should."

He gave her a look that she read as condescending, as if she was being silly. Of course she could be here because she was with him. To be sure she understood, he said, "Technically no, but if anyone asks, you're my assistant and we are here to discuss Army related matters. No one pays attention to those rules anymore, anyway."

Anna kept from rolling her eyes. As if anyone would believe that. Thankfully, Stuart steered her away from the room that was teeming with music and voices and toward a smaller, more quiet dining room. At least in here fewer people would see her. They sat at a table in the corner where the glow of the chandelier didn't reach and Anna deliberately chose the chair with her back to the room. She didn't want to be on show. The place was ornate, with statues and urns dotting the room, an oversized fireplace taking up nearly one full wall. In its past life, the building had been a spa resort for Europe's aristocracy and elite. She had heard that a lot of American officers had been to Wiesbaden before the war and thus tried to spare it from too much bombing, not out of any concern for its citizens, but out of a desire to preserve it for their own use. Whose job in the US Army was it to pick out places to save from bombs so they could be used for recreational purposes later? Anyway, they had. As she settled into her seat, Stuart summoned a waitress by snapping his fingers.

"Why don't you bring us a bottle of Henkell," he said to the woman, who stared at Anna as he spoke. Anna returned the stare, not in any sisterhood, but in defiance. No doubt the waitress had also been the subject of much drunken *Ami* attention in her job. Each of them judged the other silently, and Anna held her gaze until the woman offered a *yes, sir* and walked away.

"Ever tried Henkell?" Stuart asked. "It's from here. The 80th Infantry Division captured the warehouse when they took the city in March. There were four thousand cases of the stuff inside."

"Lucky them," Anna muttered. Under the table, she twirled the wedding band on her finger.

Stuart barreled on. "I visited the headquarters in the Biebricher Allee the other day. For State Department business. We have to keep the VIPs supplied." He laughed and waited for her impressed response.

How long could she endure Stuart's tedious boasting? What was she doing here, really? And what exactly was he expecting of her? She regretted coming, wishing she had listened to her instinct and said no, and sent him away. She would try to steer the conversation to plans for the Collecting Point. But if she were honest with herself, she would have to admit that she was also here because she wanted a taste of the finer things, such as they were these days, just for one evening. If she could get a nice meal from an *Ami*, why not? And if she were even more honest with herself, she would confess that she was here because she wanted to get Cooper's attention. She wanted to make him jealous.

"So, tell me, how are things at the Collecting Point?" Stuart offered her a Lucky Strike from a full pack. She took one and waited for him to light it, happy to have something to do with her hands.

"Things are fine. We have much to do." She exhaled the smoke from the corner of her mouth. "We are busy all the time. There never seem to be enough hours in the day." It was small talk, but she was hedging, careful not to say anything that would give Stuart ammunition. "So many people are depending on us to do the right thing."

The waitress brought the champagne and began uncorking the bottle. In another room, a burst of laughter exploded, raucous and masculine. Anna winced a little, unaccustomed to the abandon. It felt out of place. Once again she found herself on another planet, feeling alien and misplaced. Stuart raised his glass and held it up. "Cheers," he said. "To General Eisenhower. To whom we owe this lovely evening."

Anna had had enough of drinking toasts to men in uniforms, but she raised her glass. "Cheers." The champagne prickled her mouth and then turned to honey as it filled her throat. It went straight to her head, its syrupy sweetness sliding through her, leaving a trail of warm glow in its wake. She took another sip, even as she told herself to be careful. One glass would be enough. For his part, Stuart downed his whole glass in one drink and poured himself another.

"So you were saying…" He leaned back in his chair and stole a glance around the room to see who else was there and who might see him. "Things are busy at the Collecting Point."

Anna had had enough small talk. If she was going to sit here with

Stuart, she was at least going to get something out of it. She didn't know what he thought he was going to get, but she would make sure her evening wasn't wasted. She opened her eyes wide and let a slow smile slide across her face.

"Yes. But I guess that won't be for long. When are you thinking the Collecting Point will be shut down? When we have returned everything? That could take a while."

Stuart snorted. "All that stuff is going back to the States, and soon, if I have anything to say about it. Especially the paintings from the state collections. The order will be coming down any day now. Crate it up, and ship it stateside. Once that's done, there won't be much left for you all to do. That's why you need to think about moving on. I'm offering you a very fine opportunity. I trust you've had a chance to consider it?" He took a drag from his cigarette.

"But what about the paintings that were taken from private citizens? From Jews? Those need to be returned to their rightful owners."

"Good luck with that. Where do you intend to find these rightful owners? Their ashes are scattered downwind from any one of dozens of camps. You'll never find any of them. And besides, those wretches who survived have plenty of other things to worry about. Trips to Palestine and justice in the trials. That's where we're headed. A bunch of paintings? Forget it." He took another swig from his champagne. "And anyway, weren't a lot of them bought by the Nazis? What a headache. No, these paintings belong in American museums. The American people paid for them with the blood of their sons on the beaches of Normandy. They are ours."

Anna's anger rose, but she pushed it back down. "Wretches?" she echoed. "That seems a bit harsh." *Even for you.*

"Oh? What would you call them?"

Anna tapped the ash from her cigarette into the enormous glass ashtray. "Survivors. I would call them survivors."

"Tomato, tomah-to," Stuart said. "Either way, they're not going to be worried about a bunch of paintings."

"Many of them are worth a lot of money. You don't think they will come looking for their assets?" She wanted to punch him in his smug angular face.

"Those people will be generously remunerated. We'll see to that. Reparations will be paid. They will be taken care of for the rest of their lives." He took another drink. A flush spread on his cheeks.

"I don't think that's the whole issue," Anna said. "It's what the paintings represent. There are memories associated with them, family stories. They are lifelines to their identity, history, and family. A life that's gone forever. It's not the paint on the canvas, it's what was taken from them. It was the attempt to rob them of their culture." Anna took a drink for courage. "I suppose that's not something you can understand."

Stuart was up for the game. "What makes you say that?" he grinned. "You think I'm some kind of philistine? Some uncultured bureaucrat who can't possibly understand the value of art? I'll have you know I own quite a respectable collection myself. I began acquiring pieces when I got out of West Point. I care as much about art as any of you."

"Caring about art is not the same as understanding it," Anna heard herself say. "And you are not uncultured. You are just greedy. If you understood art as a collector, you would know what it means to people. But you are too eager to get your own hands on it." She took another sip.

Stuart smiled at her. "I like you," he said. "You speak your mind.

You're wrong and naive, but you say what you think, and I like that. It's a very attractive quality in a woman."

Anna regarded him for a moment. "Does your wife speak her mind, too?"

He paused before he answered, acknowledging that she had surprised him. "Not really. Military wives are not known for their opinions. In fact, things go a lot smoother if they don't have too many of them."

"But opinions are welcome in adjutants, is that right?"

Stuart raised his glass in a mock toast and smirked. "So you'll take the job?"

Anna raised an admonishing finger. "You haven't answered me. What happens to the paintings from private collections?"

"How the hell should I know? Box 'em up and put them in storage somewhere if that makes you feel better. But no one's ever coming for them, I'm telling you. How are you going to be able to provide any paper trails to prove who owns what? The whole country is flattened, and you're looking for scraps of paper to document some art sale from 1938?" He scoffed. "It's ridiculous."

"Forced sale," Anna said, stubbing her cigarette out. "It was theft, pure and simple. And now you're stealing from them again."

"You know, I think it's justified to steal from Nazis."

"Who stole it from the Jews. It's not yours to take. Or mine, or anyone's. It needs to be returned. That's what's fair."

"All's fair in love and war," Stuart said. "Who said anything about fair anyway?" He was starting to be irritated. He took another big drink and refilled his glass, holding the bottle out to refill hers. "Why don't you have another drink and calm down. I didn't bring you here to get into an argument."

Anna put a hand over her glass. "Thank you, but no." She smiled to soften the conversation. "So it's a done deal then? Shipping the art to America and closing down the Collecting Point?"

"Are you trying to talk me out of it?" Stuart leaned forward. A light trail of perspiration rimmed his hairline, and Anna smelled the smoke and alcohol on his breath. It occurred to her that the champagne had not been his first drink of the evening. "You're welcome to try, but the order is coming down within two or three weeks, tops. Then there won't be much anyone can do. I don't think any of the fellows at the CCP are stupid enough to risk their Army pensions over this. And if they are, then good riddance to bad rubbish, as they say."

Anna was about to respond when Stuart focused past her shoulder at something behind her. A confused expression took hold of his face and shifted quickly to irritation. She heard her name spoken from across the room and turned to see Cooper, in his khakis, sleeves rolled up and soaking wet.

"What the hell, Cooper?" Stuart barked.

"Excuse me, Major, but I've come to fetch Frau Klein. She is needed at home. It's urgent."

Anxiety surged through Anna's core and she instinctively pushed the chair back and stood up. Her knees felt shaky and she took a step, knocking the chair over. "What is it, Captain? What's happened?"

Cooper shook his head. "I need you to come with me. I've got a car outside." He took her elbow. "Did you have a coat?"

"Cooper, explain yourself, dammit," Stuart said, getting to his feet. "You can't come in here and..."

"Sorry, sir, but it has to be done. Anna, come on. There's no time to lose."

Anna mouthed her apology to Stuart and allowed Cooper to pull her away, barely grabbing her bag from the table in time.

When they were in the foyer, Cooper nudged her to the coat check. “I’ll be outside.”

“I don’t need my coat. I can get it later. Tell me what’s going on.”

“Get your coat, get in the car,” Cooper hissed. “Hurry up. I’ll be outside.”

Cooper unlocked the door to the back of the Collecting Point that opened onto the loading dock, and Anna stepped into the dark hallway. The rain was coming down hard and they were both soaking wet.

“What are we doing here?” Anna said. “Tell me what the hell is going on.”

They had sped down the Wilhelmstrasse from the Eagle Club, a ride of less than one kilometer. Cooper had reassured her that all was fine at home. “I said that because it’s the only way I could get you out of there.” Anna didn’t know whether to be relieved or irritated. She was, however, glad to be away from Stuart.

Anna had barely recovered, her hands still shaking from the fear that something had happened to Amalia. Cooper had driven around the back of the Collecting Point and pulled the jeep into the shadows, out of direct line of the bright spotlights that guarded the perimeter. Even inside, she still shivered both from nerves and the chill. She waited for Cooper to close the door, leaving them in near pitch darkness.

“Now will you tell me?” she whispered, not sure where he was. She heard his breathing and general movements as he dug through his pockets. When the Zippo flicked on, he was holding it between their faces.

"How was your evening?" he said. "Nice time with the major?"

"Captain." Anna was seething. "Stop playing games."

"I need to talk to you."

"What, now? Here? It couldn't wait until tomorrow?"

"I don't want anyone to see us. And where would we go this time of night? I know you've noticed there's something fishy going on around here. You think I haven't noticed, but I have. And I think you're right."

Anna was distracted by the skin on his face, how near perfect it was. Even now with a substantial five o'clock shadow taking hold, his skin was smooth and filled with color, like a man who had been out in the bracing fresh air. The glow from the lighter only accentuated this and cast jumping shadows across his brow. She tried to concentrate on what he was saying.

"Are you listening? Anna, this is serious."

She nodded, indicating she was ready for him to go on, but her mind was unsteady. She pulled on the lapels of her coat and tried to ignore the effects of the champagne coursing through her system.

"Your friend Eva. She wasn't hired just because of her qualifications. I kept meaning to tell you. I just couldn't find the right time."

Anna's attention snapped to. *Of course*. She had known there was some other reason why Eva had been hired. Why Cooper paid so much attention to her. She spoke without thinking.

"She's your girlfriend and she needs the work."

Cooper blinked his eyes into an open stare. "What? Are you crazy?" He stepped back and looked off to the side, as if speaking to an invisible person in the room with them. "You've got to be kidding me. Is that what you think? Me and Eva?"

A flush rose in Anna's cheeks helped along by the champagne. She couldn't find words to cover her embarrassment, so she opted to go on the defense instead.

"Why wouldn't I? The way you two carry on, your secret meetings and midnight outings. What else would you have me think?"

"Midnight outings?" Cooper stopped. "What midnight outings? She's not going on midnight outings with me."

"Are you sure?"

"You *are* crazy. Of course I'm sure. I don't have midnight outings with anyone. What are you talking about?"

"She sneaks out of the house in the middle of the night. She's done it a few times. Madeleine was the first to notice. She was the one who thought Eva was going to meet you."

"Oh. That's fine. I love being the subject of the *kaffeeklatsch*. What else have you all been chatting about?"

"For God's sake, forget that and tell me what is going on."

Cooper flipped the Zippo shut and Anna heard him blow on his fingers.

"Okay, listen to me. I want you to look at the Nolde painting again. And I want you to tell me without a doubt that it's the same one you logged in."

Anna swallowed hard. She knew in her bones it wasn't the same one. Cooper took her hand and guided her to the door of the storage room. He fumbled with his keys.

"Let me help," she said, taking the Zippo out of his breast pocket. It was hot to the touch, but she ignored the burn on her fingers, flipping it open and igniting the flame. She held it up to the lock so he could see.

He pulled open the door and stepped aside so Anna could go in first. A wave of cool, humid air hit her face when she stepped over the threshold, and she ran her hand along the wall, looking for the light switch.

"Wait," Cooper said, pulling the door closed behind them. "There's a flashlight in here. No overhead lights." He picked up a large Army issue flashlight that had been stowed on the bottom shelf by the door and clicked it on. Anna walked to the back and sorted through the pictures on the shelves and pulled the painting he wanted from its spot. *Man in a Green Jacket.*

"This one?" She turned the painting so Cooper could see it.

He nodded, his face wary.

"Yes." She spoke for him, turning the painting toward her and giving it a close look. Cooper held the flashlight to cast an indirect beam onto the canvas. Anna ran her finger across the ridge of blue at the edge of a cloud. She tilted the flashlight to illuminate the frame and then back to the paint near the bottom of the canvas. She ran a finger over the surface. Her eyes strained in the light and she leaned closer. She wished she had a magnifying glass or at least better lighting. As her eyes moved over the hills and valleys of paint and color, the gnawing feeling returned to the pit of her stomach. He wanted to know what she thought, so she would tell him.

"It's different," she declared with all the confidence she could muster.

Cooper's face fell. "You're sure?"

"Yes. This is not the same painting I logged in on the custody card. It looks the same, but it's a different painting."

For once, Cooper didn't argue. "How can you tell?"

She took the flashlight from him and held it over the canvas. Bending closer to the surface, she inhaled, then turned the painting over.

"Remember what I said about the tear?" She didn't wait for his answer. "I double checked the custody card. I had made a note of damage in the bottom right corner.

"Where the tear is supposed to be?"

"Yes, this one has no damage at all to the bottom right corner."

"You still could be mistaken. The custody card could be wrong."

"No, I am confident in my work." She leaned in closer and examined the painting with her nose almost touching the canvas.

"What?" Cooper was getting impatient.

Anna ignored him and continued her scrutiny. "See this here, the black shadow?" She pointed to a spot near the man's elbow, where the background met his green jacket.

Cooper leaned in further. "Yeah. So?"

"So it's black, with a little brown. It's a warmer shade. Do you see it?"

He nodded.

"So, Nolde, in the original, used a little black, but mostly blue here. That's a cool shade. He did that often; he was influenced by Van Gogh to play with the color like that." She straightened. "The original had violet strokes in the shadow here. I remember because it contrasted the green of the jacket. This brown only muddies it."

Cooper blew air through his lips. "This is pretty esoteric stuff, Frau Klein. Not sure that's going to hold up in any court of law. I was hoping for something more concrete."

Anna ran the beam of the flashlight across the surface of the painting until she found what she was looking for. "How about this?" She pointed to a spot where the frame had pushed the green paint into a little ridge along its edge. "The paint is stuck to the frame."

"So?"

"So, the person who painted this didn't have much time. They put the painting into the frame before it was fully dry. No artist would do this to their work. And anyway, it still smells pretty fresh." She held the canvas up to Cooper's nose. "For a painting that's supposedly more than twenty years old, the paint smell is strong. This isn't the same painting I logged into the inventory."

Cooper exhaled. "What on God's earth is going on?" He put the flashlight on the work bench next to her, its beam facing toward the ceiling.

"I don't know. But you knew something was wrong, that's why you brought me here, right?"

Cooper adopted the stance of a wayward child who has been caught drawing on the furniture. With the evidence in view, it was no longer possible to lie, so he sheepishly confessed.

"It bugged me a little that you said there should have been a tear on the Nolde. Not a lot, but just enough. And then when the Kirchner went missing, it bugged me a little more. And then Major Standen was talking the other day about how German Expressionists were a hot item on the US market now. Prices and demand are really picking up steam. American collectors are waiting for those paintings that vanished during the war to come on the market now. And since Nolde was forbidden from painting from 1937 on, this earlier stuff of his is in high demand."

"And Kirchner is dead," Anna added.

"Exactly. So it nagged at me—that was two shenanigans with these German Expressionists. I didn't sleep, thinking about it. I thought, *no, this is nuts*, but then I wasn't sure. In Munich they had people walking out of the Collecting Point with paintings and selling them on the black market down the street. It happens. And I don't believe anything is beyond comprehension anymore." He slumped onto the stool behind him. "I started to get worried, thinking the Kirchner had been stolen. I asked Eva about it and she claimed to know nothing, got a bit worked up if you ask me. Then, the next day, I found it, leaning up against the wall in the conservator's studio, all safe and sound. So I put it back in its place." He shifted his weight. "The thing is, no one claims to know how it got there. Not the workers in the studio, not Eva, not anyone. That can't happen. So who's to say a forged painting somehow didn't get switched out for the real deal? In the grand scheme of things, it's not that far-fetched. Especially since no one's owning up to having even touched it."

Anna processed what Cooper was saying. Without explanation, she crossed the room to find *Berlin 1913*, tucked into its slot on the shelf. She placed the painting down on the table and picked up the flashlight again. Cooper said nothing as his eyes followed the beam on the painting. Anna scanned the entire surface, finally coming to rest on a ridge of blue paint. She took a deep breath. "This right here? In the painting I logged in, the blue paint was added after the white of the cloud was dry, creating a solid edge." She ran a fingertip on the paint so he could see what she meant. "In this one, it was added when the white paint was still wet, blending the two colors. And the thickness of the paint isn't right either. This was painted by someone with little time and little paint. It's not at all the same as the one I logged in."

Not waiting for Cooper to respond, she turned the painting over to check the stamps on the back. Her voice rose a little. "And this label, it's placed too high on the back of the painting. Morgenstern put all labels on the paintings in his collection exactly even with the top of the hanger. It must have been an obsession with him. See? This is a little bit too high. Not a lot, but enough. If someone wasn't paying attention, or they were in a hurry, they could easily overlook this detail."

Cooper squinted at the label and then looked away, his eyes searching the contents of his brain for an explanation.

"You really were studying the paintings when you were inventorying?"

"Of course. First of all, the condition reports require any noticeable features to be recorded. And, second, when am I ever going to have the chance again to be alone with these beautiful things, touching them and really seeing them?" She turned the painting back over. "And anyway, it's important."

"That's why you were taking so long."

Anna picked up the Nolde painting again and placed it side by side with the Kirchner. "And see here, the puddle on the street? By the woman's foot?" She toggled the flashlight's beam between the two pictures. "It's the exact same brown as on the Nolde, applied the exact same way."

Cooper followed the beam from the Kirchner to the Nolde. "Okay…" He took a step back. "You know if you look at them side by side…"

"They could be painted by the same artist," Anna said. "When, in fact, Nolde and Kirchner had two distinct techniques." She turned the paintings over again. "But even their labels match perfectly. Slightly aged, but not too much. And placed just a little too high." Anna bit her lip. "So you believe me?"

"I do," he said to the floor. "I should have believed you the first time."

Anna paused before she spoke, considering if she was ready to make another accusation. "Do you think Eva is involved?"

Cooper shook his head. "I don't know. But it sure is strange that this all happened when she showed up."

"And why didn't you tell me anything about this before? Why didn't you include me?" She winced at her own childishness. As if two missing paintings were secondary to her jealousy.

"I didn't want to get you involved after what happened with the Schenk and Schneider case. That still might come to trial, and I wanted to be sure you were all by-the-book until then, in case they pulled you in to testify. You know how those things can go. Clearly, I made a mistake."

Anna straightened. "What do you mean, testify? I already gave my statement about the Schneider case. No one said anything to me about testifying."

"It's a long shot, but you never know. I was trying to play it safe. For your sake. You know we have a lot of eyes on us. I wanted your hands to be clean."

"You know, Stuart says we'll be closed up by the end of the year."

"He said that? To you?"

Anna nodded. "He says no one cares about this work, it's not important. The Jews who survived aren't going to come after their paintings, and anyway, the art is considered 'reparations.'"

"Stuart's a goddamned idiot. The worst kind of bureaucrat: impressed with his own bureaucracy. Not a coherent thought anywhere in that giant head of his." He looked Anna in the eye. "You impressed by him? All the talk of Nuremberg and Washington? I see you got all dressed up."

Anna ignored the comment. "You should know me better than that."

"Then why'd you go with him?"

Anna was relieved the darkness hid her being taken aback by his question. It was accusatory but also personal. "I didn't think I could refuse his offer." She stuttered a bit and then regained her footing. "And I thought I could get him to talk about his intentions for the Collecting Point. He has the ability to consider me stupid while praising me for my smarts. So I played along, stroked his ego and kept my mouth shut. Men like him are easy to maneuver." She cocked her head.

Cooper held her gaze, and for a moment, they sat without speaking. Finally he shifted, turning his attention back to the paintings on the table and averting his eyes. "And what about me? Am I easy to maneuver, too?"

"You? You're a little more of a winding road. I don't quite know where it's heading most of the time."

"Fair enough, Frau Klein."

"Why do you keep calling me that?" Anna said. "You used to call me Anna."

Cooper sank a little. "It reminds me that you're still a married woman. You are, aren't you?"

"Yes, I am."

"So you'll be Frau Klein, and I'll be Captain Cooper. Until further notice. And right now, we have a fat mess on our hands."

The room suddenly felt very small. The smell of chemicals in the air, and the humidity from the scattered bowls of water were getting to her. It was cold and damp and uncomfortable.

"I have no intention of going to Nuremberg," she whispered, "or anywhere else for that matter." She spread her hands on the table and stared at them. They looked worn and old, but she liked them.

"Good," Cooper said. "I'm glad."

His voice was soft and kind but underscored with an intensity that resonated somewhere in her core. It shook her back into the moment, and Anna turned her attention back to the painting in front of her. "The fact is that we've got two forged paintings in our possession. At least two that we know of. Someone must have the originals. What do we tell Captain Farmer?"

"Nothing for now. I need to get my head around this before we blow it open."

"What if Eva is somehow in on it? Could that be?"

Cooper shook his head. "That's what I wanted to tell you. She was vouched for by the higher ups, Farmer tells me. It's not like she just wandered in off the street; she had some brass behind her. I wanted you to know that it wasn't my idea to include her in meetings and to take her with me on field visits." He stopped to catch her eye, but Anna kept her focus on Kirchner's painted swirls. *If I look at him, I don't know what I'll do.*

As if to respond, Cooper shifted his weight away from her, just enough to be noticeable. "And anyway, no one can get a painting out of here without someone seeing it. They aren't easily concealable. And after what happened with the thefts at the Munich CCP, we clamped down on security. You've seen it yourself. The State Department is breathing down our necks, saying we can't provide proper security for the art. We can't start any of this bullshit right now. And honestly, this place is locked down tighter than Fort Knox."

Anna bent over the table, leaning on her elbows, feeling the weight of her body dragging on her. Sensing her exhaustion, Cooper stood up and offered her the stool. Anna was grateful for the seat. Eva's shoes were starting to pinch her feet. He pulled himself on top of the worktable, resting his feet on the edge of her stool.

"I'm confused," she said. "Eva never mentioned anything to me about knowing any higher ups. That seems like something she would mention, especially with the housing requisition or with Oskar. If she's so well connected, why would she keep it a secret?" She had let the news about Oskar slip, but Cooper wasn't listening.

"It's all out of whack." Cooper rubbed his eyes. "I'm well and truly in the soup this time. They're gonna send me up the river for this one."

Anna shook her head. "No. We have to find the originals and get them back."

"Easier said than done. This whole country is a shithole of corruption. And anyway, they're probably halfway to Moscow by now."

"Or Washington." Anna couldn't resist.

Cooper ignored the dig. "Can you maybe get Oskar to do some snooping around the black market? And Amalia? While you're at work? Give them a quick course in German Expressionism?"

Anna exhaled. She would have to tell him. "I don't think so."

"Why not?

"He's at the DP camp awaiting transport to some children's center in Bavaria. I was going to tell you, but…"

Cooper raised his voice. "Goddammit, Anna. You have to tell me these things. I can help you, for God's sake." He threw his hands up and rubbed his head in frustration. "Why are you so damn stubborn?"

You couldn't help with the house. This was her thought, but she didn't say it. It was pointless. "Nothing is working anymore," she muttered, "not even the simplest things. I sleep in a house of strangers.

My boy is being taken away from me. You tell me I may have to testify and face that awful man again. And Stuart, and the paintings. This mess here, and…" She stopped herself before she added Thomas to the list. *And I have to divorce my husband.* She rubbed her forehead and willed herself not to cry. The champagne had now made her even more hungry, and the hint of a headache settled behind her eyes. For a moment, she didn't register Cooper's hand resting gently on her shoulder then moving slowly to the back of her neck where he held it perfectly still. She leaned her head into his knee, the folds of his pant leg brushing her cheek. It smelled of starch and military, and the warmth of him permeated the fabric. She leaned in more, closing her eyes. His hand moved to her head and stroked her damp hair. She felt him lean forward and then press his lips to the top of her head. The gesture seemed like something from a dream, and she wasn't sure it had really happened until she felt his hands turn her face toward him.

"Listen to me now." His eyes locked into hers. "Tomorrow we will start putting this back together. The one thing we have going for us is that no one else knows. At least not yet. And whoever did this doesn't know we know. We'll figure this out. All of it," he whispered.

Anna's thoughts churned. She questioned herself one last time about her verdict on the paintings, but she knew in her gut she was right. It was true, forged paintings were not preposterous; far stranger and more terrible things happened every day. The realization reframed her perception. *The paintings are fake. Cooper and Eva are not having an affair. What I thought was true is not.* Yet, nothing had changed. It was as if the entire world had shifted, that her view of things was now from a slightly different angle. One where the light was a little better and the focus clearer.

"Now, I better get you home. It's late and you must be freezing in that dress." Cooper shifted his weight. "You look pretty, by the way."

Anna's cheeks burned. "I feel silly. This dumb dress. The dinner. This whole evening was such a bad idea."

"Not an altogether bad idea." He tucked a loose strand of her hair behind her ear, moving his index finger slowly down her neck to her collarbone.

Anna's heart never wanted to leave this room. If the world could go on and leave them both sitting together in the dank, dark storage room, it would be all right with her. "Can we stay a while longer? I need to think." She leaned her head into his knee and closed her eyes.

"Sure we can," he said, bending his head toward hers. She felt his breath on the top of her head, warm and steady.

"And anyway, you always do."

"Always do what?"

He leaned down further to whisper in her ear. "You always look pretty."

chapter twelve

Eva dropped the files in the cabinet before pushing the drawer closed. "He's letting you go back to Frankfurt?" She turned on her heel, distracting herself by sorting through the pile of papers on Cooper's desk. She had avoided making eye contact with Anna all morning. The night before, Cooper had taken care to drop Anna off around the corner so there would be no chance Eva could spot them, even though it had been after midnight. They had decided to proceed as if nothing had happened, for one day, while keeping Eva under close watch.

Cooper had said, "One day. Let's watch her for one day. After that, I have no choice but to tell Farmer, and then the shit will really hit the fan. I'll be finished."

The thought that the original paintings were lost gave Anna an even more intense stomachache than the usual one, but Cooper was less concerned. "Even if they're out there, they will turn up. Eventually. Whoever has them wants them for a reason; he's not going to keep them under his bed. These things have a way of bubbling back to the surface. I'll be out of a job by then, but it'll work out."

Anna tried not to think about Cooper and his being out of a job. She was conflicted as to Eva's involvement. Eva was the simplest and straightest line to the culprit. Over and over, Manfred Lange's name popped into her mind, unbidden and unexplained. It wasn't his party membership that nagged at her—that was so common it explained almost nothing. It was his anger at what happened during the war. He was so roiled just by the memories of the art at his museum that Eva had to calm him. Given what they all knew now about the camps, the torture, and the death marches, why was he focusing all his outrage on some paintings? And why was Eva avoiding looking Anna in the face?

"Yes, I'll go to Frankfurt tomorrow," Anna said, "to see if I can get anything else on Jacob Morgenstern."

"You're not going to let that go, are you?" Eva picked up another stack of files and carried them to the cabinet. "Do you think it's worth all this effort when there's so much left to do with the national collection and the endless field reports?" She blew at a strand of hair that had escaped from its clip.

"Cooper thinks it's worth it," Anna said. "The window is closing anyway, so if I can't find anything, I'll have to let it go. I guess they are planning to send Morgenstern's collection to Munich so all the Jewish collections will be in one place. Cooper says then it'll be up to the heirs to make a claim. Who knows when that'll happen."

Eva nodded absentmindedly, but Anna sensed she was listening more closely than she was letting on. "How was your evening?" Eva changed the subject. "Was Major Stuart nice?

"He is certainly impressed with himself," Anna laughed as she pulled a paper out of the typewriter. "I'll give him that."

Eva stopped what she was doing and turned her attention to Anna. "What's it like, the Eagle Club? It must be lovely." Her face relaxed into a wistful expression, like a child looking into a shop window at Christmas.

Anna downplayed the lavishness of the place; she felt sorry for Eva's aching for something so superficial and didn't want to rub it in. "It's all right. Not as fancy as you would think. But they do have heat and running water, and tablecloths and champagne."

Eva sighed. "I'd love to go there sometime. I know Germans are not allowed. You're so lucky that he took you there."

Anna shrugged. "To be honest, I was ready to leave."

"But you must have stayed a long time, judging by the time you got home. Or did you go somewhere else?" She changed into teasing mode in an attempt to soften Anna, who now wanted to change the subject.

"No, we were there the whole time," Anna said. "I would have left a lot sooner if it had been up to me."

"Whatever you say."

Anna started typing as a way to end the conversation. Eva was right about that; there were endless field reports. Anna thought about how years from now, some person might read the archive of their work and marvel at the sheer magnitude of documentation on the dullest things. But maybe they wouldn't seem so dull in the future.

"Well, Frau Klein, how good to see you." Stuart's cologne had preceded him, but not fast enough for Anna to make an escape.

She winced and turned to see him standing in the doorway, in his service uniform this time, hands on hips as if he had just conquered the room. Anna stood and introduced Eva who took his hand with averted eyes and then instinctively touched her hair, self-conscious and flustered. Stuart took little notice of her, instead setting his sights on Anna.

"I wanted to check on you, make sure you are okay." He sat on her desk and leaned in. "Are you?"

Anna held her breath and shot Eva a desperate look. "Yes, of course." She tried to think of a way to keep Stuart from revealing her quick and early departure with Cooper the night before. "Fraulein Lange and I are very busy already today." She smiled.

"I have to go downstairs." Eva dropped a stack of papers on Anna's desk. "I'll see you later, Anna. Excuse me, Major." She fluttered past Stuart. He still paid her no mind, as if she wasn't even in the room.

Anna saw an opportunity. "I'll go with you. If you'll excuse me, Major." She tried to push past Stuart who made no move to let her through.

Eva waved her off. "No need. I'm going down to check on the inventory." She was gone before Anna could stop her.

Stuart took the opportunity of Anna's attempted escape to catch her around the waist. He pulled her toward him and held on tight. Caught unprepared, all Anna could do was to try to push him away, but it was no use.

"Oh, you're not going to run away from me again, Anna. Not today." Stuart's cologne oozed from his skin, and the pomade in his hair gave off another, more pungent smell. Anna pushed again, harder this time. Stuart kept smiling, but his face had acquired an edge, his mouth curled slightly in subtle contempt. "You never even gave me an answer last night." He pulled her closer so she was pressed against him.

Anna leaned her torso back as far she could to escape his leering face. "Get your hands off me." She gave him the hardest push she could muster.

"Tell me you're coming to Nuremberg and I will," he said playfully. "You know, it's not really a question."

Anna's worry about Eva downstairs in the inventory room supplanted any fear of Stuart's clumsy advances. He was getting in the way. Had Eva used Stuart's appearance as an opportunity to go down to the painting stacks unobserved? Or maybe she made excuses to leave the room, thinking Anna had wanted her to. Either way, she had to get downstairs.

"Let me go, Major." Anna pushed the palm of her hand into the ribbons on his shoulder again, but he was much stronger and tightened his grip.

"Nope, not until I hear what I want to hear." One of his hands worked its way up her back and he pulled her upper body toward his face. Anna turned her head, and his lips landed on her neck where he buried his face, now grabbing at her breast with a kind of hungry desperation. A panic washed over Anna, and she pushed herself away with all her force, nearly falling backward into Cooper's desk. He looked up at her and dabbed at his lips with the back of his hand, smiling and laughing under his breath. She regained her balance, took a step forward, and delivered a full-handed slap across his face. Stuart froze, his face a combination of surprise and contemptuous amusement.

"I am not going anywhere with you," she spat. "Not to Nuremberg, that's for damn sure. Get yourself another adjutant." She rearranged her blouse, which had come unbuttoned, then took one step closer and lifted a finger to his face. "If you ever lay a hand on me again, you will live to regret it, you pig. I have work to do."

She turned and ran out the door, down the stairs, and into the bathroom. Locking herself in the stall, she sat on the toilet and buried her head in her hands. Her heart hammered in her chest so violently she thought she might die. She had struck an American officer and threatened him. Not just any officer either, but one with power over the work of the Collecting Point. Over Cooper and his career. Over her. She stood and fished around with a shaky hand in her pocket for the Lucky Strikes. Willing her hands to steady, she lit a cigarette and then climbed up on the toilet to push open the small window above the stall. The cold air exploded into the room with a clarity that felt like a slap in her face. After a few moments, her heart had slowed and the nicotine had taken hold of her nervous system. Her hand still shook, but breaths came more slowly. As her thoughts settled, a new urgency grabbed her. She took one more drag off the smoke and then stepped on the end to save the rest. *Find Eva. And warn Cooper.* She checked her watch. It was almost eleven. Stuart was likely here to meet with Farmer and probably Cooper, too. It would make sense that he stopped by Anna's office on the way to his meeting. She put the cigarette pack back in her pocket and went to the sink. Running the icy water over her wrists to steady herself, she peered into the dingy little mirror that was balanced on the shelf above the basin. "It's okay," she reassured her reflection. In English, so she would believe it.

Anna took the stairs from the basement, two at a time, weaving in between the *Amis* and workers who were moving too slowly for her liking. The door to Farmer's office had been closed, but then it usually was. The store room with the Morgenstern collection was locked, and Anna wanted to see if Cooper's keys were in their usual spot inside his desk. Eva could have had them in her pocket when she went downstairs, if indeed she was heading for the store room. Cooper's office was empty, but the lingering aroma of Stuart's cologne hung in the air. She had not been gone very long, and with the windows closed against the cold, the air did not circulate well. She pulled open the drawer and saw the familiar key ring in its usual spot. Eva knew Cooper kept them in his desk. But she also knew when he wouldn't be in his office. Anna picked through keys on the ring and found the one to the store room. While the others were old and heavy, this one was a new key that fit the lock the *Amis* had specially installed. It was an American lock, more modern than the big heavy iron ones original to the building. She took the ring in both hands and began to work the key off, keeping an eye on the hallway outside the door to make sure no one was coming. When it popped off, she quickly put it in her pocket and returned the ring to its usual spot nestled amongst the junk. At least now she had the key.

"Frau Klein, there's a man downstairs to see you." Karla appeared in the doorway. She had pushed her glasses on top of her head where they perched like a little headlamp between the two rolls of her hairdo.

Anna jumped. "Oh, *hallo*, Karla. You startled me." She shoved her hand into her pocket and closed her fist around the key. "Tell the major to go away." She rolled her eyes. "I thought I made my point."

"It's not him. This is a German. He wouldn't tell me his name."

"He wants to see me?"

"Apparently. He asked for you by name."

A chill ran down her spine. "Where is he?"

"Down in the lobby. Come on, I'll show you." They stepped into the hallway and peered over the stair railing into the foyer below. Cooper and Stuart were milling about, along with some other men she did not recognize, as they waited for the meeting to start.

"That's odd," Karla said, "he's gone. I told him to wait on the bench, but he's not there."

They stood as if waiting for some explanation to rise from the crowd below.

"What did he look like?"

Karla shrugged. "Ordinary. Old man with a suit and a mustache. Nothing exceptional about him. Slight Bavarian accent, a little dirty around the edges, and he smelled funny, like gasoline or something."

Anna paused. The man who had come to the door and questioned the children had been a little dirty and smelly, too. And now he was at her workplace. She told herself it was nothing. "If he comes back, let me know. Right now, I need to get to Cooper before he goes into that meeting."

"I'll get him for you." Karla was happy to oblige. Everyone liked an excuse to talk to Cooper. Before Anna could warn her to be subtle, Karla was barreling down the stairs.

Anna stepped back from the railing to be out of the line of sight. Through the balustrade, she saw Karla approach Cooper and speak in his ear. Cooper nodded and made his way to the stairs. Karla twitched her eyebrows at Anna before sliding her glasses onto her nose and returning to her post. No one paid her any mind, except Corporal Long who stood in the corner awaiting his shift change. He stared at

Karla, and Anna observed the girl give him a shy smile.

"What's up?" Cooper smiled as he came around the curve and bounced up to the landing. "Make it fast, I've got about one minute."

Anna pulled him toward the back end of the upstairs hallway.

"Eva said she's been downstairs, but I don't think she had the key, so I'm not sure if she went into the storage room. I took the key off your ring. It's in my pocket, and I'm going to check on everything now. Also, Major Stuart made a pass at me and I slapped him, so he's not happy. That's all. Now go." The voices from the foyer below began dwindling as the group filed into the director's office. "Go, hurry."

Cooper blinked. "Stuart did what?"

"He won't do it again, but he might take it out on you, I wanted you to know. Hurry up."

"Did he lay a hand on you?" Cooper's voice dropped.

Anna waved him off. "Doesn't matter. He won't do it again."

"Damn straight he won't." He made to go before stopping and turning back. "Did you say you slapped him?"

Anna took him by the shoulders and turned him around. "Go. I'll see you afterward." She gave him a push and he obligingly headed toward the stairs. When he came around the curve, he looked up at her, smiled, and winked. He was ready for the fight.

Anna opened the door to the store room and turned on the light. The scene was exactly as they had left it the night before: the stool still at the workbench, and the paintings sleeping soundly in their beds, oblivious to their role in the human upheaval. She closed the door behind her, went to the racks, and found the fake Nolde painting of the fake man in the fake green jacket. She ran her finger over the canvas and along the edge of the frame and found another place where the paint had buckled. Whoever had framed this was in a big hurry. The most likely scenario was that the real paintings were removed from their frames, taken off the stretchers, and replaced immediately with the fakes. Then they were somehow smuggled out of the Collecting Point. She examined the canvas. It was roughly the size of a kitchen towel. She turned the painting over, tore at the paper on the back, and examined the stretchers and the staples. She searched through the stacks and found another Nolde painting—this one much smaller—and turned it over, too. Tearing a small hole in the paper, she compared its stretchers to that of the forgery. The stretcher bars were the same, but this one had nails and not staples. She looked back at the fake. Holding it up under the naked bulb hanging over the table, she could see small holes in the frame where nails had been. But in reframing the painting, the person used staples instead of the more commonplace nails. Anna looked around. The *Amis* had staplers all around the building. A stapler was easier to conceal than a hammer and nails, and quieter, too.

She scanned the floor, stepping back to check under the table. The flashlight sat on the shelf where Cooper had left it, and she turned it on, directing its beam into the darkness under the shelves. Getting down on her hands and knees, she ran her hand along the floor. A fine layer of dirt from muddy shoes and old crates gathered under her hand. She put her head down, cheek almost on the floor and extended her arm under the shelf as far as it would reach, hoping to find something that wasn't either alive or dead. Thankfully, there were no mice or cockroaches to meet her grasp, but at the corner of the first shelf, her hand ran over something sharp. She trained the beam onto it. It was a small nail, a short one, the same kind used to secure a canvas to a stretcher. She tilted the flashlight. The nail had escaped from a small pile that had gathered in the back corner, as if swept there to be hidden or picked up later.

Pulling herself to a sitting position, she leaned against the leg of the table. From this low vantage point, the room appeared enormous, with dozens of nooks and crannies providing easy hiding spots. She ran through the scenario in her head. The original paintings had been removed from their frames and replaced by forgeries. This required both tools and time, as well as skill. Whoever it was had to have access to the room and be confident they would not be interrupted. They also had to have access to the tools, which were available in the workshop at the other end of the hall but would be missed if they were gone too long unless someone had claimed a legitimate reason for taking them. Someone with a believable reason to do so. Anna tapped her hand on her thigh to push her thoughts forward. Everything pointed to Eva. She had the access, the time, and apparently the skill. But did she have a motive? And how would she have smuggled a painting out of the Collecting Point? The bulky canvases, thick with oil paint, were not easily concealed, and the guards at the gate would not allow anything resembling a cultural object to leave the premises. And anyway, Farmer had taken to randomly checking people at the door when his time allowed. And then there was the issue of sneaking the forgeries *into* the building. It was impossible. And yet, she was certain this is how it had happened.

Anna rubbed her eyes. What if there were others? She scanned the shelves. There were more than fifty paintings in the Morgenstern collection. How could they ever be sure these were the only two? And how could they pin it on Eva—or anyone—without the original paintings? But it was the motive that gnawed at Anna. Eva had so much to lose. Anna exhaled and shook her head. Was it simple greed? Fear? Was she part of some elaborate scheme? Anna thought she would never understand people again. Until the Third Reich takeover, she had been reasonably sure that people were honest and meant what they said. The notion was ridiculously naive to her now. Everyone had ulterior motives. Everyone was running scared and angling for an advantage or hiding something. No one was to be taken at face value anymore. Not even Oskar was who he thought he was.

The thought of Oskar sent her back onto her feet. She wiped her hands on her pants and replaced the paintings on the shelves. Now that she had Cooper's key, she felt more confident about leaving the store room and trusting it would not be touched. She turned off the light, stepped into the hall, and locked the door. Heading back toward the stairs, she decided to keep going and pay a visit to the workshop.

A handful of academic types in white coats were bent over paintings and frames, one man hovered over a large book, finger running down a list. In the corner, a woman wiped a cloth on the corner of a Velasquez painting, a portrait of a lady in a heavy black dress with a complicated hairstyle and skeptical gaze. In the center of the room was a large worktable, well-lit by a series of hanging lights. Frames and parts of frames lay on the table between piles of reference books and stacks of the familiar dark green file folders the Army used alongside trays of forms and papers. Along the far wall a camera set on a tripod was focused on an empty easel, the wall behind it covered with a dark cloth. It was a mix of artist studio and bureaucracy that perfectly captured the work of the Collecting Point.

"Can I help you?" A balding man in a grimy cable-knit sweater grunted. "Are you lost?"

Anna made a face. "No, I'm not lost." She tried to think of a legitimate reason for being there. Curiosity was not welcome. She searched the worktable for an idea. "I was wondering if you have a staple gun I could borrow? Just for a moment. They need one upstairs and asked me to check."

The man rolled his eyes. "What do they need a staple gun for? They should bring down whatever needs working on and we will fix it. There are procedures and protocols for this kind of thing, you know. We can't just willy-nilly be going around stealing things."

This was a whole new level of bureaucratic thinking. Clearly, the days of free-wheeling, state-sanctioned theft were at an end. "Er, yes," she said, not sure where to go next. "I would bring it right back. It's the *Amis* that want it. What do you want me to tell them?"

The man was unimpressed. "You can tell them to bring back the one they already borrowed. I am not running a staple dispensary down here. I've only got one left and I need it. Tell them they've got a staple gun up there somewhere and they should damn well find it. If I lose this one, I have to fill out seventeen forms and wait a month to get another one. Who has time for that?"

Anna played along. "Yes, of course. If you tell me who borrowed it, then maybe I can find it and return it to you. Or at least tell them to explain themselves," she added hoping to demonstrate whose side she was on.

"It was that tall woman, the one who looks like a stork. She came down and asked for it three or four days ago. Said she'd bring it right back. Never saw her again. If she's going to show her face, she better have a staple gun in her hand," he said. "They don't like us going upstairs and bothering the higher-ups, but I will, if it's needed."

Anna made a gesture of agreement to assure the man that she was in complete understanding of his plight, thanked him, and stepped out into the hall. A thought came to her and she poked her head back through the doorway. "Is that the first time she borrowed it?"

"What, the staple gun?" the man snapped. "As far as I know." He shrugged and returned to his work before looking up again. "Wait, she was down here one other time. She borrowed a screwdriver."

"Oh?" Anna said. "Did she say what she needed it for?"

"I think it was something to do with fixing a filing cabinet. I wasn't really listening." He raised a lecturing finger. "That one she did return, I remember that much."

Anna nodded a thank you and headed for the stairs. She could hear voices in the foyer, Americans talking in low murmurs. She climbed the stairs slowly, hoping to overhear any interesting chatter. She had only made it halfway when Cooper spotted her.

chapter thirteen

"Come on, we've got to go." Cooper took Anna by the elbow and handed her a jacket. "Walk with me."

They marched shoulder to shoulder out the back door and into the rear courtyard, onward past the guard gate, and then turned left onto the side street. Anna never asked any questions when Cooper was focused on a mission he had in mind. There was no use; he never answered anyway. A stiff north wind swirled the fallen leaves, and Anna put the jacket on and held it closed around her torso. The whoosh of the wind in the trees sounded ominous to her today, whereas on other days it would have been a welcoming sound of fall. They walked around the back of the Collecting Point along the chain link fence the *Amis* had erected when the first paintings had arrived back in August. That day had been hot and humid and seemed like a different lifetime already, given all that had happened in the weeks since. In the shadow of the building, it was especially cold, the damp from the recent downpours still hanging in the air.

Cooper put a hand on her arm. "Stop," he said, and consulted his watch. "We'll wait here." He scanned the street leading back up into the leafy neighborhoods to the east.

"What are we waiting for?"

"Bender. He's coming to pick us up."

"And where are we going?"

"You'll see. Don't worry, it's nothing bad."

"You know how I feel about surprises," Anna said. She fished around in her pocket for her cigarettes and held the pack out for Cooper.

"You didn't used to smoke this much." He took one from the pack and put it in her mouth. He held the flame from his Zippo underneath the tip while she inhaled. "Is this part of the new you?"

"Keeps the hunger at bay. I managed to go all this time without making it a habit, even though everyone around me smoked like chimneys. But, what the hell." Anna shrugged.

"What the hell," Cooper agreed as he took one for himself and lit it. "I'll get you another pack." He squinted up the road again.

"Tell me where we're going," Anna pleaded.

Cooper shook his head. "If I tell you, you won't go. While we're waiting, why don't you tell me what you found out. Anything?"

Anna stepped closer, trying to not look furtive but realizing that's exactly how she appeared. "I'm glad you asked," she said. "I found nails."

He made a face of mock horror. "No."

Anna ignored him. "Under the shelf in the store room. A small pile, like they had been swept there."

Cooper shook his head, unimpressed.

Anna continued. "And the Nolde painting? The canvas is attached to the stretcher with staples, not nails. That's unusual."

"But not unheard of."

"That's true. But I visited the workshop, and they claim that someone from upstairs borrowed their staple gun a while back and had not returned it. The woman they described sounds like Eva."

Now Cooper glanced reflexively over his shoulder. He leaned in closer. "So you think she put the fake painting on the stretcher and in the frame in the store room? Right here?" He pointed at the building.

"It would make sense," Anna said. "It's easier to get a canvas out of the building when it's not on a stretcher. All you have to do is roll it up. And then…" She stopped to think.

"It would still be impossible to get something like that past the guard," Cooper said, jutting his chin in the direction of the MP standing alongside the fence at the front corner of the perimeter.

Anna stared into the distance and took a drag from her cigarette. "Yes. There must be another explanation."

"Jesus, we are making one hell of an accusation. You realize that, don't you? Borrowing a stapler is not a crime, and you know Stuart will jump all over this. I can't do anything until we have some proof. And I'm for sure not bringing it up until we've got it figured out. I can't even ask Eva, because what if she tells whoever she's connected to? And then Stuart will have my head on a platter. And my ass. And yours too, I'm sorry to say."

Anna nodded glumly. "I know. Speaking of Stuart, how was the meeting?"

"Oh, it was grand. The telegram we were worried about finally came down from Frankfurt. That's why Farmer called the meeting. There were MFA&A officers from all over Germany there. We've been ordered to ship two hundred of the paintings from the Berlin National Gallery and Kaiser Friedrich Museum, and a few others, too. Apparently, our operation here is not up to par, and Washington insists they can keep them safer stateside. The National Gallery in Washington and the Met in New York have their fingerprints all over the list that was supposedly put together by the State Department. It's nothing but plunder."

"They're claiming them as American property? Paintings belonging to German museums?"

"Oh, no, they're smarter than that. That doesn't sound so nice. They are putting them 'in trust,' if you can believe that, until such time when and *if* the German nation has earned the right to their return." He flicked the ash off his cigarette and looked around before going on. "Note the carefully placed 'if.' As if that makes us any better than the goddamned Nazis."

"But that makes no sense," Anna said. "Didn't that other officer from the State Department say what an outstanding job you're doing? In that report he gave?"

"Yeah, that's right. But that's not what State officially wanted to hear. So they sent Stuart and he gave them the exact opposite report. It's cover for them to get what they want. He said the roofs are leaking and that there are puddles everywhere. Well, of course there are, we're humidifying the air. They could get off their duffs and send us some air conditioners to take care of that, but until then, we have to make do with what we've got. As if putting irreplaceable paintings on the open seas of the North Atlantic in November is even remotely safe." He shook his head. "I can't even think about it without going into convulsions."

"And this is all Stuart's doing?"

"Oh, he's doing the bidding of some fat general. Stuart wouldn't know a Manet if it bit him on his considerable ass. He's picturing himself being toasted at some Washington reception." He took a drag off the cigarette and blew smoke out of the side of his mouth. "And he thinks you'll be there with him."

Anna laughed. "He's better off pursuing Eva. I don't know what he sees in me anyway. She would follow him in a second. And she fits the part better."

"What part?"

Anna fidgeted. "Oh, you know, mistress—or the new wife—of apparently dashing, self-important military officer who saved masterpieces from the clutches of the filthy *Krauts* while seducing a German beauty who recognizes his brilliance. Knowing how he feels about Germans, I wonder why he is pursuing German women so fervently at all."

Cooper gave a shudder. "It's a need to conquer, to keep winning. To come home with his own spoils of war. But in reality the only attractive thing about him is the possibility of a one-way ticket out of here and into the bridge clubs of Georgetown. That doesn't appeal to you?"

"I don't play bridge," Anna said. "And I may not have much left, but I have enough self-respect to stay away from him. He's not so different from the Nazi officers, convinced of his own charms. I'm glad I got to slap him."

"Yep. Maybe next time you see him, give him a good punch, too. I'll get in line right behind you. What difference does it make now, we're both in hot water." He flicked the ash from the tip of his cigarette and they watched it fall to the ground.

Cooper looked around. His mood had shifted and his voice was tight. Out of habit Anna looked around too, not knowing what she was looking for.

"Listen, Anna, I've got a few of the guys together to sign a statement denouncing the State Department's orders. I guess you can say we are mutinying. If it goes bad, it's very possible I'll be court martialed over that…if they don't get me for this forgery mess first. Things are pretty testy around here and it's going to get worse. But this order is a terrible mistake, and we won't be able to live with ourselves if we don't take a stand." He exhaled and the familiar weariness washed over him. "And this is supposed to be the peace. It was almost easier when I was dodging bombs in Italy," he muttered before recovering his resolve. He put a hand on her arm. "So you need to tell me right now if you want out. If this blows up, I can't protect you, and if you're involved, they won't look kindly on you. That's why I was trying to keep you out of it for so long. I hate to do this to you, I really do." He scanned her face, trying to read her reaction. He looked like the most friendless person in the world. But he didn't evoke Anna's pity. It was something much different. As if sensing her reaction, he cleared his throat and looked at the ground. His boot kicked at a rock and sent it tumbling into the street. "So, tell me now if you want out, and we'll never speak of it again. But my days here may be numbered either way. Do you understand?" He looked up, searching her face again, this time for her solidarity.

Without missing a beat or giving it a thought, Anna leaned in and pressed her lips to his. She had to stand on her tiptoes to reach him, and just as quickly as she raised her heels she lowered them again, her face flushing as she looked him in the eye.

"Yes," she said, "I understand."

Cooper was silent, his face registering surprise and relief. She was so close that she could hear his breath and dared not take her eyes off him. Slowly he blinked, his face melting into a smile.

"Now, who is writing this statement?" Anna whispered.

"I am. In my abundant spare time."

His mouth was so close to hers, she could have kissed him again.

Instead she said, "And I'll type it, is that the plan?"

He reached up and pushed a strand of hair off her forehead, laying it down in its place and studying the top of her head. "It's not really a statement. I like to think of it more as a manifesto. Sounds more impressive than 'disobeying an order.'"

"I don't know. Disobeying an order can be noble," Anna said. "It depends on the order, doesn't it?"

A jeep revved past them and broke the moment. Cooper threw his cigarette into the street and took a step back. "Dammit, I sure am getting sick of this goddamned Army."

"Me, too," Anna chimed in. The levity felt good and distracted her from the seriousness of the situation. Her insides vibrated with anxiety. Now she was not only risking her job, but she was risking her freedom. If she only had herself to worry about, she might feel more exhilarated to finally be part of something bigger than herself. But the cost was so steep. She thought of Amalia and Oskar and Madeleine. They depended on her. Still, she knew in her heart that she was doing exactly what she should be doing.

They stood side by side, each lost in thought. Anna could still feel the fleeting warmth of his lips. It had only been a chaste peck, but it was a leap over a gaping chasm. She was exhilarated and terrified. As if to reassure her, Cooper reached for her hand, interlaced his fingers into hers, squeezed, and then let go. It was a reciprocation of her kiss, a yes to her question. They were well and truly in it together now.

A jeep rumbled around the corner from behind the building, and Anna turned to see Bender at the wheel, grinning at them as if he knew what had just happened. Had he witnessed their moment? *Who cares? Who damn well cares?*

Bender made no indication that he had seen anything. He made room on the passenger seat by sweeping a pile of little boxes onto the floor. "Typewriter ribbons. For you, Anna," he said. "Remind me to give you those when we're done. I hear you're going to have some serious typing to do soon."

"So I've been told."

"And you're okay with that?" Bender put his hand on her arm. "You know what it means?"

Anna was resolute as she climbed into the back seat. "Yes, but Captain Cooper refuses to tell me where we are going," she said. "You'll tell me though, won't you, Corporal? You tell me everything."

Bender let out a laugh laced with sarcasm. "I do tell you everything, Frau Klein. We have no secrets. So hang on to your hat because we're going to Frankfurt."

"What, all of us? I thought I was going tomorrow?"

"Yep, all of us. You need to go anyway, and Cooper and I are going to see the friendly folks at HQ. So we thought we'd take a road trip, just the family."

"This is part of the mutiny?" Anna asked. "Is that why you are picking us up here in the side street?"

"You bet it is," Cooper said. "As our typist, you are a co-conspirator.

It won't do to be seen together. But don't worry," he turned and winked at her. "We'll have you home in time for supper."

Anna watched the jeep drive away. Her watch said almost one o'clock. Cooper and Bender promised to return by three to pick her up so she had two hours to solve the Morgenstern puzzle. She turned to face the house at Feldbergstrasse 12, the former home of Jacob Morgenstern and his family. It was in what had been a tony neighborhood of Frankfurt, now somewhat in a state of affliction, but still presenting a certain charm. The other side of the street appeared to have suffered a more direct hit than this one, where glass panes were cracked, windows boarded here and there, and a few buildings only slightly damaged. American soldiers mingled comfortably on the sidewalk and Anna guessed they were stationed at the headquarters. People moved through the street on their business, dressed smartly in clothes that were only a little worse for wear. Women carried bags, of what Anna wasn't sure since there was nothing to buy and no money to buy it with. Men were visibly outnumbered, most of them old and frail, dodging the little herds of children that roamed in the direction of an open rubble field that served as a playground. There, a pair of nuns herded them into an orderly line, admonishing them with stern tones. After a moment, the children walked quietly into a partially standing building, two nuns bookending the line at either end. Anna turned her attention back toward the Morgenstern house. It was a small but stately building with creamy yellow plaster still visible amidst its cosmetic wounds. Anna climbed the three stairs to the entrance and rang the buzzer. She had no idea what to expect or even what to say to whomever opened the door. She waited and then rang the buzzer again, stepping back to survey the upstairs windows, in case she could see someone there.

The lock turned with a loud click, and the heavy wooden door scraped open. A woman's head, wearing a scarf and thick glasses, appeared in the narrow gap.

"Yes? Can I help you?" Behind their watery lenses the eyes scanned Anna from head to toe.

Anna cleared her throat and introduced herself, extending a hand to the woman who did not offer hers. "I'm looking for information about Herr Jacob Morgenstern. This used to be his home. Would you happen to know anything about that?"

"I knew Herr Morgenstern, yes," the woman said, her voice flat. "I knew the whole family. I was their housekeeper."

Anna smiled. "Ah, good. I am working with the Americans, the ones who are finding and returning art that the Nazis stole." She stopped herself. Better not to reveal too much. The mention of valuable art made people do the strangest things.

The woman inched the door open a little more to reveal a faded flowery smock and a sturdy arm. "You mean all that stuff the *Amis* found at Neuschwanstein and in the mine?" Now it was the woman tempering her enthusiasm. "I heard about that. Was Herr Morgenstern's art in the mine, too? I've been waiting for someone to tell me that they found it."

Anna considered how to respond. "What do you know about Herr Morgenstern's collection?" She dug around in her bag for a piece of paper; taking notes would make her seem more official.

The woman opened the door a little further. "I only know it inside and out. I worked for the man for more than twenty years. First just for him, and then, when he was married, I worked for his family. They were lovely, beautiful people." She folded her arms in front of her belly, as if expecting Anna to argue with her.

"I can imagine that they were," Anna said, feeling stupid. "May I ask you a few questions? I am hoping that I can locate a family member who can claim the art work that's stored at the Collecting Point. I want very much to see the works returned to the family."

The woman's eyes narrowed. "You work for the *Amis*?"

Anna nodded. "Yes, I am a translator. And a secretary, and whatever else they need me to do at the Collecting Point in Wiesbaden."

"And the *Amis* sent you?"

"Yes, I'm here on their behalf."

The woman chewed on the inside of her cheek. A gust of wind stirred the leaves and rustled through the straggly trees that still lined the street. "You don't work for Berg do you?"

"No, I work for the *Amis*, as I said. Who is Berg?"

The woman was still considering her next move but was on the cusp of revealing something. If Anna was patient and smart, maybe there was a reward to come.

"Let's start again, shall we?" Anna smiled and extended her hand. "I'm Anna Klein." She pulled her American credentials from her bag and showed them to the woman who shied away as if they might bite her. "My sincere interest is in returning the art that belongs to the Morgenstern family to a true heir. I feel a personal responsibility to do this," she added, and then winced at her own hubris.

The woman was unimpressed. "Why? What's it to you?"

The question stopped Anna. Anything she said would sound self-serving and stink of false nobility. Why was she doing this anyway?

What *was* it to her? She tried to work her thoughts into something that made sense, in this moment, talking to this woman standing on a stoop in Frankfurt in 1945.

"Because I can?" It came out as a question, which she had not intended. What a stupid thing to say. "To be honest, I can't say. I can't sort it out in my own head. But I'm in the position to do this, and I am going to try. I hope that it's not too late." She paused. "I fear I am much too late in trying to help. And that it's not enough, of course."

The confession had only a minor effect on the woman, who pursed her lips and gripped the door, protecting her domain.

"I see. You are trying to assuage your guilt, are you? You weren't here the day the transport order came, were you? You didn't see the tears, the terror. Frau Morgenstern vomited right here in this foyer when she saw the paper. Collapsed into her own sick, she did. She couldn't stay strong in front of the children; she was so scared. A beautiful, kind woman who had nothing but joy in her heart. Never did an unkind thing to anyone. Always took care of me and my family, made sure we had enough, made sure my little ones had clothes and shoes and even treats on their birthdays. I had to pick her up and put her in the bath. The light went out of her that day. I only had her for two more weeks before they had to go. And the children..." Anger flared across her face. "There was nothing I could do for them." Tears welled in her eyes but then disappeared just as quickly. She cleared her throat.

The lists of names Anna had seen in the Gestapo's papers flashed in her mind's eye. Each one of them a human story, a person like any other. Like her. Like Amalia. The gross indignities that devolved into cruelty, sadism, and unbelievable horror. That went further into the incomprehensible, the monstrous and a sort of everyday wickedness that hung in the air all around them, groping at them but not quite reaching them as long as they kept moving. She thought she might vomit, too, but she willed the bile down. She had no idea what to say to this woman who had seen what Anna had only read on reams of sterile, bureaucratic paperwork. She offered only a weak, "I know."

"I'll not let the Morgensterns be robbed again," the woman said. "It happened once and I couldn't stop it then, but this time, no. And I don't know you from Adam. How can I trust you are who you say you are? That you're not here to take what's theirs all over again?"

"I don't know how to prove to you that I am working only in their interest. I know it's hard to believe and I don't blame you. But please trust me when I tell you that I know the Morgensterns were robbed and that's exactly what I want to prevent from happening again," Anna pleaded. Seeing she was making little headway, she tried another tack. "Look, the *Amis* have Herr Morgenstern's art. To be honest, they aren't worried about giving it back. They assume the family has perished and that this will sort itself out in due time. It's not important to them. But it is to me. I am taking a chance coming here; my boss let me, but it's the only time I can do it. I need your help. You have no reason at all to trust me, I know that. But I can show you I am serious." She dug into her bag and found the paper she had taken from the records, now folded up into a small rectangle. She unfolded it and took a look before offering it to the woman.

"Here. I went through the Gestapo papers and found the record of the family's transport in December 1944. That's what brought me here. I had to find out what happened to them. See here?" She pointed to the group of names. "Here they are. That's them, no?"

The woman went white as a bag of flour and steadied herself with one hand against the door frame. "*Gott im Himmel*," she muttered. "Yes, there they are." She stroked the paper with her index finger, running it over the names as if to touch what they represented. "Sobibor? Where is that?"

"Poland."

"So far away," the woman said, her voice almost a whisper. "How scared they must have been. How awful, those trains." She looked up at Anna, tears now flooding her eyes. She took off her glasses. "I tried everything I could to help them, but I had no means. I had no money, no place for them to go. I wanted to hide them myself, but my husband, he would have none of it. Maybe we could have managed it, in the cellar? We could have fit the four of them there, but the baby, it would have been hard. But he said no. 'Helga, it's un-German,' he said. 'It's against the Fuehrer and I won't have it.'" She mocked her husband's voice. "And I tried to find them a place, but no one would help. Everyone was scared. There were rumors that the church over there was taking in Jews, that they had some place underground." She waved a hand across the street where the nuns had been watching the children play. "I went to them, but they wouldn't help. Acted like they didn't know what I was talking about. I even tried my youngest sister; she lives on a farm out by Oppenheim. I thought they could stay in her barn. But she said no, too. She had a new baby and didn't want any trouble." She shook her head and stared into the distance, past Anna's head. "I tried," she said. "I promise I tried."

She stopped talking and Anna let the silence take hold. It was like pulling a blanket off the world; the truth was uncovered, the pain revealed to the bright sunlight where it could maybe be healed one day. But then just as quickly, the shroud of silence returned, like a fog that crept into every nook and cranny until everything was obscured again, even as the world kept turning anyway. It was a familiar, comfortable state that they had all grown accustomed to.

The woman recovered and slid her glasses back onto her nose. She opened the door all the way. "Well, I suppose you had better come in."

Anna breathed a sigh of relief, thanked the woman, and crossed the threshold into what had once been a lovely foyer, with a polished wood floor and high ceilings. A staircase with a simple balustrade rose to a second floor, bathed in sunlight from a window she couldn't see.

"Frau Huber is my name. Marta Huber," she said as she led Anna through to the kitchen. The house was clearly occupied, although there was little furniture and the walls completely bare. The smell of cooking hung in the air.

"Do you live here?" Anna asked.

"Oh, God no," Marta replied. "After the Morgensterns left, the Nazis took the house and I made myself scarce. I didn't set foot in it again until three months ago. I couldn't even walk by, it upset me so. I heard some SS officer used it for his trysts; it is, after all, a beautiful house. And the galleries here on the ground floor were wonderful for parties. But I stayed clear until all those bastards left. I still had a key—they never thought to change the locks. Why would they? I would think no one would want to come in anyway. So, after they were gone, I let myself in and started cleaning up the mess they left behind. *Schweine*. No respect for anything or anyone." She dabbed at her forehead with a napkin from the table. "And when the *Amis* came, they wanted the house for themselves. Since it was back in good shape, thanks to me, they wanted to use it for important people visiting the headquarters. I told them I came with the house, so they gave me a job as the housekeeper and caretaker. Now I cook and clean for the big *Amis*."

They sat at one end of the long kitchen table. Worn and wobbly, it made a clunking noise as it shifted each time Marta Huber leaned her elbow on it. The open window above the sink overlooked a small walled garden that was now gray and bare. Behind the garden wall rose a view of hollowed-out buildings and partially standing walls. A cast iron stove warmed the room, a steaming pot burbling on one of its burners, and a stack of bread warming alongside. Anna could not take her eyes off either.

Marta noticed Anna eyeing the pot. "Cabbage soup. With bacon. The *Amis* love my cooking. They want the real German cooking. I told them for real German cooking I'm going to need a lot more than a few sad greens and a pat of butter. So they found some bacon and brought it to me. Let me take a little home, too." She stood up and sidled her girth around the table to reach for a cup that hung from a hook above the counter. She ladled some steaming soup into the cup and set it down in front of Anna.

"Here. They won't notice. I know you're hungry. Go on. It's good. I made the stock myself with bones from the cow on my sister's farm. Of course, I didn't have all the spices handy so it's not my best, but it's serviceable."

The soup swirled inside the cup, chunks of leafy green cabbage and specks of bacon floating inside. Anna held the warmth, wrapping her hands around it and breathing in the smell. "Thank you." The soup was hot and rich, like a warm bath on a cold day. Her thoughts immediately went to Amalia. Anna would take this soup to her if there were any way; Amalia should have it and not she. But of course, that was impossible. She took another sip, grateful and guilty. The paper with the Morgensterns' transport record lay on the table between them.

Marta checked the clock on the wall. "The *Amis* will be here soon, so tell me how I can help you."

Anna put down the cup and pulled another paper and a small pencil from her bag. "I suppose you can tell me everything you know about Herr Morgenstern's collection. Do you know when he was forced to sell?"

Marta's eyes darted back and forth as she consulted her memory. "It was probably in winter of 1939. No, it was before Christmas, so late fall. The Nazis forced all the Jewish gallery owners to sell their inventories to so-called Aryan dealers or gallery owners. Herr Morgenstern sold his to Anton Berg. Well, he was forced to. Do you know him?"

Anna wrote the name down along with the date. She shook her head.

"He turned out to be a real piece of work, that one," Marta said. "He bought the art and promised to keep it in trust for the family until everything went back to normal. But of course, he sold a lot of it to other Aryans. And the Nazis took some, too. He stood to make a killing since he got it from Herr Morgenstern at bargain-basement prices. That was the law, you know. It was terrible. I am happy to know there are still some left that he didn't manage to sell."

Anna nodded her understanding as she scribbled. "We have about fifty of them," she said.

"Well, there used to be a hell of a lot more than fifty. But of course, the problem was that several of the paintings had been called degenerate by Hitler. As if he knew anything about art. Herr Morgenstern was not supposed to have those paintings either; they should have been confiscated and destroyed. But Herr Morgenstern kept them hidden. And they went in the sale to Anton Berg. Then I think Berg didn't want to be caught with them so he hid them."

"Why not just destroy the paintings himself? Or get rid of them? To be safe?" Anna took another sip of soup.

"Oh, he could never do that. They were too valuable. I'm sure he thought the Americans would buy them eventually. No, he had to hang on to them so he could sell them later."

"True. With so many of them destroyed, their value outside of Germany has gone up." Anna looked up from her notes. "Do you remember any specific paintings?"

Marta shook her head. "No, I can't say that I do." She dabbed at her temples again and stood to open the back door, which let in a pleasant cool breeze. She turned toward Anna with a finger extended. "But you know what? I remember that Herr Morgenstern had a painting, it was kind of small with a big blue sky and clouds and some funny looking women. I think it was by that crazy Kirchner—Herr Morgenstern taught me about the paintings all the time. Wanted me to learn. His enthusiasm was so infectious you couldn't help but love these paintings even though, to be honest, I thought some of them were hideous." She smiled at the memory. "Anyway. That little painting. It was his favorite. There was some question about the ownership of that one. Berg didn't want to pay for it because he said he had brought it to the gallery on commission and therefore it was already technically his. And Herr Morgenstern didn't agree. He said it belonged to the gallery and therefore to him, and he didn't want to sell it to Berg. But of course, he had no choice. So they had words over that one."

"And what happened?" Anna's heart leapt a little. The description could be a match for *Berlin 1913*, although 'sky and clouds and funny looking women' could refer to any number of Expressionist works.

Marta shrugged. "It went with all the others. I don't know what happened to it after that." She checked the clock again. "Does that help you?"

"What happened to Anton Berg?"

"He moved away at some point. I think I heard he went to Hamburg or some other place up north. By then it was 1942 and everyone was scattering. Why he would go there, I have no idea. It was worse there than it was here. But I remember feeling relieved that he was gone."

"Did he take any art with him?" Anna asked.

"I don't know, but I wouldn't think so."

"The *Amis* found these paintings in a little old cloister, out near Bensheim. Does that mean anything to you?"

"Bensheim? That makes sense. Berg had a house out there. He was a big shot, of course, with all the right Nazi credentials, so they did whatever he asked. Doesn't surprise me at all."

"You asked me when I came to the door if I was with him. Have you heard from him?"

"Not a peep. I hope he's rotting in hell. It's not right, what he did. If he's not dead, he had better not show his face here." She stood, signaling their time was up. "The *Amis* will be here for their lunch in a few minutes. They run like clockwork when there's food involved."

Anna took the last sip of the soup and Marta took the cup from her. "Good, eh? That will keep you for another day or so."

"You've been most kind," Anna said. "I can't tell you how much you helped."

"Do you want to see a picture? Of the family?" Marta didn't wait for a reply, and began digging through a small handbag she pulled from under the table. "Here." She pushed a small photo toward Anna, its edges worn and pulpy, its surface marred with creases. The square of paper lay between them, its two faces gazing up at them from another time in history. Anna picked up the photo and finally looked into Jacob Morgenstern's face. He sat on a simple wooden chair, his wife standing at his side, her hand resting on his shoulder. He was trim and wore a dark suit. His wavy hair was parted on one side, sweeping across a high forehead. He cocked his head sideways, giving the pose an informality that was helped along by the authentic grin that lit up Elizabeth Morgernstern's face. She wore a light-colored dress with a large floral pattern and stylish boots with buttons that ran in a tight row along her shin. They were the kind of boots all the fashionable ladies had worn when Anna was a child, and she remembered aching for a pair just like the ones this young, beautiful Elizabeth Morgenstern was wearing. She imagined Elizabeth and Jacob sharing an inside joke with the photographer, breaking into laughter as soon as the exposure was complete. They were young and happy, but their expressions revealed something deeper. Was it peace? Or promise? Setting out on their life together, these two people could not possibly have imagined in that moment what their fate held in store.

"That's their engagement photo," Marta said. "It's the only one I have."

"Thank you," Anna replied, pushing the photo back to Marta. She was grateful to have seen Jacob Morgenstern's face, but she could not look at him any longer for fear that she would break down. She would never forget him now.

"If that bastard Berg shows up and tries to tell the *Amis* those paintings are his, you have them come talk to me." Marta shifted gears. "Don't let him get his hands on anything. You know, some people love art for what it is, how it makes them feel when they look at it, how they understand the mind of the artist. That was Herr Morgenstern. He had an exceptional eye for great work. Berg sees money and fancy cocktail parties. He is not worthy of those paintings."

"I promise to do everything I can to find the rightful heirs." Anna extended her hand. "Thank you again."

Marta escorted Anna to the door and they said their goodbyes like old neighbors. Anna was buoyed even though the conversation had not yielded any specific results. It might just have been the cabbage soup, but she was content. With time to kill before Bender and Cooper would return to pick her up, she crossed the street to the building where the children had gone. Was it a school already set up? The front of the building was partially collapsed, so she walked around the side, across the open space they had been using as a playground. Through an open door she could hear voices, an adult admonishing for quiet and the sounds of children laughing. Just the idea of a schoolroom full of children made her happy; it was the simplest thing in the world. If Amalia and Oskar could go to school soon, things would start to feel normal again, even if it were in a half-bombed-out building. She peeked through the door. Children sat on the floor in a neat row, their legs crisscrossed, faces turned up toward the nun who spoke in soft tones at the front of the room. All at once, the little faces lit up in laughter at something the nun had said. Toothless grins and dirty knees wiggled around and one little girl leaned so hard into her neighbor that she caused the whole row of kids to topple. Anna smiled and turned away, not wanting to make her presence known.

She made her way back toward the street, navigating the loose rocks, when she heard American voices across the street. *Amis* were louder than the Germans, which made sense, of course: Their bellies were as full as their coffers. A group of officers turned the corner from the side street, a burst of laughter erupting as one pushed another, apparently the butt of a joke. Anna paid them no mind and made her way across the open lot. A gust of wind kicked up the dirt, and she squinted as it hit her in the face. As she wiped her eyes with her sleeve, she became aware that the *Amis* had gone quiet, and she blinked through the dust to see that one had stopped as the group proceeded.

"Anna?"

Oh, damn. Stuart. He was already crossing the street, walking toward her. He waved at the rest of the group to continue on and grinned his snowcapped grin at her. "What are you doing here?"

Anna blinked to get the dirt from her watering eye, rubbing it with her finger in a vain effort. She tried to keep walking, but stumbled on a loose rock and almost lost her balance. Stuart caught her elbow. "Don't tell me you've come for me?" he said. "All the way back to Frankfurt?"

"Hello, Major," she said as he steered her out of the lot and onto the sidewalk. Once they were on even ground, she took a step away from his grasp. "You're still not in Nuremberg?"

"Not yet. Some other business came up first. And I'm surprised to see you, too, after the other day. I felt you made your intentions perfectly clear." He rubbed his cheek and smiled. Anna felt the urge to slap him again already, and it had only been one minute. "But of course, it's a woman's prerogative to change her mind, and I've already recovered, anyway. And I'm having a late lunch with those gents," he said pointing at the officers who were now climbing the stairs to the door of Jacob Morgenstern's house. They would be having Marta Huber's delicious cabbage soup for lunch. "So I can't stay. I'd invite you, but we have to talk business, you understand."

Anna understood exactly what their business was. The men were all colonels at least, judging by what she could see of their uniforms. They disappeared inside, their voices trailing with them. Stuart, sensing they were now unobserved, took a step closer and tilted his head to talk directly into her ear. "I'm not going to ask why you are lurking around here, but let me tell you something. Your boys over there in Wiesbaden? They're under a direct order from State to fork over that art. You might remind them what happens to people who defy direct orders. I'll have those bastards sent straight to the stockade. No court martial needed."

Anna stepped back to escape his cologne and look him in the eye. "That's beautiful, coming from the man who told me sweet nothings about the righteous justice you're going to be doling out in Nuremberg in a few weeks."

Stuart's eyebrows twitched as his face broke into a smile. "Justice, my dear girl, is in the hands of the victors. Last time I checked, that wasn't the Germans. You play by our rules now. And those idiots in Wiesbaden are no exception. Those paintings are the prize of war and they belong in American museums. Our boys died, you understand? That's worth something to people like us. That's probably not something Germans can understand."

Anna clenched her fist and resisted slapping his face again. He was goading her, and she wouldn't fall for it. Adjusting the strap of her shoulder bag, she said, "I have to go. Enjoy your justice. I hope you choke on it." She pushed past him and crossed the street, not stopping until she was out of his sight, around the corner and along the side street. She stepped behind a low brick wall and waited. Only after she had counted to ten did she pull a Lucky Strike out of her purse and light it. No one came after her.

"I don't like that word *spoils*," Cooper said, tapping the pencil against his lip. He was sitting sideways in his seat in the jeep, resting his shoulder on the metal seat back. "What do you think?"

"How about *prize* of war instead?" Anna suggested.

"I like that," Bender said, biting into a sandwich. "*Prize*. Sounds more egotistical." The jeep was pulled over alongside the road to Wiesbaden. Bender and Cooper had brought sandwiches from the canteen at the IG Farben building, and fizzy purple drinks in glass bottles. Anna was saving hers for Amalia, feeling that two actual meals in one day was far past what she was due. She had walked almost all the way to the headquarters building so as to avoid having the three of them be seen anywhere near the Feldbergstrasse. They had encountered her up on the Furstenbergerstrasse and had turned the jeep straight out of town, not stopping until they were along a quiet section of a side road they had taken as a detour. They had a view of a rolling field in the fresh country, and the songs of chirping birds filled the open space. Here the peace had taken hold properly.

"Okay, let's go with that: *Prize of war.* Read me the sentence so far." Cooper took a drink from his soda.

Anna shuffled the papers in her lap, and when she had them in order, she held them up into the sunlight. She read in a clear and deliberate voice: "We wish to state that from our own knowledge, no historical grievance will rankle so long, or be the cause of so much justified bitterness, as the removal, for any reason, of a part of the heritage of any nation, even if that heritage may be interpreted as a prize of war." She put the papers down. "*Rankle*? Is that a word?"

Cooper nodded. "Means irritation."

Bender held up his sandwich as a point of order. "No, more like resentment. It's more like not being able to get over something. It's like a wound, not an irritation. That's more like an itch."

Cooper made a bemused expression. "Okay, Shakespeare. Resentment."

"That makes sense," Anna said. "I like it."

"We're almost there. I think maybe one more sentence and we've got it. Something that says, 'We are good Americans and that's exactly why we can't follow this order.' How about: 'And though this removal may be done with every intention of charity…'"

"Not *charity*," Bender interrupted. "Those bastards don't have any charitable intentions. Anyway, it sounds condescending. Say *altruism*. It's how they see themselves. As selfless heroes." He snorted.

Anna wrote the sentence down. "Got it." She shifted her feet, wedged uncomfortably in the cramped back seat that was cluttered with the Monuments Men field equipment: clipboards, measuring tape, and the endless boxes and tubes for supplies and plans. She put her feet up partly on the seat to stretch out her legs and rested the paper against a spare clipboard. "What exactly will you do with this document?"

"We're going to get everyone who has the guts to sign it, and then we'll deliver it to your man Stuart on a silver platter," Cooper said. "And *then* you can slap him again."

"Doesn't his threat make you nervous?" Anna asked. "You could get in a lot of trouble."

"We already went to war," Bender said. "What's a little jail time between friends?"

Anna shook her head. "It's not a joke."

"Damn straight, it's not," Cooper grumbled. "That's exactly why we've got to do it. Besides, you'll come visit me in jail, right?" He smiled at her and their eyes met. Anna couldn't help but smile back. Everything was easier with Cooper. He never played by the rules and somehow this made her feel calm. It was inexplicable, given her penchant for obeying and keeping quiet.

Cooper spread his arms and addressed an imaginary audience with the elocution of a puffed-up politician. "We are nonetheless convinced that it is our sense of duty…"

"Individually and collectively…" Bender added in his own baritone.

"…to protest against it." Cooper gestured with a flourish and bowed his head. "There. How about that? Sound okay?"

Anna re-read the sentence. "It needs more. You need a bigger finish."

"All right then. Let's think." Cooper slid out of the jeep and paced alongside it, hands clasped behind his back, face earnest. After several rounds, he stopped and leaned against the jeep, next to Anna. His voice softened as he considered the words one by one. "And state that though our obligations are to the nation to which we owe our allegiance, there are yet further obligations to common justice, decency, and the establishment of the power of right, not of expedience or might, among nations."

Anna scribbled as fast as she could, wishing for the first time in her life she had learned shorthand like her mother had told her. When the words appeared on the page, they both looked them over.

"It's lovely," Anna said.

"Among *civilized* nations," Bender said. "Say that. We are supposed to be civilized."

Cooper pointed to the spot on the page for Anna to insert the word. "Among *civilized* nations."

"Perfect," Anna said as she wrote.

"I feel like Thomas Jefferson," Bender said.

Cooper laughed and slapped his friend on the back. "That's how I'll remember you," he said, climbing into the jeep. He retrieved the boxes of typewriter ribbons from the floor and passed them to Anna. "Will you have time to type this when we get to the CCP?"

"Of course," Anna said.

"Make sure no one sees you," Cooper said. "I mean, *no one.*" He held up an admonishing finger. "Put the paper in my desk when you're finished and lock it. I believe you know where the keys are. Give the key back to me when you're done and then get the hell out of there. I want to keep your hands as clean as possible."

"Yes, boss." She shuffled the papers into her bag. "And I will visit you."

Cooper wrinkled his brow.

"In jail. I will visit you."

He smiled. "Every day?"

"Every day."

Bender laughed. "Stop it, you two. Fraternizing ain't allowed. Not even in my jeep." He reached over to the compartment in front of the passenger seat and pulled it open. "Here, I got these for you, too, Anna." He handed her three packs of Lucky Strikes. "Merry early Christmas," he said, grinding the jeep into gear. They lurched onto the road and drove the rest of the way to Wiesbaden in silence.

chapter fourteen

When Anna left the Collecting Point, she found Amalia waiting at the gate. Anna had typed up the manifesto, twice to be safe, and then put the two copies into Cooper's desk drawer. She checked the drawer's lock three times and put the key in her pocket before pulling the cover on her typewriter and making sure she had the original notes in her bag. She had considered putting them in Cooper's desk, too, but they were in her handwriting, and she thought it better to keep the papers with her. She could burn them in the stove at the house. When she had found Cooper on the loading dock, he was cleaning out the jeep, taking all the boxes and supplies into the Collecting Point. To conceal the key exchange, she had helped pull all the debris out and left the key on the back seat, where he retrieved it and put it in his pocket. They had deposited the supplies in his office and he had sent her home.

Now Anna and Amalia walked home through the cemetery, stopping here and there to study the old headstones. The cemetery was relatively untouched by war, although it was severely neglected. Another cemetery across town had been opened to accommodate all the fresh dead—the bombing victims, the starved, the suicidal, and those whom the war took in any number of ways that didn't directly involve bombs or guns. Those buried here were the historic dead who had the good fortune of missing out on the war, resting here under the tree canopy. *As if they knew better than the rest of us.* It was a peaceful walk where they encountered only a few old women tending graves, against all odds. There were no flowers, of course, but some graves were cleared of weeds and overgrowth, their scrubbed headstones announcing that this person was remembered and loved. Despite the underlying morbidness, Anna liked the place and often cut through it on her way home. The Lange house fronted it on the north end and from the windows in the living room you could see the trees sway in the wind. It was enough to soothe her turbulent mind a little each day.

She and Amalia held hands as they walked along the path, their feet crunching on the gravel. Just as Anna was about to say something about being almost home, the front door of the Lange house opened and a man exited. Anna held Amalia's shoulder to stop her walking; they paused in a patch of shade under a drooping tree. Instinctively, Anna pulled Amalia behind the tree's enormous trunk. Amalia was about to protest but then thought better of it and kept quiet. Anna peered around the tree.

Eva stood inside the opening, slightly behind the door. She waved goodbye with a stiff gesture of her hand, a forced smile on her face. The man seemed jovial and open, not at all furtive, but Anna could tell

Eva was tense. The man put on his hat and turned, buttoning his coat against the cold. Anna recognized him immediately as Herr Spitzer, the old colleague who had visited Manfred Lange. The exchange between him and Eva had not been friendly, she could tell even from a distance.

"I know that man," Amalia said a little too loudly. She was excited to contribute something to the intrigue she had picked up on.

"Yes," Anna said. "He's a friend of Eva's."

"No, I saw him at the black market with Oskar. He's the one in the car that bought all that stuff from us," Amalia said.

Anna regarded her daughter through narrowed eyes. "*Maus*, are you sure about that? How can you tell all the way from here?"

"I just can. He has the same face. And the same hat, too."

"He bought Herr Lange's books from you at the black market? Did he know what they were?"

"Not just the books. Everything. He acted normal like anyone else. Why?"

Anna turned her head to follow Spitzer's path along the sidewalk. "*Maus*, go in the house and go to our room, all right? Don't tell Fraulein Lange anything. I'll be there in a few minutes."

"But, Mama..."

"Go," Anna gave her a little push. "Everything's fine, don't worry. I forgot something at work."

Amalia complied, skipping across the street and up the stairs to the Lange's door, which she pushed open and then closed behind her without a look back. Anna took a moment to collect her thoughts. Why would Eva's boyfriend buy her father's belongings on the black market? It made no sense at all. If she needed the money it was a convoluted way to go about it. Was she hiding something? Was he?

Anna hurried on the side of the street opposite to Spitzer, who was strolling, heading east on the Johannes-Maass Strasse. Weaving in and out of headstones and the shrubs in the cemetery, she tried to go as fast as she could without drawing attention to herself, or worse, falling down. When Spitzer took a left turn, putting him on the street that defined the eastern perimeter of the cemetery, Anna abandoned her parallel track and cut through diagonally to the other end of the park, emerging at the southeastern corner where the street was busier. She was out of breath and her shoes were caked in mud. Taking a moment to compose herself, she started up the street. One last deep breath and she raised her head and lengthened her steps.

"Oh, Herr Spitzer, is it?" she exclaimed when he was within arm's reach, having approached from the opposite direction. Spitzer looked confused, then placed her, and smiled. "Frau Klein. How nice to see you." He extended a hand and smiled, ushering her out of the flow of foot traffic.

"What brings you back to Wiesbaden?" Anna asked. "Or have you been here all along?"

"No, no, I've been gone. Just got back today," he said. He retrieved a pack of cigarettes from his coat pocket and offered one to Anna, which she accepted. They were Russian cigarettes, which tasted like pure fire and dirt and scorched her lungs on the way in as well as on the way out. It was like inhaling a smokestack. She suppressed a cough.

"Sorry, they're rough, I know. It was all I could get."

She examined the smoldering tip as if it would provide some clues. "Where do you get these?"

"Mostly east of here. The closer you get to the border, the more stuff spills over."

"Does that go both ways?"

"I guess so. Why, do you have something to send to the east?"

"No," Anna lied, but she was thinking of her letter to Thomas. Sending it with a black marketeer might be the way to go, since the post was unreliable. Could he be trusted to deliver a letter without reading it? She inhaled again, bracing herself for the burn. "I guess you are well versed in the black market?" she said, deciding to pose it as an idle question.

"Not really. Why do you say that?"

"No reason. I thought that's what you were referring to. It seems I am well behind the curve on the black market," she said. "My child knows more than I do."

He laughed. "Yes, I've heard that kids are the toughest sellers. I steer clear, myself."

"You don't go?"

He shook his head. "No, never have. It makes me feel quite sleazy to even think about it. I'm an accountant, you recall. All above board."

Anna shrouded her prodding with a joke. "Not even these fantastic Russian cigarettes?"

A cloud of suspicion moved across Spitzer's face. "No. Why this line of questioning, officer?"

Anna waved the cigarette in front of her face. "Oh, no reason. I thought I was the only one." She tried to laugh it off, but Spitzer's expression had hardened. It was subtle, but it was there. She took a pull on her cigarette to buy herself time. "Anyway. I trust things are going well for you?" She coughed.

He puffed up a little. "Yes. Actually, I will be going to France next week. It looks like the Frogs can use my services, just as you suggested."

"Doing what?"

"Bookkeeping, mostly. It'll do for now." He grinned. Now Anna understood why the questions about the black market were unwelcome. Spitzer was a man who operated at the table, not under it. At least that's the image he displayed. It still didn't explain why he was buying Eva's belongings at the market and why he was lying about it.

"That is good news indeed," she granted. "I'm sorry, I've forgotten the name of the company where you worked?"

Now Spitzer was suspicious. She had overstepped. "I never said." He took a drag from his cigarette.

Anna wanted to kick herself. "I was just wondering how you and Eva met, that's all. How your paths might have crossed."

He licked his lips and paused as he scanned her face. "I worked for the museum where her father was a curator for a while. That's how we met. But then the war and the bombs. You know the story."

Anna wasn't getting any more information out of him. Instead, he turned the tables on her.

"Are you still living at the Lange house? I really should stop by and see Herr Doktor and Eva on this visit." He dropped his cigarette to the ground and put it out with his shoe.

Anna tried to conceal her surprise. "Oh, I thought that's where you are coming from now." She gestured up the street.

"No, no. Haven't been to see them yet," he lied. "But please do give Eva my best. I hope to stop by before I leave for Paris. And anyway, I will write and let them know about my placement once I'm settled."

"Yes," Anna said, twisting the tobacco out of the cigarette and stepping on the glowing ember that fell to the ground. "I had better get home. It's getting late." She extended her hand and Spitzer obliged her with a handshake. They said their goodbyes, with Spitzer promising again to visit. Anna resisted the urge to look over her shoulder until she was well down the street. When she finally turned to see, Spitzer had already disappeared.

She stood rooted to the spot. Something was wrong. Why would he lie about having been to see Eva? Yes, he was married, but Anna had already seen him there, so why did he care? Why did he deny going to the black market? Anna checked her watch. It was nearly five o'clock. If she could get to the Collecting Point before the guard shifted into nighttime mode and entry was more difficult, maybe she could still catch Cooper. Maybe he would have some answers. She accelerated to a jog for as long as her body would allow, which was only for a few steps. Soon enough, she was out of breath and had to resort back to a quick walk. Still, she made good time and found herself heading down the Wilhelmstrasse in a few minutes. The dusk was turning to dark, and the people were hurrying to wherever they spent the night. She started jogging again and said a little prayer of thanks when she spotted Corporal Long still at the guard gate. He never asked any questions and always waved her through. Anna made a perfunctory gesture with her hand to greet him as she passed the barrier.

"He's not here, Frau Klein," Long said, stepping out of the guard house. "Captain Cooper, I mean. I take it that's why you're here?"

"Oh? He left already?" She checked the time. "That's not like him."

"It didn't look like he was going for cocktail hour," Long said. "Him and Corporal Bender, they sped out of here like a bat out of hell. Not more than five minutes ago."

Anna stopped, thankful to at least catch her breath. "Do you have any idea where they were going?"

"Nope. They headed south, so could be anywhere." He pointed to his left. "Train station? Frankfurt? Air base? Who knows. Was there something I can help you with?" He smiled, knowing his offer was futile. Anna had a soft spot for Long, and she could tell he had the same for her.

"No, thank you, Corporal." She peered up at the building. A few lights glowed through the windows here and there, but most things were shut down at dark to conserve electricity. Cooper often stayed late, and it was his habit to switch lights on and off as he moved through the building. Only the bright perimeter security lights cast a foggy glow onto the building and the grounds around it.

"Do you ever do the night watch?" she asked.

"Not really," Long replied. "They leave that to the MPs. That way they can arrest people on the spot. I'm mostly here for decoration during the day."

Anna nodded. "You do make the place look nice," she said. "Well, good night." She turned to go and then stopped. "Corporal, has Fraulein Lange ever come back after hours? Would you remember if she did?"

Long scanned his memory as he chewed on his thumbnail. When a memory resurfaced, he lit up. "One time, yeah. But she was with Captain Cooper. What I mean to say is, she got here and then he showed up a minute later. She was telling me how she forgot her sweater inside and it's the only one she had and it was going to be cold that night. Could she run back in and get it. I was about to say sure— anyway, what do I care?— but then Cooper showed up, too, coming back from some field survey, and they went inside. By the time she left, I had already gone, so the night guard must have let her out."

"Did it seem like she took a long time to fetch her sweater?"

"Sure it did, but Cooper was there, too, so what could I say? My shift ended fifteen minutes later, so it's not like it was hours."

"But you didn't see her come out?"

"Nope. I didn't see anything. Why do you ask? You think something's up with them? I don't think you need worry about her, Frau Klein." He leaned in conspiratorially.

Anna felt herself blush. "No, it's not that, I'm just..." she stopped and exhaled. Long grinned at her. "I am not worried," she said, defensively.

"Good, because, first of all, everyone knows he's pretty sweet on you, and second, she's in cahoots with that Major Stuart. She set her sights pretty high, I guess."

"What are you talking about?"

"Oh, come on. Cooper? He's totally smitten. Don't say you didn't know. He thinks you hung the moon. His face goes all gooey when he talks about you."

"No, not that," Anna squirmed. "Eva. What about her and Stuart?"

"Oh, that. Stuart's the one that got her the job here. You didn't know that? Signed off on it himself. That's why I let her get her damn sweater. I figured no reason to have Stuart come after me if his squeeze got a little chilly. You never know with these people. The slightest thing gets them all up in arms. And I know we've got enough trouble." He looked around. "Cooper's told you, right? About the paintings?"

"Yes, I know about those. How do you know about Eva?"

Long hedged. "A little birdie told me. Farmer was basically forced to hire her. Didn't think much of it until Stuart started up with all his crap. Now Stuart's got them all backed into a corner. It's like you give a guy an inch, and well, you know." He looked around. "But you didn't hear that from me."

Anna was barely listening. Eva had pretended to swoon over Stuart when Anna had told her about the invitation for drinks. She had even let Anna wear her clothes, never letting on for one second that she even knew Stuart, much less owed him her job.

"Did you ever see them together?"

Long shook his head slowly. "Can't say that I did." He lifted a finger. "Wait. One night, Stuart gave her a ride home in his car. She had been here a little late, and he was just leaving. She came out and was heading toward the gate. I heard her say she had to take some items to Captain Cooper at his barracks. She was carrying some papers and stuff that looked like plans. You know, architectural plans they draw up of the old churches? He offered her a ride and she climbed in. This was maybe two weeks ago. That's the only time I saw them together. Why?"

"She said she was going to his barracks?" Anna asked. "Isn't that strange?"

"I would say so," Long agreed. "But you know, a lot of strange stuff goes on around here. It's like we make it up as we go along. Yeah, I'd say it was strange that she would take something to an officer's barracks."

"Especially since Cooper doesn't live in the barracks. He is billeted in a house on the Hellmund Strasse," she said. "That's what he told me," she added, but Long was already giving her a knowing look.

"Uh-huh. All I know is they got in the car and took off thataway." He pointed up the Wilhelmstrasse toward the Eagle Club and Eva's house. The main Army barracks were in the other direction, at the old Air Force base. Long recognized Anna's confusion. "Yep, that's what I thought, too," he said. "But here's the even weirder part. Next morning? I wasn't on duty yet, but I was getting to my post. I saw her walking in with all the same papers and junk in her hand. She told the guard that Cooper had asked her to pick it up from some other officer. But it was the same stuff."

"You said she had architectural plans? You saw them?"

"Yeah, she had one of those cardboard tubes the architects are always carrying. Those are for plans, aren't they?"

Anna's face turned hot, as if she had flipped a switch. "She had the tube on the way out and on the way in, too?"

"Yep. Like I said: She left late with Stuart and got here early the next day. I didn't think a thing about it at the time. You think she's screwing around with Stuart and never went home or to the barracks?"

Anna's heart revved to an alarming pace. She glanced at her watch. "I have to go," she said. "Thank you, Corporal."

Long grinned. "For what?"

"For answering all my questions," she called over her shoulder as she walked in the direction of the Hellmund Strasse.

Anna tried her best to tuck her freezing fingers up inside the sleeve of her threadbare coat, but it didn't help much. The sun had gone down long ago, and a cold night had set in. She had waited, sitting on the stoop of Cooper's building after no one answered the bell. But after only a few minutes, she was accosted by a group of loud and drunk GIs, who offered her a pack of cigarettes for her services and proceeded to grab at her and push her into the wall. She managed to kick one of them hard enough to send him reeling and get their attention. She told them she was waiting for Captain Cooper, knowing full well what that implied, but not caring. Let them try to mess with her knowing a superior officer might show up at any moment. The soldiers staggered on, cursing at her and calling her names, their voices echoing on the nearly empty street. An old woman sitting at a dimly lit window in the house across the street had watched the scene, and when Anna sat back down, she caught her eye. The woman spat out the window in the general direction of the Americans, and Anna smiled.

Now she decided to walk around the block, thinking it would warm her up and make her less of a sitting target for drunk soldiers looking for some fun. The wind had picked up, and with the anemic street lighting, the ruined buildings took on a frightening quality. Here and there brightly lit apartments glowed like beacons. Americans were billeted there, making a show of using their unrationed electricity with abandon. She glimpsed little vignettes through sheer curtains, an *Ami* sitting at a desk here, three officers around a table eating steaming bowls of soup there. She kept walking, checking the time to be sure she would make it back home in time for curfew. Amalia would be wondering where she was. Had she told her not to say anything about the man from the black market? She couldn't remember now.

As the minutes ticked on and her feet grew numb from the cold, she considered what she was hoping to achieve. She knew it was Eva who had replaced the painting, and now she knew how she had done it. She had rolled the canvases up inside the cardboard tubes the *Amis* used for the plans and drawings. The tubes were plentiful; Cooper had five or six stashed in his office. People were always coming and going with them, but there were strict protocols on what left the building. Stuart, for all his bureaucratic infatuation, probably didn't concern himself with such minor details. *Or he was in on the plan.* Anna chewed the inside of her cheek as she considered this possibility. She turned the corner back onto the Hellmund Strasse. Another clump of

GIs was coming at her, this group less drunk. She shoved her hands into her pockets and walked on, not daring to cross the street, as that would be an obvious avoidance tactic, which would invite their attention. This group hardly noticed her as they carried on a good-natured argument about the symptoms of various venereal diseases. She could see why they ignored her altogether.

The problem that gnawed at Anna was that even if she could reasonably argue that the Nolde and the Kirchner paintings currently stored at the Collecting Point were fakes and that Eva had switched them out, without the real paintings, she had very little leg to stand on. They could be halfway to Moscow by now. And who had painted the fakes? It had to have been some time ago; oil paint takes weeks to dry. This was a long-term plot that had been hatched well before Eva set foot in the Collecting Point. Anna couldn't get her head around it. She had decided to make one more turn around the block and then go home when a jeep sped past her and stopped abruptly in the middle of the empty road.

"Anna? What the hell? Is everything okay?" Cooper jumped out of the driver's side.

Before Cooper could get to her, she blurted out. "Did Eva ever come here at night? To see you?"

"What?" Cooper put an arm on her shoulder to guide her toward the jeep. "Eva? Come here? No. I thought we covered this already."

Anna was undeterred. "Are you sure? Have you met her somewhere after work? Somewhere else? The barracks, maybe?"

"The barracks? Why the hell would I meet her there? What are you talking about? Come on, get in the jeep. It's freezing out here." He pushed her into the passenger seat and climbed over her into the driver's side. "Let's keep moving. Less tongue-wagging that way."

Anna glanced at the woman in her dim window who was still watching the scene as Cooper put the jeep into gear. “We’ll go around the back,” Cooper said. “And you,” he pointed at Anna, “start over. Slower, this time.”

“Has she ever delivered anything to you?” Anna changed gears. “Papers from the Collecting Point?”

“No, of course not. That’s against the rules, you know that. Even I’m not that stupid,” he said. “Look, we’re going inside and then you’d better tell me what the hell is going on.”

Cooper turned the jeep into the alley behind the building, switching off the engine and letting it coast to a stop. They climbed out and Anna followed Cooper through a heavy glass door that looked to have been transferred from some other industrial building. They climbed two flights of stairs in silence, not switching on the light, and Cooper jingled through his keys at the door marked 2G. She stood on the dark landing, uneasy and nervous. She was on the verge of breaching an invisible boundary that had existed between them. She had never entered the realm of his life outside the CCP. Was he aware of the line they were crossing? Was that why his hand was unsteady? She glanced at the two closed doors that led to other apartments on the same floor and then stared at the floor. She didn’t want to give prying eyes the benefit of seeing her face. When Cooper pushed the door open, he stepped aside to let her in before closing the door quietly behind them. They had not spoken a word since they entered the building. She followed him down a narrow hallway and waited as he switched on a lamp to reveal a small living room.

“Home sweet home,” he said, closing the curtain. “Make yourself comfortable.”

A tired sofa and two chairs took up most of the small space. Books lined a shelf under the window, and a radio balanced on a small table next to a puffy green chair. A pile of English language books lay on the rickety wooden table in front of the sofa. Stale smells hung in the air, like the place had not been aired out in weeks. It was a friendly comfortable apartment with traditional decorative touches, probably a haven for whatever German family had lived here. What had happened to the people whose bed Cooper was sleeping in? She sat down on the edge of the sofa without taking off her coat.

"I have to get back soon. The curfew…" she said.

"I'll get you back safely," Cooper said. "Don't worry. Where's Amalia?"

"At home, but I didn't think I'd be gone this long. I had to come talk to you."

"About what?" Cooper held his hand over the radiator under the window. "Come on," he muttered. "Damn thing takes forever."

Anna wanted to say something about how neither radiators nor lamps worked in houses where Germans lived, but that was pointless. She wiggled her frozen toes inside her boots, ignoring the holes in her socks.

Cooper sat on the chair near the radiator. "Tell me what?" he said again. "Who is Herr Spitzer? Does he have a first name?"

"I don't know his first name," she said, "but he's a friend of Eva's. A close friend."

"So?"

Anna took a breath. "Something's not right with him."

She told Cooper about the coincidences—Spitzer's apparent relationship with Eva, Amalia recognizing him as the man from the black market, and his lying about visiting the Lange house. "I saw him come out of the house, but when I pretended to bump into him down the street, he claimed not to have been there."

Cooper squinted at her. "I'm confused. Even if he bought stuff from the kids at the black market—why does that matter?"

"Why would he buy Eva's belongings? It makes no sense."

"She needed money and he was doing her a favor? You said he's married? Maybe it's a cover to give her some money. What did he buy, exactly?"

"That's just it, it was a bunch of art books and some household items. I can't make sense of it." She inhaled and held her breath as the thought hit her. "Oh no, the rug. It's the rug."

"What do you mean? What rug?"

"Amalia said he never even unrolled the rug. It was too heavy, and Spitzer bought everything sight unseen. Put it all in his car and drove off."

"I'm still lost," Cooper said. "Try again. You really need to slow down, for my sake."

Anna leaned forward, her hands waving and punching the air to emphasize each point as she spoke. "Let's say Eva is the one who switched out the paintings at the Collecting Point. She took the real paintings and put the fakes into the original frames. Then, let's say she sold the real ones to Spitzer on the black market. That it was all a set-up, sending the children there with those things. They were a decoy for the rug. The rug that had the paintings rolled up inside."

Cooper chuckled. "That sounds pretty far-fetched, but I'll go with you for now. But tell me, Agatha Christie, how did Eva waltz out of the CCP with two oil paintings under her arm?"

"Not under her arm," Anna said, "but right under our noses." She stood and went to the desk in the far corner of the room and picked up a cardboard tube that leaned against the chair. She balanced it on her open palms as she held it out for Cooper.

"Oh, come on. In one of those? She can't leave the building with one of those, you know that. No material leaves the building."

"You know that, and I know that, but do you think someone who is visiting knows that? Someone who might already be smitten with Fraulein Lange? Someone who knows her a lot better than he's letting on?"

Cooper shook his head. "Who?"

"Stuart."

Cooper groaned. "Oh, Christ. Now you think Stuart is in on this?"

"Maybe. Or he's an unwitting accomplice. Stuart was the brass who got her the job at the CCP. He was the one who pressured Farmer to hire her. What if Eva convinced Stuart to get her the job at the CCP and he's just the means to the end? Maybe the whole thing was set up by her."

Cooper nodded, his eyes focused on a spot on the floor. "Farmer said she had already been vetted and was cleared. I never saw her Fragebogen myself, but he said her credentials were impeccable. You have something with his signature that proves Stuart got her the job?"

"Not exactly."

Cooper rolled his eyes. "Well, can you at least tell me how you know it was Stuart?"

Anna smiled. "A little birdie told me."

"Okay, you're not gonna tell me. Fine. But at least tell me how you know about the tube."

"I went to the Collecting Point earlier to look for you, but you had just left. I started chatting with Corporal Long. We got to talking about who sometimes stayed late at work, and he told me he saw Eva catch a ride with Stuart one night a couple of weeks ago. She had stayed late and come out of the building with one of these tubes and some papers with her. He heard her tell Stuart she was taking them to you. Stuart offered her a ride, which she took."

"That's nuts. There are about fifteen things against protocol in that scenario. Even Stuart knows better than that." Cooper stood and walked to the radiator, holding his hand over it again. He turned to Anna, eyes firing. "Either he's an idiot and he overlooked it or he let her get away with it because she's his mistress?"

"Or they're in on it together and that exchange was for the benefit of whomever might be listening."

"Like Corporal Long."

Anna nodded. "Who wouldn't question the actions of a senior officer."

"Especially if that senior officer was already putting the CCP in the line of fire. Everyone is avoiding tangling with that guy." He rubbed his hands together as he ruminated.

Anna jumped ahead. "She brought the tube back with her in the morning. Long saw that, too. She came in early carrying the same stuff. It was a different guard on duty, but Long had already arrived for the shift change and saw her. She probably tried to beat the shift change on purpose in case Long had noticed her the night before."

"God bless Corporal Long." Cooper collapsed onto the chair and leaned back. "I guess Eva has some explaining to do. But this is all pretty circumstantial, and you're making a very serious accusation. Not just against Eva, but against Stuart, too. And you know how much he loves us already. And anyway, you're still missing the last piece."

Ann exhaled. "I know. We need the forger and the paintings. The real ones. God knows where they are by now."

"Could still be right under our noses. Maybe in the house somewhere," Cooper offered. "Could be hanging in some major's quarters." He laughed at his own joke.

"Could be in Moscow," Anna said. "But there is one more thing. The housekeeper at Jacob Morgenstern's house told me that Morgenstern and his business partner, a man named Anton Berg, had a fight over that specific Kirchner painting. Each claimed it as his, but Morgenstern eventually won out. That can't be a coincidence either. We have to consider that this was a plot hatched a long time ago. You can't fake and replace an oil painting overnight."

Cooper started to speak, but then let her continue.

"Somehow Spitzer is involved. He says he's an accountant, but he doesn't seem like the type."

"What does that mean?"

"His clothes are too elegant, too refined. Accountants don't dress like that."

Cooper shook his head. "That's pretty weak sauce you're cooking there."

"Maybe, but something is going on with him. He's lying. It's all connected. I just can't figure out how."

They sat without speaking for a few minutes. Anna churned the events and possible explanations over in her mind. Everything returned to the fact that they needed the original paintings, they needed to catch the forger, and they needed to prove without a doubt it was Eva who had made the switch.

Anna sat up. "I think the forger has been trying to talk to me."

"What?"

"There's a man who showed up at the house and then he also came to the CCP asking for me. Amalia said he had dirty fingernails and smelled like gasoline. Karla said the same. What if they mean he smells like turpentine? They aren't that different."

"Well, where is this man?"

"I don't know. I don't know his name. I've never even seen him myself."

"Well, that's not helpful, Anna. If we're going to pin this crazy story on Eva, it's going to have to stick. Otherwise we are truly sunk. You and me both. I'm already on shaky ground. Stuart will take me down to cover his own ass. Won't even blink doing it, either. And he'll leave you on the side of the road, too, if not worse."

Anna slumped back down. She rested her elbows on her knees and buried her face in her hands. "Why can't people be normal and decent anymore? I thought Eva was my friend," she whined. "Why would she do this? God, you can't trust anyone at all."

"People are desperate. If this is true, she has a reason for doing this. It might even be a very good reason. She needs the money. She's paying a debt. Maybe she's even been coerced. Did you ever think of that?"

"I need to get home. Now I don't know what to think." She turned to Cooper. "What do we do now?"

"Keep laying low for now. We're filing the manifesto tomorrow morning; sending it to Frankfurt. That will surely bring Stuart back to town in a hurry. I'd say he'll be here by tomorrow afternoon."

"Then what?"

"Let's plan to be in my office at the same time, say at thirteen hundred. Just be going about your business and we'll meet up. If Eva is around, I'll make up some ruse that we need to leave. Then we'll decide what to do."

"Tomorrow is Wednesday." Anna shifted her weight on the sofa.

"So?"

"So, it's only three days until Oskar's transported to Bavaria. I'm so worried for him."

"I know you're worried," Cooper said, reaching for her hand. "It's going to be okay. I'm working on it. I haven't forgotten about him." He squeezed her hand. "Do you trust me?"

"But time is running out. I can't just let him go. I'll take him off the train myself if I have to." *And you can't fix everything.* Panic rose in her chest.

"It's not going to come to that. You've just got to trust me."

Anna said nothing. She did trust him. It was the bureaucratic machine that she didn't trust. It rolled over them with no exceptions and no consideration for the complexities of human lives.

"Wait, that reminds me," Cooper said. "I've got something for you."

He went into the bedroom, switching on the light as he disappeared inside. Anna could see an unmade bed and a stack of neatly pressed uniforms set on a low dresser. Books teetered on the bedside table and papers were strewn on the bed. He re-emerged with an open cardboard box, which he set on the coffee table as he lowered himself onto the sofa next to Anna. The worn cushions banked toward each other under his weight, and Anna allowed herself to lean into him. He felt warm and solid and smelled of soap. She peered into the box, which was stuffed with newspaper.

"My mom sent a care package," he said, digging through the contents. "Here. For you and Amalia." He held up two pairs of thick wool socks, one larger pair in blue, the smaller pair in yellow. "Go on, take them."

"But those are… Why are you giving them to me?" she asked. They were soft and she instinctively put them to her nose. They smelled of soap, too. Everything American smelled clean.

"I am giving them to you because she sent them specifically for you."

"You told her about us? Me and Amalia?"

"I told her I met a smart woman who is working with me and that she has a daughter and that it's going to get damned cold. I told her the German people are suffering and that the winter will take a heavy toll. That there's not enough food or clothing, and that women and children are being made to pay a heavy price for the idiocies of us men in uniform. I told her that I hoped you would be safe and that you would stay at the Collecting Point because we really need you." He cleared his throat. "And I told her that maybe one day she would meet you, too." He avoided her stare by reaching back into the box, this time producing a jar with a brown paste in it. "And this is for you, too. Do you know what this is?"

Anna was thankful to have the jar to focus on instead of what Cooper's words implied. "Peanut butter," she read from the label. "*Erdnuss Butter*. I've heard you Americans love this."

"You put it on bread, with jelly, or whatever you like. Or by itself. It'll keep you full for hours." He sifted through the box again. "Oh, and this is for Amalia." He held up a little wool sweater, dark green with little red ladybugs knitted along the bottom. There were red buttons down the front and little green bows at the ends of the sleeves. "I think it'll fit, don't you?"

Anna was stunned. She felt the urge to cry again. It was the most beautiful sweater she had ever seen. Amalia would love it, too. It would be the nicest gift she had received in a very long time. She swallowed hard. "I don't know what to say," she mumbled, her voice hoarse with emotion. "I don't deserve this." It was the first thought that came to her.

"Stop that, now. You deserve every chance to be happy. God, I wish you could see that." He shook his head. "I wish I could make you understand. Please, don't start crying. It's supposed to make you happy." He leaned into her a little more. "Think she'll like it?"

"Yes."

"Yeah, me too." He folded it in half and gave it to her. "I hope so. My mother knitted it herself."

Now the tears came. For days her emotions had swirled and she had tried to ignore them, but now there was no stopping the flood. Cooper sighed. He put his arm around her and pulled her close.

"It really is going to be okay, Anna. One way or another." He whispered into the top of her head, his breath warm on her scalp. She nodded and wiped her eyes with the back of her sleeve.

"I want to write your mother a letter, to say thank you."

"She'd like that a lot."

He smiled at her with his whole face, so close she felt his breath on her lips. She pulled him toward her. Their lips met, and this time they stayed. His hand moved to her cheek and their bodies moved instinctively toward each other. She was utterly lost, as if the kiss had swallowed her into a warm pool. She felt submerged and languid, like she had come home after a long time away. She heard his breath and dared not open her eyes in case she broke the spell. They stayed together like this for as long as they dared, and then she felt him pull away.

She sat up, averting her eyes, afraid of meeting his, in case they had come back to the reality of being in this room, in this place.

"Look, I don't quite know what to make of what's happening here. With us," Cooper said, his gaze directed at the floor between his feet. "You've gotten under my skin. But I'm not one to mess with another man's wife. And I know you're not that kind of woman either. I think maybe fate has set us on a course that we can't fully control. I know that sounds dumb." He turned to look at her, taking her hand. "I came here to do a job, that's all. Nothing more ever entered my mind. But here you are, Anna. And I'm afraid that my feelings are getting the better of me. I don't even dare acknowledge them because I know you'll probably return to your husband. And you should. I know you love him." He held up a hand to stop her interrupting. "I'm just asking you to not draw this out. I said we need you at the CCP. You are invaluable to me and to the operation. But if that work is about to end, then maybe the best thing for you to do is to go home and rebuild your life there." He started to say something more but stopped, scanning her face for a reply.

Anna's face burned. She swallowed hard. "I never asked you if there's someone waiting for you at home. I didn't want to know, honestly." It was her turn to look at the floor. A small cigarette burn along the edge of the rug made her fumble into her bag for a cigarette as a distraction. Cooper reached for her arm to stop her.

"No, there isn't. There's no one. But I want you to know, I can't go on like this much longer. Everything is changing. You know better than I do that nothing is promised."

Anna nodded. His outright decency made her feel ashamed and small. She had been comfortable in the limbo that she had allowed herself to create. Neither here nor there. But it was time. She ran a finger along her lip. Outside, a jeep engine echoed through the empty streets, and under the window the radiator gurgled. She thought of her mother for the first time in days. Since her death, Anna had felt like an orphan, waiting for some salvation. She tried to conjure that feeling now, but it wouldn't come.

"I *am* home," she said.

Cooper shook his head, confused.

"You said maybe I should go home. I think I am home."

He squeezed her hand hard, wrapping his fingers around hers. It was not a romantic gesture, more a defiant one. *We are in this mess together.* Anna wanted to never let go, but he released her hand and patted her knee. "We better get you home. Tomorrow's a big day."

"Will you give me your mother's name, so I can write to her? I'll do it as soon as I can. But I have another letter to finish first." Anna pushed herself out of the sofa's soft cushions. She held out a hand to help Cooper up. "And I'm ready for whatever's next."

Cooper let her pull him to his feet. "Me, too." His eyes flashed, but his face was drained with worry.

Anna had just turned the key in the lock, jumping as the bolt disengaged and made a click that echoed along the foggy street. She pushed the door to the Lange house open and was about to step inside when she caught something moving out of the corner of her eye. A figure stood in the shadow under the kitchen window. She turned for one last look down the road, but Cooper's jeep had already pulled away after dropping her at the end of the road to avoid any direct associations. The open door beckoned and her heart raced, but she stopped, her hand still on the key. She forced herself to look in the direction of the shape, focusing her eyes as they adjusted to the darkness.

"Frau Klein?" the voice whispered. "Don't be sacred. It's me, Oskar."

Anna collapsed into a sigh of relief before realizing what his presence in front of the house meant.

"Oh my God, Oskar. What are you doing here? You can't be here," she whispered, her eyes scanning the darkened windows of the nearby houses. She gathered him in her arms and took him inside. When she closed the door behind them, she turned to look at him. He was shivering, in nothing but a light sweater and his usual knee-length pants. He tried to hide his chills by crossing his arms, ready for the lecture he knew was coming. Anna decided to surprise him.

"So you've run away," she said, matter of fact. "It's about time. What took you so long?" The house was dark and quiet, the door to their bedroom closed. It was well after ten o'clock, and it looked like everyone was asleep.

Oskar tilted slightly toward her as if he had been braced for an onslaught that was not forthcoming. He scanned Anna's face for clues as to her disposition, unsure of what to do.

"Amalia will be so happy to see you," she continued. "But let's not wake her now. You can surprise her in the morning." She put down her bag and Cooper's package before taking off her coat.

"Where have you been?" Oskar asked, finally. "I was waiting for hours."

"Oh, you know. I had things to do," she said. "Come on, I have some of this American peanut butter stuff. We can try it together." She walked to the kitchen, tested the light switch, and then opted for the kerosene lamp that sat on the small table. "Come on," she coaxed.

"You were with the *Ami?*" Oskar asked. "He gave you that stuff?" His tone indicated he didn't approve. It might have been all right before, but it wasn't anymore. His loyalties had shifted. She sat down at the table and gestured for him to join her, which he did, perching on the edge of the stool, ready to bolt. Anna opened the jar of peanut butter and dug in with a soup spoon, offering a generous scoop to the boy.

She watched as he tried a small taste first, then a larger mouthful. A smile broke through his practiced scowl, despite his efforts to conceal it. Anna smiled back. She was happy to see him, but she knew his running away from the camp would solve nothing. They sat for a while, Oskar working on the spoonful of peanut butter and Anna considering their predicament. Cooper said he was working to help the boy, but what would happen if he had to go to Bavaria before Cooper could stop it? Or what would happen if he didn't go back to the camp? Neither scenario was a good one. She could hide him, but only for so long. They already knew where to look for him, and they would be on her doorstep first thing in the morning. It would solve nothing in the long term. A deep-seated discomfort rose from her core. To her own profound horror, she knew she was talking herself into sending him back to the camp. Not into running away, not into hiding, but into going back, into being checked off the list, and getting on the train to Bavaria. Into being a good German. There would be a way to save him still. She just had to get the right *Ami* on her side. She would make a legitimate claim for the boy, adopt him, or do whatever it took through the proper legal channels. To do that, she had to play by the rules, at least for now. She tried to convince herself that this was the righteous choice, that the days of subterfuge were over, that justice had prevailed and would prevail in the case of Oskar. She shook her head as she thought these things, disbelieving her own lies. This is what it had come to.

"I didn't run away." Oskar screwed the lid back on the jar. "I'm going back, don't worry."

"What?"

"I already tried to run away once, but they caught me. I didn't even get very far. I don't want to live on the street like before, and I can't live with you. So I'll go back to the camp and be this person they want me to be. I was never really Oskar Gruenewald anyway, that was what my German parents named me when they adopted me. Now they tell me my name is Novak. So, all right, I'll be Novak. I'll speak Polish. And I'll go live in Poland." He fidgeted with the frayed hem of his shorts. "I don't even know where Poland is."

Anna searched for words but none came. She should talk him out of it, she should tell him that she will hide him from the *Amis*, tell him it will all be all right. But the words dissolved on her tongue and there was only silence.

"So, I came to say goodbye." Oskar looked at her. "You were so nice to me, and I don't want you to get in trouble. But I wanted to tell you that I'll miss you. And Amalia, too." His jaw worked at holding back the tears that flooded his eyes. Anna took his face in her hands and wiped his cheeks.

"Oskar, you aren't going to Bavaria," she blurted. "You'll see. I'm going to fix it. I promised you I would, and I will." She shifted her gaze out the window to avert her eyes from his. He knew she was lying, and so did she.

"Oskar?" Amalia stood in the doorway, hair askew and eyes thick with sleep. "Are you back?" she whispered, her voice rising with hope.

Oskar shook his head.

"Oskar just came for a quick visit," Anna interjected. "Didn't you?"

He nodded, more to himself than anything, and offered a sweet smile to Amalia, who returned it in spades. She padded over to him and wrapped her skinny arms around his neck, burying her head into his shoulder. "I missed you."

Anna thought of the looming train ride only three days away that would put hundreds of kilometers between them and make it very likely that they would never see Oskar again. She forced herself to remember that there might be a birth mother in Poland aching for her lost son, maybe a father and brothers and sisters. None of it made her feel any better. What a mess they had made. And what a mess the peace was turning into. Maybe Cooper would still fix it, but she wasn't hopeful.

"*Maus*, you go back to bed now," she said, pulling Amalia away. There was no point in prolonging the pain. "We'll see Oskar again soon. But for now, he has to go."

Amalia resisted, but even Oskar pushed her away, eager to end the long goodbye. "I have to get back before they do the bed check," he said. "Otherwise all hell breaks loose."

Amalia, sensing they were serious, chose to not argue. She stopped in the doorway and gave Oskar a little wave, her hand by her cheek, face crinkled with worry.

When she was gone, Oskar stood and made his best big-boy expression, the one that said nothing was a big deal, that he could handle whatever came his way.

"How will you get back?" Anna asked.

"The same way I came, through the cemetery and then through the old town. I cut through the ruins in the Schwalbacher Strasse and then climb through a hole in the fence at the camp. It doesn't take long." He saw the concern on Anna's face. "Don't worry about me, Frau Klein."

"I *will* worry about you," Anna said. "Don't try to stop me." She pulled him close and squeezed him, making the silent promise to him again. As if to underscore the urgency, the clock on the mantel in the living room chimed eleven and then ticked on, unstoppable.

"You had better get going," Anna said, and she pulled her scarf from the peg in the hallway and wrapped it around his neck. "Next time I see you, I will have good news."

He nodded, mostly to placate her, she knew, and she loved him even a little more for it.

"Now get going before you wake up all the Langes, too."

Oskar put his hand on the door handle and then turned, stood on his tiptoes and kissed her on the cheek. He smiled, sweetly, embarrassed at his display. He pulled open the door and remembered something.

"Fraulein Lange. She's not here. I saw her leave earlier, while I was waiting for you. She walked that way, toward the Keller Strasse and never came back."

"She did? When?"

He shrugged. "Maybe around seven? I was waiting for you for a long time, but I don't have a watch so I don't know exactly."

"Did she see you?"

He shook his head. "No. She was in a hurry."

Anna patted his shoulder. "You go now, and be very careful." She kissed the top of his head. She wanted to tell him that she loved him, but instead she tugged on his ear and smiled. She inhaled the smell of him and tried to take a photograph in her mind. *This is how I will always remember you.*

He gave a small wave on the front step and Anna closed the door, letting the tears flow for a handful of seconds but holding back the sobs rising in her chest for Amalia's sake. By the time she looked for him through the kitchen window, he was already gone.

chapter fifteen

I haven't told you about the boy, Oskar, who was living with us. It's a long story, but he is an orphan who needed a home, so I took him in. But now he's been taken by the refugee agency, which says he was stolen from his parents in Poland. They want to re-educate him and send him back. It's a terrible story, just one of millions, but this is one I know. It has a sweet little round-cheeked face and a wicked sense of humor. And I feel powerless to change the ending. Amalia misses him terribly, as do we all. You would like him; he is smart and resourceful, with a generous nature that has somehow survived everything he has been through.

I want to make something right, at least one thing for one person. Everywhere, we are confronted with posters with horrible images from the camps, accusing and indicting us all. We deserve all the vitriol the civilized world can heap on us, of course. But how are we to go on, to put one foot in front of the other? What can we do now to make it right? I lie awake at night trying to answer this question, and I think of Amalia and now Oskar, and what the future holds for them. Maybe there is hope for them yet, but that hope must be forged from these bitter, scorched remnants. I think it must be dug up and revealed, scratched out from under the ashes and corpses and recognized. It won't present itself; it cannot float to the surface of this muck we have created. We must find it for ourselves.

Anna ran over the words in her mind as she pushed open the door to the Collecting Point. What would the day bring? She sensed a clock ticking in the background, counting the minutes to some unavoidable explosion. It was coming, but she didn't know when. She clenched her teeth and felt a dull ache in her jaw.

"There's someone upstairs to see you," Karla said from behind her desk. "And I put a file in your drawer. I need it back when you're done."

"Got it, thank you. And who's waiting for me?" Anna asked. It had to be Stuart. Cooper would be busy all morning, and Stuart was still lurking around the Collecting Point, despite his repeated promises to leave for Nuremberg. "Is Captain Cooper…?"

"Still in there." Karla nodded toward the director's office. "Since before I got here." She made a wincing face with clenched teeth. Anna returned the expression. "And I don't know who's upstairs. Frau Werner told me to warn you that someone was in the office waiting for you."

"Thanks." Anna turned to go. "Can you do something else for me?"

"Sure."

"See if you can find anything on an Anton Berg, gallery owner in Frankfurt. Aryan, worked with the Nazis. Just between us, *ja*?"

"Of course." Karla wrote down the name and put the paper in her pocket. She straightened a stack of papers by dropping the edges on the desk. "Good luck upstairs."

At first, Anna couldn't exactly place the woman sitting in the visitors' chair in Cooper's office, but when she started to speak, her words put everything into place immediately.

"Frau Klein! He's safe!" Marta Huber stood, clutching a piece of paper to her chest. "This came in the post yesterday." She waved the paper as if it were on fire. "He's safe, can you believe it?"

Anna took the paper and blinked to focus her eyes. She scanned the relevant information on the letter, *Inmate…camp…survivors…last known address…next of kin*. Her eyes darted back to the top of the page. There was the name: Jacob Morgenstern. Marta stared expectantly at Anna, her face on the verge of exploding into tears. Anna found herself embracing this woman whom she barely knew. They stood in the middle of Cooper's office, crying. Anna for a man she had never met, and Marta for a beloved friend she thought she would never see again.

"This is the most wonderful news I could ever receive," Anna finally said, offering Marta a seat. She pulled her desk chair alongside Marta and they both looked at the letter again to be sure.

"It came yesterday, like I said. I was so excited that I had to sit down right there in the middle of the post office," Marta said, excited now. "A woman had to help me off the floor. I told everyone in there, 'He's alive! My Morgenstern, he's alive.' They all glared at me like I was a damn fool. Only one woman behind the counter smiled and said how wonderful it was. And it *is* the most wonderful thing. I had to come tell you." She hugged herself and rocked back and forth in the chair, which creaked under the weight.

"I am so glad you came all this way, Frau Huber. You didn't have to do that, but it will make a big difference." Anna waved the paper. "I will need to log this into his file to be sure there's a record of it for restitution purposes. And then you'll need to keep it for a host of other things, I imagine." She moved to the file cabinet and pulled from its slot the Morgenstern file, now fat with documents and reports. "We'll need to have Captain Cooper sign off on it, too, of course." She pulled a form out of the sorter she kept on her desk and fed it into the typewriter. Frau Huber let out a long sigh as Anna began to type Jacob Morgenstern's information. It was yet another form, but this one was like a rebirth certificate. *The man we had thought dead is actually alive. Alert all relevant bureaucracies.*

"This says he's in Zeilsheim. At the camp there." She looked at Marta. "Frau Huber, he's not just safe, he's almost home."

"What?" She leaned forward to read the paper. "How did I not see that?" She shook Anna's arm. "We must go. I must see him. How do I get to Zeilsheim?" She stood as if she were going to leave right that second.

Anna thought for a moment. "I think maybe we should go together. Otherwise, they might not let you in," she said. "I don't know what the rules are." She waited a few beats, out of respect. "I don't mean to intrude, but I would like to see Herr Morgenstern, too. I can ask the *Amis* to take us." *I won't mention that someone's forging his paintings.*

"Of course, it's all right with me," Marta said. She decided to sit back down. "I can't believe it, you know? After all those sleepless nights and the worry and then the bombs. And then, oh my God, those awful photos... You've seen those, yes? From the camps?"

"It might not be an easy visit," Anna said, putting a hand on Marta's knee. "I think you should—we should—be prepared for a difficult encounter."

Marta's eyes grew as a thought came to her. "What if he blames me? What if he can't forgive me? I should have done more. I know I should have." She shook her head. "Oh, Frau Klein, maybe I can't face him. Who knows what he's been through? And his lovely wife and the children? We don't know about them, do we?" She took the paper from Anna's hand. "It doesn't say anything here about them." She put her hands to her face. "*Mein Gott*. I didn't even think. How stupid of me. What if he's lost everyone? He won't want to see me. What could I ever say after what was done to him?" She closed her eyes tight against some vision that entered her mind. Then she opened them again. "After what we've done to him." She moved her index finger back and forth between Anna and herself.

Anna nodded. Marta was exactly right. Jacob Morgenstern might spit on them and they would deserve it, too. He might refuse to see them. He might be too sick, too frail, too traumatized. When Thomas had been a young doctor at the veterans' clinic in Vienna after the Great War, he told Anna about the eyes of the men who could no longer sleep. It was as if their eyes could no longer see what was in front of them because they only saw what had happened—over and over, replaying on an endless loop that they were helpless to stop. Sleeping only made it worse. So they just sat and stared, sometimes they screamed at sights no one else could see. The camp survivors were likely going through the same horror. In that moment, Anna missed her husband with an intense ache that took her breath away. *Thomas can help them. I hope he can do at least that much.*

"Frau Klein?" Cooper stood in the doorway, eyebrows raised, waiting for an explanation.

Both women stood reflexively, Marta dropping her bag on the floor in the process.

"Captain Cooper, this is Marta Huber," Anna said. "She's the housekeeper of Jacob Morgenstern. From Frankfurt?" she prompted.

Cooper nodded perfunctorily at first and then made the connection. He extended his hand. "Ah, yes, of course. The woman from Frankfurt. *Guten Tag*."

Anna bent to pick up Marta's purse and gave it back to her. "She has good news about Herr Morgenstern." She smiled and nodded for Marta's benefit. "He survived. He's now in Zeilsheim." Marta offered the paper up to Cooper as substantiation, eager to show the American who was a good two feet taller than she.

Cooper scanned the letter. "Hmm. Well now, that is good news. You told her we have his collection?"

"Yes, when I saw her in Frankfurt. We talked about it, remember? She told me about the fight over the Kirchner between Morgenstern and his partner, this Anton Berg."

"Do you think you might go see Mr. Morgenstern, Anna? Is that possible?" he asked, looking up from the paper. "Perhaps it would be of special help," he raised his eyebrows at Anna. *Maybe he can help us*, was his message.

Anna agreed. "Frau Huber wants to go, too. But she doesn't think they'll let her in without an American."

"Of course she does," Cooper sighed. "Tell her we can go

tomorrow. Can she be here in the morning?"

"She lives in Frankfurt."

Cooper exhaled. "Fine. Tell her we'll pick her up."

Anna relayed the message to a nodding Marta who responded by embracing her so firmly that Anna had to steady herself.

"I will be ready," she whispered. When Marta released her, the tears were flowing again. She said goodbye, and Anna volunteered to escort her to the door. She shook both Cooper's hands vigorously. "Thank you, thank you," she whispered in English.

Anna took her by the elbow and walked with her toward the stairs. "Will you be all right getting home?"

"Of course. And I will be ready and waiting tomorrow."

They chatted about the logistics of arrival times and driving distance, Anna advising that Marta dress warmly for the drive in the jeep. They said goodbye at the guard gate and Anna went back inside, bounding up the steps, hardly able to believe this turn of events. She barged into Cooper's office.

"Can you believe it?"

"Believe what?" Eva stood at the filing cabinet. "What's happened?" She looked more skeptical than curious. Her jaw was set.

"Oh," Anna stammered. "Nothing."

"What did that woman want?"

Anna tried to act casual, walking to her desk and picking up her bag, which she had dropped by the chair. "Em, she was the wife of a claimant, checking on their status. Wondering what was taking so long. The usual." She began to rearrange the contents of her bag for no reason.

"Hmm." Eva stared into the filing cabinet. "She sure seemed happy about something."

Anna realized Eva could have watched the tearful scene in the office unfold without her knowing. Anna had been so distracted that she would not even have noticed Eva standing in the doorway. What had Eva seen?

"Captain Cooper was able to give her a little good news," Anna hedged, noticing the Morgenstern file on her desk and the paper with the information about Jacob Morgenstern's reappearance still in the typewriter. Eva was determinedly fingering through the files in the cabinet. "She's an emotional old woman," she said as she closed the folder on her desk behind her back.

Eva slammed the cabinet shut. "Right. Well, if you need me I'll be downstairs. Not that you will." She took the files she had pulled from the cabinet and sorted them into a stack.

"What's that supposed to mean?"

"Nothing," Eva muttered as she disappeared into the hall.

Anna watched her, thinking she might come back into the office and decide to talk. But Eva didn't return, and Anna was left to consider the events spinning in her head. She remembered the file Karla had put in her desk and pulled the drawer open to find a thick green folder that smelled of dust. She dropped the file onto her desk and positioned herself with her back to the door so she would obscure any glimpses onto her desk. She already knew what the list was, but her heart still skipped a little when she saw the title: Staedel Museum Personalakten. She smiled. Karla had gotten the museum's original German personnel files, not the documents processed by the Americans' denazification process. These were the files directly from the museum. She turned the pages, looking for the list of employees, scanning through reports about acquisitions and various administrative details going back more than a decade. The detailed personnel lists were at the very back. Anna tuned her ears to any footsteps in the hall as she ran through the names, concentrating but moving as fast as she could. Hunched over the pages, she repeated the names in her head to be sure she didn't miss anything. She turned the pages: *H, I, J*... scanning the dates. *1930-1940*. She turned the pages two at a time, and then froze when she heard the clicking of high heels in the hallway. *K*... She held her breath as the footsteps stopped. *L*... her finger ran down the page even as her left hand gathered the pages she had already perused. She checked twice. No Eva Lange had worked at the Staedel Museum in the 1930s. She closed the file and turned around. No one stood in the doorway, but a hint of hyacinth perfume hung in the air.

Amalia was waiting for Anna at the gate, sitting on the bench where she had first encountered Captain Cooper back in August, when Anna had first come to work. She watched the *Amis* going about their business, kicking her legs and scrutinizing the activity moving in and out of the gate. She saw Anna, slid to her feet, and shuffled to her side.

"What's wrong, *Maus*? What are you doing here?"

Amalia took her mother's hand. "Nothing."

This had something to do with Oskar's reappearance the night before, the picking at a scab that had just started to heal. Anna paused a beat to think of what to do. She bent down and took her daughter's chin in her hand. "How about you and I go for a walk before we go home? I have a whole pack of Lucky Strikes in my pocket. You think I can get something for them on the market?"

Amalia played it cool but brightened a little. "American cigarettes? Yes, for sure you can. They go for ten Reichsmark each. Sometimes even more. That's what Oskar told me."

"Then let's get going." She wanted to see if the man who was following her—the smelly man in the blue tie—might be lurking about today. And the walk would help her sort through what to do about Eva. How had she lied to her and to the *Amis* so easily? They had the museum records, after all. Did they really not check? Was she using a fake name? And, the thought crept up on Anna, did Eva know they were on to her?

They held hands and headed in the direction of the Marktplatz. Anna inhaled the fall afternoon air which had gotten decidedly cold, but the sun was still out and added just enough warmth to make it a pleasant afternoon. She could afford to think about something else for half an hour.

"You aren't wearing your new socks?" Anna pointed to Amalia's feet.

"Not yet. I'm saving them. I don't want to waste them on a day that's not cold enough."

Anna smiled at her daughter's logic, informed by years of scraping.

"Good idea. I am already wearing mine." She pulled her pant leg up to show Amalia. "They are very warm." It was true. Her feet weren't frozen and were now among the few things on her body that didn't ache.

The streets were busier than usual with Army traffic and the very occasional civilian car. What German had access to either the gas or the wood required to power cars, and why would they choose to use those precious resources driving around town? They must have important places to go. Mostly people were on foot or on bicycles, and occasionally, a truck loaded with supplies or people would rumble by, spewing exhaust, although no one noticed much.

They walked for a while without speaking, Amalia tugging on her mother's arm as she alternately ran ahead then slowed down and fell behind. It had been so long since the two of them had spent time together. Anna had relied so much on Oskar to watch her that he had virtually taken her place as Amalia's caretaker. They made a detour around a large pile of rubble that had been summited by a pack of boys in short pants and baggy socks, who clambered on the boulders of concrete like mountain goats, shouting to each other and laughing. In the distance, a woman's voice shouted a name with rote repetition, a mother calling her child home. Finally, one of the boys stopped laughing and peeled off the group, waving a half-hearted goodbye to his friends who stopped long enough to watch him go.

"Is that what you and Oskar did all day, too?" Anna pointed at the rubble. "Run around like little monkeys?"

Amalia smiled a fresh gap-toothed smile. "Sometimes. Or we would go exploring. The ruins in the Webergasse are the best. You can pretend cowboys and Indians there. Lots of good places to hide."

Amalia slowed her pace and let go of Anna's hand. "Mama, does Oskar really have to go live with the Polish?"

Anna took her hand and pulled her into a slow walk. Words flowed better when their bodies were moving. She thought of what she could tell Amalia. The time for soft pedaling the truth with Amalia was likely at an end. She didn't want to lie to her daughter, but she didn't know what the truth was either.

"Oskar is not a done deal yet. We're still working on him," she offered. It was a partial lie, but she hoped it would come true, so it was also a kind of prayer. She clumsily changed the subject. "Now steer me in the direction of the black market, please, young lady expert. I'd like to do a spot of shopping."

Amalia decided not to push the question, and they walked a few more blocks, leaving behind the boys, who were playing with a dead rat they had pulled from the rubble.

The market was busy but not overflowing. Mornings were reportedly the best times, when the farmers came in with their food and people waited to get the first pick. Anna scanned the periphery of the crowd for a man with a mustache and a blue tie who was doing nothing. It wasn't much to go on and yielded no results. She turned her attention to the people around her. There were stout women in sensible coats with scarves on their heads, and hunched, elderly women carrying bags in bony, papery hands. There were old men, too, with hats and dried-up faces. Here and there, Anna spotted what she thought must be an aristocrat, a duchess, or maybe even a princess, now reduced to wearing shabby wool coats, their baubles having been traded to a farmer's wife for food. These women were betrayed by their carriage, a certain way of holding their head and looking down their noses, even as they bartered for a piece of cheese alongside their former maids and house girls.

"Mama, this way," Amalia pulled her toward a small clearing. "Here. Stand here and say what you have to sell. Not really loud, but loud enough so people walking by can hear you. If you see an *Ami*, just start walking away and pretend you have nothing."

"I thought the *Amis* were the worst ones?" Anna whispered. "People say they are buying everything on the black market and sending it home to their wives."

Amalia shrugged. "I'm telling you what Oskar said. And remember, cigarettes go for ten Reichsmark. For each one."

Anna took the three packs from her bag, opened one and moved it to her coat pocket. She felt dirty already and all she was pandering were smokes. Other women had to resort to much worse. She knew of one of the girls at the Collecting Point who had lost her job and started using her children as pimps to find American soldiers for her. *Schnappers*, they called the kids who hung around doorways, soliciting GIs who walked past. She pushed the thought out of her head and said a little prayer of thanks that for now, at least, she still had a job.

"Mama, you're not doing it right. Do it like this." Amalia began accosting people who walked by, her sweet face turned up to them. "Cigarettes," she said. "*Ami* cigarettes." It wasn't an offer so much as a statement of fact. Cigarettes.

"What kind?" An old man who smelled of stale sweat and schnapps asked her.

"Lucky Strikes," Anna said, keeping her hands in her pockets.

"How much?"

"Ten Reichsmark. Each, of course," Amalia said.

"Shut up, kid; I asked her, not you."

Anna straightened and looked the man in his watery yellow eyes. "You heard her, old man. Two hundred for the pack," she added. Over his shoulder, she saw a man with a mustache look at her from among the sea of heads. She craned to follow him as he turned and disappeared.

The buyer fumbled with a stack of bills, and Anna held out her left hand wiggling her fingers. She looked past his shoulder again, but the head was gone. When he pressed two hundred notes into her hand, she pulled out the pack with her right and put them in his coat pocket. "Enjoy," she said and walked on, pushing Amalia in front of her.

"Well done, Mama," Amalia said. "You are like a professional."

"I saw it in a movie once," Anna said. A surge of adrenaline energized her, and she stood on tiptoe to get a better look over the heads of the crowd. They still had two packs to sell, so they walked around, Anna only half-paying attention to the wares being offered on folding tables, on laps, and on the palms of hands. People sold anything and everything. Cameras and furniture, blankets and plates, eggs and watches. A low mumble of voices floated in the air as people talked amongst themselves, eyes darting, hoping to stay one step ahead of any police. She didn't see the man again. Maybe she had imagined it. Maybe it wasn't the man in the blue tie.

The weather was turning dark and cold, lending an urgency to the transactions. Rain threatened from the north and the air turned damp. Anna sold the other two packs of Lucky Strikes quickly, one to a young woman with garish red lipstick and a black eye, and the other to a woman Anna saw often near Madeleine's house, sweeping the stoop of her building, an unlit cigarette always hanging from her lips. They walked home hand in hand, Anna weighed down by a can of sardines in one coat pocket, a piece of cheese in the other, and three crumbly bread rolls in her bag. Maybe things were looking up, just a little.

"Sorry I can't go with you to Zeilsheim after all." Cooper helped Anna gather her things for the drive. "Bender will take you. I've got to stay here to put out fires."

Anna climbed into the jeep. They were waiting for Bender to retrieve paperwork from the office. When word got out they were going to Frankfurt, all kinds of additional errands got piled on for people who needed papers delivered. "I need to talk to you about Eva," she said. "It's important."

Cooper was too distracted to listen. "Catch me when you get back. I've got my hands full with Major Stuart. He got here first thing. As I said, you can set your watch by that guy, he's so predictable."

"Is everything all right?"

"Also as predicted. They threatened us with court martialing. Heads may or may not have exploded from Frankfurt to Washington. Not much else we can do. Today, we'll wait and see. I want to be here when they hand down the sentences. Sorry you'll miss all the fun."

"Me too, I guess," Anna said. She shifted in her seat. "I'm not going to tell Herr Morgenstern anything about the paintings except to let him know that we have them. Do you think that's the right thing to do?"

"Good plan. Save the intrigue for later. He'll find out soon enough anyway." He shifted his weight on his feet. "How were things at the house last night?"

"Quiet. Eva wasn't there again." She took a deep breath. "You know today's Thursday."

Cooper exhaled sharply, irritated. "Yes, I'm fully aware of that." he snapped.

"But Oskar's train is going on Saturday."

"Didn't I ask you to trust me?" Cooper saw the pain on her face and softened. "Look, Anna, he's not going to Poland yet. He's going to Bavaria. It's a train ride away, and he's still under American occupation, so to speak. We will fix it. Don't panic."

"This is such bullshit," Anna muttered, surprising herself.

Cooper grinned. "Your vocabulary is improving."

"It's a good word. It seems to fit...everything." She waved her hands to indicate the world around them.

"Yes, it does. Ain't that right, Bender?" Cooper said as Bender approached, juggling a box that teetered with files.

"What's that, Captain?"

"Everything's bullshit."

Bender laughed as he dropped the box onto the back seat. "Indeed it is. I've got a whole carton of it right here." He threw a heavy blanket on top to weigh the papers down, and climbed into the driver's seat.

"Drive courteously, now. Remember to share the road." Cooper slapped his open palm on the front fender. "Good luck."

The drive to Frankfurt was becoming routine now, with Anna noticing the same things along the way: The burned barn behind the rickety farmhouse just on the outskirts of town. The large grove of trees—now bare of leaves—that always caught her eye along a wide turn to the east. The clumps of people walking—fewer of them now, too, probably because of the approaching winter. They pulled handcarts or pushed wheelbarrows, they were wrapped in blankets, or shivered against the cold winds. Hearing an approaching car, they stepped out of the street and into the muddy ditch, not bothering to even look up. Some walked toward Wiesbaden, others in the opposite direction. They passed another jeep that was pulled over on the side of the road. A woman sat in the back seat, her feet braced against the front seats, looking intently at something on her lap. A bored GI sat on the hood of the jeep, smoking. Anna's head swiveled as they passed.

"Photographer," Bender said. "*Life Magazine*. She's been all over Frankfurt this week. Wish she'd come to the CCP and snap some shots of the work that's going on there. Would be good for us."

"I've seen her before," Anna said. "She was at the concentration camp. In Buchenwald, when they marched us through after the liberation. She was taking photos of the camp. She's famous, no?"

"Who marched you through the camp?" Bender asked.

"The Americans did. Me and Thomas and all the other villagers. So we could see what had been happening. It was...unspeakable." She closed her eyes.

Bender waited a few breaths. "And you never really knew what was happening before then? Really?"

The vision of piled-up corpses flooded her mind but was quickly displaced by the one memory she would never forget as long as she lived: The smell of death and of the degradation of life—the burned flesh, the sewage under her feet, the sweat and terror of the living. It had been a bright and sunny day on the day they were marched through, but a veil of suffering and horror hung above their heads, so close you could feel it. And late in the war, when the wind came from the west, hints of that smell had seeped into her village like the icy fingers of a ghost. Invisible and fleeting, it had been easy to ignore, to explain away.

"No, I didn't know," Anna said. "I could have known, but I chose not to. Most of us did. I know it makes no sense to you. But you didn't live in the world the Nazis made for us."

"I know." Bender shifted gears and the jeep bounced down a shallow incline. He had the decency to not argue the subject, even though she knew her excuse wasn't valid. Not now, not back in the real world they lived in.

Eventually, he turned his face toward her. "Are you worried about seeing Mr. Morgenstern?"

Anna paused. "Not worried," she said, finally. "Scared. More like terrified." She rubbed the palm of her hand with her thumb. "Ashamed."

"Yeah," Bender said, "it's going to be a rough time until this heals over. If it ever does."

"I don't see how it can, I really don't," Anna sighed. "Amalia will be an old woman and it still won't be healed. I worry how she will think of me and her father. She'll wonder what we did, or what we didn't do." She stared at the passing countryside. "Our children will blame us, and rightfully so. This will never go away."

"Probably not."

"But that's the least of our worries. First, we have to pay our debt to the Jews. And even before that, we have to face them and allow them to judge us."

"You are not responsible for what happened to the Morgensterns, Anna."

"Yes, I am responsible. And I want to be held responsible. It's the only way forward." In a way, she hoped that Jacob Morgenstern would let her have it, that he would be angry at *her* for what happened to him. If he would give her the gift of his anger, it would be a relief, in a way. But her guilt wasn't the issue, not yet.

They entered the outskirts of Frankfurt, the small villages with their rubble cleared from the road into tidy piles. All towns looked the same now, with their identities scraped away. It was a world starting over. For the rest of the ride, they didn't say much, the anticipation of the meeting hanging over both of them. By the time they pulled up to the house in the Feldberg Strasse, it was nearly ten o'clock. The children in the school across the street were back outside playing in the open lot, the nuns standing guard.

The jeep had barely rolled to a stop when the front door opened and Marta shot out, nearly tripping down the steps.

"Frau Klein, thank goodness," she panted. "I have been waiting all morning."

Anna was confused. They had agreed on a ten o'clock pick-up and had pulled up right on time.

"What do you mean?" she asked, half-catching Marta to slow her momentum. "Has something happened?"

"The woman," Marta gasped. "The woman at the Collecting Point. Yesterday."

Anna shook her head and waited for more information.

"The tall one. With the hair?" Marta twirled her hand above her head to simulate a bun hairstyle. "I know her. I mean to say, I have seen her before."

"Yes?" Anna's heart jumped. Did she mean Eva?

"What's she all worked up about?" Bender asked. "Can she continue her episode in the jeep on the ride? I have to get going."

Anna directed Marta to the backseat. "We need to be going," she said in German. "Tell me on the way."

Marta nodded and used the break to catch her breath. Once they were moving again, Anna prompted her.

"Are you talking about Fraulein Lange?"

"I don't know her name. She's tall, kind of pretty in a skinny way. She was wearing a brown dress, I think. I saw her when we were walking out. She was in the hallway."

Anna hadn't noticed Eva in the hallway, but then she hadn't been paying attention. But Eva had been wearing a brown dress with her hair in an elaborate up-do that Anna had noticed.

"What about her?"

"I've seen her before. With one of the Americans that sometimes stays at the house."

Anna swallowed. "You don't mean Major Stuart?"

"Yes, I think that's his name. The one with the big teeth."

"You've seen them together?"

"She's come to the house, when he's alone. When there were no other *Amis* there. He's sent me home. Two times, she's come."

"She stayed the night with him?"

"I don't know. I went home, as I said. But it looked like that's where it was headed."

Anna relayed the conversation for Bender who started laughing. "This is better than the movies," he sputtered. "Stuart and the bean-pole. That's quite the pair."

"So he didn't just get her the job," Anna said.

"Oh, she paid for that job," Bender said. "I guess she's still paying."

Marta tugged at Anna's arm. "Frau Klein, that's not all. Major Stuart, he was staying at the house last night. At about seven o'clock, as I was putting his dinner on the table, she shows up, all flustered. They went upstairs and I tried to listen, but of course it's all in English, and anyway, my hearing is not so good. But she was very upset. I sat on the stairs and waited. Watched his dinner get cold, is what I did. And then, Frau Klein, you won't believe it. There was a knock on the door, and I open it, and who is standing there?" she paused for dramatic effect.

"Who?" Anna obliged her.

"That *Schwein*, Anton Berg. I almost slammed the door in his face. I thought to myself, why does he show up here today of all days? This news about Herr Morgenstern comes in the mail and here he is, as if he knows."

Anna hung on Marta's every word, her mind too occupied with the moving parts of the story to say anything.

"He asks me if I had heard anything about the Morgensterns. That he is going to file a claim with the *Amis*—with you, I guess—to claim the collection, since he was Herr Morgenstern's business partner. Which he wasn't really, of course. It was the Nazis that put them together. The art belongs to Herr Morgenstern."

"What did you tell him?"

"I told him he better not ever show his face at this house again. Then I lied and said I hadn't heard anything about Herr Morgenstern. He didn't believe me. He tried to push his way into the house, saying we should talk calmly, but I didn't let him past the threshold. But that's when it happened."

The jeep hit a pot hole and they bounced out of their seats. Anna steadied herself by holding onto the back seat. She was turned around in the front seat, kneeling to face Marta, who clutched the jeep's frame as they hit another pothole.

"Dammit," Bender grumbled. "Lousy infrastructure. What's she saying?"

"Go on," Anna said to Marta, waving Bender off. "What happened?"

"That woman. She was at the top of the stairs. She had heard the commotion, or she and the *Ami* were finished fighting. Anyway, she started coming down the stairs, and Berg, he saw her and he just about exploded. Yelling and shouting—standing on the street, mind you—calling her every name. She gave as good as she got, though; she ran at him. I was still standing in the doorway, so I got stuck in the middle. I was not about to let him in the house, and she was determined to get at him."

Anna tried to slow her down. "What were they saying to each other, do you remember?"

Marta nodded dutifully, like a witness for the prosecution. "Yes. He said she was an *Ami* whore, that she should be marched through the street and then shot. She said he was never to come after her again, that she had done what she said, and that she owed him *nothing*." She accentuated the last word with a nod, as if all was explained.

"And?"

"And then she pushed me aside and stepped outside with him on the front stoop, where all the neighbors can see, of course. She shut the door so I wouldn't hear. They stood outside whispering loudly for a few minutes. I couldn't hear a thing, and then the *Ami* came down the stairs wondering what was going on. I didn't want to look like I was meddling, so I went back to the kitchen. After a minute or so, she came back in, crying and holding the side of her face. She was a mess, blubbering and hysterical. The *Ami*, Stuart, he first tried to comfort her, but then he got irritated, too, and was yelling at her. In English, you understand, but he was yelling like a jealous man, and she was pleading with him. And then he struck her. Hit her right across the face, and she fell back onto the floor. He was coming after her, and she kind of scampered backward, like a crab almost, to get away from him. And then I don't know what happened to me, Frau Klein, but I took his dinner plate that was sitting there on the table—it was ice cold by now— and I just picked it up and I threw it at him. Right at his head."

"Oh, God," Anna said.

"What?" Bender pleaded. "Are you going to tell me?"

Anna ignored him. "Did the plate hit him?"

"No. It missed mostly. Just hit him on the leg. Food all over his pants."

"Oh no," Anna repeated through the hand covering her mouth.

"That's what I thought, too," Marta said. "All night I waited for them to come arrest me. Didn't sleep a wink."

"What happened then?"

"The *Ami* stopped going after her, anyway. He went upstairs, then he came back down and walked out the door. I haven't seen him since. The Fraulein, she picked herself up. I tried to help her, but she refused, even though I could see she was bleeding. I think she was so upset and embarrassed. She took her coat and left, too. That was it. I cleaned up the mess and went home. I was sure there would be MPs here this morning. I wrote you a note, to tell you what happened, in case you got here and I was gone." She rummaged in her bag and pulled out a tightly folded paper. "Here it is. Do you want it?"

"Yes, I'll take that, thank you, Frau Huber." Anna turned back around in her seat and put the paper into her own bag.

"They're not going to arrest me, are they, Frau Klein?" Marta sputtered. "What a mess. To come this far, survive Adolf and bombs and famine, and then get thrown in the clink because of some jealous *Ami* and a plate of boiled cabbage."

"They won't arrest you, don't worry," Anna said. It was an empty promise, of course, but it was likely that Stuart would prefer to avoid explaining any of this. And something more was going on anyway. Anna ruminated about what that might be.

"We're almost there. You going to tell me what's happening?" Bender pulled the jeep to a stop at an intersection.

"I could, but you won't believe it," Anna said.

chapter sixteen

The little houses of the Zeilsheim Displaced Persons Camp would have been charming in another time and place. Now, in Anna's mind, they echoed the appearance of the concentration camps, even though they didn't resemble them in any physical way. The narrow streets between the buildings were dotted with people, some moving about, some sitting on benches. Those who were moving about looked a little more robust than the skeletal ghost-like beings Anna had seen on the newsreels that the Americans made all Germans watch, but not by much. She could sense Frau Huber tense up in the back seat as they pulled through the gate, and Bender parked the jeep by the small administration building.

"Want me to go in with you?" he asked, clearly not wanting to go in with them.

"No, it's all right," Anna said. "We can manage."

"Then I'll be back in an hour. Is that enough time?"

Anna said she thought it was more than enough. "We'll wait for you outside the gate." The urge to leave was already overpowering her. She helped Marta out of the jeep and steadied her as they walked to the office door.

"Good luck," Bender said. He had become quiet and serious. "You're doing a good thing, Anna. Remember that. This is a *good thing*."

She smiled, grateful for his support. He knew her ambivalence about coming here, even after being so excited to learn about Jacob Morgenstern's survival. Now that she was about to see him face to face, she was even more conflicted. How easy it was to avert her eyes, to keep everything as words on a page, stories in a newspaper, names on a Gestapo transport list. She thought of Cooper's manifesto and the thousands of papers with endless words: orders, memos, and letters that kept the occupiers busy and had done the same for the Nazis before them. She thought, too, of her letter, folded up under her bed, unfinished, the ink on its pages nothing more than stains that would change life forever for her and Thomas and Amalia. But this, standing here at the door to the Zeilsheim Displaced Persons Camp, this was real. No amount of typing or forms or mimeographs could replace *this*. She took a deep breath and pushed the door open.

The small office had been furnished with care and attention. Desks and filing cabinets were configured into the available space, and an anemic potted plant balanced on the window sill trying to catch some sunlight. A contingent of three tiny women worked behind one shared desk, their heads bowed between teetering piles of paper. Only one looked up when they entered.

"Yes?" she said.

"Jacob Morgenstern," Marta blurted out, waving the letter with his information. "We are here to see Herr Morgenstern." She was sputtering and shaking, overcome with emotion. Anna guided her to a chair where she was happy to sit and collect herself. "Sorry," Marta mumbled. "I'm so…something. I don't even know what."

Anna slid the letter from Marta's hands. "I know. Let me do this. Take a few deep breaths."

Anna turned to the woman and explained their situation. She mentioned the letter, the Collecting Point, and the art. "And this is Frau Huber, Herr Morgenstern's long-time housekeeper. She is the one who received the letter," she added by way of finishing. Then she waited.

The woman regarded her with a flat gaze, neither interested nor dismissive, judging nor helpful. She was so slight she could have been mistaken for a child, her green wool dress oversized and hanging shapelessly to her shins. She took her time to read the letter. "I guess it's all right. I'll tell him you are here. It will be up to him to decide if he wants to see you. You will respect his decision, yes?"

"Of course," Anna said. "But please tell him that I am here about his art collection, that the Americans have…" She took a breath. "Tell him that the Americans know where it is."

"And tell him Marta Huber is here," Marta added, leaning forward in her seat.

The woman disappeared out the front door, and Anna took a seat in another chair on the other side of the small room. She and Marta stared at each other, sitting with their bags clutched on their laps, anticipating, anxious.

"Frau Huber? Can I ask you something?" Anna asked, not

waiting for a reply. "This Anton Berg, who came to the house last night, what does he look like?"

Marta inhaled and spoke on the exhale. "Oh, you know. He's nice looking enough. Not as nice looking as your Captain." She smiled. "A bit short, with dirty blond hair that's thin on top, but he thinks he's hiding that. Good teeth. Kind of a dapper dresser. Pretentious. Thinks he's better than everyone; one of those university types. You know the ones."

Anna shifted her weight forward. "Does he have a *Schmiss* on his face?" Her finger made a cross shape on her left cheek.

"Yes, that's what I mean. Fraternity type. I think those scars are so ugly. Why would anyone do that to a perfectly lovely face? Silly boys. As a mother, you can't understand it, am I right?"

"Yes," Anna said, keeping her voice steady. "And you didn't see him before yesterday? Since…since before the Morgensterns were deported?"

"That's right. He knew not to show his face, that coward. I couldn't believe when he dared show up yesterday, although I suppose it was inevitable."

Anna nodded. Marta's voice was rising and she was getting agitated again. One of the women behind the desk glared at them over her half-moon glasses.

When the door opened a few minutes later, the small woman in the big green dress announced that they should follow her. "He will see you, but you can only stay a few minutes. He is very ill and frail. You're not going to upset him, are you?"

"That is not my intention in any way," Anna said. "I hope that what we have to tell him will bring him some measure of joy. Otherwise, I would not be here."

"No, I don't imagine you would be," the woman said.

They navigated the cobblestone street, Anna holding Frau Huber by the elbow, and arrived at the door to one of the small houses that was like all the other small houses. Anna steadied herself as Marta grabbed her arm hard.

"I don't know if I can do this," she whispered.

Anna patted her hand. "You can, and you will. I am here with you. Remember how much you love him."

"That's not the problem," she breathed. "I don't know if I can show my face."

Anna patted her hand again and nodded at the woman, who had paused to wait for them.

"Please, no excitement. Stay for five or ten minutes, not more," she admonished before pushing the door open and peering inside. When she was happy that all was good, she stepped aside to let them in. "It's the first door on the left."

Anna felt faint from the rush in her head. Marta was frozen to the spot and didn't move until Anna pulled her along.

Just as it had on the outside, the inside of the house looked like it came from the pages of a picture book. Wood paneling and small windows made for a dark cocoon of a space, a cozy respite on this blustery day. Anna knocked on the first door on the left and listened for a response.

The woman in the green dress said, "You may go in. He knows you're here."

The door creaked a little as it opened to reveal a bedroom with a metal framed hospital bed pushed against the far wall. A small wooden table in the corner was piled with books and a carafe of water.

The wood floor was warmed by a worn carpet that might once have been red; it was hard to tell from the worn patches. There was no other furniture or adornment, only a weak shaft of sun that pushed through the dirty window, casting a slice of faded light onto the bed.

"Herr Morgenstern?" Anna whispered.

Marta pushed her head into the opening. "Herr Morgenstern, it's me, Marta Huber," she added.

They were met with silence, and Anna was unsure what to do. She pushed the door open a little more and Marta took a step forward.

"Over here, Marta," a voice responded. The voice was much stronger than Anna expected. "Come closer, it's all right."

Marta stepped into the room and approached the bed with hands outstretched as if she were trying to catch something. Anna followed but stood by the door after she closed it. In the dim light, the man sitting on the bed appeared as only a shadow, small and birdlike. He was sitting sideways with his back against the wall, as if the bed were a sofa, his feet swimming in thick gray wool socks extended slightly over the bed frame. An image of a shrunken Alice in Wonderland came to Anna's mind; he was so small on the rickety bed, as if it were oversized. Papery blue pajamas covered his emaciated frame, and a knitted blanket rested on his knees. The bones that were his fingers tugged repeatedly at the edge of the blanket. When he saw Marta, his face, hollow and reduced to its barest contours, shifted into an expression that was unlike anything Anna had ever seen. He began to shake as he extended a hand. Marta fell to her knees at the edge of the bed, taking his outstretched hand and sobbing into the bedsheets. Anna gripped the door handle to steady herself. Yes, she had seen the torture chambers and the gas chambers with her own eyes. She had walked past the unfathomable piles of bodies, so tattered and destroyed they looked like rags. She put a hand to her nose, remembering. Even that had been an exercise of the abstract, of the other. *Those Nazis did that to those poor people*. She had isolated and convinced herself she could have done nothing. But she was not prepared for this. The only thing that separated the living ghost sitting on the bed from her and from her family was a random fate that drew a black line between them. *Between us and them.*

No one in the room spoke, only the sounds of a few birds chirping in the bushes outside made their way inside the walls. To Anna's ears, they sounded like little whimpers.

Marta lifted her head. "For as long as I live, I will make this right," she said, wiping her nose with her hand. "I will do anything I can." She stopped crying, and Anna was relieved. This was not about Marta or Anna or their collective guilt, their shame, or their penance. Nothing could make right what happened to Jacob Morgenstern and his family. He sat, silent, looking at the woman who had taken care of his life for so long. His eyes were empty, his expression neutral. Marta stroked his hand.

"Who is this?" he finally said, focusing on Anna. His voice was clear and soft, the remnant of the elegant, smiling man she had seen in the photo. It was exactly the way his voice should sound.

Anna stepped forward. "My name is Anna Klein."

"She is with the Americans," Marta said. "She wanted to talk to you."

Jacob Morgenstern shook his head. "No more Red Cross. No more damn interviews. I don't want to talk anymore." He waved her off with a shaking hand.

"Not *those* Americans; she's with the ones who are guarding all the art." She prompted Anna to step forward.

"Herr Morgenstern, I've only come to tell you that the Americans have your art collection. I have personally inventoried and examined it and I'm making sure it is kept safe."

His eyes flashed, but he did not react other than a little snort of disdain. "What do I care about a bunch of paintings now? What use are they to me but to bring back memories of everything that was taken from me?"

Anna bit her lip. He was right. What was the point of a bunch of paint on a canvas? What did it really matter? If it meant nothing to him, it had no value. She started to speak and then stopped. It would matter again, she thought. It was rightfully his and it would be his again. But for now, she had done all she could.

"That pig, Berg. Where's he?" he muttered. "Has he shown his ugly face? I suppose he survived. The cockroaches always do." He shifted his weight on the bed and winced. "I guess as long as he doesn't get his hands on it, that will be something."

"He won't, Herr Morgenstern. I promise you that," Anna said, not answering his question.

He snorted again. "Promises."

"I will file a claim for the collection on your behalf with the Americans." *So they know you're alive. So they won't give it to the wrong person.* "It will be there when you are ready to take it."

Anna put her hand on Marta's back signaling that they should go. Marta heaved herself to her feet and leaned forward to touch Jacob Morgenstern's cheek. "The house is still there, too," she said. "It's waiting for you." He nodded and sank back into the pillows. Anna noticed a row of bread rolls sitting on the window sill. There were maybe six or seven of them, lined up like a display in a bakery.

"You say it's all there? At least what was left of it?" He looked at Anna. "I bet it's not."

"Yes, sir, I do think it is, given the sales records and accounts that were found with it in the cloister in Bensheim."

"And the Kirchner, it's still there?"

"*Berlin 1913*?" Anna asked.

Morgenstern nodded.

"Yes," she lied. But it was true, in a way. *I will get it for you, Jacob. I promise.*

Now the hint of a smile fluttered over his face and then disappeared. "Good," he said.

Marta backed away from the bed, not taking her eyes off him, as if she were leaving the presence of royalty. They said goodbye as he waved them away, lost in his memories. Anna helped Marta to the door. They stepped out into the hallway and closed the door behind them. They did not dare look at each other, instead they walked out of the building and turned toward the front gate. They walked into the gray cold, Marta stopping to vomit into a metal trash bin. Anna held her hand as they left the camp and waited for Bender.

Amalia and Madeleine huddled on the sofa in the Lange's living room, Amalia's face flushed from crying. Madeleine sat next to her, a protective arm wrapped around the girl's shoulder. All around them the room was in chaos and it took Anna several beats to take it all in. Books had been pulled from the shelf and lay scattered on the floor. The desk drawers hung open, one curtain had even been ripped from its rod and lay crumpled on the floor.

"What's happened? Have we been burgled?" Anna dropped her

bag and her keys. Madeleine shot a look over to the other side of the room, but before Anna could turn her head, someone grabbed her arm and pushed her in the direction of the sofa. Amalia let out a scream as Anna caught herself.

It was Spitzer. He gave Anna another push.

"We've been waiting for you. Take a seat," he said, his face cold.

Anna obliged, not because he told her to, but to comfort Amalia who reached out for her and huddled into her mother's side.

"What's going on?" Anna put an arm around Amalia.

"He thinks we know something about a forged painting," Madeleine hissed. "Came in here looking for money he says Eva owes him and tore the place up. I have no idea what he's talking about. Do you?"

Anna studied the man's face. The scar on his cheek was in the shadow of the light coming from the window, but she could see it very clearly. This man was Anton Berg. She knew it for sure. But she would not let on that she did. Nor would she let on to what she knew about Eva's faked museum career. If she could keep her head, he might reveal more than he intended.

"Where's Eva?" she asked.

"That's what I'd like to know, too," Berg said. "I assume you've seen her?"

Anna shook her head. "Not since yesterday. I'm sure she's fine." But she knew concern for Eva's safety was not what had brought him here.

"She didn't come to work today?"

Anna hedged. "I didn't see her. But I was very busy all day." Her heart pounded in her chest, and it took all her effort to appear calm.

He took a step closer and Amalia cowered. "Yes, that's what I've heard. Care to tell me what you were busy doing, Frau Klein?"

"CCP business, that's all," Anna said. "Why is it a concern of yours, Herr Spitzer? If it's money you're looking for, I can't help you." She was playing dumb, but she knew why he was here. He was worried Eva had decided to confess her sins to the *Amis* and implicate him. Maybe that's where she had gone. Or she had run away to protect herself from whatever mess she had gotten herself into. Next to Anna, Amalia's heart pounded so hard her body jolted with each beat.

Berg stood opposite the sofa, looming over the three of them. The room was warm, and beads of perspiration marked Berg's thinning hairline. Standing with hands on his hips, he didn't speak, his eyes darting from one side of the room to the other.

Since he wasn't talking, Anna decided to bait him. She leaned forward and rested her forearms on her thighs, making a show of having had an idea. "Maybe she's gone off and found a better job? Something that's more in line with her *actual* qualifications?"

She intended to let the remark lie, but before she knew what was happening, Berg lunged at her and pushed her backward onto the sofa, his hand under her chin squeezing her throat between his thumb and forefinger. Her head hit the wood frame of the sofa's back, and she heard Amalia scream and then begin to cry. Her arms flailed as she tried to breathe, the pain in her throat traveling quickly to her lungs like a fire. Berg's face was up against hers, his Russian cigarette breath hot against her skin.

"That whore and you, both of you, are in cahoots with the *Amis*. I'm not stupid. I didn't come through this goddamn war to be taken down by a stupid cow like her. I'm telling you, if the *Amis* come after me, you will regret it. So think about it before you do anything else stupid."

He held on for several seconds and Anna was sure she would pass out from both the pain and the lack of oxygen. Her legs kicked at the air, but his weight on her was too much. Somewhere in a distant place, she heard Madeleine shouting. He gave one last squeeze and then released his grip. Anna resurfaced, gasping for air, her ears ringing. A white glow surrounded her vision and she blinked to focus her eyes.

"I have no idea what you are talking about," she croaked, her breath still coming in constricted bursts. "Get out of here. You've made your point. Whatever you've got going on with Eva, it's no business of mine and I don't really care."

"You will care," Berg said. "Your little one, she'll tell you, won't you?" He smiled coolly at Amalia, who buried her head in Madeleine's lap.

"I'll go to the *Amis*," Anna threatened.

"No, you won't," Berg said. "They're in enough trouble as it is. No way are they going to let it come out that they allowed two paintings to be stolen out from under them."

Anna had her confession, but she still didn't let on. "There are no paintings missing from the CCP. I inventoried them all," she lied. "So I'm sure I have no idea what you are talking about."

Berg smirked at her. "Nicely done, Frau Klein. Convincing, even." He slipped his arms into his jacket and pulled it over his shoulders. "But you better find Eva, and tell her I want my money."

"Find her yourself. And now get out."

"I'll show myself out. Don't get up." He walked toward the door, which Anna had left ajar when she had entered. "Eva knows where I am. She's got until tomorrow morning." He disappeared into the street. Madeleine jumped up and went to the window, craning her neck to watch him walk away while Anna locked the door.

"*Maus*, are you all right?" She took Amalia in her arms. "Did he hurt you?" Amalia started to cry again.

"He just barged in here," Madeleine said, breathless. "Started yelling at us, making a horrible mess. Tore everything up, the beds, the sofa. He pushed me around, and Amalia, too. Was ranting about the black market, his money, shouting at her. He was here all afternoon waiting for you, Anna. What the devil is going on?"

Anna took Madeleine's hand and pulled her down on the sofa. "I'm sorry, Auntie. I can't tell you. It's a terrible mess. But it will all get sorted… I hope." She wasn't so sure.

"They were in the rug, Mama, the paintings were," Amalia said.

Anna turned to her daughter. "Say that again, *Maus*?"

"There were two paintings rolled up inside the rug that we took to the black market that day. Me and Oskar."

Anna took Amalia's hands, her eyes focused on her daughter's face. "You knew about those paintings?" Anna asked. "How did you know? Did Eva tell you?"

"No. We saw her take them out and roll them up in the rug. She didn't know we had seen her."

"Take them out? From where?"

Amalia stood up and pointed to where Anna was sitting. "From under there. They were between the cushion and the bottom of the sofa. She took them out and rolled them in the rug."

Anna held her breath for several beats before continuing. "*Maus*, why didn't you say anything?"

Amalia shook her head. "I thought we would get in trouble. And then they took Oskar away, and I thought it was because of that. I was scared."

Anna pulled Amalia close. "And that was the man who bought them from you?"

Amalia nodded, eyes wide.

"He didn't hurt you, did he?" Anna asked.

"I'm all right, Mama." The girl tugged on her braid. "Are they going to arrest you?"

"No," Anna replied. "They won't. Did you tell that man that you saw the paintings?"

"No, I didn't. I promise."

"And you are one hundred percent certain he's the same man?"

She nodded again. "Yes, because of his face." She made a gesture on her cheek with her finger.

"She didn't say anything," Madeleine said. "I was trying to stop him from scaring her, but she held tough. Very brave, she was. I had no idea what they were all talking about."

Amalia smiled a little. "I didn't want to get in trouble."

"I'm sorry, Auntie. I can't tell you more than that right now, but it will be done soon. Where is Eva, anyway?"

"I think she really is gone," Madeleine said. "I heard her rummaging around this morning early, before you got up. Lots of commotion. Then I heard the door open and close, and she was gone. You didn't realize she wasn't here this morning?"

Anna shook her head. "No, I was so distracted. I got up and left for work. I thought she was still getting dressed.

"Go take a look in her room," Madeleine said. "She's emptied the closet. And she took food with her, too."

"And Herr Lange? Where's he?"

"He's gone, too. Clothes, slippers, everything."

Anna sank back into the sofa. She tried to think where they would go. Eva going to confess to the *Amis* made no sense. They would throw the book at her. Eva was running away from Berg, most likely. And from Stuart, too, probably. Eva took her father, so that meant she wasn't planning to return. Or she was trying to keep him out of harm's way. Maybe Berg had threatened him, too.

The paintings had been right underneath their noses after all, at least the real ones had, at some point. She stood up and began pulling the cushions from the sofa.

"Now what?" Madeleine asked.

Anna got down on her knees and put her face close to the lining of the sofa's frame. It smelled of wood and old fabric. She ran her hand along the seam where the seat met the back. Dust and grime crunched under her fingernails, and she stretched her arm as far as she could into the crevice of the far corner. Something poked her skin and she pinched the object between her fingers. Holding it up in front of her face, she recognized it immediately. A tiny nail, the kind used to secure a canvas to its frame.

"I need to find Cooper." She stood up.

"What, now?" Madeleine asked. "Isn't it a bit late? And why?" She glanced at the clock on the mantel.

"Don't go, Mama," Amalia whimpered.

"Yes, what if he comes back? Or what if he follows you?" Madeleine said. "Do you have to go right now?"

"Yes," Anna said. "We'll all go. Safety in numbers."

Corporal Long was still at his post when the three of them arrived. Bundled up against the cold, Madeleine wrapped in a blanket, they had cut through the cemetery and hurried down the Wilhelmstrasse in the biting wind. Anna had spotted a few lights on the second floor where Cooper's office was, and they had hurried a little more to get there. Now they were standing at the guard house, out of breath.

"Sure, he's still here," Long said. "I can let you in, Frau Klein, but not these two. That would cost me my job, after hours and all."

"Please Corporal, just this once," Anna begged. "To get out of the cold." *And out of sight.*

Amalia stomped her foot against the cold, as if to make a point.

"I will owe you a favor," Anna pleaded, realizing too late how it sounded.

Long realized it, too. "Thanks for the offer, ma'am, but I'm not that kind of boy. You know I'd help you, but we got a long talking-to about the rules. Everything has to be by the book. All the time." He recited the instructions, but shook his head, arguing with his better angels. Anna could see he was on the cusp. He just needed a little push.

"She likes music. Classical music. She plays the cello."

"Who does?"

"Karla Albrecht. The one you have your eye on."

Long started to protest his innocence but decided it wasn't worth it. A crooked little smile pushed color into his cheeks. "Okay," he muttered.

"I thought you'd want to know. Beethoven especially. She hates all that modern stuff."

Long grinned. "Got it. Thanks."

Anna returned the grin. "Now you owe me."

Long laughed and shook his head. He glanced around and paused a few beats to make her wait. "Okay, go in. But if anyone asks, it was Cooper who let you in, not me."

"Thank you, Corporal," Anna gestured to Madeleine and Amalia to follow her into the building.

"Oh, and Frau Klein? You might tread lightly. I heard him cussing up a storm on the phone earlier. Yelling about jurisdictions and the law or something. Some MPs paid him a visit, too. It's been a rough day. Fair warning."

Anna thanked him as she ushered Madeleine and Amalia into the lobby. The lights were already dimmed and most people had left, leaving the place feeling hollow. Amalia found a bench outside the director's office, where the lights were thankfully already off, and she and Madeleine huddled onto it.

"If anyone asks…" Anna said, as she started up the stairs.

"I know, I know," Madeleine said. "Captain Cooper. I know. Hurry."

Cooper was sitting at his desk, despondent. His hair stood on end the way it did when he had been running his hands through it, which is what he did when he was thinking. The desk lamp cast a yellow glow onto the papers he was reading, and he was so immersed that he didn't hear Anna come in.

"Is everything all right, Captain?" Anna could tell that it wasn't.

"Oh hi, Anna. What are you doing here?" He checked his watch. "It's a bit late. Are you just now getting back from Frankfurt?"

"No, Bender dropped me at the house a while ago. But I need to talk to you."

"Is this about Morgenstern, because maybe it can wait? I've got a big enough headache going already." He gestured at the papers on the desk.

"What's happened now?" Anna took the chair opposite the desk and sat down.

"Orders came down. We are to pack up the two hundred paintings and ship them to Washington. They have to be ready to go immediately. We tried, we lost."

"So, those paintings belong to America now?" Now Anna felt as despondent as Cooper.

"All I know is we've come to the end of the line. It's either do this, or go to jail. And I don't want to go to jail, really. Even if you did come visit me." He looked up from his desk. "What's happened to your neck?"

Anna reached for the spot on her neck where Berg had choked her. "I need to see Oskar. Right away. He can help us with this case. He can identify Berg from the black market."

Cooper grimaced and held her gaze for a moment, perhaps hoping for a better explanation. "Does needing to see Oskar right away have something to do with those marks on your neck? Is everything all right, Anna?"

She ignored his question. "I must talk to Oskar."

"And you're not going to tell me more?"

She hesitated. She knew she would need Cooper's American authority to spring Oskar from the camp.

"He's a witness to this crime."

"Oh, good, another crime? There are so few of them around here these days." He sighed. "And anyway, how do you know?"

"He and Amalia sold the paintings on the black market. That is to say, Eva sent them to do it. She kept the paintings at the house, under the sofa cushions. They saw her take them out. They knew about it this whole time but were too scared to say anything. And anyway, they didn't know it was a crime."

"The kids sold the paintings," Cooper said, matter of fact. "Of course they did. Oskar told you this?"

"No, Amalia did. Just now. And I found this in the sofa." She pulled the nail from her pocket and held it up for Cooper.

"And does *that* have something to do with the marks on your neck?"

"Yes, a little," she said. "But, you see, Oskar is a witness to this crime. He knows that it was this man Berg who bought the paintings. When you investigate, you'll need to interview him. And for that, you need him to be here, not in some children's home in Bavaria."

"In order to investigate, we first have to admit there was a crime, which will go over like gangbusters with no actual tangible evidence. That's just what we need." Cooper shook his head.

"But you can't let them get away with this, Captain. Surely you're not suggesting that?"

"No, of course not. But it's not going to help our cause. Not one damn bit."

"But what if I told you that I think Stuart is involved? At least tangentially?"

Cooper's face lit up. "Really? Tell me more. You're cheering me up already."

Anna leaned her elbows on the desk and Cooper returned the gesture. She couldn't help but smile at their conspiratorial pose. Like children telling secrets at school.

"I told you Stuart signed off on Eva's hiring," Anna said.

"Yes, but you don't have any proof of that."

"No, not yet. But he's also guilty of fraternizing."

"Fraternizing? What with Eva? Can you prove *that*?"

"Yes, I can," said Anna, pleased with herself. "Frau Huber, the housekeeper, has seen Eva at the house in Frankfurt on occasion. She didn't witness anything herself, of course, but whenever Stuart was there and Eva showed up in the evening, she was sent home. Last night she saw Eva and Stuart get into a fight and he hit her."

"Hit who?"

"Eva. And then Frau Huber threw a plate at him and she ran out. Madeleine says Eva came home, packed up herself and her father in the middle of the night, and left first thing this morning."

"Damn. Well, okay. Where's Eva now?"

"No one knows that part. But guess who also showed up at Stuart's house last night?"

"General MacArthur?"

"Anton Berg. Morgenstern's crooked partner. He and Eva exchanged words."

"And you know it was Berg, how?"

"Frau Huber. She saw the whole thing. The man who introduced himself to me as Spitzer the accountant, is really Anton Berg the art dealer. He has a scar on his cheek, a unique one at that. No question it's the same man. See, I knew he was no accountant." She was pleased with herself.

Cooper conceded. "Frau Klein, I must say you do have a knack for this intrigue stuff. So, Berg showed up at the Morgenstern house, too? I'm just trying to keep up."

"Yes. And you know what else? Jacob Morgenstern. He asked me one question today. Only one. He asked me if the Kirchner painting was still in the collection."

"Meaning?"

"Meaning, I think, that he knew Berg was after that painting, which Frau Huber substantiates. They fought over it before Morgenstern and his family were deported. Berg really wants that painting."

Cooper leaned back. "Well, he's got it, we assume. Why's he coming after Eva now?"

"My guess is that Eva saw Frau Huber at the CCP yesterday and panicked. She ran to Stuart to tell him that Frau Huber had been here, thinking maybe that we were on to their relationship. And then Berg showed up."

"But what was Berg doing there?"

"I think he actually came to see Frau Huber and not Eva. It's possible he got wind of letters going out about the survivors? Maybe he knows that Morgenstern is in Zeilsheim, too, and feels the noose tightening. I don't think he expected to find Eva there. So when he did, she told him about Frau Huber at the CCP and panicked him, too."

"So he knows Morgenstern's alive and he thinks we're on to him. That's a pretty tight noose."

"One more thing. There's no record of any Eva Lange working at the Staedel in the 1930s. I checked the museum's own personnel files. Unless she used a different name, she was never there. She's hiding something. She lied to you, and now Berg thinks she's gone to rat him out to save herself. He came to her house looking for money he says she owes him."

Cooper whistled. "Well, now this is bad. And does *that* visit have something to do with the marks on your neck?"

"Possibly, but I'm all right, I promise."

"And Amalia?"

"They're waiting downstairs. Nobody wanted to stay home alone while I came to see you."

Cooper sat up and exhaled. "This is a great story. Really impressive. I'm convinced that what you uncovered is, in fact, what's happened. For some God-only-knows-what reason, Eva and Berg conspired to switch out the paintings with forgeries. We've still got a problem."

"No paintings."

"Bingo. No paintings, no forger, no case. Just a bunch of speculation and, if I may be honest, preposterous accusations," Cooper said. "We'll have to bring in this Berg. I'll have the administration folks find him and send some MPs for a visit. If they can find him." He pulled out his phone directory.

"I know Berg's got the paintings. He's holding onto them." Anna said. "But what about Oskar? He can corroborate the whole story." Why was Cooper paying no attention to Oskar?

"He might." Cooper ran his finger down the listing of names and phone numbers. "But that's not enough to keep him off that train to Bavaria. We don't have a case, Anna. We have accusations. And our star witnesses are two grade schoolers. It's not exactly legal *terra firma*. And anyway, these things take time."

He lifted the receiver and began dialing. "Anton Berg, you say? Speaking of *terra firma*, I'm already on shaky ground. We have to sew this up before we say anything. We'll have a chat with Herr Berg and see what he has to say. We've got to find those paintings."

Anna wanted to lunge across the desk and slap him. Why was he being so dismissive? She knew they had it right, and the urgency of it nipped at her ankles. Her mind spun in circles as she watched him finish dialing. After several seconds, he asked to be connected to the military police office. He put his hand over the mouthpiece. "First we have to find Berg. Then we'll go get him. Oh, and Frau Klein?"

"Yes?" Anna clenched her teeth.

"Be ready to go tomorrow morning at 0800. I'll pick you up at the house. Bring the duchess, too, she'll want to be a part of this." He picked up an envelope and held it next to his face as he broke into a grin. "I got a present from the MPs today. I had to move a small mountain to get it for you, but it worked. It might be my last act as an officer of the United States Army, but it will have been worth it."

Anna wrinkled her brow and was about to ask for an explanation but he shook his head.

"No questions. Just be ready."

chapter seventeen

Anna was pulling on her coat when the jeep's horn croaked outside the window. Snow had started to fall that morning, not heavy yet, but enough to stick to the ground. The house was cold and damp, and she had slept in her coat huddled with Amalia, the poker from the fireplace tucked next to her. Madeleine had slept on the sofa under three blankets she had taken from Eva's bed.

"Where are we going, Mama?" Amalia whined. "It's so cold." She hopped up and down from foot to foot, already dressed in the sweater from Cooper's mother now that is was properly cold, the wool scarf she hated tied around her head.

Cooper leaned on the horn again. Anna handed the fireplace poker to Madeleine and said a quick goodbye. They had made a plan the night before: keep the door locked and the windows shuttered; don't open the door to anyone; and if she gets too worried, come to the Collecting Point. It wasn't much of a plan, but it was all they had. All Anna could do was hope that Berg was more talk than action.

"Good morning, ladies. It's a fine day for a liberation," Cooper shouted, his breath appearing in little puffs.

"*Hallo*," Amalia said. "Nice to meet you." She was practicing her English phrases.

"Nice to *see* you," Anna corrected. She smiled at Cooper. "What are you talking about? Will you please tell us where we are going?"

Cooper said nothing as he put the jeep into gear and they lurched forward. It was early and the light was a cold steel gray that made the rubble landscape much the same color as the sky.

"Find anything?" Cooper shouted over the noise of the jeep once they were underway.

"No, nothing. I searched every corner of that house, dug through her drawers, and went through any papers I found. Closets, pillowcases, behind the books on the shelf, under the rugs. Nothing. I even turned the paintings on the wall around to see if maybe another painting was hidden behind. Can you imagine if the paintings were right under my nose this whole time?"

Cooper sighed. "I worry that the paintings are long gone. Far away from here and from prying eyes. In which case, I'm in big trouble."

"But then why is Berg still here? I think he'd be gone, too."

"Unless he was just the middle man for some other operation." Cooper shifted the jeep's gears.

"I don't think so. He wants to sell them, but it's much too soon. He has to wait for the dust to settle and for the market to get stronger.

I think we found the collection before he could move it. He didn't count on that. The paintings are wherever he is."

"I hope you're right, Sherlock." They bounced over the pock-marked pavement, and Amalia giggled in the back seat, oblivious to their conversation. Anna turned to smile at her, and, for a moment, she believed all would be well.

The roads were quiet and the ride was short. They didn't speak, each of them lost in their own thoughts. Anna resisted the urge to ask Cooper again where they were going, but as they turned onto the Schiersteiner Strasse, she began to put the pieces together.

"Is this about Oskar?" she whispered.

Cooper grinned and said nothing. When they turned into the displaced persons camp, Anna had her answer. Even Amalia had figured it out and began squirming in her seat.

"How about if I go in first?" Cooper said as they pulled up to the office at the camp. "I have this official-looking form." He held a piece of paper up to show her.

"What's that?"

"A summons to appear before the magistrate as a witness in a matter of a violation of Article 54 of the Occupational Law in the jurisdiction of Darmstadt," he thundered, grinning from ear to ear. "Let's see these UN do-gooders try to argue with *that*." He slid out of the jeep. "If I need you, I'll come get you."

Anna's heart soared. He had done it. "I'm coming, too." She climbed out after him and gestured for Amalia to stay put.

Cooper shook his head but waited for her to catch up. "Let me do the talking, at least," he grumbled.

"Yes, sir. I can't wait. But how did you get that paper so fast? You said we don't even have a case. How do you already know there will be a trial?"

"Oh, we don't have a case on Berg, but this isn't about him." Cooper said. "Young Oskar is also witness to another crime. You'll recall the case of Schenk, Schneider, and the cache of stolen art from the villa?"

"You're joking," Anna stopped walking.

"I got the case moved up. It's going to trial after all. We need Oskar, he's our star witness." He motioned for her to keep moving. "That boy just seems to attract trouble. I don't know if it's worth springing him, but since you asked me to, how could I refuse?"

Anna felt herself expand with a joy she had not felt in months. "Schenk is really going to trial?" She shuddered remembering the way Schenk had played the Americans and thrown her to the wolves at the initial hearing. He and that oily gallery owner, Schneider, had played all sides against each other to try and get access to the art at the Collecting Point. Only Oskar knew for sure who Schenk really was because Schenk was Oskar's own uncle, who had worked for the Nazis. Without Oskar, the *Amis* had no case.

"Yep. I've been working on this for a while." He waved the paper around. "Bender helped. I didn't want to let on, in case it didn't pan out. I've been lighting a fire under the prosecutors, telling them the one person who knows the whole story will be out of their jurisdiction if they don't act. They really want to nail Schenk. So, he's to be remanded into your custody as his temporary guardian. You'll have to testify, too; but Oskar's their best hope."

"Of course I'll testify." She jogged a few steps to catch up with him, but he was moving too fast, his long strides outpacing her. "So that's why you kept asking me to trust you? You were already working on this?"

"As soon as you told Bender about Oskar's problem, he told me and we got on it. Like I say, I wanted to be sure it worked. And I know you hate asking for help." He finally slowed down to allow her to catch up. "So, come on. Let's go get the boy."

Anna tried to think of something to say. "Thank you," was all she could manage. It really was going to be okay, just like Cooper said. She smiled as he held the door open. "Thank you," she repeated as they stepped into the sticky warmth of the office.

"Anna, how nice to see you." Maria Niemeyer looked up from her perch at the front counter. She smiled at Captain Cooper. Her expression shifted. "What are you doing here?"

"We've come to get Oskar," Anna bubbled. "To take him home."

Cooper slid the summons onto the counter and pointed at the relevant line.

"He's due to appear in court, as a witness to a crime," Anna clarified. "Isn't that wonderful? Can I go get him?" Anna asked. "I want to be the one to tell him."

Maria was taken aback. "Oh, but he's not here. He's gone to the train station with the others."

Anna gripped the edge of the counter to steady herself as she felt all the air leave the room. "What do you mean?"

"They're leaving for Bavaria today." She glanced at the clock. "The train leaves in twenty minutes."

"But they were supposed to leave tomorrow," Anna protested. "That's what my letter said. Saturday."

Maria shook her head. "I don't know about that. I only know they left here this morning, suitcases and all."

Panic surged through Anna's gut. She grabbed Cooper's arm and pulled him to the door. "We have to go."

"Anna, wait a minute," Maria called as she pulled papers from a file.

"Can it wait, Maria? I can't let him get away."

Maria held up a piece of paper. It was a registration paper of some kind. Anna squinted to see. She wanted only to run, but Maria waved her back to the desk, giving a quick glance to the other women at their desks, who seemed wholly disinterested in the conversation.

"I'll start the jeep," Cooper said. "We can make it, but we have to go in one minute." He disappeared into a wave of cold air that exploded through the open door.

Anna went back to the counter. "What is it?" she pleaded.

Maria leaned forward. "You're going to get him off the train?"

Anna nodded.

"And you're going to keep him?"

"Yes, of course."

"Then it might be better if..." Maria looked at Anna and then down at the paper, which Anna could see was Oskar's registration card. His face scowled at her from the photo that was stapled to the corner.

Anna followed Maria's gaze, and then the two women locked eyes.

"It seems like there's a mistake here," Maria said firmly, trying to guide Anna's reaction.

Anna bit her lip. "Perhaps I should take that with me to the train station? For identification purposes?

Maria nodded. "Yes. I think so." She picked up the paper and without taking her eyes off Anna, pulled the stapled photo off the paper and handed it her. "You keep the photo. And take this form to the man at the train. It's the only record we have of Oskar having been here at the camp, so you *mustn't lose it*." She pushed the paper into Anna's hand. "Go get him," she whispered. She pressed her lips together, picked up a stack of files, and walked away.

Anna wanted to say thank you, but she knew Maria was deflecting attention, so she turned on her heel and rushed out the door to the waiting jeep. She slid the photo into her pocket, and crumpled the registration form into her fist. She knew what Maria had done. As far as the official UNRRA record went, there was no Oskar Gruenewald anymore. She would have to figure out the rest later.

"What happened?" Cooper said, pulling Anna into the jeep. "I thought he was supposed to go tomorrow?"

Anna checked her watch. "Can we make it?"

"Oh, sure," Cooper reassured her. She glanced at him and could tell he wasn't sure at all.

The train station was across town and the weather would slow them down.

"Chicago weather," Cooper mumbled as the jeep careened out of the camp drive and along the street that had now come to life. The snow was becoming heavier, too, hitting Anna's face in wet pellets.

"Where's Oskar, Mama?" Amalia piped up from the back seat.

"He's at the train station, *Maus*. We're going to get him now. Just hang on." She did the same while Cooper took a curve too fast and slid the jeep through the accumulating snow, and ignoring more than one stop sign, waved himself through in front of the rare other car. Anna thought about what Maria had done for her. She had expunged Oskar from at least one link in the official record. He was never at the camp, and if they could get him off the train, it would, at the very least, cause a glitch in the bureaucratic continuum. If he's not on the train to Bavaria, he must be at the camp. And if he's not at the camp, he must be on the train. If nothing else, it would keep their wheels spinning for a while and buy time for her conscience to process what she had done. She took a deep breath and smiled at Amalia to reassure her. *Of course we will get Oskar back.*

They arrived at the station within ten minutes, but Anna was bristling with impatience. Her hair was wet from snow and her hands frozen from gripping the frame of the jeep to keep from falling out.

"Go," Cooper shouted, pulling up to the main entrance and pressing the summons paper into her hand. "I'll bring Amalia. We'll find you. Tell them they may not leave with Oskar on the train."

Anna ran into the main hall, nearly slipping on the wet concrete. She oriented herself and searched for Oskar's train. One look at the platforms answered her question. A group of some fifty children huddled at the far end of the station, alongside a waiting train. They were too far away for Anna to make out their faces, but she knew it had to be the children from the camp. A man in a suit and women with clipboards and khaki uniforms walked among them calling out instructions. In response, the children lined up facing the train, their backs to Anna. Their suitcases had been set to one side, piled against a column. Anna picked up her pace and started toward them just as a train arrived at the adjacent platform, blocking her view. She broke into a jog, her heartbeat accelerating. Clutching the paper in her right hand, she pushed through the sea of slow-moving people with her left. As she reached the stairs and started to descend, something familiar in the throng of people moving along the concourse caught her eye. She scanned the sea of bobbing heads and tried to find it again, backtracking up the stairs, until she saw it: the light-colored coat and green hat moving through the crowd. Even from behind, she was sure it was Berg. He was carrying a suitcase and ambling at a steady pace. The enormous clock hanging from the damaged roof ticked 8:54 a.m. Where was Berg going? If he saw Amalia with Cooper—an *Ami* officer—there's no telling what he would do. Cooper had never seen Berg, so it would be up to Amalia to recognize him, to think to tell Cooper, and to do it without drawing attention to herself. He could easily get away, right from under Cooper's nose. 8:55 now.

Anna bolted toward Oskar's platform, nearly falling over her own feet on the slippery stairs. As she descended, she tried to find his familiar tousled hair in the crowd of children, all of whom were blonde, Aryan models, so alike it was impossible to tell them apart from a distance. Her rush caused enough of a disturbance that the people waiting on the platform turned to look, and she was dimly aware of the wall of small faces now oriented toward her. She focused on the man in the suit standing at the far end by the train door, talking to someone in a Red Cross uniform.

"Oskar?" Anna said, then shouted, "Oskar Gruenewald. Where are you?" She pushed through the sea of bodies, waving the paper over her head.

"What the hell?" the man in the suit said, searching for the source of the disturbance. "You: stop!" He held his hand up at Anna.

"I am here for Oskar Gruenewald," Anna panted. "He can't go on the train." She held out the summons paper for the man's inspection.

He took it and scanned the words.

"Who are you?" he asked, irritated, trying to hand the paper back to her.

Anna skipped the introductions. "The boy is a witness to a crime that is under investigation by the Occupational Government in Hesse. He can't leave the state because he's needed to testify. That's what it says there." She jabbed at the paper with her finger.

"Frau Klein?" Oskar's voice was small and unsure. Anna turned to see him standing behind her, eyes wide and cheeks hollow.

She pulled him toward her. "I told you I would come for you, didn't I?" she said to the top of his head as she embraced him. "I told you."

"I didn't believe you."

"I know. But I did it anyway." She pulled him close as she waited.

The man in the suit acted confused and put out by the turn of events, tossing the paper back at her and scanning the platform for another person of authority to take over. Behind him, a round-bellied conductor in a faded blue uniform barked that the train was due to leave in one minute and to get all the kids aboard. The clipboard women jumped into action, reorganizing the travelers into a different line, pushing their little bodies and shouting over their heads. Some of the younger ones started to cry. Anna's heart wrenched seeing the fear and confusion on the little faces. One little girl in a blue coat and white tights reached for her, face contorted and eyes wide, but was snatched up by a uniformed woman who pushed her onto the train. Anna stepped aside out of the fray, feeling sick to her stomach. Oskar gripped her so hard around the waist she thought they might both fall over. "He's not going." She shook the summons paper at another uniformed woman who tried to pry Oskar off of her. "You can take it up with the American judge."

The woman was disinterested. "Whatever you say," she said as she yanked another child onto the bottom step of the train carriage. The scene bordered on pandemonium as the cries grew louder. Anna felt her skin crawl. She forced herself to watch as one by one they got onto the train. She would not turn away again. Not this time. She exhaled when she saw Cooper and Amalia coming down the stairs.

"Come with me," she whispered, pulling Oskar into a run toward the stairs before anyone could change their mind. Seeing Oskar, Amalia charged toward them.

"Did you see him?" Anna asked Amalia, who collided with Oskar. "Did you see the man from the black market? The one with the scar? He's here."

Amalia shook her head, gripping Oskar around the waist. "No. The man from the house? He's at the station?"

"What's going on?" Cooper came up behind Anna.

"Anton Berg." Anna said. "I saw him up on the main floor. With a suitcase. He must be leaving for somewhere." She consulted a sign above the platform. "Paris. The train to Paris."

"I don't know what he looks like," Cooper said. "Did she see him?" He turned to Amalia, who shook her head.

"Oskar, you remember the man from the black market, the one with the scar on his face? Would you recognize him? He's wearing a light-colored coat and a blue hat."

"Sure, I can spot him."

"We have to find him. He might be getting on the train to Paris."

She turned to Cooper. "He can't get on that train."

Oskar inflated. "I'll find him," he declared. He was off in a blur of knees and elbows before Anna could say anything more.

Anna took Amalia's hand and tugged at Cooper to follow them back up the stairs. Behind them, the man in the suit shouted something at her about missing the train, about explanations to the refugee agency, apologies to the nation of Poland, and other things Anna ignored. They ran up the stairs and followed Oskar who was yards ahead, waving for them to follow. He ran down the flight of stairs leading to the Paris train's platform. Anna stopped at the top to catch her breath. It would not do to come barging at Berg in a flurry, especially with a train approaching the station. As it was, Berg was sitting on a bench facing away from them, the suitcase by his side. Oskar stopped and gave Anna a questioning look. The train rumbled to a screeching stop and settled back, its doors popping open to release its passengers. The platform quickly became crowded and Anna craned her neck to keep Berg in her sights. He sat, as before, not moving. *What is he waiting for?*

She turned to Cooper. "What can we do?"

"I'll get the MP." Cooper started to jog toward the main entry. "Be right back," he called over his shoulder.

Anna and Amalia stood on the landing above the platform. The crush of passengers had reached the stairs and pushed them against the railing.

Below them, Anton Berg rose to his feet and looked around. *He is waiting for someone.* He referred to his watch and then scanned the concourse above him. Anna averted her eyes, and turned sideways in an attempt not to be spotted, but Berg saw Amalia in her green coat and then made eye contact with Anna. They locked eyes for several seconds before he bent to reach for his suitcase. In a flash, a small figure flew past him, picking up the suitcase and running along the platform, then circling back toward the stairs in a wide arc. Berg made an attempt to catch the thief, but Oskar was too fast, taking the stairs two at a time and running past Anna and Amalia to the top of the stairs and through the crowd. Berg started to give chase but changed his mind. He stopped, staring at Anna. A garbled announcement crackled over the loudspeaker and the train's engine hissed.

"*Maus*, you go catch Oskar. And then you both find Captain Cooper, quickly." Anna gave Amalia a little push without taking her eyes off Berg. The girl obliged her without asking any questions.

Anna stared back at Berg. She guessed he might take his chances and get on the train without his bag and make his escape. She moved her eyes to the clock as it ticked to 9:05. From the corner of her eye, she saw the children's train starting to move out of the station, wheels scraping along the track, its windows closed and blank. The man in the suit rubbed his forehead and watched it go.

Anna scanned the other side of the concourse for Cooper, but saw only clusters of other Americans. If Berg got on the train and it left, the hope of ever finding him was slim. Yes, the Paris authorities on the other end might arrest him on his arrival, if he made it that far. He could get off at any number of stops along the way and vanish forever. *Why is he not moving?* She caught his gaze landing on something to her left. She followed his eyes to see the tall figure of Eva and her father walking toward her. Eva wore a hat pulled down to conceal part of her face and a wool suit, the same one she had worn the day she arrived at the Collecting Point. She pulled a struggling Manfred Lange along with one hand and struggled with a bulging suitcase on the other. When she caught sight of Anna, Eva stopped in her tracks and then looked down at Berg, who finally made a move to get on the train. Somewhere a conductor's whistle shrieked, followed by a chorus of train doors slamming. As if the sound had put her in motion, Anna flew down the stairs after Berg, who vanished onto the Paris-bound train through an open door near the back. Anna ran as fast as she could alongside the carriages, scanning the windows. A conductor stood by an open door, looking at a pocket watch.

"Don't let this train leave," she shouted as she found the nearest door and climbed aboard. "There's a man on the train who's under arrest by the Americans." It would have no effect, but she said it anyway.

She ran along the narrow hallway peering into each compartment as she passed. Old women and children regarded her with the suspicion of people weary of any excitement. She raced through one carriage, then another, but Berg was nowhere. She began to backtrack, this time scouring the compartments more closely. In the middle of the second carriage, a door slid open and a hand grabbed her arm, yanking her back into the compartment with such force that she lost her footing and fell to the ground, taking Anton Berg with her. His hands grabbed and scratched at her as they both tried to regain their footing, but she fought back hard, kicking him in the ribs and stepping on his hand as she scrambled to her feet. He was slow to get up, and she gave him another kick for good measure before pulling open the compartment door and stepping out into the hall. A man coming down the hall retreated to avoid her as she pulled open the window.

"*Hilfe*!" she called, "I've been attacked." Her voice dissipated into the cold air, and she wasn't sure anyone had heard her. The part of the platform she could see was empty and only a handful of people waited for a train on the other side of the neighboring rails. She tried again.

"Help me!" she called before she sensed Berg getting to his feet. She wheeled around in time to see him lunging at her. She ducked and lurched at him with outstretched arms, ramming him hard into the compartment door. His head snapped back and struck the window, but the thud of his skull against glass was accompanied by a crunch in her shoulder. The searing pain that followed took her breath away. Berg exhaled with a groan and slid to the ground, a confused expression on his face. She had barely straightened when footsteps approached from her right and two MPs were upon them, pulling Berg to his feet. Anna stepped aside to let them pass, putting a hand to the window to steady herself. The pain in her shoulder sent her reeling, and when she tried to move her arm the agony expanded outward, washing over her head and neck. She held her breath and closed her eyes. Voices rose and the car jostled as the MP dragged Berg from the train. Once they were gone, she exhaled and opened her eyes. Cooper was walking toward her.

"Anna, my God, what happened?" He blanched at the sight of her. Taking her good arm, he guided her to the door and helped her down onto the platform. "Here, why don't you sit down?" he gestured at a bench.

Anna ignored his offer and unhooked her good arm from his. "Eva. Did you see Eva? She was here. They were supposed to meet, she and Berg. But when she saw me, she backed out."

"No, we didn't see her. I was busy racing after you."

"You have the suitcase?" Anna asked.

"Yes, we've got it, and now we've got him, too. He's little worse for wear."

A whistle pierced the air, and one by one the doors of the train to Paris slammed shut.

"Where?" Anna asked.

"Up in the ticket office."

"Let's go. I want to see."

Cooper snorted, exasperated, but he obliged. They walked together, Anna switching sides to allow her bad arm to hang between them, out of the line of jostling and bumping.

"Your shoulder looks a little off," Cooper observed.

"I know. It hurts."

"We should get you checked out first."

"No. First we check the suitcase."

Cooper shook his head, but Anna took pleasure at the hint of a gleam that flashed in his eyes. "You should be pretty happy with yourself, tackling the bad guy like that. The train was about to leave," he offered.

"We've got to find Eva and her father."

"We will. They can't have gone far."

Anna noticed that people were looking at her with concern, and she put a hand to her cheek. A gash under her eye stung when she touched it, and her fingers came away bloody. Her eye socket throbbed, too, and she felt lightheaded. They walked for what seemed like a mile until Cooper pushed open the door to the ticket office, which was dark behind closed shutters. It was several beats before Anna's eyes registered the contents of the room: desks with ledgers and binders organized into neat rows. A single bulb overhead illuminated only a small circle, and the smell of ink and paper hung in the air. Berg stood in the corner, handcuffed between two towering MPs. The suitcase sat on the floor by the door.

"Where are the children?" Anna asked. "I thought they were with you."

"I sent them home," Cooper said. "Enough excitement here. I put them in a jeep with the other MP. They'll be fine. Frau Wolf is there, right? And the MP will stay with them until I say otherwise."

Anna was relieved. Eva's whereabouts were another problem, but for now they had Berg. She walked to the suitcase. "Can we open it?"

Cooper snorted. "We won the war; we can do whatever the hell we want."

Anna started to bend down and then winced as the pain in her arm shot back up into her head.

"Let me." Cooper kicked the bag onto its side and bent over to work at the buckles.

Berg seethed in the corner, too angry to speak. Anna was pleased to see a bruise emerging on his cheekbone right above his stupid scar. His hair was a mess and there was a tear in the sleeve of his coat. He blinked rapidly, eyes focused on nothing in particular.

Cooper threw the suitcase open with enthusiasm and sent socks and undershirts rolling onto the floor. He rummaged through the contents, a toiletry kit, one pair of shoes, a handful of novels, a few shirts, and pants. The rummaging became rifling as he tossed items out, making an effort to show his disregard, until the suitcase was empty. His hands ran along the fabric lining to the edge where it attached to the body of the suitcase. He ran a fingernail along one edge and then another before stopping in the middle of the third.

"Oh," he exhaled. "Why, look here." His fingers picked at the lining until he could grasp a piece between his thumb and forefinger. The fabric made a tearing sound as it separated from the frame of the suitcase, and Cooper pulled steadily with two hands until the opening revealed something wrapped in brown paper hidden between the lining and the suitcase exterior.

"Pretty good," he said. "That's a professional job. He really must be a museum type, like he says." He pulled the package out of its hiding spot and laid it on the table. Anna's heart pounded and her arm throbbed in unison with the beats.

Cooper tugged at the cellophane tape that secured the package, separating the long seam by running the flat of his hand between the papers. He peeked into the gap and smiled.

"Merry Christmas to us," he sang as he opened the paper to reveal two canvases. A man in a green jacket gazed up at them, an inscrutable expression on his face. Cooper slid the second canvas out from underneath, and Anna exhaled and felt a burden lifted when she saw the swirly white clouds against a dark blue Berlin sky. She gave a thought to Jacob Morgenstern, and emotion overtook her like a wave of warm water. She wanted to cry, but she would not, not in front of Berg. Instead, she smiled at him.

"Those are my paintings," Berg said. "I can prove it."

"I can prove they aren't," Anna said. "Jacob Morgenstern will help me. I spoke to him myself yesterday."

Berg's face slackened just a little. He started blinking again. "I have the bill of sale," he said, his voice rising. "It was a legitimate sale."

"No, it wasn't," Anna replied. "And even if that's the case, you tampered with cultural property that was in possession of the Americans." She took a step toward him. "You know the *Amis* don't like that."

Berg glared at her, his jaw working. "I did no such thing. It was that cow, Eva. This was her idea."

Anna crossed the room in three steps and was upon Berg before anyone could stop her. "I don't believe you. No way was this her idea, you bastard. Why did you put her up to this?" she shouted. Eva was her friend. It was the one thing she knew for sure. "This is all your fault." She swung at him with her good arm, but he ducked.

Cooper stepped between her and Berg. "Okay, okay. Let's try this. There's a forger involved here. Not a great one, but a serviceable one. I expect he'll be able to tell us everything. So talk, or don't. Either way, you're done."

Berg shook his head. "You don't have any forger."

"Don't I?" Cooper crossed his arms. "You wanna place a wager on that?"

Anna stared at Cooper. *What is he talking about?* He locked eyes with Berg and smiled, expectant. Anna saw the familiar twinkle and caught on. She nodded at Berg as if she, too, knew all about the forger. "So why *did* you do it?" she asked.

"I did nothing wrong. I'm just taking what's rightfully mine." Berg spat as he spoke.

"Good, then file a claim and we'll review it," Cooper replied. "Just be clear which paintings you're claiming—the real ones or the fake ones."

He stepped back, indicating to the MPs to take Berg away. He returned the package to the suitcase. "That's about enough of this for now. Plenty of time for questions later. This is evidence," he said, patting the canvases. "See that it's kept very safe. I'll be by later to make my report." He turned to Anna. "First we need to take you to the medic. I think you've dislocated your shoulder."

They watched the MPs escort Berg from the room. Cooper closed the door behind them and turned to Anna. They both exhaled, Cooper leaning against the door.

Anna finally sat down. "So, where is this forger?"

Cooper grinned. "Beats me. Let him think we have the guy and see if it greases the wheels a little. Can't hurt, that's for sure. Now, your arm."

"It's fine as long as I don't move it. Look, we have to find Eva. She was here with her father. They were going to get on that train with Berg. We should have made him explain."

"We will, but not here."

"But there's no time to lose," she shouted, waving her arms

reflexively. The pain seared through her and she cried out. Her entire left side was on fire.

"That's it. I'm taking you to the clinic." He took her by the other arm and guided her to the door. "No arguing."

"We have to find Eva. She knows you're coming after her now, so who knows what she'll do. What if she goes back to the house with her father? She could hurt the children."

"The MP is there," Cooper said. "Don't worry. One thing at a time. You'll be useless if you don't get this fixed."

Anna let herself be pushed along and waited for him to close the door. "But that's only a solution for today," she argued.

"Well, today is all we've got." Cooper sighed. "Tomorrow is a whole other story."

Out in the train station, life continued as normal with people bustling through the ruins to get on with their lives. Already the morning's events—rescuing Oskar, the fight on the train, the paintings in the suitcase—seemed surreal. It wasn't even ten o'clock yet. Together they walked to the jeep Cooper had parked along the curb. He helped her inside, studiously avoiding touching her left arm. As they pulled away, Anna gazed up at the sky. The snow had stopped, but the clouds were so low that the vapor surrounded them, foggy and cold. She shivered as the damp air seeped through her coat and the reality of what had happened sank into her skin.

chapter eighteen

Anna cried out when the American doctor with the yellow teeth pushed her shoulder back into place. The pain burned hot all along her arm and into her body, her neck, and her face. She steadied herself on the examination table with her good arm.

"That'll be pretty sore for a while," the doctor said, tying a sling around her neck. "At least for a couple of weeks. Try not to move it. I wish I had something to stop the pain, but I'm fresh out."

"Don't worry," Anna grumbled. "I may never move it again, after that."

"Thanks, Doc. Really appreciate your bending the rules," Cooper said, picking up Anna's coat.

"Don't tell anyone." The doctor opened the door and ushered them out of the tiny exam room. "I can't make a habit of it," he admonished.

Anna thanked him as Cooper helped her put on her coat, draping it over her left shoulder. They stepped out into the freezing hallway that was decorated with large posters warning of the horrors of venereal disease. Anna glanced at the men waiting to see the doctor, sitting in the metal chairs lined up along the wall. They all averted their eyes. No wonder the *Ami* had been so kind to her; she was probably the only non-VD case he'd seen all day. A simple dislocated shoulder, even on a *Kraut*; what a nice change.

"That was fun," she mumbled as they made their way to the exit.

"I'm taking you home and you're going to lie down," Cooper lectured. "We'll deal with the rest of this mess tomorrow."

"Don't be silly. I'm fine." His doting irritated her. Perhaps another woman would have been flattered. *Does he think I like this?* She was having none of it. "Let's go to work. Don't you have things to do?"

Cooper threw up his hands. "I give up."

Before they could reach the door, it flew open, blasting frigid air into their faces. Two GIs, one carrying an old man by his arms, the other supporting his legs, maneuvered their way into the clinic.

"We need the doc," the first soldier said, his voice calm and matter-of-fact. When they got through the door, Anna saw that the man they were carrying was Manfred Lange. She gasped at the sight of him. He was ashen and unconscious.

"No Germans," Cooper said, perhaps attempting to do right by the doctor. "Take him to St. Josef's on Beethoven Strasse." He walked around them to the door and stood with his hand on the handle, ready to send them back out. Anna knew he was following protocol, but it felt heartless. He wasn't fully convinced either.

The GI was sweating from the exertion, his head glowing. He was breathing hard, trying not to drop Herr Lange, whose head flopped around alarmingly. Was he already dead?

"I know, sir, but this man is in trouble. I think it's a heart attack or a stroke or something. He fell in the street. We need a doc right now."

The commotion was sufficient for the doctor to step out of the exam room. Seeing the men, he waved them through, stepping aside to let them pass.

"Why does this always happen when you show up?" he quipped at Cooper, following the GIs inside and closing the door.

"Well, okay, let's go," Cooper said, his hand still on the doorknob.

Anna was about to argue about leaving Manfred Lange alone, but she stopped herself. Cooper had never seen Manfred Lange. Had Eva been with her father when he collapsed? Would she take a chance and turn up here, at an *Ami* clinic, looking for him? She loved him, and she would want to be with him. But Eva also knew the game with Berg was up and that she'd be implicated. Maybe she was already on the run. Had Herr Lange collapsed because she had left him behind?

"Anna?" Cooper waved a hand in front of her face. "You okay?"

"Yes," she said. "But you know, I feel a bit woozy. From the pain. Could I sit for a while?"

"Why don't I take you home? I feel like I've said this already," Cooper pleaded.

"No, I want to wait here for a minute. You go back to work. I'll be there in a few minutes. I'm worried that you're gone too long."

Cooper studied her face. "You're up to something, I can tell." He waited for an answer, but she offered none. Instead, she sat down in the chair by the front door.

"I'll be fine," she said. "Really." He had to get back to the Collecting Point, and if she stalled long enough, he would give in and go. She would wait here and hope Eva showed up. At least she would find out what happened to Herr Lange. She saw that Cooper was debating with himself about staying or going.

Cooper sighed. "Okay, but you're not supposed to be here, you know. If some brass walks in, you'll have to explain yourself, and you can leave me right out of it."

She smiled at him. "If some brass walks in, he might have to explain his reason for being here," she said, glancing at the poster on the wall behind him.

"True," Cooper conceded with a chuckle. "I don't know what you're doing, but good luck. I better see you at the CCP in one piece, and soon. Otherwise, I may start to worry about you."

"Yes, sir," she said, willing him to leave.

Cooper patted her good shoulder and stepped out into the cold. Once he was gone, she waited a few minutes, then opened the door and scanned the street in both directions. The snow was falling again, leaving little snowcaps on the piles of ruins that had once been the building next door to the rickety *Ami* clinic. She took a deep breath. It made her arm burn with pain, but the air felt good in her lungs, like a wash of cold water on sunburned skin. She stepped into the street and took stock. Eva had nowhere to go. She couldn't go home, obviously. Her planned departure had been thwarted, her partner in crime was under arrest, and now her father was ill. Would she make a run for it? She reviewed her surroundings in case Eva was lurking outside the clinic, but saw only people hurrying on their way to get out of the cold. Anna's thoughts swirled, trying to get a foothold on some fact, anything that would point to an answer to all the questions. She took a deep breath. She thought about Eva's friendship to her and her little family. Her instinct told her that Eva was caught up in something that was beyond her control. Did that excuse what she had done? Anna couldn't say, but she knew there was a good reason. She felt a kinship with this woman; they were alike in many ways. They were alone and doing the best they could to rebuild their lives. Anna inhaled and began walking. There was one place she could try.

Heading south on the Wilhelm Strasse, Anna averted her eyes from the Collecting Point, in case she was spotted. She took care to make a wide arc around any oncoming people, so as not to be jostled on her left arm. Once or twice someone bumped into her, despite seeing the sling she was wearing, and muttered only a meaningless apology as Anna gasped with pain. Once past the Collecting Point, she doglegged onto the Mainz Strasse and concentrated on the long walk ahead and on the progress her feet were making rather than the throbbing, fiery pain in her shoulder. As the stately buildings of the town gave way to the more functionary structures behind the train station, and as the road stretched out in front of her, she willed her instinct to be correct, that she would find Eva, and that somehow her friend would give an explanation that would prove her right. To be wrong meant she had once again trusted the wrong people. Or even that no one could be trusted anymore. That was a possibility she wasn't willing to accept any longer.

She walked on as the crowds thinned and she was alone on a sidewalk patched together with concrete slabs that had been taken from the hard-hit buildings along the street. Ten more minutes, she estimated. But ten turned to twenty and then thirty before she turned onto the Siegfried Ring and finally saw the main entrance to the cemetery ahead of her, the building's declarative mansard roof only slightly worse for wear. She picked up the pace as much as the pain would allow, and once again, ran through the events of the day in her head: The joy of rescuing Oskar followed by the near escape of Berg, the fight on the train, the paintings in the suitcase, and the body of Manfred Lange. The thoughts flashed in her mind like lightning strikes on a dark night.

The sound of gravel under her feet brought her back into the present, and the aroma of forest and dirt soothed her head as she walked further into the cemetery. It was overgrown and unkempt, its graves not forgotten but set aside while the living tended to the more pressing needs of survival. Concrete headstones, graced in their age by gentle mosses, stretched out in front of her. She had no idea where to go. The cemetery was much larger than she expected, and it would be possible to completely miss another visitor along its many paths and diversions. Birds chirped in the trees and the fallen leaves rustled in a light breeze. Somewhere, someone was stepping through the leaves, orchestrating a crackling that echoed through the silence. The graves immediately around her dated from before the war, and she followed their chronology in the hopes that it would take her to the place she was looking for. The influenza epidemic of 1917 was well represented, accounting for dozens of graves and family plots that bore the names of several generations, some of whom perished within the same month. The war and its bombs had the same effect, although Anna surmised those victims were not memorialized with cenotaphs and family mausoleums. And she was right; at some point the formalities had been abandoned in favor of a raw field of recent burials, unmemorialized and unceremonial. The best the fresh war dead could hope for was a soft place under the trees to lay their heads. She paused, mostly in deference to her fellow citizens but also in memory of her own mother, whose grave in Vienna she had not yet been able to visit. She imagined it to be something like this one: communal and anonymous. She allowed herself a few seconds to mourn her own loss, letting the pain take over for a handful of heartbeats, before putting it back in its place. She would be able to find it again; it was never far away.

The crunching leaves got louder, and she turned to see a tall, thin shape approaching. She almost didn't recognize Eva, with her hair matted against her head partially from the falling snow but mostly from being unkempt and having been slept on. Her eyes were glassy, and a dark bruise spread around the side of her mouth where the lip had swollen. A large gash under her right eye had bled and then stopped, leaving a puffy black slice on her cheekbone. She walked with her arms arrayed around her middle like she was in pain, stooped over into a protective stance. Had Anna not recognized her face, she would have thought it was an old woman.

"Eva?" Her heart went out to her friend. "What's happened to you?" Anna touched her arm, and Eva only barely registered her presence. Only then did Anna see the line of blood caked in her hairline all the way down to her ear. Eva noticed Anna's horror and touched her hair gingerly.

"I fell and hit my head," she said. She must have known how feeble the line sounded and turned away. She began to cry, tears streaking through the dried blood on her face. She would not meet Anna's eyes. "What are you doing here?"

"I'm looking for you. I knew you'd be here somehow."

She was tired and defeated. "I wanted to see my mother one more time. She's over there," she gestured toward a group of graves under a large tree.

"Eva, will you tell me what's going on," Anna pleaded. "Who did this to you? And why are you involved in this forgery mess?"

Eva pressed her lips together and shook her head, her eyes locked on something in the distance. She said nothing.

Anna looked around. They were completely alone, surrounded only by the remains of those who would think their human follies to be pointless and tragic. "What are you doing getting involved with that low-life Berg?"

Eva's head swiveled around and she regarded Anna with tear-filled eyes. "He wasn't always a low life."

"Do you love him, is that it? Did you do it for him?"

Eva shook her head, more in confusion than refusal. Now her eyes registered Anna's face for the first time. "Did he do that to you?" she whispered. "And your arm?"

"He got his, don't worry. I gave him a few souvenirs, too. I'll be fine, anyway. And you? Did he do this to you?" Anna reached out to touch Eva's hair, but she pulled her head away.

"It's over, Eva. The *Amis* have Berg and the paintings. The forgeries and your role in this scheme, it's all going to come out now. And you know he'll throw you to the wolves." She waited for Eva to confess, to acknowledge what she had done, but no such contrition came. Eva wasn't listening to Anna, she was absorbed by her own mind. Anna tried another way. "I can still help you, if you tell me the truth." She took Eva's hand and squeezed it to get her attention.

"Why would you steal from the *Amis*? How did you ever think you would get away with it? I am begging you to tell me."

Eva's face hardened. "I don't know what you mean," she said. "I never stole anything from the *Amis*."

Frustration bubbled up inside Anna. It was a sort of panic at being close to the truth and being told she was imagining things, that what she knew could not be true. There had been a lot of that over the last ten years. She took a breath, but her voice was tinged with anger. "No, you're right. You stole from Jacob Morgenstern. But why?"

Eva stared into the distance again. Snow landed on her cheek, melting into droplets that merged with the streaks of blood and tears. Anna's heart ached.

"If it wasn't Anton Berg, then who hit you? Was it Major Stuart?" Anna suspected it was both.

At the mention of Stuart's name, Eva's eyes darted ever so slightly, but she tried to cover it by wiping her nose with the back of her hand.

"It doesn't matter," she said. She turned her head away and watched the traffic moving along the street. Then she lowered her head. "How do you know about Major Stuart?"

Anna evaded the question. "He can't get away with this. Was this his idea? I know they won the war, but there are still laws."

"My father." Eva inhaled, stifling a sob. "He won't survive this."

"Your father?" Anna asked. Did this all have something to do with Manfred Lange? She took a chance. "He's with the doctor. I saw him." She pointed at her sling.

Eva's head spun around. "What's happened to him? Oh my God, I'll never forgive myself." Her eyes searched Anna's face.

"I thought you were together. I saw you at the train station."

"No. He said he was going home. I couldn't explain to him what was happening. I only said we had to leave. After we got to the station and I saw what was happening with you and Cooper there, I knew we were in trouble. I tried to get a car so we could leave town that way, but of course that's impossible. Our only choice was to get on the next train to anywhere, but he refused. What's happened to him?"

Manfred Lange was the only leverage Anna had. She gripped her friend by the shoulders, and felt the shivers ricocheting in her body. "Your father's very ill. He was found collapsed in the street. I can take you to him, but first, you have to tell me the truth."

For a moment, she thought Eva might crumble against the stone wall. She had gone white as the snow falling around them, and her breathing was nothing more than inhalations. Anna held on to keep her from collapsing.

"I didn't do anything," Eva gasped. She doubled over and began to sob.

Anna closed her eyes and waited for Eva to move a little further through her pain before giving it one more try. She bent down, her arm around her friend's shivering back. She pulled her close and spoke into her ear. "Listen to me. The *Amis* have the real paintings. The Kirchner and the Nolde. They were in Berg's suitcase. I saw them myself. And now they are looking for you. It's all over. You have to tell me what's going on." She squeezed Eva's hand again. "You have no choice."

Anna felt the passing of time, as if it were weighing on her more with each second. She wanted to shake her friend and get the story out of her, to hear an explanation at least, if not a confession. She was on the cusp of finding out, but she knew the truth would blow up the little piece of normality that she had found. It would all be lost—her friend, her shelter, maybe even her job. It was just a matter of waiting for the bomb to hit.

"Do you know where my father is? Is he at the house?" Eva whispered. "I want to see him. I *must* see him."

Anna straightened but said nothing.

Eva's face darkened and her jaw set as she, too, stood up. She took a deep breath and focused past Anna, as if she were addressing an unseen witness. "All right, I'll tell you. You'll hate me, but maybe you can understand why I did it." She inhaled again before continuing. "Anton Berg knew my father when they worked at the museum in Hamburg together. In 1933. You understand?"

"Not really."

"Of course you do. In 1933 every professional had to make a choice. Do what's right and stand up against the Nazi thugs, or go along to protect your livelihood, yourself, and your family." She exhaled. "My father is a very honorable man, upstanding, moral, kind, and thoughtful. Intelligent. You know that, too. But he made the choice he had to make, for us. He went along, to protect my mother and me and my brother. He didn't want to make trouble."

"Your brother?"

"He was in the Wehrmacht, the regular army. Conscripted, of course. Which was bad enough. But do you know what they did to the boys in the Wehrmacht whose parents weren't Nazi Party members?"

Anna blanched at the thought. She didn't need to know the specifics, but she knew that there were myriad creative retributions for anyone in German life who didn't go along. She didn't need to know any more. "So your father joined the Party to keep his son alive. A lot of people did that for much less decent reasons."

"Yes, he joined, but that wasn't enough for them. Because he was so knowledgeable about German art, they came after him, wanting him to consult on their so-called acquisitions. Goering himself came to his office a few times, wanting certain pieces for his collection. My father sought out the owners and completed the transactions."

"Meaning?"

"Meaning he forced the sales. He was one of the Nazis taking art from their owners, either through forced sales, or sometimes through outright theft. He became one of the thugs. Sometimes the SS had to get involved. I watched him suffer under the pressure. He should have stood up against it, but they threatened us all the time. They even put my mother into a work camp for a while. She was sixty-three years old with a heart condition. They forced her to make munitions for the war, standing in a freezing cold factory for twelve hours a day. Said it was because she had missed a Frauenschaft meeting, but it was just to keep my father in line. He had to go down to the Gestapo office and negotiate her release. After that, he did whatever they said. We came to Wiesbaden because they sent him here. By the time we got here, though, the Nazis had already taken most of the Jewish private art collections from their owners. He worked as an appraiser for the Nazi's Kulturkammer. He evaluated the art that they brought to him, didn't ask any questions, wrote a report, and sent the pieces on their way up the chain. He thought he would get work at a museum once the war was over. But of course, that couldn't happen." She exhaled, her shoulders dropping as the burden of secrecy lifted.

"And Anton Berg?"

"He worked alongside my father in Hamburg for a while. Then he became sort of a free agent, opened a gallery, and sold paintings on consignment. But he kept in touch. My father saw himself as a mentor figure to him." She snorted. "It turns out Berg always thought he knew better."

"I still don't understand what this has to do with Morgenstern's collection," Anna said. Manfred Lange's plight was so common that it was easy to gloss over it. But in light of what happened to Jacob Morgenstern and millions of his fellow Jews, she was coming to understand the real-life consequences of those sales, forced or not. Probably Manfred Lange was coming to understand them, too.

"Anton went on to be Jacob Morgenstern's Aryan business partner in Frankfurt. I had heard that Anton was here and that he had taken up with several Jewish collectors, out of necessity for them, you understand. Morgenstern's galleries were put in Berg's name after the Nuremberg law passed in '35. Anton was supposed to turn the paintings over to the Reichskulturkammer, as all Aryan gallery owners did, but he didn't. He hid them. And eventually the Nazis turned their attention elsewhere, going after other, much bigger collectors. But then when the war ended, he got wind that the *Amis* were gathering up all the Jewish art—you know all that stuff they found in the castle Neuschwanstein? That spooked him, so he decided he would replace the most valuable paintings in the collection with fakes, he'd take the real ones and sell them in Paris or in New York after the war. He figured no one would know the difference and by the time the *Amis* found the collection, he'd be long gone. He was also taking the chance that all the Morgensterns had died and that the collection would be broken up and given to museums. So, he had the forgeries made, but they weren't all that good, so he pressured the forger to fix them. It took longer than he liked, and before they were done, the *Amis* had found the stash and taken it to the Collecting Point."

Anna held up a hand to slow Eva's story and let her mind catch up. "He never counted on anyone looking at the originals and then the fakes in a short enough time frame to notice the difference. If you only had the fakes, how would you ever really know?" She ruminated on this and let her mind sort out the details. Her arm throbbed and her legs ached. She wished she could sit, but the only option was a nearby headstone. Even under the circumstances, she couldn't bring herself to use one as a stool. She cleared her throat. "And what does this have to do with you?"

"I had met Anton years ago, back in Hamburg, and we'd had a romance. I thought it was serious, but apparently, he thought differently. When the war took hold, he left, promising he'd be back. He never came back, of course, and I assumed he was dead. That's what happens, right? At least it would explain his silence. But then he turned up. Said he found my father through his old contacts. I was so happy to see him at first—and he let me be as happy as he needed. But he hadn't come to reconcile. He started to threaten me. He said he would go to the *Amis* and tell them exactly who my father was and what he'd done for the Nazis, unless I helped him get his paintings back. He gave me false work credentials and told me to get a job at the CCP. If I didn't do it, my father would go to prison. I knew the trials were starting in Nuremberg and people had gone to prison for much less here in Wiesbaden already. I was so scared."

"But Anton was just as guilty of robbing the Jews as your father, wasn't he?"

"You don't understand. Anton was a free agent. And he lies about everything. He never played by the rules, never worked for the Nazis officially. He always worked in the crevices in between, always looking for an angle. You can get away with anything if you have no scruples."

"But why not tell the *Amis* that?"

Eva shrugged. "I never had a chance. He got to me before I could think anything through. Handed me the fake papers, gave me a nice punch to the head, and told me to get the job."

Anna winced. "So, the credentials you gave the *Amis* are fake, and you have no museum experience at all." The Staedel personnel list Karla had given her had proven correct. So had Manfred Lange's Gestapo file in Darmstadt.

"No. I was a teacher. Which means, of course, that I was also a Party member like all teachers had to be. I knew enough about art to fake my way through things at the Collecting Point, but I'm no expert. I told my father that Anton got me the job to help me, and that maybe it would lead to some kind of work for him, too. He knew I was unqualified, but he thought I was doing it to help him eventually get in with the *Amis*. And anyway, any job with the *Amis* is a golden ticket. So, he helped me a little, taught me about some of the artists I saw so I could at least fake my way through conversations. In a way, he was so proud of me."

"And this is where Major Stuart comes in."

Eva started pacing between the headstones. "Getting a job with the *Amis* isn't easy." She looked at Anna. "You know that already. I had to get creative. So, I put on my best dress and did myself up as much as I could and went to the CCP and waited outside the fence. I was going to pick some *Ami* who I thought could help me. I saw Stuart leaving in a staff car and decided he was high up enough to have some pull. Luckily, he went into the Hansa Hotel, where I know the concierge. He's the son of our neighbor, and I gave him my entire ration book for the week to let me sit in the lobby, even though Germans aren't allowed. When Stuart came out of the bar, I pretended to bump into him and asked for directions to the elevator. I made up some story about visiting a colonel for a job interview, which of course, got him interested. I could tell that about him, even from a distance. He's vain and ambitious in the worst way. He's interested in anyone who might be useful to him. So the next day, I waited for him outside the hotel, pretended to bump into him again, and said I didn't get the job. I mentioned I was *desperate* for work." She stopped. "Eventually, I got him to help me get a job at the Collecting Point."

"Eventually?"

"It only took two nights," Eva said, her voice cold now. "I had him convinced that the Collecting Point needed me, what with my credentials, and he said the place needed saving from itself. So he wrote a memo based entirely on what I told him, got me a clean Fragebogen that said I was never a Nazi, and I got the job."

"And you kept seeing him?"

"When he was here, yes, I had to. He could just as easily have taken the job away. What was I supposed to do?"

"And then you switched out the paintings? Eva, this is preposterous. I can't quite understand any of it."

"Anton thinks the *Amis* are buffoons. He thought it would be easy. But as soon as I saw how closely you worked with the paintings, how attentive you were, I knew we were in trouble. I just hoped no one would look at the fakes. But then you noticed."

"And who's the forger? Where is he?"

Eva's shoulders slumped. "He's just an artist. He needed the money. He had no work the last few years. Anton paid him well. He didn't know about any of the details."

"He didn't know what the plan was? How could that be?"

"I never told him. I met with him a couple of times to pick up the forgeries. He was just an old man trying to survive."

Anna's mind flashed another memory. "Did he know your name?"

"Yes, he did. Why?"

"And he knew you worked for the *Amis*?"

"I never told him that, I promise."

"But if he knew your name, he could have easily looked up your address. And if he knew your address, he could have followed you. And he could have followed the children to the black market. And he could have asked them questions when they were sitting on the front stoop. And, unless he's a complete idiot, he probably figured out what was going on."

Eva's face tightened. "I guess."

"Tell me his name."

"Sergei Wozniak. But, Anna…"

Anna moved on. "And you snuck the real paintings out of the CCP in a cardboard tube."

"Yes, and back in again the next morning. I had to do everything one at a time, otherwise it was too much. Once I got rid of the pictures, I thought I was home free, that Anton would go away and leave my father and me alone. I knew you were suspicious. When Stuart mentioned he had met you, I encouraged him to offer you another job because I wanted your job at the CCP. That was a lie, but he believed it. And I thought if you left, I could still get away with it. And by then, you and I had become friends and I wanted the whole thing to go away. I didn't want you to find out the truth about me. And I thought I could even help you in the process, by getting you a bigger job."

"In Nuremberg," Anna said. "And you used my child to unload the paintings at the black market."

Eva took a breath and shoved her hands into her pockets. "There was no other way to do it. But then everything unraveled so fast that I didn't have time to react. And now this. And my father..." She started to cry again. "Anna, please, you have to help me. You're my only friend. They are going to lock me up for this, aren't they? And put my father in a labor camp for being a Nazi. He'll be shoveling rubble in the snow. It will kill him. I'm happy to go to jail to spare him, but I can't bear to have him revealed as a Nazi. He was a good man. I can't bear the shame of it."

"Where were you two going at the train station today?"

"Anton promised us passage to France with him, and I fell for it. Now I think he was just setting me up to take the blame in case the *Amis* caught him. But I told my father we had to leave because I had gotten a new job, a better job, and that there would be work for him there. He didn't know anything about what Anton was really like. I never told him because I didn't want him to worry. He was hopeful enough to believe me, and I had resigned myself to being beholden to Anton for the rest of my life, since we were now partners in crime. But at least my father would be safe. Or so I hoped."

Eva's anguish tugged at Anna. She was Anna's only friend, too, or so she had thought. And wouldn't Anna have done the exact same thing under the circumstances? Would she not have lied to protect her father, her husband, her child? What was the value of a bunch of paint on a canvas compared to the lives of those you love? To Eva, the paintings represented nothing more than an opportunity to protect her father. For Anton Berg, they were currency. But for Jacob

Morgenstern, the paintings were something much more valuable, they had nothing to do with money, or status, or security. And if she asked herself what she wouldn't do in order to keep her family safe, she wouldn't have an easy answer. Yes, the war was over now, and somewhere a line had to be drawn. She knew that, too. But was this where the line had to be?

"My father is a good man," Eva repeated into the falling snow.

"We were all good once," Anna said. "I don't know what we are now." Her head spun with thoughts and questions. She couldn't let Berg get away with what he had done, but that meant Eva would go down with him. If nothing else, Berg would make sure of it.

The light shifted as the sun emerged from behind a cloud, and suddenly they stood in a bright warmth that filtered through the murmuring trees. Eva's face was lifeless in the light, as if she were one of the interred who surrounded them. Anna wanted to hug her friend and tell her it would be okay, the way Cooper had done for her. But even if she said it, she couldn't possibly believe it. "Come on. I'll take you to your father," she said instead, hooking her good arm into Eva's. They set out along the snowy path together, the crunch of their rhythmic steps echoing among the departed.

chapter nineteen

Anna waved her papers at the guard on duty at the entry to the Collecting Point. He was a bright-eyed, red-headed boy who looked to be barely out of school. He smiled at her as she passed, his enthusiasm undiminished by what was becoming ankle-deep snow.

She had deposited Eva at the American clinic where Manfred Lange was stable but barely conscious. They were preparing to transport him to the German hospital and were happy to have a next-of-kin to boss around. When Anna had left the exam room where he still lay on the table, Eva was weeping over him, whispering in his ear. He stared at the ceiling, unresponsive and white as the snow falling outside the window.

"Oh my God, Frau Klein. What's happened?" Karla came out from behind her desk, arms outstretched. "Who did this to you?"

Anna avoided the contact, holding up a hand to stop her. "I'm all right. Or I will be."

Karla stepped in close. "Stuart's in there," she whispered, jutting her chin toward the small conference room. "And that Anton Berg you asked about? Big Nazi art dealer? He's living under an assumed name here in Wiesbaden. Georg Spitzer. I'm still working on the address."

Anna chuckled. "Thank you, Karla. I found him, too." She wiggled the fingers on her left hand. "Or I should say, he found me."

Karla's eyes grew wide and she stepped back, putting her hand to her mouth. "An art dealer did this to you?"

"It's an ugly business these days." Anna winked at her. "But the *Amis* are taking good care of him now." She headed up the stairs, feeling Karla's eyes follow her and letting the girl's wonderment bolster her courage.

Cooper nearly bumped into Anna as he trotted down the stairs toward her, his eyes on a paper in his hand. She stepped out of the way to avoid his bumping into her arm but knocked it into the railing in the process. The shot of pain tapped into her already raw emotions.

"Goddammit," she hissed, louder than she intended.

"Did I hurt you?" Cooper held his hands out as if trying to catch her. "Oh, Lord, I'm sorry."

"No, I did it to myself," Anna said. "It'll be better in a minute."

"I thought I told you to go home." He regarded her with worried eyes. "You look terrible, if I may say so."

"You may. But you might want to know what I've found out."

"Can it wait? I have to meet with our man Stuart in about ninety seconds." He tapped his watch. "It won't take long. He's going to give us marching orders about getting the shipment of paintings out to

Washington on Monday. It's more for his benefit than mine. I'm there in the role of best supporting actor." He stopped at the bottom of the stairs.

"There's someone upstairs to see you. He promised he wouldn't move, but keep an eye on him until I get back, would you?"

"Okay?" She was confused but started back up the stairs to his office. "It's just you and Stuart in the meeting?"

"Yeah, no one else is around. They made themselves scarce. And you know he has to get on the road to Nuremberg." He mocked Stuart's pompous inflection.

Anna watched him descend the remaining steps and disappear around the corner into his meeting. Alone in the stairwell, she wanted to cry more than anything, but she didn't. She still couldn't get her head around what Eva had done. How she had fooled them about who she really was and then let Anna and her family into her home. They shared their food, their meager belongings with an open heart. Anna knew without a doubt who Eva really was: A good daughter and a good friend. She tried to protect her father in the same way he had tried to save his family, by committing a crime for a righteous reason. Manfred Lange had been so kind to Oskar and Amalia, and to Madeleine, too. So unassuming, he was the perfect Nazi target. The vision of him lying ashen and deflated on the exam table floated into her mind. *After all that's happened, this.*

As she rounded the corner into Cooper's office, the man sitting in the chair opposite the desk turned to face her. For several seconds, they regarded each other, waiting for the inevitable.

Anna decided to go first. "Sergei Wozniak," she said.

The man stood and offered a hand. "Yes, Frau Klein."

She declined the gesture and walked instead to Cooper's side of the desk. "You are…"

"I'm turning myself in." He held up an envelope. "And returning all the money. I want to cooperate."

"You're returning the money you received to forge the two paintings?" Anna sat in Cooper's chair. Wozniak fingered the envelope with paint-stained fingers. Dirty fingers, as Amalia had noted. She noted the distinct smell of pine and licorice that wafted from his clothes. Turpentine. Beyond that, he was without distinction; an ordinary man wearing a black overcoat and a blue tie. Yet, she recognized him. "You were following me. You came here the day before yesterday to talk to me?"

"Yes. I waited in the foyer, but then so many officers came for a meeting. I got cold feet and left." He shrugged. "I'm sorry." He slid the envelope across the desk to her. "Please take it. I don't want it."

Anna stared at the bulky envelope. How much money had this mess cost Berg? She scrutinized Wozniak. He was sweating a little, even though the room was cool. Using her good hand, she picked up a pencil and slid a blank sheet of paper from the tray. "Who approached you about the forgeries?"

"Anton Berg. He paid me and gave me photos of the paintings. I painted from those." He tugged at his sleeve. "It's not the best way to go about making a painting."

"I could tell. They weren't very good fakes." She couldn't resist.

"No, they weren't." Color rose in his cheeks. "But forgery isn't my strong suit." He offered a weak smile.

"And Anton Berg picked up the paintings from you?"

"No, he disappeared. A woman came to get the paintings."

"Do you know her name?"

He collapsed a little. "Yes, it was Eva Lange. I know her father from when he worked for the Kulturkammer. I had no work, but he tried to find jobs for me. Portraits of Nazis to hang over their fireplaces, mostly. It paid well." He straightened a little. "The Langes are a good family." He didn't make any further case for Eva and Manfred, instead he pushed the envelope across the desk a little farther.

"And how did you know about me? How did you know my name?"

"I don't have much to do, so I followed Fraulein Lange home. I saw you lived there, too, and I followed you here. I saw the children go to the black market. Some mail came to your house when I was waiting for you one day, and I looked at the name after they wedged the envelope in the door. I figured you were Anna Klein."

Anna shook off the rising discomfort. "And you are willing to work with the *Amis*? To tell them the whole story?"

He sighed. "I know I'll go to jail, but I'm so tired. I'm old and I have nothing left. My sons are dead. My wife is gone, too. What is there for me now?" He looked at the envelope again.

Anna thought of Jacob Morgenstern. These men, all intertwined in ways no one could have predicted. And then there was Major Stuart, the greedy, ambitious bastard. He used the ruined landscape of Germany as his chessboard, moving pawns around to benefit and amuse himself. Maybe he believed he was doing the right thing, too, but she doubted it. Stuart was a small man whose ego needed constant feeding. For him, there was no right or wrong. There was only expediency.

"Frau Klein, excuse me. I have something for you." Karla leaned on the door frame, her eyes wide behind the oversized glasses.

"Can it wait? I'm still talking to this gentleman." Anna gestured toward Wozniak. "I'll be with you when I'm finished."

Karla grimaced and held up the papers in her hand. "Um, no. I don't think this can wait, Frau Klein." She took a step into the office.

"Karla, not now," Anna hissed. Now that she had Wozniak, she had no intention of letting him out of her sight.

Karla was undeterred. She let out a loud breath and shook the papers in her fist. "Corporal Long thinks you'll be very interested in these."

"Corporal Long? What on earth?" She glared at Karla who glowered back at her.

"He mentioned to me that you could use this information, so I found it for you," she explained in a slow staccato rhythm that emphasized each word. She shook the papers with each beat for extra drama.

Anna relented and snatched the papers from her. Her irritation was a distraction, but she forced herself to focus. Karla had handed her two sheets. The top one was the standard questionnaire all Germans had to complete, the Fragebogen asking questions about their wartime affiliations and activities. Anna had seen dozens of them and had filled one out herself. Her eyes landed on the name typed into the blank space at the top. This was Eva Lange's Fragebogen, the one Stuart had gotten for her—squeaky clean with nary a single Nazi Party meeting or act of sympathy listed. Anna's hand began to shake as she reached for the paper underneath. She scanned the page skipping ahead, but her mind filled in the details. The official American letterhead, the short and succinct message: *Introduction...exemplary qualifications...expertise...recommendation for hire*. Anna's eyes moved to the end of the text where Major Stuart had signed his name with a flourish. Anna looked up at Karla.

"I told you it couldn't wait." She was beaming.

Anna wanted to ask her how she had gotten it, but there was no time for that now. She pushed her chair back and, ignoring the pain in her shoulder, folded the papers in half and slid them into Cooper's desk drawer under the chewing gum packets and matchbooks. She threw Wozniak's envelope on top of the letters before pushing the drawer shut with her hip and locking it with Cooper's key.

"Karla, would you please keep Herr Wozniak company for a few minutes? I remembered something I need to attend to downstairs."

"Sure thing," Karla said, happy to oblige. She took a seat in Cooper's chair and locked Wozniak in her sights, as if she planned to watch his every move.

Anna stopped at the door and turned. "Herr Wozniak, I want to thank you for the offer, but this office is not in the business of taking bribes. I'll be back to talk more about your future plans. In the meantime, Fraulein Albrecht will keep an eye on you. Remember there are armed guards downstairs who will stop you from leaving, so I suggest you stay put until I return."

Wozniak slumped in his chair and stared at the floor. Anna took a deep breath and straightened her blouse with one hand, fixing where the sling had tugged it out of place. She touched her hair to check it, as if it would make any difference, tried to forget the bloody gash on her face, and headed down the stairs, her legs moving with a will of their own. With each step, her heart pounded louder behind her ears, and she was careful to keep her breath steady. At the bottom of the steps, she turned left toward the small storage room that doubled as a conference room. She put her hand to the knob, inhaled, and pushed the door open.

Stuart looked up from his seat at the table, where he was signing documents. Cooper stood with arms crossed, possibly as a way to keep from punching the major. Neither of them could have been more surprised if Eisenhower himself had barged into the room.

"Major, I'd like a word, please," Anna said.

"Frau Klein, I don't think..." Cooper began to argue but stopped when she held up a hand.

Stuart smirked. "Frau Klein, well look at you. It seems you're having a very bad day. Is this about the forgeries that you and the Captain allowed to be brought into the facility? Because if it is, no amount of explaining is going to fix this mess. What a disgrace."

"Major, I'll thank you to leave Frau Klein out of that," Cooper grumbled. "She had nothing to do with anything."

"No, I didn't, that's true," Anna said. "That was Eva Lange. You know Fraulein Lange, don't you, Major?"

Stuart's pen was still poised over the paper he had been signing. He was calculating a reply but said nothing. He wouldn't give her the satisfaction.

Anna filled the silence. "I think you do because I believe it was you who wrote a memo directing Captain Farmer to hire Eva here at the CCP. You might also have gotten her a clean questionnaire that hid her Nazi Party membership. Does this sound right to you?"

Stuart worked his jaw muscles and put the pen down. He leaned back in his chair and crossed his arms. Cooper stood frozen to the spot.

"If I understood you correctly, it sounds like you're making one hell of an accusation," Stuart said.

"Yes, sir, I am. To think that what you are reporting as the mess at the CCP, the lack of security, the criminal activity, was, in fact caused directly by your own...I'm sorry, I'm still not very good at all the legal terms." She looked to Cooper for help.

"Fraud?" Cooper volunteered.

"Yes, that's the word. And the other one, also an F word," Anna said, still looking at Cooper.

"Fraternization?" he offered.

"Yes, indeed. Fraternization and fraud. Giving a scrubbed questionnaire to your girlfriend, who was a member of the Nazi Party, in order to get her a job with the US Military government? I imagine you did it to impress her? To show her you could do it? But that's generally against the rules, isn't it?"

"I'd have to check, but I think you're right," Cooper said. He pressed his lips together to suppress a smile.

Stuart set his jaw, but the color rising in his cheeks betrayed him. "Prove it."

Anna nodded. "That's easy. I have a copy of the letter of introduction with your signature. And any quick review of wartime personnel records will reveal that Eva Lange was, in fact, a teacher in Wiesbaden after she moved here with her father. Which everyone knows means she was a party member. Which makes her squeaky-clean questionnaire a fake, too."

Cooper grinned and rocked back on his heels. "The Nazis did keep *excellent* records."

Stuart pushed his chair back and stood, throwing his pen onto the papers.

"This doesn't change the fact that two paintings downstairs in the collection are worthless fakes, and it's you people who were responsible for it," he barked, a spray of spittle raining onto the table.

"The paintings downstairs are actually originals as of about twenty minutes ago. There are a couple of fakes in police custody, and they will be explained in due course," Cooper said. "So, it looks like everything and everyone is accounted for. I'm glad to know I won't be lonely in jail. Will you visit the major, too, Frau Klein?"

Anna took a step forward. "You know, I had another thought. What if, for example, those forgeries were destroyed? And then, what if no one said anything else about this little adventure? Jacob Morgenstern will have his collection returned to him intact. And perhaps Eva Lange could get a new job, in another place, like say, in Nuremberg, as a teacher in a new school, or something less to do with valuable art objects. And then, maybe if Washington didn't hear about the forgeries, they wouldn't also have to hear about Major Stuart's involvement in this catastrophe. Because I do have proof that you set this whole ball rolling, Major. So, this seems like a good solution. That memo I have could even get destroyed," She patted her pockets with her good hand. "Now, if only I could remember where I put that memo. I would hate for it to land in the wrong hands."

Stuart stared at her. Anna held his gaze, her heart pounding in her chest so hard she was sure Stuart could hear it. But she willed herself to look at him. She thought of Jacob Morgenstern because she was sure no one had been thinking of him at all. He would get his paintings back. In the end, that was all that mattered. But if she could help Eva and take Stuart down in the process, that was even better.

Stuart picked up the cap he had set on the table beside him and tucked it under his arm.

"I have a train to catch. Captain, you know your orders. Two hundred paintings crated and ready to go on Monday. I am done with this ridiculous mess. What a headache over a bunch of stupid paintings. I'll leave you all to it." He walked around the table, but Anna stepped in front of the door, blocking his exit.

"And Fraulein Lange?"

Stuart hedged. "I've heard the schools in Nuremberg are short-handed. I can put in a good word."

"Thank you, Major. I'll hold on to that letter of yours until she's found a position, if you don't mind." She smiled and stepped aside. Stuart reached for the door, deliberately bumping her shoulder in the process. Anna let him pass, refusing to let the searing pain show on her face. Stuart disappeared into the foyer and was out the front door in three steps. Anna dared hope she would never see him again.

As soon as Stuart was gone, Cooper pushed the door closed with one hand and took her good arm in his other hand, pulling her close, their breaths intertwining. When she leaned her head into his chest, she felt his heart racing, too. She smiled. He was always so cool on the outside; but he had been just as agitated as she was. But they had done it. He wrapped her in his arms, and she felt safe, cocooned in his smell, as she listened to his heart return to a normal rhythm. Even the pain in her shoulder was comforting. She was battered, but she had survived to fight another day.

"Damn," Cooper said, pulling away. "You do look a mess, but you are something."

Anna smiled. "I hope it will work."

"Stuart saving his own ass? Yeah, that'll work." His eyes locked into hers and he started to laugh. "In a minute I'm going to ask you how you found all this out in the hour since I've seen you, but not yet. I have to recover from this first, and I want to give you my full attention."

Anna pointed at the ceiling. “There’s a forger upstairs who would also like your full attention.”

Cooper put his hand on the door knob. “Okay, but just for a few minutes. Then you’re going home, got it?”

Anna nodded. She let herself exhale. “Got it, boss.”

Anna wiggled her toes inside the new wool socks from Cooper’s mother. Her feet were finally warm and felt they might stay that way. She stacked the papers on the back of a tray that balanced on her lap. The cup Oskar had brought her steamed happily, perched on a little table he had furnished for her. She had been in bed at the Lange house for three straight days, recovering. The events of the past days had finally caught up with her and left her shivering in a panic on the bathroom floor in the middle of the night. Madeleine had found her and put her back to bed, and she had stayed there and let everyone dote on her. Cooper had come by to visit more than once, but she would not see him, deciding that it would be better for them both to clear their heads as the smoke settled. He had left chocolate bars for the children, and army blankets and American aspirin for her. In the folds of the blanket that Madeleine had brought to her, she had found a scrap of paper with the words “Get well soon. We have work to do.” He had signed it “Henry.” Which struck her as odd, since she never thought of him as “Henry.” It didn’t fit him somehow.

She tucked the blanket around her and relished its warmth as she lay on the bed, everything she needed within arm’s reach. She turned her attention back to the papers in her lap and reread what she had written:

There is so much I still want to tell you, but one thing I must tell you now that I have been avoiding. I want to tell you about the work I'm doing, and how Amalia lost a tooth, and how I spotted a forged painting and caught a thief, and how much I miss you, and the jokes Amalia tells, and how Oskar manages to find us food to eat every day. I want to tell you that some days I feel a tiny spark of hope, that I can see a hint of light under the gray, can feel its warmth and am comforted by its presence. I want to tell you that I miss us—our family, our life—in the same way I miss my mother, as a beloved who is no longer, who was taken, destroyed by the war, whom I mourn with the weight of a thousand stones on my heart. But what I must tell you is the truth, which is this: It will hurt you and for that I will forever be sorry, but Amalia and I are not coming home. We have found a safe place to land, one where the glimmer under the gray is palpable. I can feel our future here, I can sense a blooming taking hold, however small and fragile. I don't have it in me to toss aside what I have made here to return to the uncertainty of a former life that is forever changed. For that reason, I plan to file for divorce.

You don't deserve what I am inflicting on you, my dear husband. But you do deserve to be in possession of the truth, to have a clear eye on the situation. Our marriage is a casualty of this damn war, just as surely as the war was the source of our bond. Now, as a clearer light emerges, we must go our own way forward. Amalia is our tether, she will keep us connected, and I have no intention of keeping you from her. Likewise, I have no intention of returning to Kappellendorf. I wish you a happy life and take solace in the fact that the war spared us as individuals, even as it pulled us apart. I do love you, and I desperately hope, one day, you can forgive me.

She stared at the last sentence and wiped the tears from her cheeks. *Please forgive me*. She wrote her name, slid the papers into the envelope, and wrote the address of her former home with a shaking hand. In another time, she might have thought it silly to feel so nervous about a piece of paper, but now she knew better. Papers changed people's lives forever. She put the letter in her bag and took a deep breath. She felt no second thoughts encroaching, no clouds of doubt rising where she would expect. Instead she felt a release, like a balloon floating in a bright sky, catching a breeze and slipping away from a grasping hand. Before the feeling could disappear, she pulled herself up and out of the bed and swung her warm feet to the icy floor. With one hand she looped the scarf that served as her sling over her head and made her way into the living room.

Eva sat on the sofa, cradling her head in her hands. Her body shook with sobs. She had been like this all morning, ever since coming back from the hospital and announcing that her father had died in the night. The doctors called it heart failure, but Anna knew the real cause. Years of anguish and fear had taken their final toll when the old man learned his daughter had tried to save him by committing crimes herself. Madeleine sat next to Eva, stroking her back and speaking softly in her ear. It was only early afternoon, but the day already felt finished, the light so dim and gray that it never seemed to have gotten started. Anna was sad about Manfred Lange. She was sad for Eva and for Madeleine, too, who had lost a companion. And now Anna would lose her friend, too, even if all went to plan and Stuart followed through on his promise.

Amalia stood in the doorway, her little body framed in the glow coming from the kitchen light. "Mama? We made lunch," she whispered.

Anna stood and followed her into the kitchen, where Oskar sat on the stool, stirring a pot of dingy liquid that bubbled on the stove.

"I made soup from carrot tops and potato peels," he said. "I learned it at the camp. And there's still peanut butter." Oskar had been doting on Anna for the past three days, making meals, appearing with extra blankets, and being big brother to Amalia. At night, he brought her hot water to drink and pretended it was tea, each time a different flavor. It was his way of thanking her, without having to say it. But really, it was Anna who was grateful. Her little family was back together and it felt complete. Any clouds gathering on the horizon of Oskar's future were in the far distance. Anna knew they were coming, but she pushed the thoughts and the nagging image of a searching bereft and childless mother out of her mind for now. A day of reckoning might yet come, but that day was not today.

Anna peered into the pot, which actually smelled like something edible. It was warm, at least. Amalia handed her a bowl, and she ladled the soup into it. "Why don't the two of you eat in here? And then go find something to do so Fraulein can have some time."

"Will she be all right?" Amalia asked.

"Yes, she will. But now she's very sad because her father died."

"But he was an old man," Amalia said. "He lived a long life." In Amalia's world, everyone died, even young people. To be old was a privilege.

"Yes, *Maus*. It's sad even when old people die. It's no different at all."

Amalia climbed onto the other stool and joined Oskar as they slurped their soups, blowing on each spoonful first. Anna watched them for a moment, their small backs side by side hunched over their bowls, two peas back together in their pod. She filled another bowl, took a spoon from the drawer and returned to the living room.

Anna held the bowl out for Eva. "Why don't you try to eat something?"

"I can't, but thank you. You're such a good friend." Her face was strained and flushed. "I'll never be able to repay you for what you've done for me."

A big part of Anna didn't feel at all good about what she had done, maneuvering the guilty parties toward a cover-up rather than justice. Stuart deserved to be punished for what he did and so did Eva, but at what price? It would cost Cooper and likely Anna their jobs, and Cooper could have been arrested had Stuart seen fit to throw the book at him. Was that justice? It didn't feel like it. Nothing agreed to fit into neat little boxes anymore.

"You'll like Nuremberg," Anna said. "And you'll go back to teaching. Start a new life. Things will look up."

Eva nodded. "If they don't arrest me first."

"You gave the *Amis* good information about the black market and about Berg. That's useful to them. He's the one they want." The bruises and black eye Eva had sported when she was taken to the police station had helped her cause, too. The *Amis* went easy on her, but she would not be allowed to set foot in the Collecting Point ever again.

"I was such a fool," Eva said.

"You protected someone you loved. That's not foolish."

There was not much more to be said. Eva pushed the bowl toward Madeleine and urged her to eat it instead. They sat in the dim light, surrounded by Manfred Lange's books and his memory, which would soon start to fade, ever so slowly, like the winter light.

Anna took a look at her watch. "I'm going to the Collecting Point," she said. "Maybe they need some help."

"Is today the day?" Madeleine asked.

"Yes, today they pack up the paintings to be shipped to Washington." Anna shook her head. "It seems so wrong." As much as she loved being in the thick of things at the Collecting Point, she was relieved to have missed the packing of the paintings. She didn't think she could have stood to see them disappear again. And for Cooper, that feeling was certainly even worse.

"That's because it's wrong," Madeleine said.

"Yes," Anna said. "No one's happy about it."

Madeleine gave her a nudge. "You go, get some fresh air. It will do you good. We'll be fine here. When you come back, we'll have a nice little supper." She rubbed Eva's back and smiled at Anna. Madeleine knew the real reason Anna was going to the Collecting Point.

Anna pulled her coat from the peg in the foyer and managed to get her good arm into the sleeve. Madeleine helped her wrap the other side around her bad shoulder and button it. She said goodbye to the children and stepped out into the freezing cold street inhaling the icy November air.

The walk down to the Collecting Point usually took her through the cemetery and the old town until she merged onto the Wilhelmstrasse. Until a few weeks ago, the street had still been lined with a few trees, but now they were all gone, having been chopped down during the night by people desperate for firewood as the days grew colder. Today, she continued through the old town and walked to the post office. Snow flurries poked the skin on her face, and she slid her working hand into the pocket of her coat and hunched her shoulders to keep warm. The world loomed even more bleak than usual, dense clouds hanging low in the air, threatening to smother

her. It was oppressive and lonely, this weather, and it was only starting. She turned the corner and saw the light marking the makeshift post office ahead. Her stride slowed a little but she kept going, her insides fluttering. She took a deep breath and felt the cold air fill her lungs. Her eyes watered, maybe from the cold, but she wasn't sure. She put one foot in front of the other, eyes focused on the post office light. *It's going to be okay.*

"What are you doing here?" Cooper sat at his desk, leaning back in his chair, his face tired and resigned. A voice on the radio he had set up on his desk blathered on about something. Anna sat down in the chair opposite.

"I wanted to check on you," she said. "I know today wasn't an easy day."

"Well, we got it all done," Cooper said. "The boys really pitched in and did their best. Those paintings are crossing the Atlantic in down-feathered beds. It's the least we can do for them. But they are ready to go. I can only hope they will come home again. Otherwise, what's the point of any of this?"

"What was the point of anything?" Anna asked. "If people would leave well enough alone, we could all live happy lives." The air in the office was chilly and she pulled the collar of her coat around her neck. "What are you listening to anyway?"

"Armed Forces Radio. They're enlightening us about the Nuremberg trials. Tomorrow's the day."

"How ironic."

"What do you mean?"

"The Americans sit in judgment over the German people even as they commit a grave injustice against them while no one's looking," Anna said. "Even as they put that evil Alfred Rosenberg, the master art thief himself, on trial."

"He'll have his day. At least we have that going for us." Cooper leaned over and turned the volume up.

"*...it is especially fitting that Nuremberg should be the rubbelized host to this great war criminal trial. It is fitting because no other German city so symbolizes the same continuity...the same linking themes in the long dead past, and the freshly dead yesterday of German history. For Nuremberg is the story of Germany...the fabric of dictatorship and culture of a military nation...*"

Cooper exhaled. "How are you feeling?"

"Well, my arm feels better. The rest of me is doubtful." She smiled.

"Anything interesting happen since I saw you last?"

"Manfred Lange died."

"I'm sorry to hear it. How is Eva taking it?"

"Not so well."

He sat up and rummaged around on his desk. "Her papers came through. Seems there is, in fact, a position for a teacher open in Nuremberg. What do you think about that?"

Anna breathed a sigh of relief. "Well, that's good."

"And," Cooper added, "with all this State Department nonsense behind us, I think you can move back into Frau Wolf's house. All those VIPs will have moved on by next week. I filed the papers myself."

Anna was relieved. Surely these were all signs that she had done the right thing. "Thank you, Captain."

"I thought you'd like that." He straightened the papers in front of him and folded them into an envelope. "What's more, our friend

Anton Berg is singing like the pretty little canary he is. He is more than ready to talk about the goings-on of forced sales and Jewish art dealers. I think the prison food and a nice bed are doing him good. You know that's what they're saying about the fellows going on trial in Nuremberg? They're all being given the white glove treatment. I bet their breakfast was better than ours."

"I'm sure," Anna said. "But we got to have our breakfast on this side of the gallows."

Cooper chuckled as the voice on the radio droned on, oblivious.

"Tomorrow, twenty defendants will file in to hear an indictment of documented charges, an indictment signed by the representatives of the United States, Great Britain, the USSR, and France. Mr. Justice Jackson has said repeatedly that the trial will be no cut and dried affair…no mere formality to permit the winner to kill off the loser. The guilt of the defendants must be proved, for, as under our legal system, the defendants will be considered innocent until proven guilty."

"There was one other interesting thing that happened." Anna focused on the desk between them.

"Oh?"

"I went to the post office and mailed a letter."

Outside a gust of wind rattled the window pane, and cold air seeped into the room. The papers on Cooper's desk rippled slightly in the draft.

"Oh?" Cooper repeated.

She looked at him, but his eyes were now focused on a spot somewhere in the area of her elbow. "Was this letter a manifesto of sorts?"

"Yes," Anna said. "You could call it a declaration of independence, maybe."

"I see," Cooper said. "I guess this taking-a-stand business is contagious."

Another gust of wind rattled the window as if it were trying to get inside the building. Anna and Cooper sat for a while without speaking. She pictured her husband opening the letter, fumbling for his glasses, sitting at his desk, and reading it. How would he react? With sadness or confusion or rage? It would be some of each, but if she had made her case, he would come to understand. She hoped it would be enough.

"Tomorrow I'll file Jacob Morgenstern's claims for his paintings so they'll be ready for him when he comes," she said, mostly to herself. She regarded Cooper, who was staring out the window, lost in thought, his hands folded across this stomach. "What are you thinking about?"

He smiled. "Home. This weather always makes me think of Chicago."

"Is it nice there?"

He smiled and his face softened. Anna could see in the lines of his face the pain that he liked to cover with jokes and optimism. "It's beautiful," he said. "Greatest city in the world, if you ask me."

"Maybe you can tell me more about it."

"Maybe one day you'll see it for yourself."

Anna tried to imagine herself in the great American city, strolling through the canyons between its muscular skyscrapers, amongst shiny cars and well-dressed people. Going to shops and restaurants, maybe the theater or a lush park with fountains and flowers where Amalia could play in the grass while Anna read a book. *Who is with me in this picture? Am I alone? Who is waiting for me at home?* She looked at Cooper who was toying with a paper clip as he always did when he was lost in thought. The lecturing voice on the radio snapped them both back to reality.

"This trial is extraordinary for many reasons. The spectacular element enters the scene because here will be assembled at one time, in one place, the remaining, living greats of the Nazi system. But the implications of the trial are deeper, far more serious. For this is the first international criminal trial...the first criminal trial conducted by four nations...four nations which are acting outside their own countries, outside their own law.

And so tomorrow morning, the conscience of the world will be present in this courtroom..."

Cooper switched off the radio and pushed his chair back. "You want to say goodbye?"

They turned off the lights as they went downstairs. Only the light in the director's office was still on, and the dim glow from outside was too weak to illuminate the foyer. She walked among the crates lurking in the shadows, as if inspecting the troops. Tomorrow these crates and their precious cargo would go on a truck to the train station, then on Red Cross cars to the port of Le Havre in France. From there an Army transport ship would set off across the roiling waters of the Atlantic.

Anna put her hand on the rough wood of a crate, as if to give a benediction, to wish the paintings well on the journey. Yes, they were splotches of ink on canvases. They were not people, she told herself. They were objects. But the argument didn't hold up. The paintings embodied something much bigger. This blow was unspeakably sad, not just for the Monuments Men who fought against it, but also for her and for all Germans. The message was unmistakable. *You Germans don't deserve to keep your own culture. Now you know how it feels.*

"Ready?" Cooper asked, moving toward the door. His expression was mournful, the lines around his eyes deeper, his cheeks more caved.

They walked toward the exit, their footsteps reverberating between the marble walls of the empty building. She turned for one last view of the crates. This was the end of something, and things would never be the same. Behind her, Cooper held the door open and waited. She said a final goodbye and crossed the threshold of the open door. Outside, the day had finally given way to dusk. Not caring if anyone saw them, she took Cooper's hand in hers, and they stepped out into the gray together.

author's note

The Wiesbaden Manifesto was a real document written in protest against the State Department order to ship paintings from German state collections to the United States. Captain Walter Farmer, the real life director of the Wiesbaden Collecting point initiated the writing of the manifesto and outlines the operation to ship the 202 paintings – code-named Westward-Ho – in great detail in his memoir *The Safekeepers*. The paintings were worth some $80 million and included fifteen Rembrandts, six Rubens, three Rafaels, five Botticellis and five Titians. Edouard Manet's *In the Conservatory* was not on the original list, but was included to please General Eisenhower and the brass of the Third Army who had been photographed with the painting in the Merkers Mine in April of 1945.

The manifesto's authorship is credited to Captain Everett P. (Bill) Lesley with assistance from other officers. Upon its completion he is reported to have said: "I feel like Thomas Jefferson when he wrote the Declaration of Independence." He also stated in a letter that the document was not drafted, but written "of a piece," reflecting the urgency and resolve with which the Monuments Men addressed the order.

The document was signed by 24 Monuments officers, with three additional men agreeing with its statements but not signing. It is noted as the only official revolt by American soldiers against their orders in World War II and the Monuments Men pinned a copy of it inside a crate shipped back to the States. For his efforts to prevent the removal of the paintings, Captain Farmer was awarded Commander's Cross of the Federal Order of Merit, Germany's highest civilian honor, in 1996.

Although unsuccessful in its initial intention, the Manifesto's existence—it was published in both the *New Yorker* and the *New York Times*—likely shortened the paintings' stay in the US and prevented further removal of paintings from Germany. The 202 paintings shipped from Wiesbaden were returned to the German state collections four years later, after touring 13 American cities including New York, Boston, Chicago and Los Angeles, and a wildly successful exhibition at the National Gallery of Art in Washington DC, proceeds of which benefitted German war orphans.

The work of Emil Nolde and Ernst Ludwig Kirchner and other German Expressionists enjoyed great popularity immediately after the war as American collectors began scooping up newly unearthed paintings by so-called degenerate artists. The paintings that appear in this story are fictional, as is the forgery plot. However the Munich Collecting Point did have a theft problem in its early days, which underscored the potential for intrigue.

The Nuremberg trials really did start on the same day—November 20, 1945— as the shipment of paintings left the collecting point for America, an ironic juxtaposition of acts of justice and retribution. And, so-called war orphans that had been stolen from their families by the SS in wartime were rounded up by the UN authorities and sent to re-education camps before being repatriated to their home countries, their lives uprooted and obliterated a second time.

My profound thanks goes to Tanja Bernsau, PhD, art historian and expert in the workings of the Wiesbaden Collecting Point, who generously offered her time and knowledge in service of the accuracy of the historical and geographical aspects of this book.

Amanda Eyre Ward was a great teacher, reader, and reviewer who kept the pilot light going underneath the crappy first draft. My editor Caroline Tolley again pushed and asked questions and expected more from the characters and the words, making me a better writer. Elana Jackson polished, and then polished some more to create a shiny, spotless manuscript. Danielle Acee shouted the book's praises to make sure it found its readers and to keep up the troop morale. Mark Cervenka made Anna (and me) more knowledgeable about the work of German expressionists. Linda Sullivan and Katie Cervenka, thank you for bouncing ideas around and letting me talk through problems, and of course big thanks to my partner in crime Adam Fortner, without whom you would be holding a much less attractive book in your hands. Kelly Lyons, you know what you did!

Thank you to my family – my mother and father for their support and continued enthusiasm, to Erika for reminding me why I write, and to Lee for riding out the waves of self-doubt and letting me shut the door and vanish into another time and place.

Made in the USA
Las Vegas, NV
23 March 2025